Cruel Destiny and *The White Negress*

Cruel Destiny and The White Negress

Two Novels by Cléante Desgraves Valcin

EDITED BY ADAM NEMMERS
AND JEANNE JÉGOUSSO

Translated by Jeanne Jégousso
Foreword by Myriam J. A. Chancy

RUTGERS UNIVERSITY PRESS
NEW BRUNSWICK, CAMDEN, AND NEWARK, NEW JERSEY
LONDON AND OXFORD

Rutgers University Press is a department of Rutgers, The State University of New Jersey, one of the leading public research universities in the nation. By publishing worldwide, it furthers the University's mission of dedication to excellence in teaching, scholarship, research, and clinical care.

Library of Congress Cataloging-in-Publication Data

Names: Valcin, Virgile, Mme., author. | Jégousso, Jeanne, 1989– editor, translator. | Nemmers, Adam, editor. | Chancy, Myriam J. A., 1970– writer of foreword. | Valcin, Virgile, Mme. Cruelle destinée. English | Valcin, Virgile, Mme. Blanche négresse. English
Title: Cruel destiny and The white negress : two novels by Cléante Desgraves Valcin / edited by Jeanne Jégousso and Adam Nemmers ; translated by Jeanne Jégousso ; foreword by Myriam J. A. Chancy.
Description: New Brunswick : Rutgers University Press, 2024.
Identifiers: LCCN 2023051514 | ISBN 9781978837584 (paperback) | ISBN 9781978837591 (hardcover) | ISBN 9781978837607 (epub) | ISBN 9781978837614 (pdf)
Subjects: LCSH: Valcin, Virgile, Mme.— Translations into English. | Haitian fiction—20th century. | Women—Haiti—Social conditions—Fiction. | Americans—Haiti—Fiction. | Haiti—History—American occupation, 1915–1934—Fiction. | LCGFT: Novels.
Classification: LCC PQ3949.V36 C78 2024 | DDC 843/.912—dc23/eng/20240214
LC record available at https://lccn.loc.gov/2023051514

A British Cataloging-in-Publication record for this book is available from the British Library.

This collection copyright © 2024 by Rutgers, The State University of New Jersey

All rights reserved

No part of this book may be reproduced or utilized in any form or by any means, electronic or mechanical, or by any information storage and retrieval system, without written permission from the publisher. Please contact Rutgers University Press, 106 Somerset Street, New Brunswick, NJ 08901. The only exception to this prohibition is "fair use" as defined by U.S. copyright law.

References to internet websites (URLs) were accurate at the time of writing. Neither the author nor Rutgers University Press is responsible for URLs that may have expired or changed since the manuscript was prepared.

♾ The paper used in this publication meets the requirements of the American National Standard for Information Sciences—Permanence of Paper for Printed Library Materials, ANSI Z39.48-1992.

rutgersuniversitypress.org

*J'avais cessé de rêver et commençais à éprouver un soulagement inav-
ouable à ne pas être eux, à ne pas être pris pour eux. (I had stopped
dreaming and began to feel an unspeakable relief for not being them,
for not being mistaken for them.)*

— *Fabienne Kanor,* Louisiane

Contents

Foreword

Être américains en Haïti, depuis 1915 ... c'est se promener en pleine paix
avec des machines-guns braquées sur de pauvres étudiants en grève; être
américains, enfin, c'est vivre d'abondance, mourir d'indigestion à côté
de l'haïtien dont les tripes se sont rapetissées à force de privations.

[To be American in Haiti, since 1915 ... is to walk about in an atmo-
sphere of peace with machine guns pointed on defenseless students on
strike; to be American, finally, is to live extravagantly, to die of indigestion
beside the Haitian whose intestines have shrunk from deprivation.]
— *Virgile Valcin*, La Blanche négresse

When I first discovered the work of Cléante Desgraves (aka Virgile Valcin) as I began composing my text on the work of Haitian women novel-
ists in reaction to the 1994 U.S. military intervention in Port-au-Prince
which deployed troops from the city in which I was then living, Nashville,
I was struck by the fact that Desgraves, Haiti's first woman novelist, penned
both her novels, *Cruelle destinée* (1929) and *La Blanche négresse* (1934) during the U.S. Occupation of 1915–1934. I was struck not so much by the
genre of the novels, which could be classified as romance and thereby be
easily dismissed as trite or inconsequential, speaking only out of a nar-
row space of class privilege more consonant with works from the Victo-
rian period, but in the ways Desgraves ingenuously utilized the vehicle of

sentimentality to investigate questions of raced identity, gender, nation-
alism, and sovereignty. Both novels address colorism and class in Haiti,
particularly in urban Port-au-Prince, as a means to think about the impo-
sition of American racial parameters through the Occupation, while also
questioning whether Haitian women could liberate themselves from patriarchal norms already enmeshed in Haitian society. She echoed, without
perhaps having knowledge of them, the works of female Harlem Renaissance writers in the United States, also taking up themes concerning
racial passing, class, and gender mobility in their writings, particularly
Nella Larsen in works like *Quicksand* (1928) and *Passing* (1929) or Zora
Neale Hurston in *Their Eyes Were Watching God* (1937).

We know, of course, that Hurston spent time in Haiti, writing the latter novel in Port-au-Prince as she studied the language as well as the rituals of Vodou for her book *Tell My Horse* (1938), but less is known about
whether she had exchanges with local writers like Valcin and they with
her. Unlike Harlem Renaissance women writers such as Larsen, Hurston,
and others, who are now widely read as a result of the work of Black women
writers and scholars emerging in the 1980s to the present, Haitian women,
for lack of accessibility, that is, translation into English, have largely
remained in obscurity, despite their entanglements with history and their
examination of a society evolving under the twin forces of colonialism and
occupation. Like all Haitian women writers writing out of Haitian space
who were to follow her, from her contemporary, Annie Desroy (*Le Joug*,
1934), to current writers such as Yanick Lahens, she responded to the times,
incorporating them into the very fabric of her plots. In the case, particularly, of *La Blanche négresse/The White Negress*, the novels struck a chord
in the world of Haitian intellectuals.

This struck chord was signaled by the fact that Jean Price-Mars, father
of Haitian "indigénisme" took the time to pen a preface to the latter, in
which he extolled its virtues, stating that she had "poured all her heart into
it, a heart aching from the bruises from which we have all suffered for
nineteen years while our Homeland has been occupied by the American

Military Forces and by the occult power of American Finance" (see preface to *The White Negress*). In short, he stated, "Her novel is also a slice of
contemporary history." It comes, then, as less of a surprise, to read in Valcin's work, the sharp critique of American occupiers with which I began
this foreword, a critique that manages in an economical few lines to both
reflect the violence of military occupation and the privation rather than
progress that it occasioned for future generations (students) and those
already dispossessed of their land and its fruits (the poor). In this novel,
Valcin also weaves into her fictional narrative references to debates of the
day advanced by very real political and intellectual figures, such as Price-
Mars (as well as historian Pradel Pompilus and historian/novelist Stephen
Alexis, father of Jacques Stephen Alexis) who represent, then and now, pos-
sibilities for shedding Haiti's colonial inheritance in favor of its revolutionary path. Valcin's work, then, is not entirely what it seems. The
"marriage plot" or conventional romance novel are vehicles for larger
issues pertinent to us today and Haiti's grappling with a complex history
of revolution, occupation, and dispossession, themes that animate theo-
ries of postcolonialism, but which are seldom given a considered space in
the unfolding present.

We cannot begin to properly understand the importance of Valcin's
work at such multiple crossroads without the translation here made available to a wider readership. Such translation makes possible the examination of how Valcin's work can be understood, as I have argued in *Framing
Silence* as the beginning point of a Haitian women's literary tradition
marked by its interests in the political life and survival of the Haitian
people while also critiquing its patriarchal underpinnings and colonial
vestiges. It can assist scholars and students of Haitian literature to better
understand how the works being produced by Haitian American women
writers in English are themselves part of a genealogy that begins with Valcin and, for many, continues in the tradition of observing and comment-
ing on the politics surrounding their production. Such a translation also
makes the work accessible to assess how it participates in a national literary

tradition that is no longer localized in Port-au-Prince but spins out into transnational realities as far as Europe, and into the depths of the Americas. It also opens the door to an examination of how the text may interact with those by African American writers of the Harlem Renaissance and, ultimately, to that penned by other Caribbean writers in the region at this time also creating under the shadow of "manifest destiny," while also taking into account its class positionality. Such comparative analyses may also uncover a more complex, dynamic inheritance for African Diasporic literary letters and women's literature more largely in terms of novels of the domestic. More importantly, it creates a space to consider the merits of Valcin's oeuvre on its own grounds and to appreciate the work, in context, for beginning to voice the realities of a sector of Haitian women at a time when all Haitian women were largely silenced, ignored, and violently repressed, for what it dared to say.

Myriam J. A. Chancy
Los Angeles, CA
April 11, 2023

Introduction

The claim of a literary first, when not specious or tenuous, still leaves the abiding question of significance. What does it mean—what does it matter—that Cléante Desgraves Valcin was the first published female Haitian novelist, and that this volume includes the first English-language translation of her works?[1] Perhaps a better query asks why a Haitian woman had not published a novel in the centuries before 1929, and why such an important literary figure, from such an important era, has for so long been inaccessible to Anglophone (and especially U.S.) audiences. As the Haitian writer Myriam J. A. Chancy explains, the absence of Haitian women such as Valcin has not been through accident or neglect. Rather: "Women have consistently been written out of both the historical and literary records of Haiti" (Chancy 13)—to which I would add they have been doubly written out of the historical literary record of Haiti. She continues to explain that "Haitian women writers have been forced to articulate their marginalization on multiple fronts: the experience of the

1. During our research, we identified several names for the author (among them Mme Virgile Valcin, Cléanthe Valcin, Cléante Desgraves, Cléante Desgraves Valcin). Rather than utilize her husband's name (Mme Virgile Valcin), as is often the custom in French publication, we have chosen to employ the most common spelling for her first name and decided to include her maiden name as well as her married name in order to provide full agency to the author.

Haitian woman is defined by exile within her own country, for she is alienated from the means to assert at once feminine and feminist identities at the same time that she undergoes the same colonial experiences as her male counterparts" (Chancy 13). Reversing this legacy of internal exile and marginalization, then, requires an intentional re-centering of women, their identities, and their experiences, projecting their voices and positing their lives as essential to any full and accurate understanding of the Haitian nation.

To wit, in this volume we present the first English-language translation of Valcin's novels *Cruelle destinée* (*Cruel Destiny*, 1929) and *La Blanche négresse* (*The White Negress*, 1934), which amount to a mere portion of Valcin's rich life and oeuvre. Born in 1891 Port-au-Prince to an American mother and Haitian father, Desgraves was educated at the Pensionnat des Demoiselles and trained as a teacher during her adolescence. Her 1917 marriage to Virgile Valcin resulted in two children and her emergence onto the Haitian literary scene, chiefly through his ownership of a printing press closely affiliated with the Haitian government. She first tried her hand at poetry, publishing a collection of verse, *Fleurs et Pleurs*, in 1924, before turning to fiction by penning a number of short stories and the aforementioned novels in the span of a decade. In post-Occupation Haiti, Valcin became a frequent contributor to various journals, including *La Semeuse*, *Le Temps*, and *Voix des Femmes*, the last of which highlights her work with feminist activism across the Caribbean. In the third stage of her life, she became a prominent feminist figure on both local and regional stages, serving as president of the Haitian Women's League for Social Action and representing Haiti at the 10th General Assembly of Women in 1955. Valcin died just a year after that Assembly and a year before Haitian women gained the right to vote, leaving behind a literary legacy carried on by female Haitian writers such as Chancy, Edwidge Danticat, Évelyne Trouillot, and Marie Vieux-Chauvet.

In some ways, *Cruel Destiny* serves as an inchoate draft of Valcin's later novel, as both center on romantic melodrama, sordid revelations, and the difficult choices one makes when traversing the vicissitudes of love. Yet the earlier novel has value in its own right, as an allegorical exploration of Haiti's colonial heritage and the incongruency of the Franco-Haitian special relationship in the modern age. Adeline and Armand's near-miss incest—established in Paris and exported to Port-au-Prince—highlights the danger of backward-looking foreign liaisons, especially those whose provenance has not been fully scrutinized (a theme that recurs in her later novel as well). As if to underscore the connection, *Cruel Destiny* draws heavily from the French literary tradition, mining the sentimental vein of romanticism a la Alexandre Dumas and Victor Hugo, or perhaps the later naturalism of Guy de Maupassant and Émile Zola. Even amid strange interjections and flourishes, Valcin's novels read as if they'd been written a century earlier, and bear little trace of literary modernism, much less the influence of her contemporaries in France, the United States, or the Caribbean. Valcin's novel of five years later, *The White Negress*, also belongs to the genre of Occupation literature, the body of Haitian letters written during the nineteen-year period (1915–1934) when the United States invaded the island and forcibly superintended Haitian affairs. This neocolonial intervention, ostensibly conducted to stabilize the Republic and for the benefit of the Haitian people, resulted in the U.S. takeover of Haitian government, banks, and industry and the arrival of rapacious American business interests that exploited Haiti's natural resources and people. Haitian culture was also a site of hostile takeover, as the United States sought to displace France as the dominant power in the region, secularizing Haitian education, implementing American English as the lingua franca, and installing an American-style racial hierarchy. No wonder that Valcin's latter novel is conversant with the New Negro and Negritude movements that swept the Caribbean and United States during the early decades of the twentieth century, often in reaction to systems of U.S./white supremacy.

To appreciate the apparent discrepancy between the form and prose of Valcin's novels, one must consider the milieu in which they were composed. *Cruel Destiny* is a strangely ahistorical novel, apparently written without regard to technology, geography, or current events surrounding the plot, emerging as an allegory or commentary rather than chronicle. By contrast, *The White Negress* is very much situated in the 1920s and 1930s, with mentions of airplanes, automobiles, yo-yos, popular music, and the names of dozens of real-life people who populated Haiti during this era. Here the difference between 1929 and 1934 is crucial—the former date of publication, during the thick of U.S. Occupation, meant that Valcin and other writers had to be careful in composition and especially publication. Yvette Gindine notes that "Although the Yankee had since 1915 become a ubiquitous military and civilian presence in Haiti's daily life, censorship, imposed or self-administered, prevented his being depicted directly until the last phase of detente (1930–1934)" (41). Thus Valcin's 1929 *Cruel Destiny*, written under the vigilance of U.S. censors, allegorically critiques Haiti's relationship with its former colonizer, France, while her 1934 *The White Negress* offers a full-fledged condemnation of the U.S. invaders, concluding with a mass of Haitians rejoicing at the Yankees' departure. Similarly, while carpetbagging U.S. authors like the fictional Yen Leabrook (based on William Seabrook) churned out exploitative bestsellers for the American market, it was not until the wane of the Occupation that the backlog of Haitian-authored novels made their way to the Haitian public: Léon Laleau's *Le Choc* (1932), Stephen Alexis's *Le Nègre Masqué* (1933), Annie Desroy's *Le Joug* (1934), and Maurice Casseus's *Viejo* (1935). Little, if any of this literature has emerged into English-language corpus; Haitian protest literature, like the Occupation itself, is rarely acknowledged in American (literary) history, even as the impact of those two decades on Haiti proved indelible.

As the title of Valcin's first novel indicates, a facile, outsider's view might consider Haiti and its people as "cursed," especially given the frequent tribulations that have plagued the western portion of Hispaniola: French colonization, the Taíno genocide and mass enslavement of Africans; the bloody, brutal, decades-long struggle for Haitian independence; and the hurricanes and earthquakes that have ravaged the nation in centuries since. These intertwined narratives of sin and expiation are at play throughout the novels—especially in *Cruel Destiny*, with its discussion of nuns and convents, its deathbed confessions and frequent allusions to Mount Calvary and the Garden of Eden. Indeed, *Cruel Destiny* repeatedly meditates on the consequences of original sin, and subjects both Junie and Adeline to mysterious illnesses and premature deaths as fallen women. But *The White Negress* reverses the curse, as it were, refusing to trope upon its would-be tragic mulatta (Laurence) and instead relating the downfall and suicide of the American Robert Watson, who shoots himself with ignominy after discovering his wife has a small percentage of Black ancestry. In this way Valcin inverts the source of Haiti's misfortunes, laying the blame upon the (neo)colonizing nations and men (like Watson and Gaston Renaudy) who dissemble and dominate, rather than the many Haitian characters who suffer through no fault of their own.

Valcin seems to have written for a primarily Franco-Haitian audience, as evinced by her choice of language and narrator's use of the pronoun "we" throughout the novels. Both narrators position themselves as an au courante Haitian woman who, like Valcin herself, is intimately familiar with the goings-on of Haitian society, journalism, and politics, down to the ongoing plays and muckraking newspapers of Port-au-Prince. At other times, as when describing the native flora of Haiti, Valcin seems to address a foreign audience unfamiliar with the Republic. In *Cruel Destiny*, for instance, the narrator reveals that "in Haiti, flowers are always in season. We see them everywhere and all the time, sometimes puny in winter, but in May the gardens and the valleys are oh so magical!" Directly addressing the reader, she queries, "You know probably how expensive orchids are?" and continues to explain that "the hills are covered with them, they abound, unsuspected, unknown. At the bottom of our mountains, the peasants for whom they shine ignore their value, and we, the townspeople, cannot easily reach them." Throughout her novels Valcin writes in a formal French rather than the more commonplace Haitian Creole—although passages of dialogue in *The White Negress* show her facility with that language as well. While the predominant mode is sentimental melodrama, Valcin is also attuned to journalistic and sociological dimensions in offering a portrait of the Haitian mise-en-scène during the U.S. Occupation. Writing in his preface to *The White Negress*, Jean Price-Mars called the novel "a slice of contemporary history," observing that Valcin "weaved the action of the drama with all the social, political, and worldly material with which Haitian life was kneaded during these heavy years" (see preface to *The White Negress*).

The novels' most salient ideology is their robust feminism (often situated in league with Haiti's resistance to colonialism), best displayed via the subversive disquisition on the question of how much obedience a young woman owes to her parents and husband. In *Cruel Destiny* Adeline's mother forbids her "to say that you are engaged," telling her daughter, "You mustn't choose a husband for yourself. This is up to your father and me." *The White Negress* similarly features Raoul Desvallons telling her daughter Laurence that "You must be obedient to your husband" and her stepmother, Lucienne, cautioning that "You've fallen too deep into feminism." But both heroines push back against their parents. Adeline protests that "Times have changed . . . Parents shouldn't choose a husband for me . . . it doesn't happen anymore." Laurence similarly chafes at her yoke of "obedience": "Oh! If you could know how much this word hurt me when the mayor pronounced, it . . . It's time for the institution of marriage to no longer turn a free woman into an oppressed one. Thanks to my marriage, I am a slave whom only divorce will set free." *The White Negress*, in particular, endorses a strain of modern feminism that defines a woman as self-sufficient and independent of her assumed identity as wife and mother. Even after Robert leaves her, Laurence refuses to return to her former lover, the Haitian lawyer Guy Vanel, instead delivering a passionate speech denouncing marriage and embracing her status as a widow and single mother:

> Marriage should not be the only goal, the only ambition of a woman. There are many other goals a woman can aim for which give as much happiness as marriage (when it gives any) . . .
>
> The lawyer who defends the widow, the orphan, who rehabilitates the innocent unjustly condemned, the doctor who saves a child from the claws of death and lays him cured in the arms of his mother, these women, aren't they happy? Did they look for their happiness only in marriage?

In this stirring speech, Laurence likens herself to a nun, nurse, or lawyer (one might be tempted to include a novelist), three of the few professions open at the time to Haitian women. At the end of the novel, the remaining three characters, all female, stand and join with the youth of Port-au-Prince in singing "La Dessalinienne" after the Yankee occupiers have departed. The patriotic scene altogether rejects the necessity of colonialism and paternalism alike, instead positing a robust and autonomous feminism in line with Valcin's own ideology and the trajectory of her personal life after penning the novel.

In *Cruel Destiny* no racial conflict is mentioned: the characters are all Haitian, and though they're variously described as "dark," "brunette," and "high yellow," their color poses no romantic obstacle. In contrast, *The White Negress*, with its cast of American and French characters, features all manner of racial prejudice; race becomes *the* issue that makes and breaks marriages, consistent with the Jim Crow climate of Haiti under U.S. Occupation. According to the novel's Haitians, race is a problem introduced by the Americans; as the president of the fictional Haitian-American Club, Emile Jérôme, argues, "There is no colorism in Haiti, this word is a stepping-stone for the exploiters," as "many Haitians, knowing the Yankees' hatred of Black people, decided the least dark would receive the most respect from the occupier." The novel's Americans certainly demonstrate a hatred of Black people, with Robert calling Guy a "vulgar pickaninny" and Miss Jefferson declaring that Laurence had better kill herself than live as a "white negress." To an extent racial prejudice cuts both ways; Guy's uncle, peeved that his nephew has eschewed the "many educated and honest Haitian women from good families, many of whom deserve to be called your wife" advises Guy to "break . . . off" his liaison with the "white girl." But in the denouement, when the "white girl" is revealed to be partially "Black," Valcin offers a reversal through the triumph of racial essentialism. As Nadève Ménard observes, "Although at the end of the novel Laurence signifies herself as Haitian, her biological mother actually had roots in Martinique, not Haiti. What is important then, is not nationality, but race. Laurence's 'black blood' legitimizes her Haitianness" (Ménard 157). In the same way Laurence's substantial monetary inheritance—taken from both her Black uncle and her white husband—signals a return to the pre-Occupation status quo, when whites were prohibited from owning property and Blackness was considered an essential component of Haitian identity.

This brief Introduction can only gesture to a few of the characters, conflicts, and themes that the reader will encounter in these novels. We hope that this volume is not merely a translation of the first published novel by a Haitian woman, but a continuation of and catalyst for many translated novels composed by Haitians of all genders, ages, styles, and eras. For too long Haiti has been a locus only of misery and penury in the imagination of the English-speaking world, the Pearl of the Antilles having been tainted by writers like Seabrook, who made a fortune peddling lurid tales of werewolves, cannibals, and zombies to credulous American audiences. May it be that introducing Anglophone readers to the vital perspective of Cléante Desgraves Valcin helps offer a corrective to that enduring astigmatism.

Adam Nemmers

WORKS CITED

Chancy, Miriam J. A. *Framing Silence: Revolutionary Novels by Haitian Women*. Rutgers University Press, 1997.

Ménard, Nadève. *The Occupied Novel: The Representation of Foreigners in Haitian Novels Written during the U.S. Occupation, 1915–1934*. 2002. University of Pennsylvania, PhD dissertation. *ProQuest*, https://repository.upenn.edu/dissertations/AAI3054979/.

Translator's Note

To the best of our knowledge, no manuscripts or drafts of the novels written by Cléante Desgraves Valcin, Haiti's first woman novelist, subsisted. It is therefore difficult to estimate how much editorial support the author received, if any. The first editions of 1929 for *Cruel Destiny* and 1934 for *The White Negress*, on which we relied to establish this first English translation, both included errata stipulating at the very end that "a few insignificant typos" remained in the texts. Even if our primary concern was to be as close as possible from the original French text, to preserve Valcin's unique and challenging style, the mistakes and inconsistencies addressed in the erratum and/or left in the texts have been corrected, as long as they did not change the meaning of a sentence and were superficial (such as spelling or agreement of a past participle). The structure of the text is unchanged, apart from the addition of asterisks, signaling an ellipsis in the narrative. The characters' lists included before each novel are not in the original publications and were added to help the reader identify and remember the main protagonists, and as a pedagogical tool to facilitate the discussion of these works of fiction in the classroom.

Attentive to the linguistic and sociohistorical background of the novels, that of a postcolonial Haiti living under its first American occupation, words and dialogue in Haitian Creole have been kept in the texts and translated into footnotes when they could not be understood in context.

Indeed, the use of Creole often gave valuable unspoken information about the character speaking (such as their socioeconomic status or the intention to exclude French or American protagonists from a conversation) or describe cultural and religious rituals specific to Haiti. We also decided to retain the specific vocabulary and language used by Valcin to describe racial identities, stereotypes, and ideologies inherited from French imperialism and the American Occupation, as it was necessary to best convey the author's critics of racial inequalities and prejudices during her lifetime.

On numerous occasions, Valcin quotes from the Bible and from famous works of literature—among others, French philosophers Voltaire and Blaise Pascal. Their English renditions, when the source could be identified, was taken from reputable English translations which were referenced in a footnote. In the few occurrences we were unable to recognize and/or were unsure if they were notable citations, we kept the quotation marks used by the author, hoping others might recognize the segments we could not descry.

Overall, in this first English translation of Cléante Desgraves Valcin's novels, we aimed at conserving the specific vocabulary which would have been chosen by an author during the first half of the twentieth century, and at propounding the style, voice, and literary expertise of Haiti's first woman author.

Jeanne Jégousso

Portrait of Cléante D. Valcin. Photographer unknown. Source: Valcin,
Virgile. *La Blanche négresse*. Port-au-Prince: V. Valcin, 1934.

Cruel Destiny

List of Characters (in order of appearance)

Madeleine and Jane Rougerot: Rougerot daughters

Junie Rougerot: Mother of Madeleine, Jane, Armand, and Bébé

Julien Rougerot: Absent father

Armand Rougerot: Only son of the Rougerot family

Bébé: Youngest child of Junie

Henri Rougerot: Rich uncle

Adeline Renaudy: School friend of Jane and Madeleine, eldest
    Renaudy daughter, fiancée of Armand (changes name to Claire
    Closebourg)

Jules Renaudy: Father of Adeline, Rose, and Roland

Mireille Renaudy: Mother of Adeline, Rose, and Roland

Rose and Roland Renaudy: Younger siblings of Adeline

Marie and Louise Guitton: Cousins of Adeline, Rose, and Roland

Gaston Durieu: Wealthy employer

CHAPTER I

– "Madeleine? . . . Jane? . . . Did you see your father leave?"

 – "Yes," said Jane to her mother, "Daddy kissed me, crying, and told me he is coming back in fifteen minutes. . . ."

 – "Where was I? Where was Madeleine? What time was it? Why did no one call us? Oh my God! Oh my God!"

Jane, who did not understand Madame Rougerot's panic, did not give much importance to her questions, so she ran to her older sister to tell her that their mother was angry because Monsieur Rougerot had not asked her on a walk. Madeleine, who was wiser, was going to ask her mother for an explanation when she entered her room like a gust of wind:

 – "Your father . . ."

 – "What is happening Mom?"

 – "Read!"

 – "Mom . . . What's all this distress I find you in?"

 – "Read this letter, and you will know everything."

The child took the note handed to her by the sorrowful woman and read:

My dear Junie,

I am ruined, as you already know; I am leaving to elude the shame which, sooner or later, will inevitably fall upon my house.

You are a brave woman; I know you will survive my departure and provide for our children.

I flee, because I could not even pay my debts in five years; if I were to cling on to this business which shoves me every day more into the abyss, I would face prison.

My poor wife, if you knew how many letters, how many threats I receive each day from my creditors! Alas! One is always in the wrong when one owes money, but the hearts of creditors are made of stone, their smile is a crevice of Hell, even their pity is poisoned . . . They know that I lost twenty thousand dollars in coffee transactions; they know my business could pick up at any moment, but they want to slaughter me. I am writing you not to be forgiven, not by you nor by society, I am a coward, I know it, but when I shall return to this country to pay my debts, I will ask society to redeem my faults and ask forgiveness for the pains you are enduring.

I am leaving, Junie, but I will remain here in thought, in spirit to watch over you, and my dear Madeleine and Jane.

When the next one is born, you shall talk to him often about me, so he does not think himself an orphan. Be honest with my daughters about my situation even though they are young, and above all tell them, assure them that I am not a thief. And if you see any doubt in their eyes, you must, out of pity, defend me. I kiss their little feet and hold you in my heart.

Good-bye.
Julien

Madeleine finished reading without really understanding the meaning of these words, brought together on paper by shame and pain, but what crushed her heart was the thought that her father, her beloved father, was now far away. That is why, without a word, she fainted at her mother's feet.

– "Madeleine! Madeleine! . . . ," cried out Mme[1] Rougerot, "come back to your senses, your father will be back tomorrow . . ."

Jane let out a desperate cry which alerted the nearest neighbor, Mme Dubourg.

– "What is the matter?" she said worryingly.

– "Madame," said Madeleine, whose fainting had subsided, "if you know where my father is, tell him that we will assist him in his work . . . tell him . . ."

– "She is delirious," said the neighbor in a low voice, "call a doctor, Madame, your child may be under the influence of some emotion . . ."

– "Alas!"

– "Where is M. Rougerot?"

– "Alas!"

– "Madame, we cannot leave this child in this state, I am going to apply poultices to her, hold her writhing limbs . . . Child, take this infusion . . . Yes, it will do you good . . . Do not cry . . ."

– "Oh! On the contrary, let her cry. Tears are good for a heart full of sorrow, look I too am crying, Madame Dubourg, to comfort myself. Madame Dubourg, this child is not delirious . . . Read this," said Junie.

She handed her the calamitous letter and continued:

– "Even though I am trying to hide the state of my heart, everything betrays me, and I am pleased to find a soul sister to entrust with my torments."

– "Poor woman! You are right to confide in me, you will not regret having done so, so much will my heart grow to share your sorrows, to make them my own."

1. "Mrs." in French.

She hastily read half of the letter then, putting it down, she added:

– "Since the situation has come to this, we must do something
other than lament. Give me your most precious possessions,
including your jewelry, the children's belongings as well as some
family heirlooms you hold dear."

– "Here are the keys," said the abandoned woman in a daze, "do
as you see fit."

Mme Dubourg wanted to be useful to the Rougerot family, but an inner
voice commanded her not to pilfer what now belonged to the creditors, in
the absence of her fugitive husband.

She stood there, indecisive, when Junie, unable to take it any longer, let
out a heartrending cry and fainted.

A few neighbors came running and, finding Mme Dubourg attending
to the child, questioned her.

– "I believe she just learned the death of a parent . . . It is nerve-
racking . . . It will surely go away," said Mme Dubourg.

After a few minutes, Mme Rougerot started to regain consciousness
little by little. She felt a warm, comforting hand holding hers.

– "Ah! It is you, Madame," she said, "it is you here, caring for me,
thank you. God bless you! . . . where is Madeleine? What happened
to my little Jane?"

– "Do not worry, they are at my house, my housekeeper is taking
care of them."

– "Oh! Thank you once again!"

– "Be brave and say like Jacob: the Lord gave, and the Lord has
taken away; blessed be the name of the Lord."

– "You are a saint . . . Yes, God took everything away from me, I
do not wish to keep anything except the jewels my dying mother
bequeathed to me, and the portraits of various family members that

would be worthless to the creditors . . . these jewels? Alas! I would have left it behind if my mother had not told me: "They belonged to your great-grandmother, may they be passed intact to my grand-children." Ah! Powerful are the oaths we make to the dying!"

———

The following day, Julien Rougerot's store was sealed and eight days later the newspapers of Port-au-Prince announced that his private effects were to be sold at an auction.

Everything sold: the house looked like a vast cemetery after the sale. Not a piece of furniture did not find a buyer, not a utensil was too used to be sold . . . On the contrary, the auction ended when there was nothing left to sell . . .

The bankrupt's house became a veritable bric-a-brac waiting for the order coming from one of the creditors to be chipped away, or should I say to be liquidated.

With a house empty of any furniture, Madame Rougerot left with her two children, without bread, and told Mme Dubourg she was leaving for the countryside.

– "To the countryside? Sure, but toward which area are you heading to?" enquired Mme Dubourg.

– "Near Diquini."[2]

– "Where exactly?"

– "My second home."

– "Why not spend a few days here, I am alone, and your children have provided me company ever since they moved in with me."

– "No, I will certainly come back to Port-au-Prince, and I will give you, or rather I will give myself the pleasure of spending a few days with you then. Right now, I need the outdoors, I need the

2. Haitian locality situated near Thor le Volant and Garde Cote.

comfort of nature to spend these hours so differently from those I
relished from my birth to the departure of my husband."

Mme Dubourg did not contradict her; she climbed on a truck, accompanied by her children each carrying a small suitcase. She wept bitterly,
but the children, distracted by the sight of the blue sea alongside the road,
smiled and gradually returned to the natural cheerfulness of young
children.

The truck stopped, started moving forward, then stopped again:
"Bizoton!"[3] yelled a passenger. The word snapped Mme Rougerot out of
her daydream.

   – "Children, another stop, and you will arrive in Thor. That is
   where we will get off, do you understand me?"

She was still crying, her neighbors, although moved by her tears, did
not dare question her; her pain was so intense that they all shared it without knowing the cause.

Finally, they arrived in Thor, where she remembered the bridge,
immortalized by the terrible railway accident that had bereaved her some
time ago. There, she had seen the lifeless body of her brother, his limbs
scattered, disfigured, lying in the arms of her elderly mother, who, mad
with pain, was gathering up the pieces of flesh crushed by the railway like
the crazy Défilée.[4] There, Junie had seen so many other people fulfilling
the same duty toward so many other victims that she couldn't take it anymore. She had fainted; she had been taken to a nearby neighborhood.
Here she was again, at the same place, not to mourn a dead brother, but
the shame of her husband, the most infamous pain of her life, the death
of her honor.

3. Bizoton is a communal section in the Western Department of Haiti.
4. Défilée, also known as Dédée Bazile or Défilée la folle, is a popular figure of the
times of the Haitian Revolution. The legend says that she is the one who found the
lifeless body of Emperor Dessalines, who was a leader of the Haitian Revolution and
the first ruler of the newly independent Haiti.

– "Mom," said Madeleine suddenly, "you are crying too much, you are going to be sick."

– "Alas! Dear child, can one suddenly divert the waters of a river? Well, true tears are like them, whatever the reason, you cannot stop crying when, in your heart, you have a violent sorrow and a bitter memory. Ah! If I told you that here, I cried tears of blood, all my tears, would you believe me?"

– "You? . . . Here!" cried out the children.

– "Yes."

– "Why?"

– "Your heart is too small for big sorrows . . . Do not question me further."

The heart has unpredictable movements which it sometimes regrets afterward, but one is not always strong enough to repress its outbursts, especially when suffering. However, if in spite of everything, we can stop it in time to spare another suffering heart, we must do it; otherwise, we would be selfish.

– "Poor mother," said the girls

– "We need to keep going, children. Diquini is farther down the road, we must walk a little farther before . . ."

– "Finding the house," they added.

– "Alas!"

Mme Rougerot did not have a house within reach; she was wandering in search of shelter. She arrived to Diquini and settled under a tree.

– "Where is the house?" asked the youngest.

– "Here we are, children."

– "I do not see it . . ."

– "This thick foliage will be our roof, this trunk cut down by a charitable hand, look at it well, will be used as a seat by day and a pillow by night . . . See the numerous mango trees that no hand has

planted, and which present us with their ripe fruits; listen to the
sound of the nearby river which invites us to drink its crystal-clear
waters, to cool our bodies, to feel the air that caresses the cheeks, it
can only be a welcome beverage for our lungs damaged by the heat
of the city . . . and we will not be alone . . . small birds are nesting in
these trees."

– "What of the Bogeyman, if Bluebeard, if the Ogre and the
Ogress the children talked about the other day . . . ," said Jane,
afraid.

– "Demons do not chase the poor . . ."

– "What if it rains?"

– "Ah, no! It is not going to rain. God would not expose two
children to the elements, and if it rains, the foliage will protect us . . ."

– "And our feet?"

– "The Lord will dry them."

– "Poor mother dearest!"

They spent the night under the shiny stars, without fear or whisper.

The next day, the unfortunate woman left her children, after saying a
short prayer to the Lord, and ran in search of a thatched house. An unsuc-
cessful quest! A futile pain! She came back to find her little girls huddled
together, trying to turn two weaknesses into one strength against the fear
engendered by their mother's departure.

Learning of their misery, Mme Dubourg arrived in her car to beg them
to come live with her. Junie refused:

– "If I was alone, perhaps, but I have two girls . . ."

– "I would be a second mother to them, and you would grant
them permission to share with me the filial love with which they
surround you."

Junie, seeing the insistence of Mme Dubourg, packed up, and by God
what tremendous luggage! She returned to Port-au-Prince after sending a

heartfelt thank-you to the big mango tree that had sheltered her and her poor children for two nights.

> – "*Adieu* meadows, woods, river, *adieu!*" she said to herself, "farewell and thank you!"

M. Dubourg, to put her at her ease, had given her a little house, shaded with flowers, built in his courtyard with the ground floor being used as his garage.

Before Dubourg's marriage, the house was his cozy bachelor pad. It was left furnished and often, when his wife wanted to exchange her noisy life for a calmer one, she went there, leaving her villa and her expensive furniture, and staying there for days with the dreams of a young girl in her heart. In the evening they stayed there late, she and her husband leaning on the only window or on the little balcony, whispering to each other like two fiancés. At times, they imagined themselves newly married, in the midst of their honeymoon in some remote part of Pétion-Ville.[5] Exchanging tender words, full of warm affection, they would lean against each other, and weep with happiness. Oh well, they had just sacrificed their nest of love to the pressing need of a poor family, they felt happy, oh! yes, happy to be able to accommodate people who only yesterday lived in opulence, who now were victims of life's ups and downs.

Madame Rougerot and her children had been living with Monsieur and Madame Dubourg for a month when the latter, upon leaving a ball, was struck down by bronchopneumonia.[6] The continuous and devoted care of three doctors could not ward off the illness, which worsened and turned this young and beautiful woman into a sad corpse in less than four days.

---

5. Eastern suburb of Port-au-Prince, the capital city of Haiti.
6. Subtype of pneumonia.

M. Dubourg, lonely, inconsolable, did not want to continue living in
Haiti and one day said to Junie:

– "My poor friend, I'm leaving in six months, do me the honor of
accepting a small allowance which will allow you to live, even though
modestly with your children, to live all the same and raise them."

– "No, Monsieur Dubourg, find me some work, it will be the
best income you could give me. Recommend me to someone, while
withholding my real name since my husband brought upon it
the cruelest shame."

– "What type of work? You will run a shop?"

– "What else can I do? I have only ever done that."

– "Poor woman!"

– "Yes, pity me, but do not leave me fending alone for myself
when you go away."

– "I just offered you . . ."

– "Let's not talk about it anymore, my dear Monsieur Dubourg, I
want, if I can redeem myself, to do it by working; I am full of energy,
so why not work to overcome my misery? To make a living?"

– "You are right."

– "Your wife, your beloved guardian has been dead for eight days,
I cannot stay here any longer . . . I must leave."

– "Where?"

– "I do not know, but Mme Dubourg had told me to find work
before her death, and I have a hundred gourdes[7] worth of labor left. . . .
I will not be able to keep sewing since I am not very good at it."

– "And you have enough work to earn a hundred gourdes?"

– "Yes, I had reimagined myself as a seamstress, but your wife
oversaw the pattern . . ."

– "My dear poor wife! She passed away too soon . . ."

7. Currency of Haiti.

Yes, she had died too soon, Junie thought, for she had taken care of the unfortunate woman's two children and had dreamed of turning them into true little queens.

M. Dubourg felt more grief every day for the death of his wife, so he spent hours huddled in an armchair between the small intimate objects that had belonged to the deceased. There was the pink silk dress she had worn on the evening of the ball, here the villainous coat which had not been able to protect her against the cold, close to her, her nude silk stockings, her silver satin shoes, still redolent of her perfume; on a table her fan made of ostrich feathers, her jewels, her various small bottles of lotions, extracts, milks, the variety of jars of cream, paste, powder, alas! All accounted for and ready to meet the needs of the departed. Everything was there intact, only she was missing.

The rose she used to wear on her shoulder was still shining, attached to the vanity, and seemed to disregard the pain of the husband.

> – "Oh!" he cried out one day, mad with discouragement, "my darling wife, why do you lock yourself in a cold tomb when you have my warm arm to support your frail head, you have my heart to receive your confidences, you have my strength to support your weakness . . . It is very cold a tomb, why do you prefer it to our little home, over there at the back of the courtyard?"

"It is so warm even in the depths of winter and still cool in summer since we open our window and our door which overlooks the little balcony . . . Come back, poor swallow, which the mist has chased away, come, and take back your place in the shared nest, a warm ray of sunshine awaits you there . . ."

Then, almost fainting, he collapsed into an armchair. Men's pain, however great, is always silent, but when a man cries and complains out loud and you are sure he is not doing it to make you feel sorry for himself or for a concerned party to see his sensitivity, his pain is so strong that it borders on madness.

Men do not like to show their tears, and often when seeing us shed tears because of their injustices, their inconstancy, or their selfishness, they laugh at our pain and compare us to wind-up dolls that laugh and cry according to the whim of their owner . . . Now, they do not cry unless their suffering overcomes their pride, which often holds so many tears at the corner of their eyes and buries the explosion of sobs in their torn chests. Oh! these proud men, what tears they hide while laughing!

M. Dubourg fell into despair at the death of his wife, and he had not sought, like some widowers, on the very day of the funeral, a friendly hand to dry his tears, tears of a moment, fake tears! No, he loved his wife beyond the grave, and respected her memory which remained intense in his poor heart. His once cheerful house was now only open to a few visitors. He eased his pain a little by covering Madeleine and Jane with his paternal affection, so it was with heartbreak that he said to them one day:

– "My dear girls, I have recommended your mother to a friend who will give her work tomorrow, so she will be able to support you. For me, I am giving you a small donation which will be deposited in the bank, and from which we can withdraw on your behalf if necessary. I am leaving, and if you ever have some free time, pay a visit to my wife. I will come back to retrieve her when the Haitian soil has had enough of her flesh. My poor wife had two homelands: Haiti and France; one took her flesh, the other will have her bones. Yes, I will return to collect her remains, to lay them where so many members of my family already sleep and where I will sleep."

– "Monsieur Dubourg," said Mme Rougerot, "how can I show you my gratitude!"

– "You and your children will write me sometimes, and it will be enough for me."

– "Oh! Allow me to believe that you are my brother, even though we are not of the same race and our skins are far from similar."

    – "When the divine judgment comes, there will be no race, no
nationality, no colors, no wealth, no poverty; there are only poor
sinners returning from a long exile, waiting for their judgment, and
the decision of the Lord. My sister? Yes, you are my sister . . ."

They kissed. Sweet are the bonds of a man and a woman united only
by friendship! They shared some tears and went on their way.

Junie was to start the next day as manager at a new shop. M. Dubourg
asked her to leave her children with him, so he would not be alone.

Madeleine and Jane did so much and so well that they managed to cheer
up their always worried protector. After five months of mourning, you
could run into him walking around with his protégés. Sometimes
you could see him in his living room listening to a plaintive melody
which his wife had taught Madeleine; the notes fell on his heart like
anointing oil.

    – "Continue," he used to say softly, "continue, Madeleine, so I
can keep dreaming . . ."

With his eyes closed, he pictured his wife, a child again, playing this
melody with a few imperfections but playing it anyway.

    – "How beautiful, how sublime," he murmured with tears in his
voice.
    – "Ah!" replied the young artist, "I am closing the piano since
you are crying."
    – "No, this sad instrument that reminds me of my wife was
closed for five months, saving the perfume of her fingers, and I must
get drunk on this perfume blowing in gusts. No, you must study,
Madeleine, or you will lose your touch and deprive me of your
melodious notes. I still see my better half next to you, teaching you;
I think I still hear her in Weber's *Dernière pensée*.[8] Ah! Give me the

8. Violon and piano piece by German composer Carl Maria von Weber (1786–1826).

illusion of being myself . . . Can't you see that I am the shadow of whom I was five months ago?"

Madeleine was not happy, either, despite the great pleasures she found at Dubourg's. Her eyes were still watery even when she did her best to entertain her protector.

She often tried to be cheerful to make Dubourg smile, but her own heart was heavy with grief. She thought:

– "Perhaps when I eat copiously at M. Dubourg's table, when I drink sparkling wine, when I sleep in a soft bed, my father begs for a piece of bread which no one gives him, he is thirsty in a burning dessert. He is tormented by the fear of ferocious beasts, he sleeps on the barren earth using his bare arm as a pillow."

As she was crying one evening, sunken in an armchair, her sister Jane was moved by her grief and asked her:

– "Why are you crying, are you sick?"

– "It is worse than sickness, Jane, I am grieving, I want to see my father."

– "He is in his bedroom, go see him."

Madeleine suddenly grabbed her sister's arm and shook it, hurting her:

– "Say, don't you know that our father is away, that our father's name is Julien Rougerot? Do you know this, yes or no?"

– "You are right, Madeleine, but M. Dubourg is also our daddy dearest? . . ."

– "Yes . . . however, when I say 'daddy,' a word so sweet which comes out of the depths of my heart, know that it is about the other man, the absent, the exiled . . . I may be ungrateful, but what do you want? Filial attachments are so powerful that no other can ever replace them."

– "Don't you love M. Dubourg?"

– "I am very grateful to him, and I wish him the very best in the world: health."

– "I am leaving with him."

– "You cannot. Coward! How? You would leave your mother behind in her misery, when she needs our help, you would flee our home because there is no more bread and enjoy a false happiness in France?

"No, do not be the deserter who gives up the fight on the eve of victory and who is ashamed the next day, and cannot return to his home to be honored after having suffered. No, stay with us under fire, the days of glory are near: Mom is working, Daddy is coming back, we will find ourselves happy soon . . . No, don't go, poor discouraged soldier, the fight will end, wait, do not desert."

Jane, confused, bent under the weight of these words which Madeleine's lofty wisdom had inspired in her, did not answer, but tears drowned her face.

The two little girls threw themselves on each other's hearts and promised not to leave their mother after the departure of their protector.

CHAPTER II

– "Christmas! What a beautiful day to have a baby!" exclaimed Madame Rougerot.

A pink and healthy newborn was crying in a small wicker cradle placed near her bed.

– "Be quiet, poor *chérie*, you should laugh instead. Why begin life with tears? I named you Armand, didn't I? In memory of my dear and good friend. Ah! you won't know him . . . And Julien? Will you see him at least one day? I prefer not to remember that he is so far away. Ah! I told you not to cry, now tears are coming out of my burning eyes and splashing on your nappies . . . No, I want to celebrate your arrival in the world which coincides with that of the son of God. You resemble him but you lack grandeur and magnificence. He was born poor like you, but he is God, and you are a wretched creature, a rag of flesh for whom baptism will soon lead toward a Christian life . . . You will be happy, I hope."

The next day, Jane and Madeleine, who had sung at Midnight Mass and had stayed with the nuns after the ceremony, were very happy to see their family had grown with a little brother.

As they put their shoes near their beds so Baby Jesus could leave presents there, they assumed that Madame Rougerot had found the baby in her own shoes, after having also placed hers near her bed.

– "Oh! I got a doll!" exclaimed Jane.

– "And me, a sewing basket," said Madeleine joyfully. "You see, Jane, I confided to Mom that I wouldn't like to have a doll this year. It seems that the Good Lord heard me."

– "As for me, I like, rather I prefer, the doll. But the person among us who has the most luck is Mom because she found a baby in her shoes," said the little girl.

– "Mom's baby is our brother, Jane, we played a role in Mom's finding him! Oh Christmas! What a beautiful day!"

– "Sure, it is beautiful. But everything is amiss since Father is not here to welcome him with us. He may never know this dear child if death surprises him in a foreign land."

– "Poor child," said the sad, tight-lipped mother, "your pain equals mine, but I wanted to appear strong to prevent you from crying on this beautiful Christmas day. But here we are, Jane who never cries, Jane the incarnation of gaiety and pranks, is sobbing beside the cradle... No, my children, don't, don't cry over this child who is already miserable enough. No, don't cry. A sudden ray of hope fills the depths of my heart. I want you to hope, too, for there is no youth without hope... Who knows if this child won't wash away the shame of our family by paying our debts if my efforts remain fruitless? I will try to pay them off before he does, but if death surprises me in the arduous and unbridled battle I am waging to live, then you, Madeleine, will continue the fight until Armand comes of age. When the time comes, pass him the torn, almost destroyed, banner so he may repair it and ensure the victory of the family. You will thus have accomplished a pious deed."

– "I'm young, but I feel capable of great things. Armand doesn't count, he's so small," said Madeleine.

– "One must always base one's great hopes on a man, even if he is only an infant," replied Madame Rougerot. "A chrysalis today, tomorrow a butterfly! The child who emancipates himself to be useful to his family and to himself, who gains his freedom not to abuse it but to do for his ruined, poor, or infirm parents what they should have done for him, is practically a hero.

"Parents should not be blamed if they have fulfilled their child-rearing duties for as long as they can. Armand, you will be our protector," she continued, pressing the little one to her heart.

M. Henri Rougerot, Julien's old uncle, was displeased by Armand's birth. He accused Junie of having ruined her husband by incessantly purchasing extravagant clothing. He welcomed the news with these callous, transactional words: "This female still gives birth? When one has no fortune, one must limit one's offspring. My nephew is more ruined today than yesterday, and tomorrow he will be more so than today."

Henri was an angry bachelor and an insufferable dotard accustomed to living in filth, deprived of all comforts. He found it excessively funny that a person could buy more than one bed, even if the family consisted of several members.

What was his surprise, one day, to learn that Julien had received an order for three suits and twelve shirts for his personal use! He protested so much against what he called a "vast exaggeration" that he fell out with his nephew. That's why he remained indifferent to the ruin of the poor family.

Junie's business was flourishing day after day, but she was still unable to pay her debts, which had been reduced by half due to the sale of her furniture by the creditors.

– "They leave me the rest of the debt as one throws a bone to a dog. They think I am a poor woman. Ah! They don't know who they're dealing with, I don't want it, I hate other people's belongings. If my husband had made me aware of his situation, I would have bravely thrown myself into the fight with him, but no! He placed me on a pedestal built on sand and pride and surrounded me with poisonous flowers. This pedestal was not solid, Julien, you had to give me your hand to help me come down slowly to avoid this fatal fall. When I married you, I promised to help you if you ever needed my help, but you did not give me the opportunity to be useful to the community at the height of our troubles."

"Julien, you didn't trust my courage, you left me idle next to the work in peril, you let a sentry sleep at the approach of danger, with the certainty that the worst was averted. Ah! How angry I am with you for that, how angry I am with you! You satisfied my most secret desires, and when I pointed out to you that your business was going down, you laughed at me and closed my mouth with a kiss. When I offered you my help, you mocked me and asked me what I could do that you had not already done. When I offered to work for you as secretary, you placed this iron bar between work and me: 'Your children! Who will take care of them the way you do!'

"You didn't want me to know about your debts, alas! And here you are on the run, leaving them to me. When I suggested you sell our car, since it was more of a luxury than a necessity, you became outraged. So, I thought I hadn't really understood our real situation, and that I was truly crazy, as you so often told me . . . Julien, why didn't you make me your muse? A man married under the laws of the community must get advice from his wife before doing anything impacting their life together as the blessings, like the misfortunes, resulting from the acts of one of the spouses, fall inevitably on the community."

"There are marriages, some that love did not create, and others that love alone built, in which a contract guaranties that each spouse is independent and solely responsible for their interests.

There again, these spouses, although independent, must still have the most basic courtesy, the most natural feeling of confraternity to join their two brains, their two energies, and their two hearts when having to accomplish serious tasks. But this was not our case; our interests were only shared under the law."

"There are so many follies single men wouldn't make if only a feminine voice sometimes rose in the silence of their homes to say no. That voice might sound like a prayer of supplication but would, in reality, be a powerful order." And that's how the unfortunate woman spoke to herself.

Junie was still without news of her husband when, more sad than sick, she went to bed. The doctor prescribed her a trip to the countryside.

– "Alas! How can I return to the countryside if I can't guarantee in advance the proper functioning of my business?"

Eventually, a cousin offered to help, and Junie left her the management of her operation.

Armand was six months old, but he had grown so strong they would have thought him twelve. The fresh air gave him a complexion like the beautiful peaches of Kenscoff. He lived freely among the flowers and the bushes; he watched the dead leaves fall from the tall trees and tried to catch them before they landed near him. Oh! What a vigorous effort he made!

His mother sat him down on the bare, warm ground to get him used to misery, which would only become more severe because inside her, alas! Another little one grew. Yes, she felt the baby, ready to scream. She couldn't lie to herself anymore: she was going to be a mother.

The sun, with its golden coat, barely showed the folds on the horizon when, for the second time in less than two years, Madame Rougerot heard the cries of a newborn baby in her room.

– "It's a girl," said a matron, "a big girl!"

– "Poor child," said the woman in a deep sigh. "Who will take pity on her, who will be just enough to pardon her for her shameful birth?"

– "The Good Lord!" said the midwife.

– "Oh! Yes, Prémice, yes, for he gave her to me."

The poor woman withdrew inward and devoted herself entirely to her last two children, since M. Henri Rougerot had placed the older ones in a boarding school at Lalue and was responsible for their monthly payments.

The poor baby girl was growing up, she was three months old, nameless, and unbaptized, like a little wild beast in the woods. Junie harbored the sweet hope of finding a charitable person to give the child to, someone who would raise the baby secretly and who would allow Junie to go and kiss her sometimes while saying: "My daughter!" Alas! This friend, this sister, this saint did not appear.

Upon learning that her business was beginning to decline, Junie begged her employer to terminate the contract she signed with him to manage the store. She could no longer resume her work; she was exhausted.

– "I'm without bread, it's true, but I won't have any new debts," she wrote wistfully in a letter to her employer.

Without bread. Yes, she could no longer feed her two babies. Her breasts were empty, anemia had dried up her milk.

To feed someone, you must feed yourself, for it's your life—a poisoned life—that you pass drop by drop to the little one you want to save from hunger. Because of her deprivation, Mme Rougerot's illness became more serious, even life threatening.

One day, however, when she was feeling better, Prémice led her to a chaise lounge. Junie had sat there with her two children for almost an hour when the good woman stormed in, took "Bébé" hastily and left, saying:

> – "Here they come!"
>
> – "Here they come!" repeated Madame Rougerot daftly. "I don't understand these words, so devoid of meaning for me. I expect nothing and no one. Here they come! Ah! If only it was my children, my other children of whom I have been so deprived!"
>
> – "Mom, where are you?" cried out Madeleine and Jane.
>
> – "Them! Yes, it is them, I am so happy! I thought I would die without seeing them again. Oh! May they never know my sin!"
>
> – "Mom," they cried louder.
>
> – "My dear children!"

She wanted to stand up to kiss them, but she lacked strength, and her head fell heavily on the back of the chaise lounge. She let out a little cry of pain.

> – "Are you hurt?" said Madeleine sadly.
>
> – "No, I'm simply happy."
>
> – "And sick, aren't you? Do you know . . . I have good news. Here is a letter from Daddy."

This time, Junie screamed in despair and turned her head away. No, she was no longer worthy of the absent man. No, she couldn't dare to look at this writing which, like the all-seeing eye of God, seemed to penetrate her secret.

The two little girls did not know why their mother was so moved and above all so sad. There was a heavy silence during which all of Junie's blood seemed to rush to her already so sick heart. It was Jane who ended it:

> – "Mom, I don't like your house, it's not beautiful and besides, there's no furniture, no mirrors? Is there a large yard? I am going to look around."

– "No, no, don't do that, please don't go into the yard," Junie begged in stupor.

– "What is it, Mom? Calm down, Jane won't go into the yard," concluded the eldest.

– "Yes," said the unfortunate woman with relief, "there is . . . there is . . . a . . . a . . ."

– "A ferocious beast?" finally said Jane.

– "Less than that . . ."

– "A dog?"

– "More than that . . ."

Fear had driven her almost mad, so she was raving, saying sentences the children could not understand.

– "My dear little ones, there are children who live modestly and without bread in the countryside, without clothes, without any of the joys of childhood . . . To think that they could have been like you if fate had been on their side. If you ever come back to these parts, bring them bread, clothes, toys, and a bit of your grace."

As she said those words, she thought of Bébé, "baby" as Prémice called her, whom she was to abandon soon, without parents, unknown to anyone who could ease her misery. Perched on Madeleine's legs, Armand watched the conversation without understanding a thing. She had brought him a big wooden horse and candies.

M. Rougerot's letter lay there on the sick woman's only table, unopened for more than an hour, which surprised the children. They pointed it out to the dying woman.

– "I will open it," she said, "I will open it, but first let me prepare myself . . ."

She opened it and read it. She cried. Why was she crying today more than yesterday, since Julien's letter announced his imminent return with a fortune earned in a foreign land? Julien was coming back and had five thousand dollars! Why wasn't she happy? No, because of her child, this poor martyr whom she was obliged to hide, would not share this happiness.

———

Her daughters were long gone, and she was still crying. When night fell, drowning her bedroom in its cold darkness, she was still crying, the fateful letter in her hand, smeared with tears, all crumpled with . . . shame!

Armand was hungry and began to cry, Bébé was latching at the breast, trying to feed herself, but alas! She suddenly flew into a rage and there was a desperate uproar in the dark bedroom. Hunger and death reigned there. Prémice had gone out in search of a piece of bread for Armand and a bit of sugar to sweeten the poppyseed tea she had made to stave off Bébé's hunger and soothe her cries.

– "Charity for my poor family," she said to passers-by who did not believe her. Three hours had already passed, and she had yet to come back. No, she would not return until she had enough to ease the misery of her unfortunate guests.

Oh! To see a three-month-old baby angry at an empty breast which she instinctively latched on with force, with annoyance, with rage, to try to appease in vain the extreme hunger tormenting her, is something that breaks the heart. Prémice, the brave peasant, witnessed this terrifying and painful scene almost every day.

Finally, when she returned, all was asleep, things and beings. Twenty centimes was her bounty. Prémice was a dairy farmer, but she only had one cow who no longer gave her milk—she was pregnant—and who was anemic, barren for lack of nutritious pasture. As a result, the poor woman was without support. Her man, tired of suffering, had joined the exodus of workers to Cuba and had not returned for a long time.

Junie saw each day end with a little hope, as she kept telling herself that she would find help at the dawn of the following day. But no, days all born and died without bringing the assistance she was waiting for patiently. No milk for Bébé, no bread for Armand, no broth and medicine for the dying woman. Nothing. Nothing in the house, not even sunlight, because Prémice left the only door closed to protect Junie from the winds coming down the mountain. When the latter, under the weight of her suffocating illness, asked for fresh air or a ray of sunshine, the only things she could have free of charge, the peasant woman, kind but cautious, replied idiotically:

– "No, the winds!"

Sometimes Junie rebelled, fuming with rage before the apathy of her protectress who, despite being devoted to her patient, condemned her to the most terrible asphyxiation:

– I am suffocating, Prémice, you must allow a person whose lungs are wheezing. I suffer from a lung disease, and I'm breathing stale air. I'm killing my children, Prémice, I'm poisoning you and I'm dying in pain . . . Open the door!

At other times she begged her, trying to break the harsh surveillance with her tears:

– "Prémice, can't you see I'm suffocating? Whether "the winds," as you say, precipitate my death or not, I must die soon, this evening probably. At least allow me to die peacefully, without the struggle to gasp for air . . ."

– "Alright," replied the ignorant woman, "I'll open the door"— there was only one door and a window—"but if your disease worsens, you will be the one your parents will blame."

– "My parents!" said Junie, more than revolted, "my parents! Come on then, I have no one else but my children and you!"

– "And your uncle, M. Henri?"

– "Don't talk about him, Prémice, I forbid it. My uncle is waiting for me to die to advertise his false generosity . . . Ah! Why shouldn't my death remain as unknown as my terrible suffering? No, I do not want a pompous funeral. I am a destitute woman; my burial will not be that of a rich person."

She said these things with sincerity and without hatred, not wanting
to blame her uncle for her destiny. One evening, the most dreadful of those
she had experienced, she called Prémice and gave her Bébé. She was unable
to take it any longer. Drawing the peasant woman to her bed, she whispered in her ear . . . She had placed a piece of paper on the child's chest
with a gold and diamond brooch, a jewel Madame Dubourg had been able
to save from the auction held at Junie's house some time before. On the
note, she had written a name, her daughter's real name. Prémice left.
The dying woman, mad with pain, called her back:

> – Let me kiss her, let me hug her one last time, and then quickly
> run and take her to her second mother . . . Prémice, promise me,
> whatever happens, never tell anyone the name of the woman who
> gave birth to this unfortunate baby, and that of her father . . .
> When Julien returns, I will already be dead, I will only have to
> answer to God, to God alone."
> – "He's coming back tomorrow."
> – "Yes, I will have finished my pilgrimage."
> – "Don't say that, Madame Rougerot."
> – "Oh! Bah . . . Prémice, take the child and leave with her,"
> said the martyr woman with a heroic resignation. Then, extending
> her hand:
> – "Be happy, Bébé!"

She turned her head away, so as not to see this piece of herself leave,
and fainted. Prémice returned an hour later. Beings and things slept in
silence. Tormented by the thought of telling Madame Rougerot what had
happened, Prémice decided it best to watch over the patient:

> – "Madame," she said, "I went to the alley and saw no one. Bébé
> was in a big basket, sleeping soundly. I entered the yard and met a
> maid. 'Is Madame here?' I said, trembling. 'She's out, wait for her,

she'll be back home soon.' I was afraid the child would wake up and cry. I put down the basket with a thousand precautions and pretended to wait. The housekeeper went to get me a chair. I was leaving when I ran into the lady. I approached her with these words:

'I left a basket with a letter for you, Madame.'
'Who sent them?' she asked curiously.
'My mistress.'
'Your mistress has a name?'
'I forgot it because I have only been at her service since this morning.'
'Oh! Well, I'll wait for the answer.'
'I'm in a hurry, I'll be back tomorrow morning.'
'That is fine.'"

The moving story of the anxious peasant was received in complete silence.

– "Madame Rougerot! Madame, Madame!"

She bent over and took Junie's hand. Alas! She was stiff and cold . . . Prémice let go of the deceased's hand in a stupor. Her scream woke up little Armand, who had been put to sleep by hunger:

– "Mom!" said the child instinctively, bringing his fingers to his pale mouth.

He was afraid of the dead woman who had become the shadow of herself. He wanted to be taken away from his mother. Prémice, herself distraught, took him in her arms.

The neighbors came running. Warned, the old uncle had the corpse taken away immediately. The next day, oh irony of fate! Curious people gathered near the chapel of the Sacred Heart in Turgeau[1] to see a large,

1. Turgeau is part of Port-au-Prince's Gingerbread District.

very large, convoy pass by. The funeral carriage disappeared under a blanket of flowers. Under their black lace coats, the horses showed only their feet and the tips of their shiny hooves. The flowers? Oh! They were everywhere: on and inside the funeral coach, with ribbons, strips of tulle, so many furbelows indispensable to vanity. A man said:

> – "When one has so much money, one should invent some balm to protect from death."
> – "Alas!" whispered another, "many of those who go away thus adorned are also those killed by hunger and privations of all kinds . . . Some rich people abandon their own to the most dreadful misery and then prepare a sumptuous grave for them. Alas! Those who did not have a roof over their head while being full of life and who passed overwhelmed by misfortunes, find a palace to protect their remains and worms that feed from them."

They were back from the Necropolis and the children were still crying, still crying.

> – "Quiet now," said M. Henri. "Junie was no longer useful to you."
> – "A mother is always useful," Madeleine retorted, "even if she is impotent and you have to sacrifice everything you have to take care of her: pleasures, possessions, health, life . . . Feeling that she loves you is already a blessing, but knowing that you owe her your life is immeasurable."
> – "Don't worry little one, your mom is better off in her beautiful tomb than in Mam'zelle[2] Prémice's shack."
> – "How does the wealth and size of her vault matter to her? Does she have the immensity of the heavens for her home? My mother has

---

2. Colloquial form of *Mademoiselle*, "Miss" in English.

suffered too much for God not to have given her a place, a good place, beside to his throne."

– "The nuns teach you a lot of morals. Luckily, I don't owe them a penny. They never asked you to become a nun?"

– "You are joking, Uncle Henri, you are joking on the day when my soul suffers as it has never suffered in my life. You cannot know how I suffer, and you do not know how happy my mother would be if she had lived ten more years . . . I wish to work hard to rehabilitate her after leaving school. If it had been the Lord's will, I would not have become a little dressed doll who expects everything from her parents or from a husband. No. I would have been a young girl who works and brings her share to the home which gave her so much. But God took my mother, and my father must come back to care for Armand. I'm going to enter a convent. They do so many beautiful things there. I'll work for the poor, and Jane will come with me, she's the youngest and my only friend. We'll go together."

– "Don't do this, child. You will regret it."

– "Only God knows!"

– "So, you loved Junie more than your father?"

– "I never said that!"

– "Well! Julien arrives tonight or tomorrow, so why are you so sad?"

Madeleine did not answer and continued to cry next to Jane and Armand, who was already consoled. It is true that if the youngest had cried while his sisters were grieving, it was only to get his milk.

Now that he had been fed, he laughed at his stuffed animal, a little dog he had loved as soon as he'd arrived at his uncle's house. Children love change, and Armand felt happy surrounded with his wooden horse—a witness to his past miseries—a pretty ball, and a thousand other trinkets that the old man bought him to distract him.

CHAPTER III

Peeping through the louvered window, Julien realized that a death had occurred.

– "Too late!" he cried out, "too late!"

Madeleine and Jane jumped into his arms:

– "Daddy, you must know since you're crying, you know, don't you?"

– "Yes, all these chairs, these candelabra, these scattered flower petals on the floor, these wall hangings, this smell of new wood, of turpentine,[1] of formalin,[2] make me understand that not long ago, someone was there, lying down lifeless. But do tell . . . tell me that it's not Junie, that it's not my uncle Henri that . . ."

At these words, he saw the old man holding out his arms to him.

– "Oh!" he said, "so she was the one that was just buried . . . She would come out running at the sound of my voice. She would come and cry on my chest . . . if she were here. It's her, is not it? Is it Junie?"

1. A pine-based resin.
2. A strong scented liquid meant to preserve dead beings.

Madeleine uttered a cry that left him in no doubt. He was confused, remorseful, and in tears. But at the sight of Armand, whom he did not yet know, he regained his composure:

– "My son! My son! My dear child."

He hugged him tightly while the child looked at him, astonished, without trying to detach himself from his father. Then came Armand's bedtime. It was he who fulfilled this role for the first time, and every evening since then. He put the child to sleep while wiping his eyes, hesitating between his duty and the desire to flee the house which now seemed so empty because of the absence of his wife.

Still grieving, Madeleine and Jane returned to the boarding school a few days later.

M. Julien Rougerot paid his debts and resumed his business, this time with more experience and less excess.

He placed Armand in the care of Saint-Louis de Gonzague, a Catholic school whose praise was second to none, and devoted himself entirely to the education of his three children.

What had become of Bébé? Mystery!

Whom had Junie entrusted her to? Daedalus!

Where was Prémice? No one knew!

CHAPTER IV

Madeleine and Jane were finishing their studies at the school Sainte Rose de Lima when a beautiful little eight-year-old girl was placed in the establishment and took a liking to them. They too felt how much this child was dear to them, so their souls were very saddened after their final exams not only because they were going to leave the boarding school where they had spent the best part of their lives, but mostly because they had to leave behind the affectionate Adeline Renaudy.

Since leaving Sainte Rose, Madeleine and Jane had never seen the friend we mentioned above again, and little by little her memory had faded. In the meantime, Adeline Renaudy had grown up and left the school where she had cheerfully spent her childhood. She was now a young girl full of charms, a pretty brunette, as the tropics produce, an authentic daughter of the sun with incomparably dark hair. Two beacons of light, fringed by a velvety shadow, lit up her joyful and malicious face.

Svelte, slender, she wore her clothes with a grace that reminded people of those mysterious mythological goddesses represented in gilded frames.

Well, Adeline was a little fairy who turned the heads of the young people and who, mockingly, sent them smiles that were sometimes welcoming, sometimes repulsive. She knew she was beautiful; they sang it to her so often! She took immense pleasure in making her admirers suffer. In addition, she was rich and saw each suitor as an ambitious one. A dowry, a large dowry, is something so rare in Haiti. She repeated these words to herself with pride. In Haiti, one marries the woman they love without ever demanding a dowry (with rare exceptions).

M. and Mme Renaudy had three children, of whom Adeline was the eldest and the most spoiled. Roland and Rose, the other two, were much younger and looked nothing like her. They were high yellow and chubby, while Adeline was dark and thin.

– "Oh! I'm sixteen today! So many flowers! So many presents! I am very happy!"

These are the words with which the young Adeline woke up one morning in January and then, her heart swollen with joy and pride, she ran to kiss her parents, who were waiting for her to wake up to celebrate.

– "We are gifting you a trip to Europe," said M. Renaudy, "a group of nuns is leaving Port-au-Prince in April on the *Macoris*, you will be going with them, won't you Adeline?"

Stunned, the young girl could not believe her ears. Oh! To see Paris! Paris the marvelous city! To see this corner of the world known to all dreams, to walk on the enchanted soil, to smell the invigorating air of Europe, to finally live the life of the Parisians! Wasn't she in a dream? Wasn't it a maddening dream, a deceptive mirage that toyed with her being? Why, was she dreaming while awake? No, she was not dreaming.

———

It was April. Here she was, installed in a cabin, here she was, on the open sea, far from all those who loved her, with only their hearts as their compasses. France! Paris! Why was Paris so far away, and her heart so tormented? She was ill with fear and expectation. No, she could only stay a fortnight longer without seeing France and her precious jewel of which everyone wants a piece: Paris!

Finally, one morning, the sky which had been a little cloudy the day before became serene, and Le Havre appeared in the midst of a bright ray of sunshine.

– "I'm in France," cried Adeline, moved to tears, "I'm in the heart of the second homeland of all!"

A few hours later, Paris, her Paris, finally welcomed her. How to describe the joy, the immense intoxication which filled her whole soul and made her cry with contentment!

The night came. She thought Paris was in flames, as the electric bulbs projected their light, sometimes bright, sometimes softened by some streetlamp. When she went to bed, she thought that everything around her was phosphorescent and bathed her in a soft light.

– "Paris," she said as one says a prayer, "may I draw from you all that you can give! I want to enjoy your charms until, tired, swooning, I felt the need to leave!"

She fell asleep, a smile on her lips, and joy in her heart.

The young girl was happy too. She wrote to her parents, to her friends, and she often said to herself in soulful monologues:

– "How happy I am," she said one evening. "My soul is light and delighted, it seems that I have never cried. When I'll wish to remember what suffering feels like, I will not be able to . . ."

Poor Adeline! She did not know that the future would be unpleasant to her one day. Her life would change, of course, she would become more beautiful, more radiant next to a fiancé and later in the arms of a husband, then an adored wife, she would feel within her the first heartbeats of a little stranger . . . unknown, but how dear and how long awaited! Then, one day, O blessed day! In a cradle, she would see a very small brown or pink head returning her motherly smile. And there, very close by, her husband, moved by emotion, admiring the little living flower, this part of himself and of his beloved.

Finally, old, now a grandmother, there she is surrounded by grandchildren, telling them a thousand stories. This is how Adeline imagined her life, without thinking that the future, this bitter and sweet word, is an uncertain path built on moving sands—under which there is a chasm—which will open under your feet when you least expect it, and which becomes firm when you feel that one more step is precipitating you into the abyss.

Adeline had just spent a year in Paris when she received a letter from her parents calling her back to Haiti. She was happy because nostalgia was already gripping her heart. In Paris, she was an ordinary person, people saw her pass wrapped in her pretty silk or woolen coat without stopping to look at her, without telling her how pretty and richly dressed she was. No one knew her.

Ah! No, she had to change her life, go back and show her compatriots how many beautiful dresses she had bought. She only had to go to the two movie theaters in Port-au-Prince to show off her rich outfits, which would create tears of envy there, whereas in Paris, they left the greatest socialites and the most modest workers indifferent. Eventually, tired of being able to cause neither the envy nor the jealousy of others, Adeline decided to adopt only two outfits per season, as many French women do.

Every day, the young girl ran to the shops to buy a thousand little things to bring back to her country.

– "It's funny," she thought looking at a richly dressed young man the day before her departure, "my heart beats for this gentleman. What if I loved him? But a woman does not approach a man to confess her love to him . . . How unfair are social convenances! I'm going to tell him that I love him . . ."

The young girl pulled herself together and felt daunted by thinking that for a second she had the urge to cry out her love to this stranger. She, at whose feet a thousand love confessions came to die each day, admissions she laughed at. Now a stranger had stolen her heart, paralyzed her pride, bruised her dreams. Yes, she loved this indifferent young man who had just entered the store where she herself was standing. Their gazes met like two flashes of lightning. They stared at each other for a minute, attracted to each other, then Armand Rougerot, for that's who he was, came up to Adeline:

   – "Hello, Mademoiselle," he said, "it seems to me that I've already met you in Haiti. Excuse me if I do not remember your name or where I met you."
   – "You are mistaken, Monsieur, I've never met you," she said, affecting an air of superiority.
   – "Excuse me, then, excuse me. You know, when you're on a foreign land, away from your family—especially for an unlimited time—you're always happy to meet a person you bumped into there. We seek in everyone a compatriot, an exiled countryman who also suffers from nostalgia. One searches for a soulmate to share one's happiness and one's pain, to wipe away one's tears. The mirage is so believable that you quickly imagine you carry a part of your homeland, of your absent homeland."
   – "Oh! To find someone who walked on the land of your ancestors, who cried and laughed there, who saw your flag flying during the most agonizing hours as well as the most beautiful days, who knows that we are lying when we say that Haitians are cannibals and that the most enlightened dance is Vaudou. Oh, to find in a foreign land someone who can say in front of a thousand Europeans that the Haitian elite rivals that of the largest countries of the world and that it is not the Americans, our great friends, who showed us the way to school; that Pétion, more than a century ago bestowed us with a high school which still thrives, and which provides elites to my country. To find someone is something relieving, something I always crave . . . I am Haitian, Mademoiselle, and I'm proud to be."

– "I, too, am Haitian."

– "Oh! I was not mistaken," said Armand with tears in his voice. He held her hands.

– "Excuse me," slipped Mademoiselle Renaudy, "you are compromising me, Monsieur, there are a thousand buyers who can see us . . . who are already looking at us . . ."

– "Let's get out of here, shall we?"

They went to the Bois de Boulogne and sat close together. The young girl pretended to get up after five minutes, but Armand objected.

– "I'm telling you, Monsieur, we are being watched," concluded Adeline.

– "We're not doing anything wrong, Mademoiselle, we're talking. You can't be indifferent to my love . . . Can't you see that I love you?"

– "Monsieur!"

– "Please, tell me your name, I love you, I love you, can't you see that I am madly in love with you?"

– "Enough!" said Adeline with authority. Then, gathering herself, she lowered her voice to say these words full of tenderness:

– "Why is your stay here unlimited? Why not leave tomorrow? . . ."

– "Alas! I can't. I must become a lawyer before returning to Haiti. My father and my sisters want me to have extraordinary qualities. I, too, once had this ambition, but everything disappears in the light of your eyes . . . Yes, I want to leave without my diploma, I want to leave with you tomorrow. Isn't tomorrow the day of your departure? I feel it in my heart. Oh, tell me your name . . . May it cure my pain."

– "Adeline Renaudy."

– "Adeline Renaudy! Oh, what a lovely name! Adeline! May this name be engraved forever in my heart!"

– "Poor young man!" let out the overwrought girl.

– "It's understood, I'm leaving tomorrow. Will you allow it? Order and I'll follow you like a dog follows its master."

– "No, you will stay, Monsieur. One does not break the dreams of their parents that way; be constant . . . and soon, you will be a lawyer, I wish you that."

– "But I love you . . . do you share my love?"

– "Oh! Monsieur!"

– "Do you love me a little? Oh! Don't tell me no, don't break the heart of an orphan who yearns for a mother's tenderness . . . Adeline, be that mother, fulfill the sterile desire that has tortured me for so long. I have sisters who spoil me a lot, but I need a different love to fill the big void I feel in my heart despite everything. Adeline, I don't have a mother, do you want to be my mother?"

– "Yes . . ."

– "Oh! Let us seal our oath with this ring that I wear on my finger . . . I am Armand Rougerot. Armand Rougerot, remember this name . . . Here is my portrait."

– "How can someone forget the name of the one they love? They should only hear it once!"

He put the ring on the left ring finger of Adeline, who did not refuse this secret engagement.

– "For life!" they said in a love duet.
– "For life!" echoed the little birds.

Now, as they felt dear to each other, they were each thinking: How could we have lived so long without knowing each other, since it seems that we are each other's soul mate?

They had risen. Where were they going? They did not know. They hadn't spoken to each other for a long time and had been walking aimlessly, when Armand broke the silence with this exclamation:

– "Where did you get the brooch that holds your scarf? I have the same one on my tie . . ."

– "My mother gave it to me . . ."

– "It's strange, Adeline, it's also my mother who gave me mine as an inheritance. She had two; the other got lost, according to Daddy and my sisters."

– "What makes them unusual is the number 13 made of tiny diamonds. Mine gets everyone's attention, Armand."

– "Mine too!"

– "It's my talisman, I never leave it behind."

– "Yes, a lucky charm, but rare and expensive, huh?"

– "Armand," said the young girl abruptly, "our tête-à-tête has gone on long enough . . . I feel bad for my parents, who would never want to believe I would do what I'm doing now. I want to remain worthy of the trust they have placed in my seriousness. I won't see you again before I leave. I will see you again in Haiti. Leave!"

Armand protested, but Adeline held firm.

– "If you really love me, do not compromise my name and my dignity as a young girl. We've already shown ourselves in public . . . You don't bruise the flowers that adorn your boudoir, you take care of them, so they don't fade too quickly . . . go away."

– "You're right, Adeline. I don't want your parents to be told that you were promiscuous in France and that I compromised the reputation of an honest girl. Let's part ways, but not without swearing the most inviolable fidelity."

– "I swear to love you always," said Adeline resolutely.

– "I swear it too," said Armand, moved.

They went their separate ways. But Armand had only taken a few steps before he called his fiancée back to tell her he would be returning to Haiti in August of the same year, immediately after the July exams.

The next day, the young girl boarded the *Macoris*.

– "Au revoir, Paris," she said, "good-bye beautiful museums, beautiful monuments, good-bye Versailles and your illuminated fountains, real enchantment, real magic. Good-bye to all of you, things and beings, you have charmed me so much, I'll cherish these memories!"

She said these words with gratitude, because she had received nothing but affection and joy in Paris. The proof? She carried a hundred photographs in her suitcase, pictures of the people to whom she had been introduced and of the marvelous things she had seen and which she had enjoyed. She was grateful to this Paris which had shared a little of its life, which had polished her already so distinguished manners!

– "Oh!" she said to the French women traveling to Haiti for the first time, "I have some of your France in the folds of my dress and in the depths of my heart. My eyes are still full of your beautiful things! May you find in my country, not artificial marvels but panoramas: a blue sky, sunsets, the most majestic moonlit evenings you will ever see. You will never see the trees bereft of leaves, the rosebushes without flowers even in the dead of winter. You will never see houses stingy of welcome or hearts deprived of love. We love the French in Haiti!

"When summer covers the towns with its veil of fire, you will seek asylum in the countryside and the villages: in Pétion-Ville or Kenscoff if you are in Port-au-Prince; in Pivert if you live in Saint-Marc; in Plaisance if you are in Cap-Haïtien; in l'Islet if you live in Les Cayes . . . so on and so forth. There you will await the return of autumn in the company of the little inhabitants of the air who will charm you with their melodies.

"You will go to Furey—Oh! Trust me—where you will find Continental temperatures and where you will see pine trees whose highs rival the tops of your skyscrapers. I am probably exaggerating, but you can judge for yourselves."

A few days later, Adeline was with her family, which had two new members: Marie and Louise Guitton, Madame Renaudy's nieces whose mother had just passed away. Adeline was hostile to these children who, she said, deprived her of some of her parents' affection. However, little by little, her animosity subsided. Hadn't she too shared the affection she had reserved to her family? Armand, was he not the sovereign of her heart? So, she had her revenge.

The orphans—children brought up with care—did so much and so well that they ended up defeating Adeline's hostility and earning her warmest friendship.

———

It was May. Wildflowers—there are so many in Haiti—adorned the small ravine that borders Pétion-Ville when one is north of the Saint-Pierre's Chapelle and faces east to the end of Rue X.

> – "Let's go out!" said Adeline to the four other children, "let's go and strip Mother Nature of her ornaments; let's rob her of her beautiful flower's garlands, her tufts of jasmine, her moonflowers smiling at the sun. Tomorrow is Sunday, we'll fill the salons with them, and we'll entwine them with the 'civilized' flowers, that is to say our roses, our beautiful red roses . . ."

They left. Oh! What a charming sight! The pretty white butterflies of June, free, hatched a month earlier in a chimerical and mad flight, left their shelter, all happy, joyful, and ready for their short and fatal destiny. One could already see here and there that some without wings, without antennae, who without heads, were dying on the ground, beaten down by the children. The hands of these kids were white with the fine dust left by the touch of butterflies' wings.

Half an hour later, the ground was covered with corpses, but thousands of other little beings, freshly hatched, were being chased by these reckless murderers.

"Poor little white butterflies!" thought Adeline. "Why is your life so fragile and our game so brutal?"

– "Let's go," she said aloud, "these corpses disgust and sadden me." *Why don't I have wings too? Me, to be less fragile, to fly toward my lover! God gave them wings to fly and die under our feet. Oh! If I had any, it would be to live, to make happy the one who loves me and whom I adore, to tell him that he is my golden calf, my only idol!*

CHAPTER V

– "What's wrong, my daughter?" asked Mireille, seeing Adeline's eyes all red. "You cried. Why?"

Adeline let her tears fall freely on her mother's chest:

– "Mom, Mom, I'm in pain . . ."

– "Well, what's wrong with you?"

– "I'm in love."

– "Oh!"

– "Don't start scolding me, listen to me instead."

– "I don't understand you . . ."

– "I got engaged to Armand, and here is the ring he gave me to seal our oath."

– "Adeline, I . . ."

– "I promised my hand to Armand, I tell you, and soon he will write to Daddy to confirm what I . . ."

– "I understand you less and less, so please be quiet. First of all, you talk to me about your Armand as if he were someone I know. Who is this Armand you are talking about? Does he only have a first name?"

– "Armand Rougerot. I know that you already accept my choice . . ."

– "Don't worry . . . I don't know the young man."

– "He is a good man: educated, kind, sweet, thrifty, handsome, affectionate."

Mme Renaudy interrupted her:

– "Enough with the qualities, Adeline."

But she was thinking that this child's heart is now trapped in a vice, oh Lord! May this young man be decent, for if it were otherwise this little one would die of grief. She addressed bitter reproaches to her daughter:

– "You shouldn't have promised yourself to this young man whose parents we don't know. And what truly grieves me is that you accepted a jewel from him."

– "I do not consider the ring a piece of jewelry. It is only the thing that unites our oath. Armand could have given me a flower, a straw, a trifle that I would keep just as preciously. This ring is important to me, Mom. My fiancé and I, we have sworn on it to always love each other. I also have his portrait, there next to my heart."

– "Poor child!"

Mireille took the girl's head in her hands and kissed her forehead, which was burning with fever:

– "You're sick, Adeline, go to bed."

– "So, you accept?" said the young child.

– "I forbid you to say that you are engaged. You mustn't choose a husband for yourself. This is up to your father and me."

Adeline protested:

– "Times have changed, it's not the parents . . ."

Then, calming down:

– "It's Armand I love . . . it's him that I'm going to marry. Parents shouldn't choose a husband for me . . . it doesn't happen anymore . . . I don't want . . . I don't want . . ."

– "I don't recognize you . . . Adeline, enough."

– "I will marry Armand."

Madame Renaudy left her, ran to her bedroom, knelt in front of her crucifix, and prayed for a long time, asking that peace return to her child.

– "Mireille," said M. Renaudy, crossing the threshold of the bedroom, "I received a marriage proposal for Adeline, but I decided that the marriage will not take place. I do not know the young man, but I know his father. His past isn't spotless."

– "Sons should not, if they are honest, suffer from their parents' faults. In good conscience, Jules, is this young man responsible for his father's past?"

– "Yes, of course. When you have a family, your bad behavior shouldn't undermine the foundations of the genealogical foundation your ancestors built for you. I don't want M. Armand Rougerot because his father is a . . ."

– "Don't finish, Jules, think that "mastering others is strength. Mastering yourself is true power." Don't say anything bad about the man who will become our son-in-law . . ."

– "My son-in-law? So, are you supporting him? Do you know him?"

– "Sure, I know him, he is a decent young man."

– "Well, I don't want him for my daughter."

– "Are you going, like a vile Cerberus, to place yourself between happiness and Adeline?"

– "This marriage is not proper. Come on then. A Renaudy does not marry a Rougerot. Mireille, you are a bad mother, and you will be responsible for this child's misfortune by your cruel weakness . . .

I love Adeline very much, but I will not allow my fatherly love to be a blindness and thereby compromise my daughter's future. Mireille, she will suffer one day if she marries this man, she will suffer when she discovers this past which forever tarnishes her name and that of her children. Adeline is proud; think about it."

   – "One forgets so quickly . . ."

   – "History never forgets!"

   – "Are you kidding! What does she have to do with the debts this unfortunate man had? Debts, alas, which led to his exile. He redeemed himself since he is still in business. Besides, trade debts don't matter . . ."

   – "What! Are you talking nonsense—we should pardon M. Rougerot? Adeline shall not marry him."

   – "Adeline will die . . ."

   – "Too bad. I'll bury her."

   – "Jules!"

   – "Yes!"

   – "You're tough . . ."

   – "And you, you are too soft."

   – "You're playing on words," she said, wiping her eyes.

They heard a scream in the next room: Adeline had fallen on the floor, unconscious. Bright red blood bled from her head, which had a deep wound.

   – "You see," said Mireille, shouting at her husband, "that's the result of your cruel words, she heard everything."

The young girl remained unconscious for almost an hour, then, little by little, she opened her eyes.

She did not speak, but her gaze showed her silent pain. She was lying like a wounded animal which, unable to speak, points to its bruised paws, licking them, and asking you for help.

After eight days of complete silence, whether intended or not, Adeline rebelled energetically against her doctor's treatment:

> – "Let me die doctor, I don't want to take anything anymore . . . Don't dress my wound anymore. Let it become infected so that it takes me away quickly . . ."

These choppy words, pronounced with the greatest discouragement, fell on the hearts of M. and Mme Renaudy like molten lead. They visibly suffered, so the doctor guessed that the young girl was more sad than sick. He prescribed fresh air and plenty of distractions. They were already in Pétion-Ville, so where could they find a better climate? What distractions had to be created for her to relax her mind? She refused to do anything and took pleasure in shutting herself up in her room for entire days, alone, lying between her clammy sheets with the portrait of her beloved.

Mireille, hesitating, suggested that Adeline go to Kenscoff.

> – "No," said the old man, "no, Mireille, Kenscoff is too deserted this time of the year. And this child would mope under the tall trees at the bottom of the valleys to hide the tears she's poorly holding back."
>
> – "And why does this matter to you?" cried out the furious young girl, "only my mother feels a little pity for my pain. Father, I want to die since you want it . . . I don't need any distraction."
>
> – "I have listened to you enough and I'm ordering you to be quiet," retorted M. Renaudy. "Yes, enough . . . You have fallen in love with a young man whose name is not worthy of ours. It is up to me to tell you that you have chosen badly; and if, despite my advice, you persist in nourishing this unhappy love, it is because you have no pity for my old age and no respect for the name you bear."
>
> – "Your name? My name? I will point out to you that the stain that soils the Rougerot's name cannot reach yours since by law, when marrying Armand, I will replace my name by his . . ."

– "Oh! Don't worry, you will only be Mme Armand Rougerot after Mlle[1] Renaudy has publicly announced she agrees to be his wife and has signed the marriage certificate with the officiant and the witnesses . . . but I don't want this misalliance."

Mireille, who had been silent for a while, got up abruptly and came to stand between the father and his daughter, placing one hand on each of their shoulders:

– "Enough of this, Adeline. You are only a fool to believe that the violence of your words can overcome Jules's resistance. Look, look at this hurt old man, the most tender of fathers, who suffers and cries . . . Look!"

Adeline got out of bed—pain, joy, or fear paralyzes us or gives us superhuman strength—and ran to kneel in front of M. Renaudy, whose sobs broke the silence of the room:

– "Sorry!"
– "Get up," said the old man, "and be M. Rougerot's wife tomorrow, this very evening if you want. I can't tolerate your arrogance any longer. Shameful daughter, try to be a loving wife and a devoted mother . . ."
– "Daddy, I shall enter a convent . . ."

On second thought, Jules shook his head:

– "No, you would be a bad nun, you are not made for the cloister and do not have the vocation . . . You would come to—when it will certainly be too late—to regret the pleasures of this world."

He left her and went to weep in his study. He replied to Armand's letter an hour later:

1. Miss in French.

Monsieur,

I received the letter by which you ask the hand of my daughter Adeline. I'll give the answer to your father who, you told me, must come and talk to me about your request.

Best regards.
J. Renaudy

Armand, who had spent the last month waiting feverishly, felt a pang in his heart when his servant handed him the envelope. He stared in amazement at the address, the brutal handwriting of which contrasted sharply with the dreams he had cherished during this wait. Oh! How he trembled with despair at this long-awaited answer! How he was afraid of discovering a refusal! Finally, taking his courage in both hands, he opened the fateful letter and read the two terse sentences.

Armand, heartbroken, withdrew into himself and waited desperately for his father's answer, which was to arrive soon. Eight days later, he read this:

My Son,

I met with M. Renaudy about your marriage proposal. He received me with rare distinction and granted me Mlle Adeline's hand for you. The girl looks very nice and is already very dear to me, for she is the portrait of your sister Jane. Rejoice, my dear Armand, and try to come back immediately after your exams to become officially engaged to Mlle Renaudy.

To you, my son, my best wishes.
Julien Rougerot

The young man felt all his blood rush to his heart. He looked around and saw no one; he rang for his servant:

– "Jérôme, I'm happy, do you know that?"

The servant did not understand and opened his eyes wide; he wondered if his master had suddenly gone mad, but Armand guessed his thought and said to him:

> – "No, I'm not crazy, Jérôme. I love and I'm loved, and my request has been accepted. I'm going to get married, and I . . . I . . ."

He was delirious. Half an hour later, he was walking around Paris to find a soul mate to share his happiness with. It was in vain, all those he rubbed shoulders with were unknown to him and passed by indifferently, without even guessing at his joy.

The month of August had just dawned with its heavy storms and its impetuous winds when Armand landed in Haiti, finding his father in charge of the affairs of M. Henri Rougerot, who had passed away, and finding his sisters as sweet and as devoted as he had left them. How happy they were to see him again, he whom their old uncle had exiled to punish him for his misbehavior and thus depriving him of their care! How he must have suffered in Paris, alone, young, far from any family affection!

They still remembered that day when their little brother, in despair, waved his handkerchief in a cruel farewell from the boat which was carrying him away.

Henri Rougerot himself—no doubt touched by the tears of the other parents—had furtively wiped his eyes, before saying these very words:

> – "Take comfort, my friends, soon in this same place, you will shed tears of joy to welcome him. The return will be sweeter to you than the departure is cruel . . . but I won't be here."

These words became a prophecy: Henri had been dead for a while, and now Madeleine and Jane had tearful eyes at the sight of their little protégé. Julien was dumbfounded, but he looked at his son with poorly disguised pride. The young girls wanted Armand to tell them all about the life he had led in Europe, his arrival, his stay, his departure, they wanted to hear it all. He began to tell his parents about the thousand events of his trip and his stay in Paris. As he saw them touched by his story, he doubled his ardor and wished to be pitied.

> – "I almost died of grief when I landed, when I found myself in a crowd of people who were indifferent to me and had no interest in me. When evening came, I went to bed in a large dormitory in the company of a hundred children who looked at me in astonishment. I cast a long glance over the vast room and could not hold back loud cries: 'I want my sisters,' I cried out through my sobs. The other boarders laughed at my grief and their laughter increased my pain. Then they consoled me, seeing that I was sincerely sad. Little by little, I got used to university, and became one of the most esteemed students thanks to my diligent work . . ."

Julien put an end to his children's private conversation by inviting Armand to go out with him, which they did. The Renaudy family, as we remember, had been living in Pétion-Ville for some time, so it was easy for Adeline, knowing of Armand's arrival, to organize a little party which, without being given in honor of the young man, was nevertheless a pretext to celebrate his return as it was planned precisely on the day when the two families were to meet. Armand's visit was scheduled at four o'clock and the party at five.

It was a Sunday. All of Adeline's friends were on vacation, but as soon as they had finished dinner, they headed to the Renaudys's huge courtyard to have fun to their heart's content.

When Julien and Armand Rougerot arrived at M. Renaudy's, they noticed an air of gaiety which made the liveliest impression on them.

The old man kept his word, and appeared seemingly satisfied with the conversation: he then invited his guests to drink a glass of champagne with the family, much to the delight of the future fiancés.

Adeline asked her father for permission to invite Armand to stay and attend her little party, a request which was accepted on both sides. As a result, the young couple had the opportunity to speak to each other freely, without witnesses, in a love duet. Many children and young people, like them, walked around and from time to time sent them smiles and congratulations.

They talked to each other in low voices, without worrying about others, forgetting everything that wasn't their love. The sweeter things they said to each other, the more it came to them, so when the evening covered the courtyard with its dark coat, they were heartbroken as they said good-bye. Their hands remained together for a long time, in defiance of the fierce looks that the old man cast at the young girl.

It was Armand who slowly let go of his beloved's hand to take leave of his parents-in-law, because he didn't want his first visit to become an inconvenience.

Adeline watched him leave without flinching, but her heart sank as he walked away.

The joy she felt the whole afternoon was gone. Armand was gone, the party had to end. So, she pretended to have a migraine and went up to her room.

– "Oh!" said some of the guests, "since Adeline is ill, we can't go on dancing even though our party has nothing to do with the main house."

– "Yes!" said the other children, "big and small, let's clear the place; Adeline needs to rest."

The noises of the party did not reach the young girl's room, since everything took place at the back of the courtyard which was four hundred feet long.

These children had set up the place in such a way that you thought you were in some old-growth forest, far from any habitation. No chairs, no tables, just tree trunks to replace them. No rugs, no doilies, the foliage took their place. They had even created a spring, thanks to a big garden hose hidden under some branches and attached to the service pipe, which then became a river that disappeared in the distance.

The young girls were dressed in Brazilian outfits and made mules trot with mad merriment. Young people dressed like Brazilians also made a thousand courtesies to the distinguished Amazons; they helped them get off their mules and offered them fruit. Oranges, mangos, caimitos, figs, Spanish limes, etc. tempting like Eve's apple, adorned the wicker baskets placed sometimes on the ground, sometimes on stakes, and increased the children's appetite.

Everyone parted ways, knowing Adeline's discomfort, and promising to meet again soon.

– "Excuse me, Mom, said the young girl a few minutes after the party, entering her mother's room, I was immodest with Armand, I know it because Daddy looked at me with an air that made me feel wrong, but I couldn't resist the urge to be with my fiancé.

– "Yet your father didn't tell me anything and I didn't know . . ."

– "Well," continued Adeline, "go talk to him about it to find out if he's angry or not."

– "He's not angry at all, I can assure you . . . However, if that were the case, I would be able to smooth things over."

– "Oh! Mom, you love me! You love me so much!"

– "Yes, but promise me to be more docile," concluded Mme Renaudy with severity.

At these words Mireille left her daughter to see her husband, who was moping in his study.

– "Jules," she said, "why are you staying alone with a pile of newspapers and books that you don't read? Dinner is served, so let's go eat."

– "Yes, yes," said the old man sadly, getting up and following his wife.

Adeline, who had already sat down at the table, got up at the sight of her father and ran to take his arm.

– "No, Adeline, no, leave me," said M. Renaudy.

– "Why are you pushing me away, Daddy?" asked the girl worriedly.

She threw herself into the arms of the old man, who did not react to her embrace.

– "Oh! No," exclaimed Mireille, "you are causing this child too much pain; she didn't do anything to you."

Encouraged by her mother's reproaches, the young girl thought it her duty to tell her father all the sentiments that flooded her heart.

– "Father, since you don't want me to marry Armand, I will obey you, but I will die! Yes, yes, I want to die. I cannot live without the one to whom I have promised my life and unwavering fidelity. You can stop me from getting married, but you cannot force me to live. I am in charge of my life."

– "Be quiet," said Mireille, "why these exaltations which do not lead to anything? Only your father here has the right to *want*. Your duty is to obey."

– "Oh really!" chanted the girl, "the one who has duties, if they are not a slave, must also have rights. It is my duty, as you say, to obey my parents, but no one can take away my right to die."

– "Well, we want, no, we command you to live," said Madame Renaudy.

– "I won't do anything harmful but sorrow will take me away . . . Who can cure those who wish to die? My soul is already dying, my body is suffering from it fatally," continued the young girl.

– "Oh!" cried out Mireille, "how one suffers from children who have been spoiled too much! I am being punished for being unable to be as severe as I am kind to you, Adeline. Until yesterday, I thought I would make you happy by giving in to your most secret desires, but I see that I have made you unhappy."

– "Mireille," resumed M. Renaudy, "I'm glad you have finally come around to my daily reproaches. Not knowing how to say *no* to children when their fantasies go beyond the limit of little treats made for them, is to ruin their future. Who loves Adeline more than me? Who cares more about her health? Who watches over her every move? Well, were it not for your stubbornness and her insolence—a consequence of your care—I would have never accepted M. Rougerot into my family!"

"But alas! We can't always do what we want! Adeline would be an eternal torment to me if I persisted in my refusal. But I ask her in return, if I don't also have the right to suffer from her choice since she forced me to accept it. So, what is she complaining about? I'm too old to fight," he said, facing the girl who was crying. "No Adeline, don't cry, be happy . . ."

– "Daddy, Daddy, please! Sorry!" suddenly said Mademoiselle Renaudy, whose heart was split between passion and duty. "I am suffering," she continued, "I suffer horribly from lying when I tell you that I will live without this marriage . . . I feel that I cannot not love Armand. I will agree to leave him if you tell me how to forget him. Even if someone were to say to me: 'Armand stole, burnt, murdered, Armand doesn't love you,' I would always love him."

M. Renaudy took pity on this violent passion, so he decided, no matter the circumstances, to no longer oppose this marriage.

Mireille, who had never really been against Adeline's wish, felt relieved when her husband said these words full of real tenderness and absolute sincerity.

– "I want," he said, opening his arms to his daughter, "to put all of this behind us and for you to be happy. You will marry M. Rougerot."

– "Are you telling the truth, Daddy?" asked the anxious girl.

– "But yes, yes . . ."

– "Oh!" said the joyful child, "grant me your forgiveness, please, Daddy, smile at me, show me you still love me a little by allowing me to sit on your knees as I did when I was very small."

– "Poor child!" said Madame Renaudy.

– "Yes, Mom, pity me, I'm in pain."

– "It's over, I said," repeated the old man, "It's over . . . let's forget what happened."

CHAPTER VI

Madeleine and Jane embroidered a pretty pink silk dress for Adeline, and they asked her to wear it on the day she would be officially engaged with their brother. The bride-to-be was touched by this sign of sisterhood, so she asked and obtained her parents' permission to go visit her future sisters-in-law as a thank you.

Mireille offered to go with her and suggested that Adeline take advantage of their visit in Port-au-Prince to visit some friends. The young girl was happy about Madame Renaudy's idea, so she asked enthusiastically about the time of their visit.

– "We will go this afternoon at four o'clock," replied Mireille, "I will call M. Rougerot Sr. to announce our visit."

– "Oh Mom," said Adeline gratefully, "you love me, you desire my happiness!"

– "Did you doubt it?"

– "No, but I suffer so much that everything makes me fear . . ."

– "Fear what?"

– "Say, Mom," said the young girl, taking her mom's hands in hers, "say, can you feel how much I love Armand? I should have kept quiet, no doubt, I should have had enough scruples not to tell you so directly, but you are my mother, to whom do you want me to open my whole soul? Into what soul do you want me to pour its overflow if not in yours? A mother, isn't she the friend of happy days as well as sad ones? If I don't have to tell you my little secret, my only secret, whom am I going to tell it to? Whom will be indulgent enough to listen to me whisper to her, morning, afternoon, and evening, only one name, only one: Armand! Oh! Dear mother, protect me, protect me."

– "But are you in danger? Calm down, Adeline, you know very well that your father will be angry to learn that you're discussing our little past misunderstanding. Isn't everything settled? Aren't you going to get engaged very soon? And what are you complaining about?"

– "Alas! It is reluctantly that Dad . . ."

– "Oh, you're wrong," Mireille said quickly, interrupting her, "you're wrong. He agreed, it's over."

– "I don't know, it looks like there's an evil spirit, an incubus, between happiness and me."

– "Don't worry, darling daughter. Enjoy life and being adored by all of us."

Three o'clock rang.

– "Are you going to get dressed, Adeline?" Madame Renaudy asked the young girl upon hearing the three loud strokes of the clock. "You must be beautiful, more than ever," she continued playfully, "so that Armand would see that he has chosen the prettiest girl in Port-au-Prince."

They went their separate ways to get ready. The driver had already cleaned the vehicle immaculately so that passing children looked at each other in the doors; it was as shiny as the strips of steel lying here and there. The car cushions, covered with finely embroidered cases, waited, while prying and envious eyes looked at them.

How everyone envied the young girl! Even some of her friends wondered why Adeline was so blessed by God. They resented her for her happiness.

Finally, it was time to go, and Madame Renaudy and her daughter were ready.

> – "Four o'clock! Are you ready, Adeline?" said Mireille from her bedroom to her daughter.
> – "Yes, I'm just waiting for you, darling mom."
> – "Well, let's go, because I too am absolutely ready."

They met at the top of the stairs and went down hand in hand, but they paused briefly in the living room to look at each other in the large mirror before going out.

CHAPTER VII

In Haiti, flowers are always in season. We see them everywhere and all the time, sometimes puny in winter, but in May the gardens and the valleys are oh so magical! Even the forests adorn themselves with the rarest, most precious flowers. What, are you smiling, readers? Well, no, large numbers of tourists have discovered varieties of orchids of great beauty in the depths of the Selle mountains, on the side of New Touraine,[1] and in many other places. You know probably how expensive orchids are? The hills are covered with them, they abound, unsuspected, unknown. At the bottom of our mountains, the peasants for whom they shine ignore their value, and we, the townspeople, cannot easily reach them. It is true that we have so many other flowers to catch our eyes!

That's why Mme Renaudy and her daughter were able to come down from Pétion-Ville this afternoon, at the end of August, to bring Armand's family a big bouquet of rare flowers among which bloomed the most beautiful roses they had ever seen.

– "Oh!" said Julien, noticing these ladies laden with their gift, "how nice, really!"

1. A department of Haiti just outside of Port-au-Prince, near present-day Kenscoff.

– "May they show my sincere gratitude," replied Adeline. "Thank you for the dress, thank you!"

– "Our pleasure, "said Madeleine and Jane quickly, "we will be the ones thanking you if you do us the honor of wearing it on the day of your engagement."

– "Of course, I will wear it!" said Adeline confidently, "it's so pretty!"

– "Oh! Thank you, Adeline, we will be grateful to you."

– "But Armand, where is he?" said the bride.

– "He left at half past one, so twenty minutes before you called us," said M. Rougerot.

– "It's unfortunate," said Mireille, "Adeline and I would really like to shake his hand."

– "You may wait for him," said Jane.

– "Impossible," replied Madame Renaudy, "we have to pay other visits before going back to Pétion-Ville."

Adeline felt slightly annoyed to miss her fiancé at his house, so when Madeleine served drinks, she barely touched her glass. She wondered why destiny was so desperate to demolish the big house of cards she had built? Why were her dreams fading away one after another? She who, before loving, had never known anything but pleasures and enjoyments, now she faced immense difficulties at every step.

Finally, after many signs of courtesy from both sides, they left with the promise of meeting again soon to officially celebrate the engagement of Armand and Adeline.

Eight days later, at dawn, beribboned baskets of flowers were delivered to Madame Renaudy's. The flowers, lovingly entwined, lilting, rose, showing sometimes the gold of their stamens, sometimes the colorful shades of their petals. They seemed to smile, happy to bring joy to a young girl's heart, happy to be the messengers of Love, Friendship, Sympathy, Decency.

They were everywhere: in the living rooms, in the bedrooms, in the door-
ways, on the ceilings, on the floor, and in people's smiles.

The day passed and flowers kept coming almost without interruption,
so around five thirty, the reception room took the appearance of a flower
market.

The crystal of glasses and floral centerpieces competed with the ver-
meil of the trays where slices of pies from Vienne and a thousand other
fine candies offered themselves to the gaze of the guests. The servants, in
livery, impatient, awaited the signal from their masters to begin service,
but Adeline had not yet gone down to the drawing room where Armand,
his father, and his sisters were seated. Five o'clock rang. Roland and Rose
ran to fetch the young girl, they met her as she was coming down holding
M. Renaudy's arm. All rose to greet them. All eyes were on the bride whose
dress shone like a star in the depths of the heavens.

Lowering her eyes, she timidly accepted a thousand compliments.
Armand, visibly moved, cast a furtive glance from time to time at the one
who was soon to be his wife, his dearest half, the mother of his children.
What! This young girl, with such a pure gaze, such a sweet smile, such a
big heart, he wondered, was going to be his, his alone, to share his joys as
well as his sorrows? Why did God grant him so many favors? To him rather
than to another? What had he done to deserve so much glory?

Oh! If one day he had to pay for this illegitimate happiness, what would
become of him? He was scared. Suddenly, he became sad, tears rushed to
his eyes, but a smile from the young fiancée fought them back.

  – "How stupid I am!" he thought, also smiling, "Adeline loves
  me, why was I thinking about all these things that make me suffer
  so much?"

The young girl saw him daydreaming and wanted to know the cause.

  – "Why are you sad?" she said softly, "while my heart overflowed
  with joy, while I would like you to understand all my happiness.

Here, look at me, Armand, don't you see the love in my eyes? Can't you see that?"

– "Yes, you're right, Adeline, I'm sad, but all my worries are about you."

– "From me?" asked the young girl with surprise, "from me, Armand? What have I done to you?"

– "Nothing, I was thinking about the day I would lose you."

– "Silence," she said with relief and smiling, "I thought I had done something to you; we can't leave each other, we can't die when our hearts are so full of love."

– "Would you like to dance with me? Perhaps, the magic of this music will make me forget my worries. I love you so much that I already suffer from thinking that I will probably not be able to satisfy your every wish, that I will make you upset one day. I want you to be happy, the happiest woman, I want your most secret desires to be my orders. I am your slave, you already know it, but I want my life to show a passivity never suspected in a man. Adeline, I will live only by you and for you, I swear to you, oh my goddess . . ."

– "Armand, let's not think about what we'll do . . . let's just think about our engagement today."

– "The future is the master of every destiny," said the young man gravely, "how can I not talk about it?"

– "Yes, but God is the master of everything, beings and things. Quick, let's dance!"

They had risen but were not dancing, while happy couples, talking to each other in low voices, whirled around, ensorcelled by a beautiful waltz.

The band of Duroseau and Sons outdid themselves. The piano, played by Duroseau Sr., echoed the soul of the musician in the accompaniment of the pieces performed, while the violins wept under the bows of his sons. The notes, soft, sweet, sometimes also frenzied during joyful meringues, fell from the bows with grace, reminding them of a concert of angels.

Little garlands of colored bulbs hung languorously from the palisades, from the front of the house, and sparkled over the guests.

Dawn was already lighting up the horizon when the musicians, tired, announced the end of the ball with this popular meringue which in our house invites the dancers to leave: "Good evening, ladies, we are going to sleep!"

The young couples, delirious, were still dancing, some wearing only their overcoats, others their coats or their scarves. M. and Mme Renaudy watched them, smiling. "How happy they are!" they thought.

Five o'clock! The room gradually emptied of people.

Louise and Marie Guitton, who had danced for the first time, were at the height of happiness; they joined Roland and Rose to share their excitement.

– "Marie," said Louise with emotion, "how happy I was to dance and to hear twenty adorers soliciting the honor of taking a walk with me with such sweet words . . ."

– "Flattering words!" said Marie, laughing, "the same that comes from all male lips that address all the young ladies in the same tone."

– "Oh! If only I were Adeline!"

– "Are you jealous of our cousin?"

– "No, but I would also like someone who thinks me the best among a thousand other girls and chooses me for his companion. It's an honor, so think about it, sister. I would like to have my Armand like Adeline."

– "Silence, it's madness, when a young man chooses a fiancée, it's not because he compared her to all the other young girls and found her more worthy, he simply followed his heart. There are so many unfortunate choices!"

CHAPTER VIII

The next day, Mireille and Adeline, exhausted, had stayed in bed late. Someone knocked on the girls' door.

– "Who is it?" said Mireille with a start.

– "It's me," answered Gertrude, the housekeeper of the family, "Madame sent me to Mademoiselle."

– "Come in, Gertrude, I'm being lazy."

– "Mademoiselle Adeline is rather tired," said the servant.

– "Ah! Yes, you are right, but, Gertrude, what do you want from me?"

– "Madame wants to know how Mademoiselle is doing."

– "Good. Tell her that I will come down and kiss her later. What is Daddy doing?"

– "Monsieur just went out."

– "Went out? Went out? Daddy is out?" asked the bride in amazement. "Where did he go? Quick, Gertrude, hand me a dress, my shoes. Oh! How scared I am! Grab my comb, so I can run to Mom."

– "Mademoiselle Adeline is very excited!" thought the maid while following her mistress's orders, "her young gentleman seems very calm."

Mademoiselle Renaudy hurried, did it so well that she ended up being ready in ten minutes.

– "Mom," she said at the threshold of the bedroom, "why did Daddy go out so early this morning?"

Mireille, frightened by her child's confusion, looked at her without being able to answer her.

– "Mom," continued Adeline, "where did my father go?"
– "Come on, my dear child," said Mme Renaudy, "you are going crazy . . . Explain to me why you are so worried by Jules's absence."
– "I'm afraid he went to renege on his word . . ."
– "Madness! This is what you think about the day after your engagement."
– "Mom, tell me I was wrong, that my concerns are vain."
– "Let's talk about something else: the success of the party, the satisfaction of the guests, the bewitching music that our friends played, the pleasure that your father and I experienced when seeing you cheerful, happy at last standing next to your chosen one . . ."
– "Oh! Yes," said Adeline, "the evening was so captivating that I believed for a moment that life is made of nothing but ultimate joys."
– "Ah! No, darling daughter, each joy is followed by a displeasure and vice versa. You could even say that one complements the other, but we must expect these reversals without fear because "What God does is done well."
– "So, I'll suffer more than I've suffered before Daddy accepted Armand, because today I'm happy?"
– "I didn't say that . . . Adeline, will you leave me alone?"
– "Remember that I still don't know why my father went to Port-au-Prince . . ."
– "You will know in an hour or two."

The half-worried, half-reassured young child kissed her mother and ran to find the children who were making the engagement party last by feasting on the leftover sweets and emptying the bottles of liquor that hadn't been completely finished.

– "When are you going to get engaged again?" Roland asked his sister. "Rose and I would like to have this party again next Sunday."

– "Child!" said Mademoiselle Renaudy, taking him by the wrists, "were you happy last night?"

– "Yes, I danced with Jacqueline Bernard, Rose's friend."

– "Bravo! Are you a big man now?"

– "I 'Charlestonned.'"

– "And you, Rose, are you happy?" continued the bride.

– "Yes, but tears came to my eyes when, at the end of the party, I saw Louise crying, crying heavily, over there, at the back of the garden."

– "What happened to her? Oh!" said Adeline, "Mom is right to say that sorrows rub shoulders with happiness. Who could believe that tears felt down here, when the most enchanting music brought so much gaiety to this house? Who could imagine that a heart, amid so many happy souls, would tear itself apart in the silence of its grief?"

– "I thought I saw Louise," resumed the young girl aloud, "divinely pretty in the arms of a cavalier, dancing a beautiful waltz. Her smile didn't seem mixed with sadness . . . Rose, are you sure you saw our cousin cry last night?"

– "You can ask her."

– "Yes, I want to know what happened. Where is she?"

– "She was with us five minutes ago," said Marie.

– "Poor Louise!" muttered Adeline.

She was about to go meet her cousin when she saw her father get out of his car with a small package in his hand; forgetting all about her cousin and her grief, she ran to throw herself in M. Renaudy's arms and took him into the drawing room.

– "Is this package for me? I'm sure it's another piece of jewelry you're bringing me here . . . tell me, Daddy, whose package is this?"

Without saying a word, the old man gave it to her; she opened it. Oh surprise! Oh immense joy! A river of fine pearls smiled at her from the bottom of the box.

– "Ah! Thank you, Daddy, thank you, how pretty!"

– "Where is your mother?" asked M. Renaudy, smiling.

– "She must be in her room, I left her there not long ago."

– "Here I am!" replied Mireille who, tiptoeing, had come to stand behind them, "I saw everything, heard everything . . . Jules, I must point out to you that you spoil this child too much while seeming to blame me for my own weakness for her."

– "Oh!" said Adeline, "spoil me because I'm going to be leaving soon. I will no longer be the queen of your hearts . . . Father, Mother, I'm jealous of those who will remain close to you after my marriage."

– "We will never stop loving you," replied M. and Mme Renaudy.

– "How to can I live without you?" said the young girl sadly.

– "Armand will make you forget that you miss our presence," said Mireille, "and little by little you will get used to living away from those to whom you are so dear. Yes, darling daughter, this separation is as cruel to us as your happiness intoxicates us with joy. We must adapt to the circumstances of life, alas! However contradictory they may be in order to have a joyful existence."

The young girl sensed that her dreams were built on sand, and she wondered if the immense affection she enjoyed so freely in her father's house was also waiting for her in the matrimonial home. Admittedly, love, the violent love of the first days of marriage, was going to celebrate her, but would friendship, trust, abnegation also be present there? She was about to leave a house where she was the center of attention, where everyone anticipated her most secret desire in order to satisfy them, for another where one day she would have to be creative to cheer up a worried husband, to lessen the boredom—oh! The cruel boredom caused in the home by the presence of a person you no longer love but to whom duty binds you.

The stronger the love, it seems, the more the indifference is felt among the spouses who, before their union, did not ask themselves if they esteemed each other a little, if after the hurricane of their violent passions they could find calm in the shade of friendship.

Adeline, the little madwoman, the former little trickster, had become worried since her engagement: her dreams one by one were giving way to a troubling reality.

The pearl necklace lay abandoned on one of the tables in the living room; the young girl took it without enthusiasm and put it to her armoire, from which it was not to come out for a long time.

CHAPTER IX

Marie and Louise, who had left school three months earlier, had not yet decided on a professional apprenticeship. Louise dreamed of being a pharmacist and Marie a typist, but M. Renaudy was slow to agree to them, so when October came around, the young girls were horribly bored.

Adeline herself was focused on the preparations for her wedding, which was to take place in the first half of November. Her future sisters-in-law, Madeleine and Jane, often came to fetch her for long walks; the fiancée often also spent entire days preparing some cheerful little things, such as cushions, doilies, skeins of yarn, etc., which were soon to adorn her house.

One day, Marie and her sister were given permission by Mireille to take a walk through the woods in the company of several other young girls. Two hours later, they came back tired but with their hands full of flowers and fruits that they wanted to offer to the bride.

– "We donate all our provisions to you, Adeline," they said cheerfully to their cousin.

As she looked at them with an indifferent air, Marie and Louise asked her the reason nervously:

– "Are you sick, Adeline?"
– "No, I'm sad, immensely sad . . ."

– "You?" said the really surprised young girls, "you the most spoiled girl in the world? Come on!"

– "You upset me, you two . . . You're taking my place here."

– "Us? How?" said abruptly the eldest of the orphans.

– "When I leave, Mom, who loves you so much, will surely give you my pretty room."

– "Be quiet, little madwoman," said Mireille, who had noticed how angry Marie was, "enough, my children," she continued, turning to her nieces, "you know that Adeline has always been a spoiled child and will remain so until the day of her marriage, it is not necessary to pay attention to what she says."

– "Spoiled or not," replied Marie, "Adeline must know that pride is the sin God punishes the most, she must be able to spare our egos of we two orphans, who were given hospitality. We never envied her happiness, we never said that she was too admired, we who have neither father nor mother. Why does she not have more sympathy for our situation as orphans, as wards of our aunt, our mother's sister?

"I swear I've never done anything that would be against Adeline's happiness," she continued, putting her hand over her heart, "I swear I always used the enjoyments generously given to me here in moderation . . . I never believed myself to be her equal and never measured myself against her, knowing fully well that my role is secondary . . . You, Louise, did you deviate from the plan I drew for you when you arrived here? Did you hurt our cousin? Answer me."

– "I'm not defending myself," said Louise, moved, and her eyes full of tears . . . "But I'll point out to you that Adeline is complaining mostly about our presence here, at her place."

– "It's fair. However, Adeline, your selfishness drives us out of this house the moment you leave it yourself. We will leave promptly."

– "I have listened enough, my children," resumed Mireille, quiet now. "Marie," she continued gently, "it would make me really happy if, forgetting Adeline's reproaches, you allowed her to kiss you and ask your forgiveness."

The young girl, angry, hurt, tortured, did not answer, but Adeline, regretting her unfortunate gesture, ran to throw herself in her cousin's arms, saying:

– "I ask your forgiveness, Marie, and you, too, Louise, I see my words offended you so much."

– "Who knows how long it took for the smoldering fire, unable to take it any longer, to ignite today?" said young Marie. "Oh! We were mistaken, my sister and I, to believe you had any affection for us!"

– "But I love you, my cousins, I love you!"

– "Thanks!" replied the two sisters ironically.

Louise, we must say, was more appalled than offended. She kept her eyes lowered, as she could not bear the fiancée's gaze. Adeline noticed it and questioned her:

– "What about you, Louise, do you forgive me?"

Petrified, the orphan, to whom this question was addressed, wept silently. Why did she have this guilty attitude? Why was she suffering from her cousin and her aunt's gaze, while her sister, her head held high, grave, was answering to Adeline's unfair reproaches? What a labyrinth!

They all left, each went their own way, but Marie followed her sister, who went to sit on a bench in a small garden:

– "Are you alright? I, on the other hand, am entirely in touch with reality," said the eldest Mademoiselle Guitton, "how I suffer from being under my aunt's roof."

– "What do you want us to do?" asked Louise.

– "I haven't lost. I am going to write to Aunt Régine to ask for her hospitality."

– "Remember that before dying, our mother took us by the hands and handed us over to Aunt Mireille."

– "Yes, and she was right to think her sister would protect us, but she had done so without thinking of our cousin's selfishness, without thinking, alas! that the loss of a mother condemns the hearts of orphans to the cruelest sufferings. I'm not complaining, Louise, about my fate, I know that God will hold Adeline account- able for the many injustices she has done to us because her parents adopted us."

– "Marie, I can feel the hatred in your voice. Please forgive our cousin the misfortune of being too spoiled . . ."

– "Me? Hate the daughter of our benefactors? No, but only leav- ing this house can heal my wounded self-esteem, injured by her reproaches. Our father, who worked so hard in the past, should have left us a little inheritance, but God did not want it that way. We'll have to be self-sufficient."

– "We will work for it."

– "Oh! yes, Louise, our uncle didn't want us to do it sooner, but since we don't have an inheritance, work alone will make us independent. We will go to Aunt Régine, on the condition that we're free to be useful to ourselves, to enjoy her solely moral protection and the happiness of caring for her. Yes, her infirmity gives us the opportunity to show her all the devotion of which we are capable."

– "Oh! Marie, these things weigh on me . . . ," said Louise, sud- denly. "I feel so sad I could die, it seems that my heart can no longer suffer. Why can't I die?"

– "Discouragement is a sign of weakness. We must live by follow- ing our mother's footsteps, she always was a strong woman, whom death surprised amidst her duties, despite our father's mistreatment."

– "Poor mother!" cried Louise, sobbing. She took this evocation as an opportunity to shed the tears she had been holding back for too long.

She placed her head on her sister's shoulder and wept for a long time; when she sat back up, her sister's bodice was completely wet.

Why was she so upset? Did she love her cousin after all, and didn't want to leave her despite the wrongs she had done her? Alas no, she was crying because she felt guilty toward her aunt's daughter, because she kept a secret in heart, a secret Adeline seemed to have discovered . . . a secret, my God, which diminished her in her own eyes, a secret, in short, which made her the hidden enemy, the rival of the fiancée. Yes, she had loved Armand with passion ever since she saw him for the first time.

After trying to suppress this forbidden love, after debating for days between the happiness of loving and the horror of the harm she was inflicting to her cousin's heart, she had abandoned herself to the passion which filled her soul with sweet pain.

That's why she was overwhelmed when Adeline, her eyes red with tears, her heart overflowing with pain, had aimed her reproaches at her.

Her love was guilty, so be it! But was it prejudicial to Adeline's? Didn't she have the right to follow of her heart? Wasn't this unrequited love responsible for her sad days, sleepless nights, and troubled awakenings? Didn't she suffer from loving without being loved, from feeling her lips bereft of kisses when all she had to do was hold them out to Armand, and he to pluck these ripe fruits ready to fall?

In the evening, Louise, perplexed and under the influence of her injured love, ran to the Saint-Pierre Chapel, wanting to go to confession. She wanted to tell a priest the state of her heart, but all the confessionals were occupied: crowds of peasants massed around the holy courts were piously waiting for their turn to blame themselves before returning to the heights of Pétion-Ville. It was six o'clock in the evening.

She left the church without having poured out the overflow of her soul into the heart of one of God's ministers.

The next day, the two young girls used all their knowledge to write a beautiful and moving letter to their old aunt Régine Guitton, asking her for hospitality. They were almost done when the doorbell rang.

– "It's him!" murmured Louise to her sister, "Oh! My heart! It's him . . . I'm dying under the weight of my emotion."

– "Him? Who are you talking about, dear sister?"

– "Marie . . . I must reveal a secret to you . . . Can't you guess it already?"

– "Alas! I would not dare to . . ."

– "I love."

– "Who?"

– "I love . . . Oh! forgive my love . . ."

– "But then, who do you love? Is it wrong to love?"

Louise didn't answer. Her sister guessed what was petrifying her so much, but she could not convince herself of it. She continued to kindly question her:

– "Whom do you love? Give me the alms of your confession because your silence weighs on me, tears my soul . . ."

– "Doesn't your heart beat in unison with mine? How do you not feel how much I love Armand Rougerot?"

– "Oh, unfortunate girl! It was at you that Adeline's reproaches were aimed, you?"

– "Marie, don't judge me too harshly. I love but I am not loved . . . Armand doesn't know . . ."

– "But why love this man who is not available? Do you want your love for him to be adulterous?"

– "I'm not asking him to love me . . . I love him because I have no choice, because I can't live without thinking about him. I love him, as one loves the One, the One no one sees but feels everywhere."

– "Heathen, Louise, how dare you comparing a man to the Lord? Ah! You are going crazy . . ."

– "Yes, put me in the straitjacket, have me committed, let me kill myself, but don't stop me from loving Armand in the silence of my heart."

– "Louise, be reasonable, you can't continue to abuse our aunt's hospitality while taking away her daughter's happiness. We can't stay here any longer, because if Adeline agrees to keep quiet when your love for Armand is harmless to her, she won't fail to defend herself like a ferocious beast as soon as she sees her happiness seriously threatened. The fight would be terrible!"

The girl fell silent for a moment before continuing:

– "I pity you, dear sister; go pack your suitcases, I'll post the letter tomorrow at the latest. We're leaving this house; do you hear me?"

– "Yes, we must be honorable even when falling from grace."

– "Falling? Falling? You have fallen, Louise!"

– "Alas! Yes, since I cannot overcome my guilty passion and I feel I would gladly throw myself into the arms of this man who does not love me. The thought alone is a disgrace, I know it, but I cannot resist."

– "Why don't you take it back, since you know full well that you are doing wrong?"

– "I'm telling you, Armand doesn't know I love him."

– "Well, you must sever your engagement . . ."

– "One can only sever what has been united. Armand doesn't love me."

– "Poor sister! You're mad, completely insane," said Marie sadly.

CHAPTER X

Régine Guitton was a rude, rich, and disabled spinster. She had several servants working for her, but none of them liked her for she was stingy. Despite her many servants, it often happened that she lacked something that she badly needed, and it annoyed her so much that she complained about it to her young nieces in almost all her letters.

Régine had many faults due to her old age and her serious illness, but she also had unsuspected qualities. She often had numerous young girls at her bedside, girls who talked to her about their little secrets. She gave advice, always good ones, and was discreet regarding her friends. However, despite the many visits she received, she was sometimes alone, sadly alone, abandoned for hours on end to her infirmity. She wept for a long time, she regretted not having a devoted little relative at her bedside, a soul mate who could be a balm for her moral suffering.

Wealth does not cure the illnesses of the mind and the heart. Only the affection, the devotion, the altruism of a loved one can if not cure them, at least alleviate them.

Although Miss Régine was very fortunate, she was not happy, so it was with great pleasure she received and read her little nieces' letter. She replied the very same day. She was even more pleased with these children's request because she thought of them as her own. She had raised their father, M. Guitton, had married him, and had seen them born. And today, they, like strangers, were asking for her hospitality, while imposing an ultimatum on her: permission to work to make a living or else.

Marie waited feverishly for Régine's answer while her youngest let time pass, daydreaming. Roland and Rose often interrupted her futile dreams, but she went back to them as soon as the children were gone.

When the response arrived, Marie felt relieved of the weight she carried in her heart and, quickly, she said to her sister:

– "My aunt Régine accepted our proposals, let's go say good-bye to the Renaudy family."

– "Oh yes!" said the other sister bravely, "yes, the sight of Adeline is like a dagger to me, or rather like the eagle which ate part of poor Prometheus's liver for eternity. We must leave . . ."

– "One never loves a rival!" said Marie ironically.

– "I don't hate my cousin, oh no! On the contrary, I am ashamed of her, I fear to upset her happiness."

– "So, what are you doing taking her fiancé away from her?"

– "Marie, please don't make fun of me, don't insult my sad love, which is content to stay sterile. No, I'm not hurting my cousin, only I suffer."

– "Adeline is a saint!"

– "And I'm a heroine! Yes, I say it without false modesty: to love without being loved is heroism."

– "Do you want to give me immense pleasure?"

– "Yes."

– "Well, don't talk to me about your forbidden love anymore."

– "I swear to you not to talk to you about it again, whatever it costs me. I will suffer in silence."

– "Dear God, have pity on my sister," cried out Marie nervously, lifting her eyes to Heaven, "free her from this passion which crushes her under its yoke like the most vulgar tyrant would have done to a martyr. Mother," she continued, weeping, "implore God's help for this child whose madness saddens me."

Then, taking both of her sister's hands:

– "Louise, darling, understand what you are doing, tell yourself that you have no reason to be ungrateful to the family that adopted us since the death of our father and our mother. Listen, little sister, promise me to go kneel in front of the Tabernacle and to sincerely ask the Good Lord to help you forget . . . Forgetting is necessary, indispensable to the souls chained by strong passions."

– "Don't ask me the impossible . . . Who is harmed by my love, who, since it is only silence and sacrifice? Isn't it a fire that only consumes me? Well, don't ask me to heal, because my illness is the only good thing in my life. I suffer, oh! God only knows how much and since when, yet I never complained. If I allowed myself to make this confession to you, it is only because I weakened for a moment under the weight of your interrogations, being only human, fragile."

An hour later, the two young girls were in Madame Renaudy's salon, where destiny had brought together all the members of the family. Their aunt became worried, seeing they were wearing their hats, and questioned them:

– "Where are you going, my children?"

– "We are here to announce to you, to all of you, that we received a letter from our old aunt. She is asking us to come live with her."

– "Oh! No," protested Adeline, "you must stay with Mom and Dad! They will be so lonely after my wedding."

– "It's too late," said Marie haughtily, "we'll come back to visit our parents, but our place is no longer here: it's with the one who raised our father and watched over our early childhood."

– "I thought you forgave me for my little joke the other day, but you're still angry with me. Louise, my little friend, you at least, stay with Mom and Dad, stay with Rose, who won't have anyone to walk with."

– "I must follow my older sister," said Louise, her eyes lowered and full of tears.

– "I don't want you to go away," replied Mireille with authority, "you were given to me by your mother, my younger sister, on her deathbed ... Now, how dare you come to me to announce your departure?"

– "My aunt," added Marie, "we have always followed your orders, but accept today that we ask you, despite your refusal, for permission to go and find Aunt Régine, who is infirm and old ..."

– "Yes, but she was able to live quite well without your care until now."

– "Each hour weakens her more: she needs a caring hand to soften her last moments and this duty falls on us."

– "You feel the urgency of this duty a little late," said Madame Renaudy in a tone of reproach that hurt the young girls.

– "We are ungrateful, oh! yes, my aunt," said Marie, "so we leave bent under the weight of shame."

– "My poor nieces!" cried out the old man with sadness, "why do you abandon me to my old age? You say that Régine is ill and old, but I, don't I also have all the ailments and am I not old too? Think about it."

After a few minutes of icy silence, M. Renaudy resumed:

– "Have you thought about it, my children?"

They answered together, without hesitation:

– "Yes, we are leaving, Uncle."

– "Well, so be it! Go, but if in your race toward this other horizon, a storm bursts and surprises you, remember that our house is an open port where you can come and wait for the return of the sun. Our affection, like a beacon in the middle of the night, will guide you and will bring you back to our shore . . . Go! Oh! My heart bleeds!"

– "Thank you, thank you, *au revoir*!" they said achingly.

Roland and Rose threw themselves in the arms of their cousins:

– "No, no, don't go, don't leave us."
– "We will be back. We'll be back . . ."
– "Good-bye!" said Adeline painfully.
– "Good-bye!" answered Louise and Marie.

Mireille remained silent, but her whole soul was torn with pain.

CHAPTER XI

Absence always played an important role in Louise's life, for she was able to passionately love her perfect love, the ruler of her heart, without having to hide it. How happy she was when finally, alone, embracing the void, she cried out:

– "Armand, how I love you! Dear Armand, my beloved!"

She poured all her soul into these words that were so sweet but that her fiancé would never hear. Armand! This name summed up her whole life, it was imprinted in her heart and on her lips.

Mademoiselle Régine, with whom the two sisters had been for two months, saw the enamored girl daydreaming, and she asked her the reason.

– "Louise, you are always dreaming, are you heartbroken? You never smile when you come back from work. You cannot live on your preoccupations, or even your occupations; you must enjoy the fruits of your labor.

"Marie and you forced me to let you work. I accepted, but God knows how my heart bleeds when I see you go out every morning in search of bread, when I should be providing for all your needs. I have some wealth, my children, use it, please, since I cannot enjoy it myself.

"They say I am stingy, alas! No, I only want, that when I die, all of you, my heirs, receive a share of this comfort which will protect you from adversity. If from now on you agree to let me share my income with you, know that this will not diminish the inheritance I intend to bequeath to you and to my other little nephews and nieces."

– "Thank you," said the girl, with tenderness, "I feel all the sincerity of your offer, but allow my sister and me to continue to work while enjoying your largesse. Work, my aunt, chases away the bad thoughts that idleness creates in us. I am heartbroken, yes, dear aunt, but the more I think about it, the more I suffer."

– "Confide in me, dear child."

– "Alas! No, I swore to Marie not to speak of this impossible love which fills my whole soul in equal measure with pain and happiness."

– "An impossible love!" repeated Régine without understanding.

– "Yes, impossible, forbidden since the man I love is not free."

– "Oh! Let's not really talk about it," said the old lady.

– "My God!" thought Louise, "everyone is pitiless in my opinion, and you, will you remain insensitive? Won't you protect me against the irony of Destiny? You gave me a loving, passionate soul, you put this impossible love in my heart, so grant me, if not the happiness of being loved, at least the courage to always love Armand, all my life, never expecting one look in return, and without complaining. My aunt," she continued in a low voice, "you know how to pray, ask the Good Lord to alleviate my pain . . ."

– "You know very well that it is a sin to ask the Lord for the impossible."

– "Since when is the Good Lord no longer the Being whom nothing can resist? The word 'impossible' is meaningless in Heaven."

– "Louise, I will pray that you forget."

– "No, I can't, I don't want to forget."

She left her aunt and went to lock herself in her room. There, she could give free rein to the tears that soaked her eyelids. There, alone, she wanted to talk in the language of the gods to the one her heart had chosen.

Yes, why shouldn't she tell him that she loved him since he hadn't been able to guess it? Why shouldn't her suffering heart sing her pain since God had given her poetry as a confidant? Wasn't poetry made of sweet emotions and bitter despair?

She sat down at her bedroom table, took out a sheet of paper and wrote:

No, I won't say that I love you too much
But I love you enough to suffer without truce:
I love you and I suffer and never a sob
Has not betrayed my love which can only be a dream.

I love you, but no, I don't love you . . .
I adore you and feel an unspeakable intoxication
To sing my love for myself alone in a low voice
Without daring to hope for a caress from you!

A handshake in which we say to ourselves
Words unspoken but which a lover guesses,
Without daring to hope for a look that reads
Love, true love, this divine flame . . .

Without daring to hope that one day—tomorrow, tonight
Perhaps—O my beloved, my dear beloved!—your soul
Will have for my blind and powerless love
A thought, alas! . . . to revive my flame.

I love you and can only silence the impulses
Of my heart which could tell you so many things!

Thousands of dreams animate my twenties
And are extinguished in me as the roses die.

My soul is yours, O sublime oppressor!
Always oppress it, always oppress it,
For its slavery soothes its pain,
For its slavery soothes its pain,
And having you as a master is his only caress.

I am guilty, but what can my will do,
Against the dreadful destiny that wants me to love you,
And who finally wants my only voluptuousness
Either to suffer without complaint and to even succumb?

After having written this epistle, she remained immersed in a long dream. How could she send these unfortunate verses to their recipient? She thought about it for a long, long time, then she had an idea: since she went out to go to work every day, she would take the letter to the post office herself. And she did.

CHAPTER XII

Adeline endured her cousins' absence with an indifference that astonished Armand, and when they happened to talk about it, she always found a way to change the topic. As for Roland and Rose, they seemed to miss the company of the Guitton girls, whose names they constantly mentioned.

M. and Mme Renaudy languished with pain and were sick to see their house become painfully darker after the departure of the young girls. No more music, no more singing! Adeline preferred the sweet but selfish music made by two loving hearts. Yes, it was in her gaze, in her smiles, in her soul that she was singing now, and Armand alone heard it.

– "I love you!" she said in a low voice to her beloved, "I love you! I would like to prove to you my devotion with a sacrifice!"

– "Yes, I know, Adeline. Just knowing that you will be mine, mine alone, that I will bow down one day before you like the Muslims before Allah, fills me with an immense happiness."

– "No, you will love me as one loves his wife!"

He took her hands, almost hurting her because of his passion. He asked her to tell him how much she loved him:

– "Will you still love me? For your whole life? Tell me yes, repeat to me this binding word, this blessed word."

– "Oh! yes, all my life," repeated the exhilarated girl.

When it was time to leave, what additional happy words were not whispered?

———

One day, Armand and his sisters were invited to dine at M. and Mme Renaudy's to celebrate Rose's birthday.

Mireille, who liked to see cheerful young people, had planned a little party around four o'clock in the afternoon, which kept the guests dancing for three hours.

At seven o'clock, Jane and Madeleine asked their brother to take them home to Port-au-Prince, where their father was a bit under the weather and completely alone. Adeline tried to prevent them from leaving so soon—their departure was taking her fiancé away from her—but she recanted after hearing the young girls' valid excuses to leave while the ball was more and more enchanting.

Adeline walked them to the front gate, and so that she wouldn't be alone on the way back—there was a very great distance from the fence to the house—she took Roland's hand and included him in their little group.

– "Good-bye, little sister," said Miss Rougerot, getting in the car, "see you next Sunday, this time at our place."

– "Yes, in eight days Rose and I will visit to play with M. Rougerot's mimosas. Does he still like to garden?"

– "That's why he's sick recently. He walked too much in the damp. Ah! Armand," they continued with a half-stern, half-playful expression, "could you let go of Adeline's hand which you are pressing so much? It is now all red."

– "My sisters, it is with a broken heart that I follow you . . ."

That said, he sat next to the driver and waved his dear fiancée a sad and sweet farewell, while tearful Adeline watched a part of herself gradually slip away.

– "Let's go back," she said to her brother, "why are we standing here staring into emptiness? Roland, don't you see that the sweetest joys precede the greatest heartbreaks?"

– "Villains! They left too quickly."

– "No, Roland, no, they are not mean: in life, the happiness of one soul ends where that of another begins, or there would be too many people happy, and no one would feel the need to pray. How many dreams did I not have when I was your age? Yesterday my heart was an unshakeable hearth of joys of all kinds, and today, disillusioned, I cry, my brother, I cry because I suffer."

– "Oh! Dear sister, what is the matter with you?"

– "Nothing really, but it seems that a misfortune is going to happen to me, I feel that I will never see again these people who are so dear to me."

– "Poor Adeline!"

– "Yes, poor me! Why am I so sad? Won't I be seeing my fiancé in two days?"

– "Yes, in two days."

– "Maybe never!"

– "Ah! Don't say that. Armand will bring you sweets and you'll give me some . . ."

– "Roland, are you thinking about trivialities while I confess my fears to you? Be quiet and let's go home. Ah! How unhappy I am! How I fear the future!"

She was already walking along the alley when she heard a strange voice coming from the street, calling her while Roland was fleeing:

– "Mademoiselle, Mademoiselle, do I have the honor of speaking to Mademoiselle Adeline Renaudy?"

The young girl hesitated for a moment, then, impelled by curiosity, she replied resolutely:

– "Yes, what do you want with her?"
– "I have a letter for her."

Her words immediately were followed by actions. Adeline, still hesitant, stretched out her hand and grabbed the envelope from the stranger's hands.

– "Who are you?" she asked, staring at the woman. "Come in, my parents are here. Who are you?"
– "I am the one who wants to spare you irreparable harm and eternal remorse."
– "Tell me, who are you? Who are you?"
– "*Au revoir*! Good-bye!"

The enigmatic messenger, still unknown, backed away and disappeared into the darkness of Pétion-Ville.

– "Is she a demon? Is she a good soul? I don't know, but I'm afraid," said the unhappy child to herself.

She hid the mysterious letter in the folds of her scarf and walked back down the main aisle all by herself and went to the drawing room where, oh irony of humanity! Cheerful, mad couples were dancing to their heart's content.

No one noticed her trouble; she went up to her pretty room, where a framed photo of her picking flowers smiled at her, as if making fun of her concerns.

– "You," she said, staring at the portrait, "you're the girl with foolish dreams, I'm the martyr of reality. You have fragrant flowers in your hands, my heart is full of them, too, but mine are poisonous."

In her madness, she believed the photo was no longer smiling.

– "Oh!" she said, "things have a soul since you help me to suffer."

The dreadful envelope was still in her hands, but she couldn't dare to read it, her heart telling her that it was hiding a terrible secret.

Finally, tired of getting lost in conjectures, pushed by anxiety and curiosity, she tore open the large envelope, took out the letter, and read:

My poor Adeline,

The pain you will feel reading my letter will be equal to the pain that plagues me when I write it to you, but you will forgive me for causing you pain in the present to save you the most bitter remorse in the future, after that an irreparable evil will have covered you with your own contempt.

You are not M. and Mme Renaudy's daughter. (Cry, Adeline, yes, cry as much as you can: tears relieve great pain). You are the daughter of the late Mme Julien Rougerot, the mother of . . . Ah! If I could this time conceal this name which you must guess but do not dare to pronounce. If I could, dear child, not say to you that you are the sister of Armand Rougerot, I would be at peace! But then, what would be the purpose of my letter?

To tell you that he is your brother is also to tell you that a marriage between you and him is incest . . . Following the absence of her husband, Madame Rougerot, your mother, found herself in a shameful situation because of someone whose name she never mentioned and, to hide her shame, she came to seek asylum in the depths of the woods. There, a little calmer, but deprived of comfort, she fell ill immediately after your birth, which took place in the secret of my poor cottage.

Oh! How cruel it is for me to tell you, my poor Adeline, that without bread for your brother, without milk for you, without medicine for herself, I would go out and stay for hours begging across the countryside for the things our neighbors often also lacked: ten sous! Sometimes I came home with a bit of bread, other times, alas, with nothing in my basket!

I was a milkmaid; the little money I earned each week was not enough to meet the needs of the house.

But who am I? Who am I, after all?

A poor peasant woman who was honored to have given hospitality to Madame Rougerot, mistreated by destiny.

The day your mother felt she was dying, she called me and said: "Take Bébé—that was your name—let me kiss her and go, drop her off at Mme Renaudy's door." She who was then holidaying in a luxurious villa in Diquini.

How it pained her not to have any children! She complained to anyone who wanted to listen and shared her sterile maternal affection with all the children she met. When M. Renaudy used to see Armand, who was often hungry, walk by, he stopped him, caressed his little brown head and gave him sweets that the poor child devoured . . . But do sweet almonds appease hunger?

I've added to my letter a medallion representing your poor mother before the birth of your brother and a seemingly very old photo of her picking up flowers as a young girl.

Good-bye.

> – "It's my portrait," said Adeline painfully, staring at the medallion, "it's me . . . am I going to go crazy? I feel something boiling in my head like the crackle of bullets which, during the civil wars of yesteryear, made me tremble so much . . . I can no longer collect my thoughts; I am going mad; I am gradually losing my mind, and I cannot hold it back. Oh! How I suffered when I wanted to catch a dragonfly fleeing away! I cannot even cry at the loss of my sanity. The burning tears of yesteryear I shed capriciously, tears of a pampered child, still gather in my eyes so that I cry! I'm paralyzed and

stupefied but I don't suffer because I can't feel my heart beating anymore . . . I don't have a heart anymore.

"My heart of twenty springs, why do ice cubes prevent you from beating? Why has the winter of hope descended on your pulsations? Ah, how I would like to die!"

The rosewood of her bed reflected her face, and she recoiled in horror, thinking she saw a ghost: "Help!" she said in a sob before fainting.

Nobody heard her.

Half an hour later, someone knocked on her door.

– "Adeline," said Mireille, worried, "why did you run away from the party? Everyone is asking for you."

Madame Renaudy's voice brought her back to reality, she rubbed her eyes, numbed by her indisposition. She hid the photographs and the mysterious letter under her pillow and, stumbling, went to open the door which she had double-locked.

Before she had time to explain herself, Mireille excused her with these words full of frank tenderness:

– "I see you're ill, Adeline, but why didn't you tell us when you left the living room?"

– "I have a little . . . a . . . a migraine."

– "I'm going to tell those young girls who are still dancing madly."

– "No, they must not suffer from my sickness; let them have fun, one day they will not even be able to enjoy themselves because of suffering, everything will be taken away from them; they will be insensitive, inert, no longer able to laugh or cry, unable even to find, in pain, a reason to live; they will all be dead . . . while alive!"

– "Adeline, you're delirious."

– "Yes, since I'm crazy . . ."

– "Crazy? Are you crazy, Adeline?"

– "Can you tell me why you loved me so much, why do you still love me?"

– "Because you are my child, my first maternal affection."

Without a word, Adeline looked at her intensely. Frightened, Mireille lowered her head but raised it almost immediately.

– "So?"

The young girl understood everything with this gesture of semi-failure and, courageous, heroic, she placed a kiss on the forehead of her adoptive mother, gently dismissing her:

– "It is indecent none of us are with those we invited; go meet them while I am going to ask sleep for a remedy for my distressing migraine."

Adeline walked her to the door. They kissed again and parted ways.

CHAPTER XIII

The heart has, in a hidden corner, a seed of ingratitude ready to germinate at the slightest circumstance; one can prevent this unhappy seed from growing with vigorous and incessant efforts, and eventually annihilate it, but it takes very little for the seed to be reborn as if by magic.

After two days of a partial nervous inertia, Adeline realized that she was starting to live again; her heart, which seemed dead, was coming back to life little by little but was coming back to life only to suffer. Yes, she felt it beating painfully.

The source of her tears, mostly dried up by stupor, still let drops fall on her cheeks from time to time, shiny and warm drops: she lived, again.

But why was this inert heart yesterday so insensitive, lifeless, reborn today with not only pain but almost resentment?

Sorrow had made her ungrateful, yes, she resented M. Renaudy, she resented Mireille, she resented all those to whom fate had bound her so closely and, to excuse herself in her own eyes, she accused her adoptive parents of wanting to marry her to her brother to get rid of her.

The old man and his wife quickly noticed the young girl's indifference toward them and even toward Armand:

– "Are you sick?" they asked her often.

– "Mireille," said Jules to his wife one day, "I am wondering . . . what if—I may be wrong–Adeline knows that we are not her natural parents . . ."

– "Enough, be quiet . . . who could have told her?"

– "Ah! Humanity is ugly and jealous."

Then, after some reflection, he continued painfully:

– "Who knows if, among the rare people who know this secret, there isn't one who envies her? Adeline suffers in silence in her pride, Adeline is unhappy."

– "So?"

– "I questioned her a thousand times and a thousand times also I came up against her angry silence. Adeline knows she's not our daughter."

– "Oh! Stop talking, I'm telling you she could hear you."

– "Our secret is no longer a secret, believe me."

– "Yes, since you reveal it to the walls: don't they have ears?"

Suddenly, the creak of a piece of furniture made them aware that someone was there, very close to them, spying on them, listening to them. Madame Renaudy, frightened, ran to check but found no one and nothing in the next room! However, angsty, they scrutinized every nook and cranny of the apartment. No, they weren't mistaken; they had heard a strange noise, someone had been there.

– "Oh! It's you," they said relaxing, "it's you, Tchéco, who surprised us! May you never betray us. Where is your mistress? Say, she wasn't with you? Oh! Say quickly."

The dog—for these pressing questions were addressed to Armand's dog—shook its tail and went out. Madame Renaudy followed him; he went straight to the young fiancée who was seated in a little enclosure where several vegetable plants grew, and laid down at her feet.

– "Why are you here alone?" said Mireille. "Don't you know Armand will be here in an hour? Go make yourself beautiful. It's getting colder and you'll easily catch a cold, let's go home."

The girl smiled at her and whispered:

– "Mother-Mireille, may I stay in the garden for a while longer? I feel so happy to be Nature's guest; look at these seeds that we sowed only a week ago, they are already germinating. Oh! These miniature cabbages, these beets, these carrots, which raise their little leafy heads toward the sky, show us God's presence when we doubt it. Let me enjoy this picture."

– "No, don't stay alone like this, let's go, dear daughter."

The poor child got up, gave her mother her arm and left with her.

– "Armand is really my mother's son," she repeated to herself twenty times a minute. M. Renaudy himself confirmed it to her by the careless conversation he had had with his wife.

When they had parted ways, one to go get dressed, the other to keep her husband company, Adeline took Tchéco in her arms and confided in him.

– "Your mistress is unhappy," she said with anguish, "your master is her brother and her fiancé at the same time, do you know that?"

The animal, as if to sympathize with her pain, uttered little plaintive cries that went straight to young Adeline's heart:

– "Yes, pity me, Tchéco, pity me, because all my dreams have vanished, all my desires are dead. My pride, this veritable diadem that adorned my head, is today at my feet, bruised, broken, annihilated! My poor Armand," she continued with anguish, "why did I find you if I must leave you?

"To confess to everyone that you are my brother is to sully the honor of your family, it is to disgrace you, it is to break the hearts of my sisters . . . It is to awaken a dormant fault, it is filling the heart of a cheated husband with rage, it is soiling the memory of an unhappy wife, it is finally telling everyone, friends and enemies, that I am a child of adultery!

"Ah no, this cruel confession would have too many unpleasant consequences: I will remain silent, but, to you Armand, I will one day tell you I am your sister, so you can love me as a brother . . ."

Tchéco watched her speak attentively and remained motionless, placed against Mademoiselle Renaudy's chest like a child.

– "Comfort me, my favorite dog, comfort me," she repeated.

Armand, the recipient of Louise's lament, felt mortally intrigued and—inconstant like all men—he started to fall in love with this stranger. He kissed the mysterious and beloved poem a hundred times a day, and a hundred times also at night. He often caught himself thinking of the unhappy young girl.

Forgetting the promise he had made to Adeline, to love her as a pagan loves his God, he spent hours imagining the young stranger in a halo of beauty.

Who could have loved him to the point of sacrifice when Adeline, his fiancée, his future wife, the future mother of his children had become almost hostile to him? She refused his kisses while greedy, feverish, sadly unknown lips wanted to be united with his? Why was this woman or young girl hiding to love him, when his heart was ready to be hers?

However, as he did not know the one who loved him so much, he forgot her little by little, he forgot her so completely that the poem which had moved his heart so much had become only a vague memory: Adeline alone occupied his thoughts.

CHAPTER XIV

It was the end of October. Armand, happy, anxious, was waiting for the day that was to bond him to Miss Renaudy, even though she seemed to fear him. The young man noticed it, and he began to study his fiancée to convince himself.

– "Adeline," he suddenly said to her one evening, "why do you love me less and less every day?"

– "You are wrong, Armand, I would give my life to prove my devotion to you. Are we not of the same flesh?"

– "Yes, married, we will be of one and the same flesh, you are right, but you no longer love me like you used to at the beginning of our engagement."

– "I love you more, but I love you with a different love."

– "You intrigue me! Tell me how is your love?"

– "Don't question me, please."

– "Your words are an unfathomable mystery to me, so, despite everything, must I tell you these words which burn my heart and my mouth: Why do you love me less and less every day?"

– "Armand! Have pity on a heart that can't even hope to get out of the maze where darkness and the fangs of death keep it."

– "Are you unhappy?"

– "Pity me!"

– "Confide your sorrow to me," said the young man on his knees, "I promise you silence, the silence of a priest. You darken my horizon with your visage of Mater Dolorosa,[1] Adeline you are my sun, so shine on my horizon. I hurt you, no doubt, well, you have punished me enough, your painful attitude has tortured me for days, forgive me now, absolve me."

– "I don't want you to question me."

– "You loved? Why do I care! Are you ruined? My arm is strong and tough. You do not love me anymore? Too bad, I love you. So why are you suffering?"

Adeline was silent while he, mad, desperate, lost himself in a soliloquy the poor girl did not listen to. Then, as he no longer knew what he was saying, he fell silent and wept for a long time, his head on his . . . sister's knees.

– "Don't cry Armand, I love you so much!"

– "No, you don't love me anymore, you suffer from loving me."

– "If only you knew!"

– "Yes! I want to know."

– "Don't say a word, *chéri*."

– "No, I won't be silenced until you tell me your secret."

– "Can't you guess when I'm joking?"

– "Don't play with my sanity . . . I'm not crazy, Adeline."

– "I was joking. Your tears?"

– "Crocodile tears! Your complaints?"

– "Jokes!" she said, smiling.

– "Did I misunderstand you? Am I in a dream?"

1. Religious artistic representation of the Virgin Mary and the seven sorrows of her life.

– "I wanted to test you, I wanted to see if my tears would move you."

– "You can't prank a soul like that, I'm going to complain to your parents."

– "No, they would scold me. Do you know that all my sorrows come from knowing I will leave them forever?"

– "We will see them every day."

– "It will not be enough, they have been so good to me, and I am leaving them without showing my gratitude to them, without giving them any compensation."

– "They did their duty; parents must instruct, educate their children, provide for their needs and prepare a path for them without hoping of personally drawing profit from it. No, sometimes their only satisfaction lies in seeing the well-being of the fruits of their love, thanks to the guidance they have given them.

"Your parents, Adeline, would be too happy to see you go honestly toward the nest of love that awaits you. You will find in me not only a husband who will respect your filial sensitivity, but a brother who will love everything you love and hate everything you hate."

– "Yes, you will be a brother to me."

– "More than a brother: a pagan whose idol you will be."

– "Not that! Not that, Armand!"

– "Adeline," he said with rage, "kiss me, kiss me."

– "No, no, no!"

He grabbed her hands furiously, threw her head back, and dropped a rain of kisses on the lips of the young girl who, cruelly happy, drank the poisoned honey.

– "My God," said Adeline to herself, when Armand had let go of her hands, "may the rest of my life be spent in seeking forgiveness for this moment of oblivion!"

Seven o'clock struck from the big clock of the only church in Pétion-Ville. Armand got up; at the same moment M. and Mme Renaudy appeared:

– "Armand," said the old man, "what time do you have? It seems that the clock of Saint-Pierre is mistaken."

– "It's ahead."

– "On the contrary, on the contrary, my dear, it is behind."

– "I must leave then," said the young man.

M. Renaudy pretended not to hear him and affected an air of astonishment when he came to shake his hand.

– "Are you leaving already?"

– "Yes . . . Good-bye."

He said good-bye to his future parents-in-law, kissed Adeline's slender hand, and left with bitter satisfaction in his heart.

CHAPTER XV

Mme Renaudy was occupied by the preparations for her daughter's wedding: waxing the hardwood floors, cleaning the furniture, polishing the silverware herself, placing various ornaments here and there so that her home would be extremely joyful in three days, for in three days, Adeline was to be Armand Rougerot's wife. All the servants were on deck. Jean, the gardener, would have given five years of his life so that his roses were prettier and more numerous to celebrate Mademoiselle Adeline. He wanted them in the living rooms, in the bedrooms, but he preferred them, welcoming, on the entrance flower beds, walking the visitors in and giving him good publicity.

– "How pretty your roses are!" the friends of the family often said to him. "How do you make them so beautiful?"

Jean, his heart swollen with pride, replied:

– "I have a secret!" He was laughing in his gray beard, and delirious with happiness.

The poor gardener, who had worked more than twenty-five years for the Renaudys, was like a member of the family; he knew all the little secrets, all the joys and all the quirks. When they were in mourning, he was sad, too, and when they were celebrating, he was the first to feel happy.

– "Mamzell Adeline is getting married," he said to himself. "I am going to give her all my flowers."

No one ever corrected him for believing that the garden was his property. He cultivated it with all his soul.

Armand promptly arrived at Madame Renaudy's at four o'clock. He urged to see her, and a maid warned her.

– "Let him in," said Mireille, decorating her boudoir.

– "Where, Madame?"

– "Right here. Are you afraid, Gertrude, to let him see me at work?"

The servant left and returned with the young man.

– "Madame," he said, taking her two hands, "I am in pain. I have made myself unworthy of your daughter: she no longer loves me. Let me run away. After time diminishes her resentment, I will come to ask her forgiveness."

– "Armand!"

– "Yes, blame me!"

– "What did you do to your fiancée?"

– "I betrayed her."

– "Well, why are you complaining?"

– "Because I assume that in the heart of young girls like Adeline, there is forgiveness and kindness."

Madame Renaudy, without answering him, rang for Gertrude, who appeared immediately.

– "Call me Mademoiselle Adeline," she said with authority.

– "No," begged Armand, "no Madame, please."

– "I want it, so that right here you have a discussion with her. I wanted to assume, for a moment, that you were joking, but no, you are guilty . . . You betrayed Adeline, you say, how?"

He was silent and an exasperated Mireille pressed him to answer.

The maid, who had left despite the young man's disapproval, reappeared a minute later to announce that Mademoiselle Renaudy had arrived.

A sepulchral silence descended on the boudoir where, mockingly, the little blue flowers the bride's mother had just placed on a table laughed at her and at Armand.

Adeline, barely back from Mount Calvary, looked tired, her hands laden with wild—but beautiful—flowers she had picked on her way. We must add right away that Pétion-Ville's Calvary was located on the top of a high mountain, and you had to walk, walk for a long time through the woods before arriving at the foot of a big white cross, a cross one could easily see from a long distance, but which one could reach only with tremendous difficulty.

This cross is still there today, a witness to so many complaints and so often moistened by the tears of pilgrims.

> – "What?" said the young girl in surprise. "Armand is with you, Mom? I was far from knowing he was so close to me."
>
> – "Yes, he needs to talk to you."
>
> – "Of course," said the young man trying to regain his composure. "I came to ask you to go out with me this afternoon. Although you are not ready, I will wait for you. Go get dressed, go . . ."

Mireille looked at him persistently as if to ask him if he were mad, but he pretended not to understand and tried to prevent Madame Renaudy from speaking to Adeline by continuously speaking himself.

> – "But where are you going? Or rather, where are we going?" asked the girl.
>
> – "To see those who must conduct our marriage . . ."
>
> – "Ah! Yes . . ."
>
> – "Will you be ready in twenty minutes?"

– "Yes, if Mom gives me permission. However, we should have announced ourselves."

– "Well, no, this visit is simply for friendship. Haven't we shown the necessary politeness already?"

– "It's true."

– "I'm not opposed to you going out. Go out, Adeline, make yourself pretty, but you, Armand, stay to talk to me."

She waited until her daughter had left to question him:

– "Explain to me what just happened, please. Are you . . ."

– "Crazy? Isn't it the word your lips hold, Madame? Well, no, I'm not crazy."

– "Crazy or not, Monsieur, you must give me the key to the mystery that Adeline and you have been living for some time. I don't want to be a character in a farce I don't understand. My daughter will be back in twenty minutes, and you will, in front of her and her father whom I am about to call, repeat what you told me."

– "Madame!"

– "I believe you a gentleman . . ."

M. Renaudy, arriving, heard these words and was extremely surprised:

– "What is it? Oh! I shudder. Armand, what is it?"

– "Monsieur!" answered the groom.

– "M. Rougerot has just told me our daughter no longer loves him; I called Adeline so he could explain, but he preferred to act like he was crazy and spouted a thousand nonsenses to this poor child."

At the same moment, Mademoiselle Renaudy, who had no interest in the walk, came back:

– "Armand, I'm sorry I can't go out this afternoon because Louise and Marie, my cousins, are visiting us for the first time since they left. They are even bringing me a small present."

– "Well, let's go to the garden."

– "No," said the old man, grabbing Armand's arm, "you will stay here to tell your fiancée what you said to my wife earlier. You are misleading us and making our child miserable. Coward, you hurt a heart and don't even have the gentlemanliness to confess your crime. I condemn you! Defend yourself if Adeline's grief doesn't come from you."

– "Daddy, don't blame my fiancé."

– "Why do you love to the point of sacrifice the one who does not even pity your tears?" said M. Renaudy.

– "Don't defend me, my poor Adeline, your father is right, I am a coward."

– "Well, what do you say, Adeline?" asked M. Renaudy.

– "Armand is unhappy, I know it very well, but I can't do anything about his illness," continued the young girl sadly.

– "He blames you! He blames you; you know? He says you don't love him anymore."

– "Poor Armand! Father, have mercy on him; he is so unhappy!"

– "Defend yourself," said the old man firmly.

– "I was joking," said the young man, taking his fiancée's hands, "let's go out, let's walk in the garden, let's ask the flowers the secret of their happiness."

– "Alas! There isn't a single one left, Jean cut them all off yesterday and Mom took them to the cemetery."

– "Adeline, there are still some who, unsuspected, mischievous, hide under the brushwood and wait for engaged couples passing by; our revenge is that their smell often announces their mischiefs. Let's go find them, these beautiful and shy violets; let's search the bushes together, we'll find there the four-leaf clovers that bring good luck."

They went out.

– "Adeline," said the young man in the garden, "let me kiss you, let me ask your forgiveness, my lips on your lips."

– "No, no, please, no."

– "Do you forget that in three days you will be mine, mine alone?"

– "In three days, but . . ."

– "But do you still refuse a kiss from your fiancé? Adeline, remember our caresses? Why do you love me less as our wedding day approaches?"

– "I love you Armand, believe me."

– "Prove it to me by letting me rest my head on your heart to hear its beat, let me kiss your eyelids from which fall these unjustified tears. You see I'm not even asking you the reason for your tears, I leave you the freedom to suffer from a harm that I did not cause, but which is your delight . . . I respect your secret, Adeline, even if it makes me suffer horribly, but at least grant me a kiss, even if it is the most bitter one. I could still lie to myself and believe that you love me a little."

– "Armand!"

– "What did I do to you? Tell me, Adeline, have I made myself unworthy of you by some bad action?"

– "Oh! No, no."

– "Swear it to me."

– "I swear. Armand, forgive me. It's just the opposite."

– "So why don't you love me anymore? Adeline, *chérie*, I love you, I adore you, you are my only reason for living. Lie to me. Tell me you still love me, lie to me."

– "Calm down, Armand, come here. Tomorrow, at ten o'clock in the morning, I'll tell you what makes me suffer. If you really love me, don't question me anymore. *Au revoir.*"

– "Good-bye, Adeline," said the young man desperately, "good-bye!" He choked out a sob, "you'll never see me again."

CHAPTER XVI

The girl immediately went up to her room and locked herself in to cry. Then, when dinner time arrived, Mireille sent for her, but she refused any food, pretending a little fatigue and a painful stomach.

She was there, lost in cruel reflections, when Rose came to ask the reason for her absence at the dinner.

– "What's the matter, dear sister?"

– "I am tired, Rosette; come kiss me, call Roland so I can also press him against my heart."

– "Oh! Why are your eyes full of tears?"

– "Rose," said the young girl, hugging the child with an affection mixed with pain, "I love you, I regret leaving you all! How cruel is this separation to me!"

– "Poor sister!"

– "Yes, I'm unhappy, I'm leaving . . ."

– "Don't go, Adeline."

– "I must, *chérie*, but it is not without regret that I leave."

– "Tell Armand to come live with us after your wedding."

– "Child, child whom I love, be quiet and kiss me . . ."

Soon, the whole family was gathered in the young girl's bedroom; she had collapsed in an armchair.

– "Adeline," said M. and Mme Renaudy, "here is Roland, who wanted to know why you didn't have dinner . . . Are you better? Would you like a cup of hot milk?"

– "No, I just want to sleep. I'm already falling asleep."

She stood up, kissed her parents one after the other, and began to undress, thus inviting them to leave.

– "We're leaving, Adeline, good night," said Mireille, who left the room followed by her husband and her children.

As soon as she found herself alone, Mademoiselle Renaudy got dressed hastily and sat at her little desk to write.

– "Destiny," she said, head in both hands, "what am I? You take me, throw me, pick me up, throw me away and I can do nothing against your spoiled child's fantasy: I am not even a valuable rattle in your hands!"

Then she wrote:

My dear Armand,

I know to what existence I condemn you by recusing myself from your love, and I also know all the depth of the sorrow from which you are going to suffer upon reading this letter, but I can no longer pretend, no longer keep secret what my lips tried to tell you a thousand times. I would like not to be me, but alas! I cannot redo my life, I can no longer not be the daughter of Madame Rougerot, your mother. Yes, Armand, the one who gave birth to Madeleine and Jane was also the one who gave us life . . . I am your sister, a poor peasant woman told me this secret to save me from disgrace, she told me in a letter I still have there. There Armand, standing between happiness and us.

I probably should have had enough courage to tell you face-to-face that the blood that flows in your veins is also the one that runs in mine, but

I'm a coward, only my pen can break the walls that stand between my secret and you.

Adieu, darling Armand, adieu. Try to be happy; alone in the world now, I'll forget our criminal love in a foreign country. Adieu.

Adeline

She sealed the letter without rereading it, took another sheet from her diary and wrote down these words:

My Benefactors,

I thank you for all the blessings you have given me, from my birth to this day and I ask your forgiveness for my ingratitude. Yes, pardon me, for I am fleeing away from you when it would have been so sweet for me to support you in your old age. Alas! I can no longer live a lie: Armand is my brother; I can't marry him.

I'm probably not telling you anything new, but to explain my exile to you, I must give you the reason.

Why didn't you tell me this yourself, in time to prevent me from suffering and leaving? Mystery.

Adieu then, my dear parents, the only ones I know besides my mother's children, that poor woman who was Madame Julien Rougerot . . .

Your adopted daughter,
Adeline

The pen fell from her frail hand, which was shaking with emotion. What! She was going to leave a house where love surrounded her, for the indifference and uncertainty of the streets? What would become of her in a foreign country, without a job, without a relative? She had money, a gift from Madame Renaudy for her marriage, but does wealth guide the steps of a young girl in life?

She rose, and abruptly seized the medallion on which Madame Roug-erot was smiling, kissed it with love and bitterness, saying:

– "My mother, my real mother, protect me."

Then, opening a drawer, she grabbed the little gold and diamond brooch which had so easily caught Armand's attention the day they had met for the first time in Europe.

It must be remembered that this brooch was the one Junie, dying, had placed on Bébé's clothes, the one which held a small piece of paper on which were written these simple words: "Have pity on Adeline and give her this jewel."

– "You," she said, "you will be my traveling companion, my tal-isman, as I told my brother when I saw his."

She took down a small painting where all the members of the Renaudy family were together and where each child cheerfully showed off the beauty of their features: she had her doll and was laughing, Roland had his racket, Rose a bunch of flowers. Marie and Louise, one her dog, the other her cat. As for the old man and his wife, they watched smiling the playful joy of those to whom, thanks to their ease, they had given a happy childhood, free from all worries.

The word "concern" used to be incompatible with children, but alas! How many I see now who, at ten years old, are already thinking with dread about the future? Times have changed everything, even the souls of children.

They were a happy family, Adeline admitted it to herself as she stared at the painting, this irrefutable witness to her former happiness.

– "Oh! How sweet life was to me! How I loved this life that tor-tures me today! No orphan has ever known the pleasures I was given, no adoptee has ever felt so indispensable to her adopters as I do. Never a word, never a gesture, never a thought from my adoptive parents made me suspect that I had no right to be so proud and so determined. Ah! Marie and Louise were more deserving than me! I almost chased them away, their aunt not daring to take them very seriously since I'd complained about their presence in the house.

"Pardon, pardon, my poor friends, pardon, you were at home here, I'm the stranger who was given hospitality, a hospitality I proudly abused, pardon."

Adeline would have liked to see the Mesdemoiselles Guitton again to tell them her secret, she would have liked to throw herself into their arms to cry but no, she had sworn not to let anyone know her secret, except the interested parties: her adoptive parents and Armand.

She placed the painting at the bottom of a briefcase where she had stored other small things. Everything was silent, sleeping; a grave-like silence surrounded Pétion-Ville for hours now, a silence only interrupted from time to time by nocturnal birds and insects which let their shrill cries be heard in the distance.

The hours were long, interminable; it seemed like they were at least a thousand minutes long or that her clock wasn't ticking. Only eleven o'clock! No, the clock of Saint-Pierre was lying, it had to be four o'clock in the morning so that she could leave forever the house where she had known her greatest joy as well as her greatest pain.

Adeline's heart was now tormented not only by the pain caused by the impossibility of her marriage to Armand, but by the desire to know her father, her real father, and by the imminent separation from her adoptive parents. Who was the father of this young girl whom another had loved? Why was M. Renaudy attached to this child by such solid ties? Adeline was, without her knowing it, the daughter of his brother, M. Gaston Renaudy, whom politics had exiled for twenty years . . . Oh coincidence of life!

He had refused to acknowledge the paternity of this child to avoid the wickedness of his wife, who had promised to have the baby taken and to poison the unfortunate Junie. A month after the birth of poor Adeline, the civil war had forced him to leave Port-au-Prince with Madame Gaston.

The exiled man, after he became a widower ten years later, had written quickly to many friends asking for news of his child, but alas! Junie had been dead for a long time and no one, except Prémice, knew of the existence of the one who was soon to be the young, the delicious Mademoiselle Adeline Renaudy.

CHAPTER XVII

Pondering his most horrible disappointment, Armand returned to Babiole, where he found Blanco, the dog he got to replace Tchéco, who stayed with Adeline in Pétion-Ville. The sleeping animal woke up, recognized his footsteps in the alley, and ran to greet him.

– "Go away," said the young man spitefully, "you too are surely deceiving me, you don't love me . . . I've had enough of insincere caresses, leave me alone."

– "Armand," replied M. Rougerot, "instead of the poor dog who was questioningly looking at his master, why are you pushing away your faithful friend? Can't you see that this dog is suffering from your brutal actions toward him?"

– "Can Blanco's suffering equal mine? Oh! Why am I not this dog that I mistreat and who is ready again to lick my hand? Why do I have a soul since it makes me suffer so much?"

– "Are you in pain, Armand?"

– "Considerably."

– "I know you don't like gambling . . . but youth, curiosity, a simple moment of forgetfulness can . . ."

– "Daddy, please, you know I don't gamble."

– "Did you lose money in any other way?"

– "Why do you think only the loss of money to be the cause of my suffering? Ah! If only fortune alleviated this severe pain, I would run away from here, I would go work in the United States and return in twenty years with millions to buy the love of Mademoiselle Renaudy, but . . ."

– "What are you saying, Armand?" interrupted Monsieur Rougerot. "Did I hear you correctly?"

– "Yes, Adeline doesn't love me."

– "Armand!"

– "Adeline doesn't love me. Adeline doesn't love me."

– "You are a passionate man."

The young man recoiled.

– "Ah! You, too, you blame me? To whom, then, should I complain since I have no mother? It seems that a mother's heart is the only source from which one is sure to draw consolation and find a tomb in which to bury one's secrets. Oh! Why didn't God give me a mother since all children have one? Why don't I have a mother?"

– "Yours is dead," said Rougerot sadly, "but I have replaced her advantageously . . . Haven't I always spoiled you, you, our youngest child? Didn't the letters I wrote to you when you were away testify that I suffered from your absence and that I longed for your return? Why are you complaining today that the heart of a father is hard as a stone?"

– "I didn't say that," protested the young man.

– "You have more than said it, Armand, and it pains me . . . You are mistaken, all of you who believe that a father, to be severe, loses the sensitivity that God himself has given him. He loves his children, but desperate times call for desperate measures: the more a mother spoils her children, the less a father should. I'm not saying that the sensitivity of mothers is not a noble and very natural feeling, but, when it is excessive, it is more than a plague. It is a cancer.

Your mother," he continued gently, "would not have loved you more than me, Armand, believe me. Confide in me: Why do you say that Mademoiselle Renaudy no longer loves you?"

– "The spark I had seen in her eyes in Paris, and which had attracted me, is gone. Her lips, her dark lips which she gave to me, reminding me of a plum I use to nibble, are now forbidden; her heart, the wellspring of love and assurance from which once I drew endlessly, has now dried up."

– "Did you find a note, a word, or a gesture rather which makes you think she loves another man?"

– "No. Oh! No."

– "Well, I'm right to say that you are governed by passion. I will see your fiancée tomorrow and tell her about your strange allegations."

– "My fiancée? My fiancée?"

– "I'm talking about Mademoiselle Adeline Renaudy."

– "My fiancée? No, please do not repeat these two words, they are so cruelly sweet to me. When I said them to her, taking her hands in mind, and looking into her eyes, I saw angels with golden wings pass by, I saw myself, with them, enjoying celestial beatitudes, but tonight these words burn the lips like acid."

– "I thought you had a more noble soul, but it is matter over mind with you. Would you like this young girl, forgetting her piety and her modesty, to give you her lips voluptuously and reserve no surprises in marriage? I admire her modesty myself, and I con-gratulate her for it."

– "Daddy!"

– "Yes, Mademoiselle Renaudy is not just any young girl, please respect the delicacy of her feelings."

– "Good-bye, Father," said the young man with the deepest discouragement.

– "Where are you going?"

– "To sleep."

– "One does not sleep with a soul so tormented."

– "I'm going to bed."

– "Everything is settled, isn't it?" said M. Rougerot, softening his voice. "Forget what you just said to me, will you?"

– "Yes."

– "Forget the words you uttered regarding poor Adeline."

– "Yes."

– "See you tomorrow then."

– "See you tomorrow."

The two men went to their rooms.

– "Blanco," said Armand to the dog who was waiting for him at his doorstep. "Blanco, *pardon*, you are my only love, my only friend."

Tears rolled down his face and the animal licked them drop by drop. Then he moved away from his faithful companion and went to the balcony to watch the last light of evening twilight die away. He gazed at the great dark woods surrounding Babiole, grabbed powerful binoculars, drew close to him a corner of the moving blue night, which seemed to him as calm as a lake. He raised his head toward the starry sky and saw the moon which, victorious from battle with large clouds, rose, rose slowly, throwing its slivered honey on Port-au-Prince.

– "My country," he said abruptly, "you are more beautiful this evening than ever, your sky is purer than that of Greece and your mountains prettier than those of Switzerland: I love you at last! Haiti, my sweet homeland, you are my fiancée, it is you alone that I love now, it is after you alone that I will sigh since I must depart from you forever to forget Adeline."

He sent a kiss to this nature that troubled him so much and went back to his room to write this letter:

Adeline,

You will read this letter when I am far away. I can feel how much your soul is haunted by the dreadful thought that only two nights and a day separate us from our wedding, but I break the chain which attached you to me.

Adeline, why can't you pretend? If you did not suffer, if your heart could tolerate my loving you without your sharing my feelings, I would not run away, for I love you enough to be satisfied with a little friendship from your heart, but my love makes you suffer; you don't want to be loved.

Adeline, the kings had their jesters, poor beings, alas! Who were obliged to laugh and make people laugh even when they had a sad heart themselves . . . Why won't you even let me to fill the role of jester in your heart? Your suffering shows how odious my love is to you, even though it does not ask for the honor of being shared.

Good-bye,
Armand

He sat still for a moment, his head resting on the table and his eyes full of warm tears that smeared the letter he had just finished. Then, gathering his strength, mastering his pain, he began another one:

Dear Father and Sisters,

My soul has always been very open to you, but this time I was able to hide in its deepest recesses my plan to flee Adeline and leave Haiti forever.

I would like to kiss you all before leaving, but I fear that your tears joining mine would hold me back and force me to marry a heartless bride.

Adeline doesn't love me and suffers from my love. I leave her so she can be happy.

Tell yourself, my dear parents, that I am an ungrateful child so you won't suffer from my departure, for I should not have placed my passion and my despair above my filial and fraternal love.

Good-bye,
Armand

P.S. Do not reclaim the belongings I sent to Miss Renaudy.

Once more,
Armand

– "It's over," he said with a painful sigh. "I'm breaking up with those I love more than myself. Ah! If I were sure that my presence would be indifferent to Adeline's heart, I wouldn't go away, but she doesn't want to see me anymore.

"My God, which crime did I commit as to disgust Adeline? Does she know I received a love letter from an unknown woman? Does she know, alas, that I spent hours, days, sleepless nights, dwelling on the author of this poem? Even so, I wouldn't deserve the fate she has imposed on me; she mustn't forget that there are no completely faithful men . . . Yes, I've been unfaithful in spirit, but like the Prodigal Son, have I not knelt a thousand times at her feet to ask her forgiveness?

"I would prefer her reproaches to this silence, to these painful looks which scrutinize my thoughts, which tear the veil of my secret. Ah! Who is this woman who took away the happiness of being loved by Adeline and who in return does not even give me the right to know her?

"I flee from you, too, heartless stranger," he said with anger, "I flee from you, your love is not sincere; I was curious, that's all."

He got up, leaving the letter addressed to his father and his sisters on his desk, taking the one which was intended for Adeline and leaving the room, his overcoat on his arm and a small briefcase in his hand.

In the courtyard, half lit by thin silvery rays blocked by the tall trees of the orchard, he raised his eyes toward his sisters' windows and wept for a long time:

– *"Adieu,"* he said quite loudly, "good-bye, my dear little mothers!"

They could have heard him if they had not been fully asleep, exhausted by the preparations for their brother's forthcoming wedding.

Julien couldn't go to bed, for he saw light in Armand's room. He was so worried and exhausted that cunning Morpheus took advantage of his weakness to get a hold of him. He reigned in regions where reality is forgotten. There, Rougerot saw Armand, happy, satisfied, walking Mademoiselle Renaudy to the Town Hall, then to Saint-Pierre Chapel. He saw them, happy, in the salons of M. and Mme Renaudy, surrounded by relatives and friends. Junie, his poor Junie herself, was there too . . . showering her daughter-in-law with thousands of caresses . . . But why was she wearing a mourning lace veil at her son's wedding? Why didn't she come to him since they hadn't seen each other for twenty years?

His heart was pounding when Blanco's barks woke him up. He felt relieved of the weight of the nightmare, but he fell back into the dreadful reality.

He went to his window, and worryingly noticed that the dog was tied to a tree.

– "Servius," he said to his stable boy from the window, "why did you tie Blanco to a tree?"

The young man, who was awake since he had just received Armand's letter for Adeline and a thousand instructions, did not think he had to answer since it was so late.

Julien, intrigued, came down with a small lantern and ran to see what happened to the animal.

– "Blanco, my poor Blanco," he said, "what is the matter?"

The dog, who was not used to being tied up at night, felt a sweet satisfaction when Julien removed the chain from his neck. He licked the hand that had freed him and, sniffing the ground, followed his master's trail. He lost him at the gates, from where, an hour ago, the object of his faithful dog's affection had driven away.

Mad with grief, he retraced his steps, went up to Armand's room where M. Rougerot was making the same observations as Blanco. Armand was gone and his briefcase was missing.

The young man's bed was intact, and the room was mournfully sad.

CHAPTER XVIII

Three hours after writing the heartbreaking letters, Adeline knocked on the door of Jean, the old servant whose presence had become indispensable to the Renaudys during his twenty-five years of service.

The old man, hearing the trembling voice of the young girl, assumed the worst and, shaking himself, he grabbed a lighted piece of pine—a real peasant candle—and ran to his little mistress.

– "Mam'zelle Adeline, what's the matter?"

– "Jean, you served the house for more than twenty-five years, so you know that M. and Mme Renaudy are not my real parents?"

– "Mam'zelle! Mam'zelle! Who told you? Madame will die of grief if she knows that you know . . . Oh! Oh! Oh! Who said that to Mam'zelle?"

– "Jean, lead me to the chapel and then turn off this 'wood-pine,' I don't need any light here, where everything is safe. I will be leaving late this dark night, alone with a stranger. No, I must only have the light of my conscience to guide me."

– "Where is Mam'zelle going? A stranger?"

– "The driver."

– "But . . ."

– "But I'm leaving, that's all."

– "Why?"

– "You already know why."

– "And?"

– "And I'm not marrying my brother."

– "Mam'zelle's brother?" he repeated in amazement but pretending to know everything already.

We must say quickly that Jean did not know that Armand was Adeline's brother, but he was aware that the latter was not Madame Renaudy's daughter. He pretended to know the mystery of the blood ties that united the betrothed out of pride: he always boasted of knowing, through his seniority, of all the family's comings and goings. It would be a disgrace for him if someone outside the house knew a secret he didn't. So, when Adeline said those cruel words to him, he didn't take notice.

– "Jean, you knew that Armand is my brother, and you were going to let me marry him? Ah! You are a dishonest man."

– "Pardon, pardon," he said plainly.

He was asking forgiveness for a fault he had not committed: his pride took the blame for it.

– "Jean," resumed Adeline, "I forgive you, because you are a simpleton; you probably don't know incest is a heinous crime, but 'they' . . . What motive did they have?"

– "Sorry for them too!"

– "Never!"

– "You can refuse this union without having to leave."

– "Let's go!" she said with an authority that admitted no reply.

When they arrived at the square, the poor young girl saw the gardener's face and said:

– "Jean, I know Armand's mother was my mother, but who, and where, is my father?"

– "That I don't know, I don't know, nobody knows ... it's a mystery, Mam'zelle."

– "Ah! It pains me not to know the tree of which I am the fruit! Father, who are you? I would like to know you."

– "God is good!" stupidly said the old man. "You will meet him one day."

– "Yes, I hope so, Jean. I really hope so."

She looked at the Place du Champ de Mars for a long time and discovered a black and motionless mass in the grayish shadow stretching over the square.

– "Is that your car, M. Johnson?" she said calmly, trying to control her trembling voice.

– "Yes, Mademoiselle."

– "Are you sure that you have everything?"

– "Don't worry."

– "Well, let's go."

Then, turning to the old man, who was crying:

– "You will give this letter to my fiancé at sunset and give the other to my parents. If questioned, Jean, you will say you do not know anything ..."

– "Understood."

– "Here's a little bit of money to buy yourself a small souvenir, and *adieu*."

Jean sadly kissed the hand that Adeline generously held out to him.

– "May the Lord grant you happiness in your voluntary exile!"

– "*Adieu*," they both said desperately. The car screeched and disappeared into the distance in a cloud of dust.

CHAPTER XIX

Mademoiselle Renaudy was taken to Cap-Haïtien,[1] where she boarded a ship which took her to France. There, she felt lighter, relieved of the weight of her torments, but another issue troubled her: What should she do to live? A Renaudy could not be a servant or a simple worker. She eventually changed her name and looked for work, as she had very little of Mireille's money left.

She was sometimes a seamstress, sometimes a milliner, sometimes a saleswoman, but since she was not used to work, she fell ill from fatigue and went to the hospital. After her convalescence, she changed her name to Claire Closebourg, and continued torturing her little brown and velvety hands with difficult manual labor to earn her daily bread.

Oh! How sad she was in the evening when it was time to go to bed. Where were those she once kissed tenderly before falling asleep? Why was she alone and so unhappy when her heart was so desperate for affection? Why was she condemned to live alone in a hotel room, when she had a brother, sisters, and who knows, a father?

She spent hours seated at her table in bitter reflection . . . then the dawn's golden rays pierced the darkness of the room; she realized she had spent another night sleepless.

1. City located on the northern coast of Haiti with a complex history.

The poor child lived like that for a long time, turning work into the only compass of her miserable life, and prayer into her only consolation. Little by little, she bravely acclimated herself to the solitude which was now necessary to her; she even noticed she suffered when she was among the crowd. Paris was no longer the city of pleasures she had once known; it was an ordinary city where she had come to ask that her sorrows be forgotten. She could not find in her heart the gentle impulses, the enthusiasm of the past: everything in her had changed, alas, even her name.

One evening, as she was reading the newspaper to distract herself a little, she noticed this ad which intrigued her very much:

Job offer. Wealthy old man without children is looking for an educated young woman, also without children, to fulfill the role of governess, and personal lector as well.—Lots of benefits and high salary.

Contact G. D., general delivery.

Paris, on the___of____

Adeline, anxious, ran to grab her pen and wrote to the old man, who hired her at his service three days later, without even requesting a Certificate of Character.

A week later, the young girl noticed that she was not treated as a servant but as a friend, a protegee:

> – "Mademoiselle Claire," her employer, M. Gaston Durieu, often said to her, "may you read for me a little? You have such a good diction that I would like to hear you read all the time. I am afraid I'm taking advantage of your generosity, but I get so much pleasure from doing so."
>
> – "It's my duty, Monsieur."
>
> – "No, Mademoiselle Claire, no, you are doing me a favor, you are providing me with a useful distraction for my torn soul, damaged more than twenty years ago."

Adeline, or rather Claire Closebourg, protested, telling him that she was only a humble servant, but Durieu begged her to ignore her real role.

The young girl went out of her way to embellish the house so that it would be pleasant to the old man who, despite being old, had a young soul and was eager for beautiful things. One day, however, she had forgotten to replace a bouquet placed the day before on her employer's desk. The latter sadly pointed out to her the dead petals which were scattered on his blotter:

– "Mademoiselle Claire, I feel ten years older when I find myself in the presence of wilted flowers . . ."

– "Excuse me," she said, confused and her eyes red with tears, "I regret giving you the opportunity to make this just observation. You are so good to me!"

– "I'm not angry, Mademoiselle, simply saddened: old people and toddlers alike love to be spoiled! Me especially, Mademoiselle Claire, I need you to make me forget how much I suffered."

– "You, Monsieur? Have you suffered?"

– "Too much."

– "Oh! What I would do to rid your heart of the memory of your misfortunes!"

– "Well, allow me to enjoy your talents: sit at the piano and play me a beautiful piece."

Claire Closebourg, as we must now call her, was already playing a beautiful piece by Chopin, eager to please the man she loved like a father, when he stopped her with his hand:

– "No, play something by Occide Jeanty,[2] Justin Elie,[3] Ludovic Lamothe,[4] I have a mazurka[5] by my old friend Desgraves, play it for me . . ."

2. Occide Jeanty (1860–1936) was a Haitian trumpeter, pianist and composer.
3. Justin Elie (1883–1931) was a Haitian pianist, clarinetist, and composer.
4. Ludovic Lamothe (1882–1953) was a Haitian pianist, clarinetist, and composer.
5. Polish folkdance music.

– "What! You have a lot of Haitian works. Do you know my country?"

– "I'm from Haiti."

– "You?" exclaimed Mademoiselle Closebourg, happy to find in France a compatriot with a generous heart.

– "Yes, but politics forced me to leave this blessed land for an interminable exile. Alas! I conspired to free my country from sucking vampires, but my political party was defeated, and I was outlawed. Since then, I never returned to Haiti, where I have strong ties. I suffer, Mademoiselle Claire, I suffer a lot when I think of those I left there and whom I might never ever see again. I live here without relatives, like an exile, without ever receiving a letter from my country telling me about my family. They don't even know Gaston Durieu . . . a name I borrowed and was saddled with after it preserved my life. I kept my head on my shoulders, this old white head for which some had offered to pay four thousand gourdes to whoever would bring it to them . . ."

Claire listened religiously to the old man's story; he opened his poor heart to her, encouraged by her tenderness:

– "Mademoiselle Closebourg," he continued, "do you believe me now when I tell you that I am unhappy?"

– "I will try, Monsieur, to make your life, if not pleasant, at least acceptable."

– "Oh! How devoted you are to me, Mademoiselle Claire! Promise me you'll never leave me, never, never."

– "Oh! Never! I will share your joys and, even more, your sorrows."

– "How I love you, dear child!"

M. Durieu, in the secret of his heart, would often wonder for hours why he was so attached to this young girl, but the longer they lived together, the more indispensable they became to each other.

– "Mademoiselle Claire," said Gaston Durieu during a rainy evening, "I'm bored; the raindrops fall on my heart like so many stab wounds . . . what should I do to distract myself?"

– "Do you want to hear some music?"

– "No!"

– "Should I read you Haiti's newspapers?"

– "Yes."

But as soon as she begun to read *Le Nouvelliste*,[6] she fell unconscious on the floor.

– "What's happening?" cried M. Durieu in pain.

The young girl could not answer him, she was shaking, and her face was as pale as that of a dying woman.

– "Claire, Claire," he said desperately, without getting an answer.

The servants rushed up and gave the governess smelling salts. She gradually regained consciousness.

When she was completely recovered, the old man—who never even thought of reading the newspaper—questioned her on the source of her terrible concussion:

– "What did you read that moved you so much?"

– "Alas! The one who raised me just died after losing her husband . . ."

– "Who was she?"

– "Madame Jules Renaudy."

– "Claire, Claire, how I suffer. Jules and his wife were my closest relatives . . ."

– "So, we are both struck to the heart."

– "Yes, my daughter, yes. Oh! Let me cry, let me cry alone."

– "Why don't we do it together?"

6. Daily Haitian newspaper founded in 1898 by Guillaume Chéraquit.

They stayed close to each other for a long time in mute pain.

Armand, let's remember, had left Babiole for an unknown destination almost at the same that time his fiancée had fled the country. It was their parents who received the letters they had sent to each other. Julien had remained dumbfounded by the young girl's revelations, unsure if he was holding the proof of the irrefutable truth:

  – "What? Junie committed a sin? Junie, whose virtue I always praised? No, no, it's impossible," he cried.

From time to time, he reread the mysterious letter, hoping to discover another name in lieu of his wife's, but alas! The five letters were there, clearly legible, forming this name once so sweet to his heart: Junie! Oh! How he would have liked to deceive himself!

After a moment, he screamed into the void the word of forgiveness that the dead woman's ghost surely needed to go away forever:

  – "I absolve you, my poor Junie, I forgive you, because you had to, like a drowned man clings to a branch, also cling to your virtue before this fall you could not survive. I had left you with two children, without bread, and in charge of a failing business. I lost my honor on one side while trying to save it on the other. I fled prison and I lost your virtue."

Then, taking his revolver, he paced it to his heart and fired.

Jane and Madeleine, maddened with terror, had come running to find their father, their only support, in a pool of blood.

His fingers clenched, M. Rougerot still held the damning letter as well as the one containing his son's farewell.

Madeleine, a little more in control of herself, knelt beside the corpse and took them away; they were stained with blood, but still readable.

  – "Jane," she had said resolutely, "no one else should ever know why our father killed himself."

She had just uttered these words when a dense crowd of neighbors gathered in the sad room, some trying to help, others trying to discover the reason for this despair.

Walls have ears!

The next day, every single Port-au-Prince newspaper announced that M. Rougerot had killed himself upon the receipt of a letter which had revealed a horrible secret to him, and another in which his son bid him good-bye.

After the funeral, Jane and her sister went to seek asylum in a convent, in the most overwhelming despair.

M. and Mme Renaudy, also overwhelmed, had withdrawn from social life, trying to bury their grief in prayer and mortifications, asking God for forgiveness, for not having been able to stop the orphans Mme Guitton had entrusted to them, but they were driven away by Adeline's pride.

The old man died soon after.

CHAPTER XX

After learning about Mme Renaudy's death, Mademoiselle Closebourg—Adeline Renaudy—dressed solely in black and no longer played music.

– "Mademoiselle Claire," Gaston said to her one day, "I can't get used to the idea that you are my governess; be a little like my child since I don't any . . . share my sorrows with me."

– "Alas! Monsieur, my role as governess is enough for me."

– "I am sad, and you are, too, don't you see that there is a communion of circumstances, of feelings and thoughts between us? I am unhappy, I have already told you so, and I feel that you, too, are suffering from a secret illness.

"I am selfish, I am absorbing your youth and abusing your devotion. How many times have I seen you tired, discouraged, but smiling to please me! I never asked you to leave this apartment which lacks fresh, pure air for your young lungs. No, go for a walk, go and enjoy the renewal of nature and the springtime of your life. Leave me with my gray sky, leave me."

– "It's me who doesn't want to go out on Thursday, since it is your servants' free day."

– "Claire, enough, you're not my maid."

– "I am not ashamed of this word, Monsieur."

– "Alas! I have lost a child who would be about your age today, what if I asked you to replace her?"

– "I would decline this honor!"

– "Claire!"

– "Yes, I was already adopted, and it brought me bad luck . . . Since we are sharing, I will tell you, Monsieur, that my name is not Claire Closebourg, and that a great sadness led me to Europe."

– "Poor child!"

– "My name is Adeline Renaudy!"

The old man jumped hearing this name; he did not question the young girl, not wanting to interrupt her confession.

– "My name is Adeline Renaudy, I'm telling you, I am the child of sin, adopted by M. and Mme Jules Renaudy.

"I was secretly conceived in poverty by my mother, Mme Julien Rougerot, she asked for asylum in a deep tomb trying to hide her shame from her husband. When she died, a peasant took me away and gave me, according to my mother's dying wish, to this woman I mourn today out of gratitude.

"Jules Renaudy and his wife made me the most envied girl in Port-au-Prince and the most pampered in the family. They spoiled me so much that I became willful and disagreeable despite being only sixteen years old. They sent me here, in France, as soon as I finished school . . . Oh! I'm afraid to finish . . .

– "Adeline, continue, please . . ."

– "When I arrived in Paris, I saw a young man and I fell in love with him . . . he loved me too. We got engaged, and two days before our wedding, I had to leave him . . ."

Tears cut her off.

– "Poor child! Why didn't you marry this young man?"

– "Because the one who had given birth to me had conceived him a year before me."

– "He was your brother?"

– "Yes, and my parents did not tell me a marriage between us was impossible."

– "Do not overwhelm your adoptive parents, Adeline, perhaps they did not know whose child you were."

– "My mother, poor Junie, wrote them a note when she was dying."

– "Unsigned, probably . . ."

– "Ah! You're right . . . she was married."

– "Who is your father?"

– "A wretched man, a man who, taking advantage of a woman's weakness, gave her a piece of bread in exchange for her honor. A man without a conscience, an executioner. If I'm unhappy, it's thanks to him. How many times here, after my exile from my bene-factors, have I gone to bed without bread after a day of walking under the sun, looking for work? I should have at least met him to shout at him: I am hungry, I have no mother, and I am the fruit of your loins; you didn't raise me, you didn't take care of me, I'm hun-gry, give me something to eat since I'm a piece of you, your blood runs through my veins . . ."

– "Adeline, I've never seen you so angry."

– "Ah! I am angry at the thought that I am condemned to be like a wandering Jewess if unsatisfied by my work, you put an end to my mission here. I did not ask to be born. I did not ask to have a father, why—I am not ashamed to admit it to you—must I be tor-mented by the desire to know the wretched man?"

– "Pity him, Adeline."

– "After making my mother suffer, he makes me suffer. When I am crying the most, I kiss the medallion where my mother smiles, and I feel soothed, but I have nothing of him, nothing, he abandoned me . . ."

– "Adeline, don't blame your father, he must be very unhappy. He must have made many futile attempts."

– "I was not hidden in Haiti like I am here. If he had looked for me, he would have found me."

– "This father is to be pitied; I'm telling you . . ."

– "Think about it, Monsieur, I get up, go to bed, always wake up with the cruel desire to know my mother's killer, to strike him down with my vengeful gaze and to die at his feet so that he understands the full depth of my resentment."

– "After hearing your vociferations, how do you expect that this man, who has perhaps spent his whole life suffering, would deepen his pain by admitting to be the horrible father you are looking for? Why not let the culprit die in silence?"

– "Oh! To see him, to see him only to die afterward!" said the young girl soulfully.

– "If you saw an old man in front of you and he said to you: 'I am your . . .'"

– "Father! My father!" cried out Adeline, throwing herself in M. Durieu's arms.

– "My daughter! My poor child, pardon, pardon! I am your father since Mme Julien Rougerot was your mother and I am the brother of the man who adopted you. My name is Gaston Renaudy."

– "My father! Pardon!" asked the young girl falling on her knees.

– "Get up and love me, that's enough for me."

– "So Jules Renaudy and his wife were my aunt and uncle?"

– "Yes, my child."

– "But why didn't they ever tell you about me?"

– "In order to flee Haiti, I had changed my name and I had never written to them . . . However, Junie wanted you to be a little at home by leaving you with them, knowing they were my relatives."

– "Oh! How ungrateful I was in incriminating them!"

– "I'm sure they didn't know you were my child."

– "Dear father, we will never leave each other. You will take me to Port-au-Prince to weep on my mother's grave and on the graves of those who loved me to the point of sacrifice."

CHAPTER XXI

– "Poor Adeline," said M. Durieu (now known again as Gaston Renaudy), "before leaving this land where we met one another, let's go to the grave of M. and Mme Dubourg to lay wreaths of flowers."

   – "Who were they?"

   – "Your mother and your sisters' protectors, my most devoted friends."

   – "Oh! I regret not knowing them."

   – "You bear the name of Madame Dubourg and your . . . your brother that of her husband."

   – "May God grant me the pleasure of seeing them in Heaven!" said Mademoiselle Renaudy gratefully.

After having fulfilled their pious duty, father and daughter embarked for Port-au-Prince, where they were happy to find a few relatives.

Gaston, who had always been tormented by nostalgia, felt a deep contentment in Haiti, contemplating the verdant nature next to his beloved daughter.

   – "Adeline, come and see this corner of the sky on which the dying sun lays its last rays. The sea has become quite phosphorescent;

look, Adeline, look at these flowers which defy winter and tell me if
our country is not the most beautiful of all!"

And so, the old man fell into ecstasies every day in front of the beauty
of our Caribbean island which he was forced to leave twenty years ago.

Despite her father's fortune, Adeline lived humbly, isolated, finding real
happiness only in the accomplishment of work and the elevation of her
soul to God. She hadn't even tried to discover what had become of Armand,
telling herself that a moment of weakness might cause her to lose the fruit
of all the mortifications she endured since her initial departure. She no
longer expected anything from life since it seemed not to have been created to enjoy the pleasures of the world. On the contrary, she wanted the
rest of her life to be redemption for her past pride and ardent passions.
She often knelt on the cold flagstones of a church and wept for hours on
end, imploring God's forgiveness for her guilty love.

As for the old man, he had found the way back to long lost pleasures;
he often went to the Cercle, the club, in the evening and only returned at
night, which hurt poor Adeline's heart.

Sometimes, she would wait for him, alone, lying on a couch between a
dog she had tied up and a pile of newspapers. Other times, she would fall
asleep leaning on the table, a pen in her hand, while writing to distract
herself. Although rich, she now was the most unhappy girl in the world,
so she often asked the Lord to take her to him so she could return to the
homeland for which she was destined. She was sincere.

God heard her earnest prayers. Adeline fell ill with an inflammation of
the chest. M. Gaston exhausted the limits of medical science to save his only
companion, this child whom he could not legally recognize under the law,
but to whom a happy coincidence had given his name. Thanks to his wealth,
he consulted all the preeminent doctors in the capital, foreigners and Haitians, but alas! Neither money nor diligent care cures an illness when God
calls the one who suffers to him, and Adeline's condition worsened.

– "Father," she said one evening, "what's the use of worrying like this? Since you are coming back to life, I will pray that God softens it for you, but let me die and be as happy . . ."

– "Life without you, Adeline, will be as bitter as my exile."

– "Great mortifications must be opposed by great passions; therefore, I tell you, my sins, which are many, are forgiven—for I loved much. I would have been vile and contemptible if I had continued to love Armand knowing he was my brother but no, as soon as I learned the truth, I did not hesitate to leave him forever and to offer my life as a sacrifice to expiate a crime I unconsciously committed.

"I want to see God in person, I want to kneel at his feet and hear from his divine lips the words 'forgiveness' and 'mercy.'"

– "Adeline, live for me . . ."

– "I'm doomed . . . The doctors already told you, but who knows?"

The old man lowered his head to cry. Someone rang the doorbell.

– "Mesdemoiselles Louise and Marie Guitton," announced a servant.

– "Oh! Happiness," said the dying woman, "happiness to see them again before dying. Tell them to come in right away, right away. Louise," she called, "Louise, come in . . . Marie, my poor Marie . . ."

Upon entering the room lit only by a candle, the young girls could not look at Adeline because death had already marked her features.

– "Louise, Marie," said the poor girl, "I don't see you, where are you? I need to talk to you, to open my heart to you. Rose," she said to her adoptive sister who was at her bedside since her illness, "light the big bulb so I can see my dear cousins."

When the light had spread over the room, drowning it with its dazzling rays, the two sisters involuntarily uttered a little cry of astonishment in the presence of the humble patient who, with her emaciated face and her bruised limbs, had replaced the proud Adeline:

– "You? You?"

– "My cousins!"

– "Pardon!" said Louise in her ear. "I loved your fiancé. Was that why you chased me and my sister away?"

– "Poor Louise! Oh! Why didn't you tell me earlier?"

– "Let's forget everything, shall we?"

They kissed and wept together.

– "We came to help your nurse, Adeline," announced the Guitton girls.

– "Oh, thank you," and turning to M. Renaudy:

– "Father, I almost forgot to introduce you to my cousins . . ."

– "I am moved, Mesdemoiselles, by the help you have just offered my daughter, and I am even happier to meet the children of Mme Guitton, the sister-in-law of my brother, Jules."

– "Oh! Did you know our mother?"

– "Yes, I am M. Gaston Renaudy."

– "We are happy to meet a member of our family, Monsieur."

They shook hands affectionately.

Seven o'clock struck. The doorbell rang again:

– "A gentleman wants to see Mademoiselle Renaudy," announced the housekeeper.

– "It's probably a relative," said Adeline, "tell him to come in."

Armand, for it was he, suddenly found himself at the dying woman's bedside. No one recognized him, not even Adeline.

They looked at him with surprise when the poor young girl, staring at the stranger's tiepin, exclaimed:

– "Armand!"

– "Adeline!"

– "Brother!"

– "How did you recognize me?"

– "I recognized the brooch with the number 13 on your tie."

– "Adeline, what's wrong with you?"

– "I'm dying."

– "No, no, I don't want to. Why did you leave me without revealing to me the secret of your birth? I only learned about it after returning to Haiti which I had also left, because . . ."

Mademoiselle Renaudy interrupted him:

– "Let's not relive the past, it was too cruel to us, let's talk about the future, the happy days that await us over here, all over here . . . I am your sister, Armand, did you know?"

– "I was told."

– "You must believe it. I am your mother's daughter."

She held out her hand to him, a feverish, frail hand. The young man kissed it.

– "Armand, may my death be the expiation of our sins!"

Mad with pain, the young man drew his pistol and held it to his head. Adeline, already chilled by death, had enough courage to stop him.

– "Coward! You have no right to mix my death with scandal. You are my brother. Since I lead a turbulent life, I want a peaceful death."

He dropped the weapon, which misfired into the ceiling. Louise let out a cry.

– "Come," said the dying virgin to Louise.

She took her hand, placed it in Armand's:

– "Be together!"

Armand had a look of surprise and revolt, but the dying woman took her pin with number 13, placed it to Louise's bodice, and said:

– "I am giving you this jewel, may it bring you happiness, Louise, and may Armand make you happy in marriage. Armand, grant me one last request. You must marry this young girl, who has loved you for almost ten years."

– "Oh!" thought Rougerot, "here is the author of the poem which intrigued me so much."

But he remained almost indifferent toward Mademoiselle Guitton, wanting neither to displease his sister nor promise to marry her.

Then, realizing that her brother had not answered her, Adeline pressed him:

– "Armand, it's time for me to go . . . answer me . . . will you marry Louise?"

– "Yes," he said with sobs in his voice.

– "Oh! Thank you . . . call Rose and Roland, call Marie, Father, oh Father, gather around me and take my last breath . . . death's cold has reached my knees . . . it is rising rapidly . . . My Savior, lead my steps toward the new homeland. My father, my poor father, come near me. Ah! It's over, my heart freezes: *adieu* to you all! I want my last thoughts to be only for Heaven. My Lord, lead me . . . My Lord . . . My . . ."

She passed away with this sacred name on her lips and serenity on her face.

– "*Requiescant in pace*,"[1] a priest said twenty-four hours later, ending the song of the dead. "*Requiescant in pace!*" echoed two altar boys.

---

1. Latin for "rest in peace."

Then the body of the one who had been the innocent victim of a cruel destiny passed through the wide-opened gates of the Sacred Heart.

A month later, the same priest sang the *Magnificat*, asking the Good Lord to cast his holy blessing on a couple who had just gotten married.

The newlyweds?

Armand and Louise.

The White Negress

Preface to *The White Negress*

Among the less predictable consequences of the American Occupation of Haiti, it is not paradoxical to see a radiant and sudden bloom of our literature, of which a few pathetic[1] novels will bear witness to our most distant posterity of the reaction of our souls in the face of the brutality of this situation.

The White Negress that Madame Virgile Valcin presents today for advertising partakes of the same nobility of feeling.

It is a psychological drama. A moving drama which shows the harsh instinct of possession, the tenderness of the father, a husband's affection[2] toward pride, vanity, and the psychosis of racial prejudice.

An American in Port-au-Prince, a man 100 percent dominated by this prejudice and serving on the land of Haiti, marries a woman of his race and whom he has every reason to believe to be authentically white, learns one day that the one to whom he gave his name and whom he loves passionately and from whom he has an adorable little daughter—the flesh of his flesh—is tainted by Black blood. We must wonder about what moral torture, what ravaging, what atrocious suffering his tortured soul is suddenly assailed by, when confronted with such contradictory feelings.

---

1. Producing an effect upon the emotions; moving, stirring, affecting (*obsolete*).
2. Favorable or kindly disposition toward a person or thing (*obsolete*).

Such is, briefly summarized, the topic of *The White Negress*.

Madame Virgile Valcin not only wrote this book with the talent of an informed storyteller, but she poured all her heart into it, a heart aching from the bruises from which we have all suffered for nineteen years while our homeland has been occupied by the American military forces and by the occult power of American finance. With the skill that befits such a delicate task, she has weaved the action of the drama within all the social, political, and mundane material with which Haitian life was kneaded during these heavy years. From this point of view, her novel is also a slice of contemporary history, and the reader will not be surprised to encounter, during the story, a touch of criticism on the men and things that occupied public attention in the news.

It is this amalgam of fiction and realism, mixed with a certain poetic taste, that gives *The White Negress* the endearing interest which characterizes this book from the first to the last page.

I am certain that, in this country where there are so many very gifted women who dare not face the uncertainties of publicity, the fine effort, the concern for art and beauty to which Madame Valcin's novel bears witness, will find the welcoming audience that it deserves.

April 27, 1934
Dr. Price-Mars

List of Characters (in order of appearance)

Raoul Desvallons: French, father of Laurence

Anna Desvallons: Dies during childbirth, mother of Laurence

Laurence Desvallons: French, daughter of the Desvallons

Myrtana Durand: Haitian, friend of Laurence

Yen Leabrook: American, works at the Central School of Agriculture

Lucienne Monfort: French, marries Raoul, stepmother of Laurence

M. Ménard: French, father of Anna

Guy Vanel: Haitian, lawyer, informal fiancé of Laurence

Robert Watson: American, works at the Central School of
   Agriculture

CHAPTER I

– "Doctor," Raoul Desvallons said desperately, "is it true nothing else can be done to save my wife?"

–"I tried everything, my friend; who knows? . . . A reaction can still happen . . . but . . ."

– "Say no more, what you are about to say may be too cruel, I want to keep hope alive, try something once more . . ."

– "My friend, my poor friend," the doctor said gravely while holding the husband's hands, "be brave, Madame Desvallons wants to talk to you . . . go see her, but try not to tire her too much, she's already so weak!"

The poor husband, his back bent under the weight of the pain, approached the bed quietly and knelt.

– "Dear, dear Anna, talk to me, I'm listening, open your seventeen-year-old heart to the desperate man I am. Where will I find words powerful enough to describe to you the pain that grasps me? Oh! Speak, my beloved; I will be happy hearing your warm voice, your voice that I love, your voice that no other voice resembles. Say the words I told you repeatedly yesterday, the words that change a heart full of doubt into a trusting heart, a disconsolate soul into a happy soul; speak, oh! Speak the way you did when I saw you the first time, speaking like an adored wife speaks to her husband . . . I am not hearing you. Your suborned silence scares me Anna . . . speak now . . ."

The poor woman was probably listening to him, as from her closed eyes came warm, heavy tears, tears, the only testimony of her love and her regrets. She could neither speak nor move.

The new mother had been silent for an hour, when suddenly she whispered:

    – "Raoul, my regret, my only regret is about my little girl!"

    – "Ah! This is what the doctor talked about . . . the reaction . . . is happening . . . Because she speaks, she is saved . . . Oh! Quickly, somebody call Dr. Marchand, call him . . . tell him she speaks . . . Oh! Hurry, hurry . . . ," cried the sad man.

Kneeling next to the dying woman, he told her his sorrows, his fears, his plans. Madame Desvallons was under no illusions, and wanting to take advantage of the little strength God had given back to her, she pronounced her last wishes, placing her hand on his mouth while making a sign signaling to let her speak, she who was going to speak for the very last time.

    – "Name my daughter Laurence," she began, "I like this name, be a devoted protector to her and tell her my last thought was for her. My dear Raoul, our happiness did not last long! I want to live! But . . ."

    – "Anna, Anna . . . you will live . . . you . . ."

    – "Let me speak, I have so much to say! Alas! I can feel the weakness that rendered me mute earlier coming back; Raoul . . . allow me to say good-bye to Laurence, to hold her with the strength I have left before it leaves me. Quick . . . bring her to me, if you wait for even five minutes, it will be too late . . ."

    – "It is not true . . . you are going to live . . ."

The nurse near the little white cradle held the newborn baby, and gave her to Mme Desvallons, who hugged her while crying tears of happiness:

– "My daughter! My child . . . be happy, you will live . . ."

All her courage was depleted by the embrace!

– "Brave, I am not afraid anymore . . . *Adieu* . . ." She abruptly stopped talking. Worried, Desvallons leaned toward her and embraced her last sigh in the sweetest and cruelest of kisses.

Dr. Marchand, who had returned to the mother's bedside a few minutes earlier, felt her pulse, then, discouraged and dumbfounded, released the poor white arm and turned to Raoul:

– "I pity you, my friend! I did everything I could to save her . . . My deepest sympathy . . ."
– "Thank you, thank you for your devotion. Thank you."

In one jaunt, the doctor reached Rue Servandoni (where his car was parked) and promised himself to come back in three days to attend his poor client's funeral at the old church of Saint-Sulpice.[1]

With the doctor gone, Raoul fell into a deep state of meditation: he remembered all the beautiful walks he had taken through the "infamous and marvelous Paris" as a student. He remembered the day he told Anna he loved her, and she promised to spend the rest of her life with him. These detailed memories were still alive within him: he could see them flash before his eyes—oh sweet vision! All the exquisite things they had seen together during their brief engagement. He remembered every word they had shared during their honeymoon spent in Montmorency,[2] he especially remembered the promise they made to love one another until death did them part. Until death! How distant those words had seemed to him!

---

1. The second-largest Roman Catholic church in Paris, dating to 1646.
2. A small commune in the northern Paris suburbs.

And they were at the end of their first and only year of marriage . . . they had promised to love the sweet baby girl who slept in the cradle to which he himself had tied ribbons while his wife added laces and tulle! And why, in front of the same cradle where they had happily imagined so many plans, hand in hand, eye to eye, did he find today only a shrouded body and a poor crying man?

Alas! Had they believed too much in happiness, in the future, in life? So many couples had gotten married twenty, thirty years ago and were still living . . . Were happy! . . .

> – "I want to go back to the past, to my past," he said, "but my past was only yesterday, alas! Why should I remember anything before the time of my engagement and my marriage? Before I had lived? I don't know, I don't remember anything . . . Had I lived? . . ."

Yes, he had lived, and what a life! Born from a degenerate father, he had spent his childhood consoling his sad mother by telling himself he would be happier when he was a man, but death, this executioner that struck him again today, had taken his mother away the day he had found a job. All his plans had collapsed with the passing of this woman, for whom the poor adolescent had wished nothing but a peaceful old age. His despair was endless, to keep living was an injustice to him. What did he expect from this life that had tormented him and taken away his mother, this life his father exploited with the revolting lucidity of people who "do evil, who know they are doing evil, and who do it anyway"?

Three years later, his father died. Who would want to believe that this death had been as cruel as that of the unfortunate woman? The deceased was scrawny, useless to his country, to society, useless to his family, a man who had worked for his own ruin, both physical and moral, but he was his father! He said: "Farewell, pleasure!" He had been sincere in uttering this cry, but he had not thought of the imperious need young people feel, the need to band together to live life, which seems like an oyster or rolled-out red carpet.

"Farewell, pleasure!" He had thrown himself into his schooling to fight against some subconscious forces trying to take hold of him.

No, he had wanted to be the master of his brain, and to come out of this ordeal with a calmer soul, a hardened body . . . what if there was a war? He would enroll, and offer a strong arm, a brain full of serious things to his country, to brave France, "everyone's second homeland."

At that time, he lived in the "Boul' Mich"[3] with fellow students. He could still picture his cheap little room, where three small iron beds stood next to each other, an old, threadbare sofa, a chair, a table, and some books . . . That was all, they were so poor!

He remembered in great detail the day he had seen Anna for the first time, oh happy day!

It was in the Luxembourg Garden, one summer afternoon. Tired after a whole day of tedious work, and wanting to clear up his head, he had come to see the sparrows fly, the flowers smile, the fountains weep, and hear students cooing sentimentality to their lovers . . .

Time had mostly healed his double grief; he had already been deprived of his mother for five years, and it had been two years since his unfortunate father had passed.

He had been in the garden for half an hour when he saw a young girl accompanied by someone who must have been her father. She did not have the insolent attitude of some of the young ladies in Paris's Latin Quarter . . . She had just arrived from New York:

- "Which park is this?" she asked suddenly.
- "It is the Luxembourg Garden," said the man.
- "What is the name of the long street we walked on earlier?"
- "It is the Boulevard Saint-Germain."
- "What about the street where we bought books?"
- "It is the Rue Monge."

3. Short for Boulevard Saint-Michel, a street located in the Latin Quarter of Paris.

– "And the place where you bought me flowers and a pretty bird?"

– "It is the Quai aux Fleurs."

– "And the big courtyard from which people carrying books were coming out this morning?"

– "The Sorbonne . . ."

– "Oh! How splendid . . . Over there, in America, everything is huge, but . . ."

They stopped to make plans:

– "Here, Daddy, take me to the opera to see Faust, take me to the Comédie-Française[4] to see a classic in this sweet and soft language . . ."

– "Come on, you can speak it."

– "Not perfectly. The teacher I had in America was conscientious, but I had no one to speak French with. When he left, I was very sad . . ."

– "Poor little flower, transplanted into a climate that was not yours! Aren't you happy to be back in France, Anna?"

– "Oh! Yes, even though I cried a lot when I left . . ."

– "Departures are always sad, we always feel regret when leaving a place, even if we only spend a few hours there, even if it is a land of exile, since no land has ever given anything but bitterness.

"Dangerous criminals come back from the Devil's Island in Cayenne[5] with fond memories; recently one of them published his recollections written at the penitentiary, in the newspaper *La Croix* . . ."

– "What? Missing jail?"

---

4. French theater company founded in 1680.
5. A French penal colony located in Cayenne (French Guyana's main city) that operated from 1852 to 1952.

– "It was not the prison he was missing. It was the strong friend-
ships he was able to develop in the world of convicts, or perhaps a
prison officer who had a word of pity for him, when an inmate was
picking on him, what do I know?"

– "Dear, dear father, I love you so very much for bringing me
here. Oh! Paris is so beautiful!"

– "New York as well . . ."

– "Paris is pretty in a different way, Father. Here there are houses;
in New York, there are colossal buildings which, like merchan-
dise, show off their insolent majesty and their silly desire to impress
the gaze of the astonished tourist . . ."

She had laughed, and Raoul had seen her perfect white teeth.

Anna and her father had started walking again, without noticing that
someone was watching their every move. It was Raoul Desvallons.

– "Oh Paris!" she said once more. Like a chorus, these words
came back to her lips twenty times during the walk. Then, as if to
tell a secret, she had taken her father's arm:

– "Let's walk slowly, I am going to tell you about an event that
happened last year.

"We were invited, my uncle, my aunt, and I, to spend two
weeks in Georgia at the Blaksons's, who were celebrating the birth
of their firstborn. We took a plane . . . it was the first time I had left
New York. There is no need to tell you how happy I was during my
first flight. I felt like I was going toward the Lord and was finally
going to meet him. Oh! To see the beautiful steel bird carrying me
away, scraping the roofs of buildings of New York with its wings. To
me, it was as fascinating as it was prodigious."

She had stopped smiling and had become serious again.

– "The trip passed without incident. I rejoiced, but I heard a
distant thrum during landing; it grew gradually louder, and it

turned into a frightening tumult in less than five minutes. I clung
to my aunt's skirt, who was also worried.

"The American pilot told us in his calmest voice—in English:

"'Don't be afraid, it must be a n——[6] being lynched ... Every time
I land here, I witness a lynching and I'm always very happy about it,
one must see that before turning twenty ... It is very interesting.'

"The word 'lynching' was unknown to me, or maybe I did not
understand the pilot's babble.

"A car, driven by Monsieur Blakson himself, was waiting for us
in a tall grass field.

"I did not know him.

– "'Meet my niece Anna,' said my aunt, 'she enjoyed the trip ...
she's been living with me for nine years, ever since my sister was
sent to a sanatorium ...'

"Without saying a word, the American took my little hand,
almost crushing it in a strong handshake. My poor hand! He burst
out laughing; I was upset, and thought that a Frenchman—you,
for instance—would never do such a thing. But the car left full
blast, I forgave him, and decided to leave my worries behind. The
roar of the car prevented me from hearing the clamor of the crowd.
Alas! I was wrong, the house we were going to was located near a
square, and this square was precisely the location chosen to be the
theater of the crime ... and what a crime!

"Under a beautiful tree, probably centenarian, someone had
placed a heap of dry, green twigs, taken here and there from all the
valuable plants that adorn the square. I saw men, dirty, drunk, their
bodies drenched in sweat. The drooling mouths, where flies were also
going to get drunk, seized a poor Black man already chained, lifted
him two meters above the piles of wood, and tied him to the trunk.

6. Literal translation of the French. Valcin purposely uses this ethnic slur to high-
light and insist upon the extreme racism of her American protagonists.

"The unfortunate man tried to defend himself, without success. He insulted the white savages and showed these disciples of Torquemada[7] and Jimenez[8] how bravely Black men die.

"'Murderers!' he said, 'you call yourself civilized, you do what the primitives never did, you kidnap young girls, children, defenseless old men, and demand ransoms to return them to their families or you kill them . . . Murderers, I spit in your face . . .' which he did when he had finished talking . . .

"He had just spat in the face of the man closer to him: a white man.

"Mad with rage, the American drew his knife, and cut out the Black man's tongue. The poor man stopped speaking, since he no longer had a tongue, but he began to laugh . . . a reaction that exasperated the crowd, who did not know what to invent to prolong his torture.

Everyone shared their opinion, but no one listened. Each of them felt offended for the person who had been spat upon. Ferocious scoundrels approached, doused the Black man with gasoline, and set fire to the stake . . . The man was still laughing. The fire slowly rose and rose, almost reaching his feet. He was still laughing. They added twigs. He was still laughing. They fanned the flames; he was still laughing. The executioners, angered by his laughter, his last act of bravado, threw their torches at him . . .

"His pants caught fire, he was still laughing, but soon after his body, his poor Black body, was nothing but a blaze. He used all his strength to expel all the resentment that gripped his soul in one final burst of laughter."

The little girl fell silent. Sickened by this cruel memory. Monsieur Ménard asked her to go home, as this story had upset him. He was pale.

---

7. Thomas of Torquemada (1420–1498) was a Spanish cleric and the first Grand Inquisitor.
8. Francisco Jiménez de Cisneros (1495–1517) was a Spanish cardinal, statesman, and Grand Inquisitor.

A month later, Raoul Desvallons had the pleasure of being introduced to Mademoiselle Anna Ménard and her father. Thanks to his brilliant qualities of mind and heart, he had no difficulty earning the friendship of this honorable family. He asked for and obtained Anna's hand, though she was still a child, and they got married.

During this trip down memory lane, Desvallons had fallen asleep next to his late wife's corpse. Sleep had made him as oblivious as the innocent orphan in the next room.

Afraid he had fainted, his family woke him up.

Alas! This brutal return to reality was too cruel to him. He ran from the bed to the cradle, and from the cradle to the bed where roses had been placed, roses which slowly shed their petals, giving back their little souls to Nature.

How he wished his coffin could be next to Anna's . . . but who would take care of Laurence?

———

Ten years had passed. Laurence was now a beautiful little girl, a little wild, thanks to her father's numerous treats. They lived in a relatively nice apartment in the Rue Royale, but Raoul had sent his daughter to boarding school, where she could learn good breeding and manners. The separation from his only reason to live was heartbreaking . . .

Laurence rebelled, but the brave man held on. Tired of fighting, she ended up accepting the austerity of boarding school life, a situation she hoped to overcome one day.

Hardship: who hasn't had one in their life!

Desvallons, who thought he was ready for the fight, was surprised to feel sad in the absence of his child. Loneliness weighed on him when he returned in the evening from the Compagnie du Gaz[9] where he worked. This separation was a new test. Often, he wandered through Vincennes,

9. Gas company.

Saint-Cloud, Suresnes;[10] other times, he visited museums, eager to increase his extensive knowledge.

One Sunday afternoon, Raoul decided to retrace the last steps that he and his wife took. He started on the Rue Royale, stopped for a moment on the Place de la Concorde to buy a small bouquet of violets, walked near the horses of Marly, and continued past the Champs-Elysées until he reached the Place de l'Étoile.

He was about to lay his bouquet on the Tomb of the Unknown Soldier,[11] when a young girl, a real fairy, crying heavy tears, appeared next to him. She also had flowers for the illustrious stranger.

Raoul did not want to admit that this presence had deeply moved him. However, when he got home, he began to feel sorry for the beautiful young girl, regretting that he had not asked the cause of her tears . . . It would have been an indiscretion, of course, but he thought a word of pity might have relieved her inconsolable soul.

During eight consecutive days, he had repeated the same walk, trying in vain to find the beautiful nymph.

Why did he want to see this person he didn't know again? Why did he catch himself thinking about her? Why this connection between the tearful face of a stranger, met by chance at a public monument, and the confusion he felt? He had seen so many women cry without being moved by their tears, and even in his widowhood he had remained stoic. Why did the painful expression of those two eyes full of tears remain so vivid?

———

A month had passed. Desvallons was wandering one morning in front of the Hôtel de Ville[12] in Neuilly, when he saw from a distance a silhouette looming near the Church of Saint-Pierre:[13]

10. Communes in Paris.
11. A memorial to all the soldiers who have died for France, located under the Arc de Triomphe in Paris.
12. City hall of Paris.
13. Saint-Pierre de Montmartre, one of the oldest churches in Paris.

– "It's her," he murmured, "joy!" The young girl quickly entered the holy temple and kneeled in front of the altar. Raoul followed suit. She did not notice. But, when she left the church and arrived at the Rue Rigaud where she lived, her beautiful blue eyes stared at the enquiring face of the young widower, who said to her hesitantly:

– "Please forgive me, Miss, but I cannot resist asking you if you are the sister of my college friend, Jacques Lavoisier . . . My name is Raoul Desvallons . . ."

– "No sir, I am Lucienne Monfort . . . I had a brother, too, but alas! He died during the Great War . . ."

Her eyes became heavy with tears.

– "My brother was my only family," she continued, "it was with great sadness I learned from his superior that he had died, and that his body was missing. That is why I visit the Tomb of the Unknown Soldier and bring flowers when I want to cry. I tell myself that the one who lies here in all his glory might be the brother I lost. It is crazy but it brings me comfort."

– "If I asked you, Miss, to give me your permission to fill the void left in your heart by your brother's passing? . . . I am a lonely widower . . ."

She stared at him but did not reply. They had been walking together for the last five minutes when Lucienne came to an abrupt stop.

– "This is where I live . . . Good-bye, sir."
– "No answer? Not even a promise? Nothing?"
– "I will think about it . . ."
– "Where might I see you again?"
– "Here . . . in eight days . . ."

Desvallons returned home with a happy heart; the only thing that seemed an obstacle to him was how to talk to Laurence about Lucienne.

He dreaded this moment because he knew his daughter strongly believed he would never remarry. He had often said so himself. He thought Laurence was going to scream, to complain. But things turned out differently when her father told her about his project during a day off. She simply said:

> – "Father, if this marriage makes you happy, I wholeheartedly support it. I already give my friendship to the woman who will become your wife. But, if you were to suffer because of her, my hatred would know no bounds . . ."

What could Raoul say to this ultimatum? Isn't marriage a gamble from which you always come out with a prize, a prize which can be very trivial or very important? Who knew if behind Lucienne's deep beautiful eyes there was not some malice? Who could guess if under her appearance of detachment, of simplicity, a simplicity that almost borders on complacence, was not hiding a desire for luxury, a fickle desire, one of those desires that make women run from store to store looking for trinkets? How could he know? He had seen many sheep turn into wolves. Didn't demons start out as angels? Didn't Satan, their leader, stand next to God's throne before his rebellion? Doesn't the most beautiful day often end with the strongest storm?

When Laurence was sent to the convent, her eyes were full of tears, she had the impression that her happiness had been taken away. Never in her life had she felt so unhappy. What? Her father was going to let a stranger come between him and her? Was he lying when he told her that his heart belonged to her? Was there room for another woman? Would this new presence in the paternal home diminish her rights?

In January, Raoul and Lucienne decided to get married in early March.

Days passed, the life of the little girl remaining unchanged. The Mother Superior soon noticed her sad expression:

> – "Laurence, why the long face? If you have grief, why don't you open your little heart to me? Am I not your mother? Is your educa-

tion not entrusted to me? If you knew how much you pain me, you would come to me with confidence, and throw yourself into my arms to share your sufferings with me . . . you are suffering, aren't you?"

– "It is nothing, Mother," she said before bursting into tears. Mother Superior took the girl's hand in hers.

– "Come on, look me in the eyes. . . . Only lower your head before me when you are at fault and, praise the Lord, you have not committed anything to be ashamed of. Talk to me. I am listening . . . Speak."

This last word was said in a semi-affectionate, semi-stern tone. The headmistress couldn't allow a student to spend all her time moping around for no apparent reason. Besides, what could be wrong with a ten-year-old? It had been a long time since she had overcome separation from her father. What was she complaining about now?

She was studious and well-behaved, oh! So well behaved as to earn the right to spend two nights and a pleasant day with her father at the end of each month. Her teachers were amazed at how quickly she had adapted to the harsh discipline of the establishment.

– "Well," said the headmistress, looking at the mute child, I am going to ask for Monsieur Desvallons, and you will tell me what is bothering you in front of him."

– "But I am suffering because of him," the girl cried out.

– "Because of Monsieur Desvallons? Explain yourself . . ."

– "He wants to remarry . . ."

– "Well!"

– "He always told me he would remember my mother forever . . ."

– "Laurence, be honest. Are you claiming the rights of the deceased as your own? Do you think this marriage will rob you of your father's affection? Do not be unfair, my girl, this man has the right to include a woman in his life, a woman who will be a new

mother for you, who will give you advice, and whose generous presence would be a comfort to you, if a storm were to cross your path.
Life is not always beautiful, dear child, what if your father were to
pass away? What if. . . ."

– "Oh, I would simply die."

– "Well. That's good. But you mustn't be hostile to the mother
Monsieur Desvallons is going to give you. The Good Lord always
does well. Your recriminations, even if just, will not do anything
against His will. It's over now, isn't it? Your friends are waiting for
you. There, live, wipe your eyes, and go play. Try to put on a happy
face so that on the day of the wedding you will look splendid in
your beautiful dress, pink, blue, white, or green . . . how pretty you
will be! How exquisite the candies will be, and your affectionate
mom, and charming dad."

The Mother Superior had not preached to no end; Laurence had changed
since that day. The idea of her permanent return to her father's house after
graduation seemed to her less painful. A well-raised person does not
impose her will unto others, she thought, as the priest had said in a ser-
mon the other day. She was resigned to her fate.

That is why, when her father sent for her so she could attend his wedding, she left the boarding school without a tear.

However, when she entered her father's bedroom and looked around . . .
alas! She realized the large portrait of her mother was gone, which tore
her heart. She quickly understood that the deceased had lost the right to
be ranked first in Raoul's house: the dead do not have a home, "they only
have their pains . . ."

Monsieur Desvallons had thoughtfully decided to place the large photograph in the pretty bedroom saved for Laurence after graduation.

She was touched by this kind gesture. She later forgot what she had initially considered an affront to Anna's memory.

– "Well," said her father, "how do you like your new mother?"

Before she could answer, he added:

- – "Kind? Beautiful? Charming?"
- – "Oh! Yes, very . . ."
- – "Isn't it right you are going to love her?"

Once again, she did not have time to answer. The car taking her to the wedding had just honked outside, while the newlyweds' automobile idled and purred.

––––––

It was 1925. Five years had passed since Raoul Desvallons married Mlle[14] Lucienne Monfort. But bad luck, a harsh, tenacious, enraged bad luck, seemed to be following them.

Usually in control, Desvallons had fallen seriously ill, a disease which left him somewhat addled, and then he resigned from the Compagnie du Gaz.

For the last three months, he had barely been able to support his family. He was no longer able to afford the luxury of the beautiful apartment located in the Rue Royale, so he had rented a modest place in the Rue de la Convention.

After brilliantly passing her senior final exams, Laurence returned to her father's home, where unfortunately bad luck had arrived first. Since she had only spent her days off in the Rue Royale, the young girl did not notice the disadvantages of their new lodging. Only Mme Desvallons suffered from it. So what! To live in the Rue de la Convention, empty of distractions, after having known the splendid Rue Royale, with its endless comings and goings, its diamonds, its shops with coats and dresses at five, six, twenty thousand francs, and so forth! It was dreadful, intolerable!

Rue Royale! It's a wonderland when the Yankees, men and women, parade ostentatiously, with snobbery to throw their dollars around . . . Who, in their life, would not want to witness an "American raid" at the

14. Miss in French.

luxurious Samaritaine,[15] in the shops of the Rue de la Paix and the Rue Royale, of the Avenue de l'Opéra, the Grands Boulevards? They wanted to purchase all of Paris . . .

Seeing American tourists go by is a real diversion for those who don't have the time to go see a comedy at the theatres.

In short, Lucienne was not happy, alas! She must cook by herself, wax the wooden floors. She had not anticipated all these difficulties when Raoul had promised her happiness if she married him.

———

When Desvallons comes home in the evening, after a day of futile attempts, a day during which he knocked on every door to ask for work, he finds in lieu of his Lucienne, the Lucienne of the good old days, a woman with a closed face, a woman angered by nothing and everything, a woman who does not respond to his most ardent caresses:

– "My dear, leave me alone, I am exhausted . . . Don't you know I do everything by myself here? One does not make love in a state of misery."

Lacking strength, he only murmurs:

– "My darling, I visited all of Paris hoping to find a job, but. . . ."

She interrupts him:

– "Didn't you quit your steady job? Well! What are you complaining about? What can you tell me I don't know? . . ."

– "Ah! Despite the affront that had been done to me, I should have continued to work in this company? The fear of destitution has deprived you of any sense of nobility!"

– "What do I know?"

15. A large department store located near the Louvre in Paris.

– "My poor darling, be patient, more fortunate days will come back. The clouds will go away."

– "Alas! . . . in the meantime, my hands hurt . . ."

These little revolts of Mme Desvallons pained the poor man, who was fortunately supported by Laurence's affection.

– "Father," she says, "one day, allow me to work, I want to be a typist to help with the basic needs of the household."

He doesn't answer, but he pulls the child to his chest and cries into her hair.

The next day, oh happy day! While he is having lunch next to Lucienne, the doorbell rings. It's the postman . . . The postman! But what can he bring? It's been so long since anyone wrote to him: nobody writes to unfortunate people . . . However, something tells him that this envelope, this pretty blue envelope conceals a surprise. "Surprise," what a pretty word!

And here is a man, discouraged yesterday, who starts hoping again just because a common postman gives him a letter.

Laurence and Madame Desvallons look at him in amazement; they cannot understand the many happy thoughts filling the sad man's mind, why so much hesitation? The letter has been lying there for five minutes now, like a poor thing no one cares about. Yet he believes, he knows, he is sure that his salvation depends on this envelope . . . (The heart experiences doubts, and fears disappointments, even amid the greatest happiness. Would the hope of happiness be sweeter than happiness itself?)

This letter! It can only contain. . . . A letter from his friend Dubois, who works in Haiti. He had promised to find him a job on this marvelous island.

Where does this fear come from, the fear of opening an envelope? He cannot doubt anymore, he has just seen the advertisement in large letters "Drink the coffee of Haiti, it's the best" next to the stamps glued to the envelope and bearing the image of the Haitian president. Such happiness!

Gone are the doubts . . . gone all the dreary days with a woman he adores, but from whom he does not expect any caress, because love does not get along with misery, as she says. And his daughter, so affectionate, so joyful despite the suffering . . .

In this kind child, he can already see a strong woman. One who will survive the moral and bodily miseries without stigmata or scars. She already has an ideal: it is to love all that is good, all that is beautiful, it is not to ask life for more than it could give.

She loves poetry, music, she loves flowers, the sky, the sea, she loves God and all the beautiful things he has done. But she knows the Lord was born poor, that he worked, that he suffered, she loves the poor, labor, she is neither afraid of suffering nor death. Raoul opens the letter, oh sweet emotion! There are still people who remember unfortunates like us!

> – "Lucienne," he says happily, "we are leaving for Haiti . . . Dubois found something for me there."
> – "Well! What? A promise . . . It's so far from reality . . . Besides, going to Africa doesn't tempt me . . ."
> – "Africa? But you are mistaken, my friend. Haiti is one of the four islands of the Greater Antilles, an island where the sun shines on flowers and leaves, summer and winter alike. Dubois described it to me, it's mostly an agricultural country, a paradise."

Laurence laughs, saying:

> – "A Robinson Crusoe[16] type of island?"

Him, joyful:

> – "We will not be alone like the character of Daniel Defoe, who was stranded alone; in Haiti, we will find a civilized people who

16. Reference to the novel *Robinson Crusoe* (1719) written by Daniel Defoe, which features a castaway stranded on a deserted Caribbean Island for twenty-eight years.

speak our language with ease, with a refinement and some turns of phrase unsuspected among Blacks."

Lucienne, won over little by little by the prospect of leaving poverty behind her and going directly to fortune, says after reading the letter:

> – "Well! Let's go right away. When we have earned a few thousand dollars, fifty, a hundred thousand, for example, we will become snowbirds: after the winter, we will return to the regions we had deserted because it was too cold. We will return to our beloved France, to the heart of our dear Paris. Paris will be happy to see us again, it will hold out its arms to us, those arms which are inclement to us today. It will smile on us . . . Paris always smiles on the rich . . . Rich! We will be so rich I already picture myself in the Bois[17] in my beautiful automobile, contemplating the large white swans swallowing little frogs in the lakes. I see us at the Longchamp races,[18] betting five thousand, ten thousand francs, on this horse and this one . . . I see us at the opera, in the best box.

> "We will buy a residence in Dauville or Biarritz for the summer, and in the winter, we will go to Nice,[19] we . . . oh, what will we do? Let's go . . ."

> – "Is this Charlot's *Gold Rush*?"[20] says Laurence, amused, "what if we do not earn this fortune you are already counting on, dear stepmother?"

> – "Shut up, crazy girl, Dubois wrote to us that Haiti is never insensitive to the miseries of foreigners. On the contrary, she is always more merciful to them than to her children. Haiti, he says, is the *refugium peccatorum*[21] of all those who do not have a dime.

17. Short for the Bois de Boulogne, a large public park in Paris.
18. A horse-racing venue in the Bois de Boulogne.
19. French resort cities.
20. "Charlot" is short for Charlie Chaplin.
21. Latin for Refuge of Sinners, a Roman Catholic title for the Virgin Mary.

That's why even the stupidest Americans who barely graduated from elementary school can buy an engineering degree from some old men who no longer need it, and then be hired as 'experts' . . ."

– "Experts?" says Laurence.

– "Yes, according to Dubois, it's a title given to Americans who don't have one. There are experts in grass, in 'rat control.' In the art of earning bribes, of letting people rot in prison . . . I do not remember the rest . . ."

– "That's stupid. Thank God Dad has a real diploma: he is really an engineer. He studied . . ."

– "Yes, my child, I still have vivid memories of my life as a student at 'Boul' Mich,'" adds Raoul.

These sweet memories are now mixed with others, which make him suffer. He remembers the beautiful child he one day saw, on a walk with her father in the Luxembourg Garden. He remembers the nymph who briefly shared his life, but whom he finds alive in Laurence.

He whispers, "Poor Anna!"

———

People frantically wave their handkerchiefs at the Orsay train station. It is 10:59 P.M. Those staying cry as much as those leaving.

– "Good-bye!" they cry out. Good-bye! Alas! Many will never see each other again . . .

The train leaves. A man and two women bend over the door to send one last kiss to a poor old man who is crying, and who is returning alone in the cold and uncertain night.

There are five passengers in the compartment, and all of them have tears in their eyes.

A sob here, a cry there, quickly silenced by the noise coming from the locomotive's blastpipe.

– "Poor grandfather!" Laurence whispers, "I regret leaving him behind!" (She cries.) "Oh! How I suffer!" Lucienne consoles her:

– "Your great-aunt, isn't she coming back from New York soon? M. Ménard will not be sad for much longer . . . Doesn't he also have a son in Canada who is rumored to be very rich?"

– "Yes, but we never heard from him."

– "I wish I'd known him. Grandfather always told me that this man and Mum had the same mother . . ."

– "How? Or rather: What? What do you mean?"

Raoul replies quickly:

– "My little one, he was married twice like me; he had children with the two women, while me . . . or rather you, you don't . . ."

– "Silence! Laurence is enough for us. She is also my daughter."

– "Thank you, Mom," says Mlle Desvallons, flattered.

She kisses her, and Lucienne returns her caress, but, curious, she inquires to her husband:

– "Who was the mother of Anna and the man from Canada?"

– "A stranger M. Ménard met in the islands . . . ," said Raoul.

She senses that one more question would be an indiscretion. She places her arm underneath her head, like a second pillow on top of the one she got at the train station and falls asleep peacefully. A smile on her pink lips. Sweet dreams, divinely beautiful.

Laurence and her father follow her example, but they are awakened from time to time by a man shouting in a loudspeaker at each station: "Passengers for X or Z, get off the train . . . ," etc. Then it's Bordeaux, the Garonne, it's the steamer that shakes, it's the Atlantic.

There are many stops in various countries, but finally, it is Haiti! Haiti the marvelous, the pearl of the Caribbean.

Did we dream? Can a country be so green, with such a bright sun in the middle of December?

Haiti, it is a magical island, it is truly the paradise described by Dubois. Their enthusiasm knows no bounds.

They arrive in Cap Haitian.[22] Tomorrow, they will land in Port-au-Prince. Tomorrow! It's a few hours away; such an immense happiness!

The day shone. They overslept, and now the boat's siren announces Port-au-Prince.

Lucienne, who at the beginning of the trip had imagined a few white-washed huts in Haiti, filthy huts where barely clothed Blacks live promiscuously, now feels moved by the beautiful mansions she sees in the distance. She sees black and yellow gentlemen coming to the boat to welcome a relative or a friend, who knows?

Dubois has just arrived with a very distinguished young Haitian named Guy Vanel, a twenty-four-year-old lawyer, already famous. Laurence is shaken when she notices him, but she does not pay attention to this new feeling.

However, she feels her hand tremble when he is introduced to her. He squeezes her hand delicately. Her heart is beating faster than ever. What does all this mean? Is it the climate? Mystery.

———

By a very strange coincidence, the house rented by Dubois for the Desvallons is next to Mme Vanel's, the young lawyer's mother.

Strong relations soon develop between the two families.

Guy Vanel is a good musician, but what he likes the most is to recite epics, loving, passionate verses into which he pours his soul . . . his soul which rises toward the greatest ideals . . .

In Haiti, white foreigners quickly make friends, and the Desvallons became pillars of Port-au-Prince's social life in less than a year.

22. Short for Cap-Haïtien, a commune on the northwest coast of Haiti.

Many solicited an invitation to their "happy hours," during which the most exquisite cakes and the tastiest liqueurs were always served. The scents coming from the flowerbeds delighted the guests of the salons lit *a giorno*.[23] Laurence's smile, an even more beautiful and delicate flower, captivated the most hardened hearts. But none of her admirers had been able to impress her as much as Guy.

Raoul and his wife also took great pleasure in chatting with him. They often invited him to stay after their guests had left so they could continue celebrating in strict intimacy.

With their melodious voices, Lucienne and Laurence then sang romances, sometimes cheerful, sometimes melancholic, until they brought tears to your eyes. Guy recited verses, his own sometimes, those he composed for the little fairy of his dreams in the silence of his room, verses overflowing with enthusiasm, mad, impassioned verses. Often, they did not separate until the very next day, around two o'clock in the morning.

Monsieur Desvallons himself, using his slow and tired memory, often managed to remember a poem and recite it.

How charmed they all were, the French as much as the young Haitian! They were as happy as they were surprised. They had never suspected that a Haitian could possess so many qualities, although their friend Dubois had written about it. They considered the young lawyer according to his rank and forgot that he was neither the same color nor the same race as them. Among those who visited the Desvallons were a few U.S.-Haitian treaty "officials" and many Yankee civilians.

Two of them, Watson and Leabrook, offered to find Desvallons a job in Damiens, at the Central School of Agriculture directed by M. Geo Freeman, an American.

At the time, Damiens was the promised land of any worthless American in the United States, due to the growing unemployment rate there.[24]

23. Italian: by daylight.
24. i.e., the Great Depression in the United States.

This disguised emigration of unemployed Americans illustrated Yankee audacity and cunning.

Most of them, having no title, nevertheless called themselves doctors or experts . . .

Desvallons was a merchant, but his business went slowly: no cash.

Americans don't buy anything in Haiti; everything comes to them free of charge, and they are the ones who have the highest salaries . . .

The 1915 Haitian American Convention says something like this: "The Financial Adviser will pay American employees, will pay himself, etc. with funds from the Haitian Treasury for his expenses and the payment of his employees are still very low in Haiti . . ."[25]

After mulling this over, Desvallons (perhaps pushed by his wife) terminated the contract he had signed with his friend Dubois, as co-partner of the corner store Au Bazar Français.[26]

As a result, he immediately started in the "paradise" of American experts: Damiens.

His house became a small cosmopolitan city where people of different nationalities discussed the news of the world.

Soon they started a literary and political circle: Haiti-France-America. Thanks to this group of interesting men, the circle quickly grew.

After an honest election, Guy Vanel became the president of the association; a young American was elected secretary, but since she did not speak French, they conducted a random draw, and this delicate role fell to Mlle Myrtana Durand, a smart and cultured Haitian woman.

---

25. Indeed, Article V states that "All sums collected and received by the General Receiver shall be applied, first to the payment of the salaries and allowances of the General Receiver, his assistants and employees and expenses of the Receiver-ship, including the salary and expenses of the Financial Adviser, which salaries will be determined by previous agreement; second, to the interest and sinking fund of the public debt of the Republic of Haiti; and, third, to the maintenance of the constabulary referred to in Article X, and then the remainder to the Haitian Government for purposes of current expenses." In this way Americans were paid first and Haitians, if any monies remained, last.
26. The French Bazaar.

(The parents of this young girl had an income of five hundred dollars a month . . . Very few families had not completely lost their fortune in the payment of high taxes and fines since the arrival of the Americans in Haiti.)

Five hundred dollars a year! This added a jewel to the crown that the clubmen had woven for Myrtana . . . the taste for luxury was beginning to develop rapidly in Haiti. We saw people splurge to own a car, to live in the heights of Port-au-Prince, where people have the reputation of being rich. The occupier was aped with rage. Sportsmanship fascinated young people. They arrived at the salons in shirtsleeves and sports shoes . . . the fine French manners that were once so dear to us were gradually disappearing . . . during this time, alas! All our resources, as if attracted by a powerful magnet, went toward the Yankees' pockets.

Guy Vanel, whose efficiency was already proven, had brought the association to a higher level. Neither "yes-men" nor wallflowers were admitted there . . . Each one, in their field, had to showcase their expertise during the activities of the circle, to speak like Americans.

There was a session every fortnight and a detailed report would be made at the end of each year.

Among the clubmen were former MPs, from the Parliament dissolved a few years earlier by the occupier Waller, with the consent of President Dartiguenave.[27] The MPs used the meetings to "shoot arrows," golden arrows at the Americans . . . who "picked them up" and sent them back after having stripped them of their precious metal . . .

M. and Mme Desvallons, wanting to be neutral until the end, in the useless but intelligent quarrel between the Americans and the Haitians, pretended to understand nothing.

---

27. Littleton Waller (1956–1926) was a United States Marine Corps officer. Philippe Sudré Dartiguenave (1863–1926) served as president of Haiti from 12 August 1915 to 15 May 1922.

Leabrook and Watson were the most zealous participants the circle could have. They found material for refutation in all the lectures, in all the speeches delivered at the association.

We must say right away that they were very educated and spoke French correctly.

The former was married, but Robert Watson rather liked the bachelor's life, the great adventures, the long journeys. However, for several days, he found himself thinking about Laurence when he was away from her. Him! For whom a woman's heart was just a toy: he had broken so many of them without remorse!

CHAPTER II

When the time came to celebrate the first anniversary of the Club with a solemn gathering, Guy went to the Desvallons's house, hoping to receive their advice on how to enhance the prestige of the upcoming event.

It was Laurence who received him, as her father and mother were absent.

– "Monsieur Vanel," she said, "what a wonderful program!"

– "Outstanding!"

– "Please, do sit down. You look distraught!"

– "Don't pay me any mind."

– "Are you all right?"

– "Nothing. . . . It's nothing, Mlle Laurence. Well . . . why not confess to you right now?"

– "You are on the verge of tears . . . Please talk to me."

– "Laurence, dear, dear Laurence, can't you guess that I love you?"

– "Oh! Say no more!"

– "I love you . . ."

– "Monsieur! Monsieur!" she said while retreating.

– "Do not leave . . . Listen to me."

He took her hands and drew her closer to him. He wished he could say charming, sentimental words to her, words no one had said before him, but he could only repeat these: "I love you!"

I love you, I love you . . . I love you! Oh sweet chorus! This sentence, so simple, seemed to contain all his unspoken thoughts. I love you! These words, so old yet always so new, these words said in cottages and in palaces, in the most sordid sewers and in the most austere cloisters, these words the Carthusians, the Poor Clares, the Carmelites[1] repeat in the most beautiful canticles, who can deny their depth?

I love you! Universal words! The admirer whispers them, the lover, the husband, the seducer pronounces them . . . They are sometimes used in a lie, and quite often they cause suffering, but there are so many other words that deceive and martyrize the heart without ever intoxicating it . . .

> – "Laurence," he went on, "I love you, and I am asking you to become the mother of my children, my beloved companion. Answer me. Do you love me? Oh! How your answer would soothe me!"

Moved to tears, the sweet young girl only made a gesture, an eloquent one, a mute confession: she rested her beautiful blonde head on Vanel's chest, and wept while he repeated: "I love you . . ."

Lucienne entered the room, astonished:

> – "M. Vanel, I find it hard to understand your behavior. Explain yourself."
>
> – "Madame, I do apologize. It is my honor to ask you permission to marry Mlle Desvallons."
>
> – "Laurence is too young, way too young . . . and Raoul is in no hurry to marry her off."
>
> – "I will wait . . . Madame."
>
> – "You know very well, dear Monsieur, that I alone cannot decide on such a delicate question. Come back tomorrow, it would give me time to talk to my husband about it."
>
> – "Thank you, I place my trust in you."

---

1. Members of various Catholic orders.

– "I make no promises . . ."

– "It's true . . . . See you tomorrow, then."

She turned to the young girl and said to her:

– "Leave the room, Laurence. I'll call you back in a few minutes.
I am quite angry at you. And you, you mustn't see her before our
meeting tomorrow," she told Guy after Mademoiselle Desvallons
had left.

– "Very well, Madame," promised the famous lawyer, "very
well . . ."

– "What is well?"

– "Yes."

– "Yes what?"

– "I won't see Mlle Desvallons until tomorrow."

– "Ah! Good, I take your word for it."

– "Lying disgusts me."

– "Splendid! Good-bye, Monsieur."

He bowed and left.

After the young man's departure, Lucienne went to find Laurence and
said to her sternly:

– "What did you know about this?"

– "Nothing until this morning, Mom. I knew nothing of M.
Vanel's feelings for me. I could see he enjoyed my company, but I
was far from thinking that he wanted to marry me. He had never
said anything about his love for me. I only sensed I did not displease him . . . and for my part, I had given him all my sympathy.
Voilà."

– "And why did I find you with your head resting on his heart?
This is bad, my child, very bad."

– "What is?" asked Raoul, just arriving.

Laurence bravely confessed:

– "Dad, only that Guy Vanel wants to marry me."

– "It is serious, little one, what are you going to do with your toys? It's very serious."

– "Not really."

– "A young bride of sixteen years of age! . . . Ah! No."

– "I'm not sixteen anymore, Dad, in three weeks . . ."

Lucienne cut her short:

– "At that age, I played with dolls and ran from Rue Rigaud to the Porte-Maillot with my young companions."

– "Because my father . . . didn't love you, then . . ."

– "Laurence," says M. Desvallons, "I admire your honesty, but I do not plan on marrying you in Haiti."

– "Why?" she dared ask.

– "Because I do not wish to stay here all my life, and I would suffer terribly if only two of us were to leave this country, instead three, like in Paris."

– "On the contrary, there will be more of us. There will be Guy and perhaps our children. People have many in Haiti: Madame Renand has ten, Mme Tiburce twelve, Mme Rex thirteen . . . I wouldn't want so many, but I would like to have two, three, or maybe even four . . ."

– "You are too young to get married," he said, stroking her head.

– "But my mother . . ."

– "Alas, your absence would be too great for me to bear."

– "The Scriptures say: 'Therefore a woman shall leave her . . .'"[2]

___

2. Ephesians 5:31 "For this cause shall a man leave his father and mother, and shall be joined unto his wife, and they two shall be one flesh".

– "Ungrateful girl, go . . ." (He smiled.) "What, would you leave me?"

– "It's a yes! Thank you, Dad . . ."

– "Not so fast. Let me think it over and go play . . ."

He had insisted on this last word, but he thought: "One plays at sixteen, but one also gets married . . ."

He could not see why he should oppose the marriage of these young people. Wasn't Anna Menard sixteen when she became his wife? If death had taken her away from him, her age had nothing to do with it.

Wasn't Guy the natural representative of the honest and studious youth of Haiti? Was he not from an honorable family?

When Vanel returned the next day, his request was granted.

Desvallons asked the interested parties to keep their engagement secret, as it was not to be officially announced for another six months.

After a few days, however, everyone knew they loved each other. The young girl confided in her good friend Myrtana, and Lucienne told all of her own closest acquaintances.

Leabrook and Watson got wind of it later on. They arrived one day at Madame Desvallons's and found the bride-to-be conversing with Myrtana in the garden.

– "Mlle Laurence," said Watson without preamble, "I missed you, so I came."

– "Flattering," replied the young girl, laughing, "would you like to have tea with us in a moment?"

– "No, I do not want to."

– "Well, in that case, sit down here, and be as good as gold."'

– "I love you."

– "Why are you telling me this?"

– "I do not know."

– "I am engaged, don't pretend to ignore it."

– "I have millions . . . to come. Him, no."

– "I will marry Guy Vanel."

– "I have diamonds . . ."

– "He has my word."

– "I am white."

– "Silence, now this is stupid."

– "Well?"

– "Well, I dream of art, of beauty, of poetry, of youth."

– "Two million dollars would amply supplement them. When my father dies, I will inherit half a million, and then, when my childless uncle passes, I will receive the other million and a half. I place them at your disposal."

– "Thanks! Pick them up quickly, because I am going to trample them . . ."

– "I am tenacious, Mlle Laurence, very tenacious."

– "Me too."

– "The fight will be terrible between us."

– "Terrible."

– "Be careful."

– "I am not afraid of you."

Myrtana had been listening for a long time without saying a word, but it seemed to her that the discussion had gone on too long. She gently advised Leabrook:

– "Do tell your friend that one does not make a love declaration with threats."

– "We do as we can," replied the American. "When I fail to make myself loved with kisses, I use a whip. It's curious, there are women who cannot make love without being flogged . . . Mlle Laurence must belong to this category . . ."

– "Monsieur Watson," cried out Laurence suddenly, "I like your gaiety. As a tennis partner, you are admirable, but you are not a suitable match. And you certainly won't be a model spouse. Forget about it, and let's stay friends, shall we?"

– "The dreams of an American always become reality. I will marry you before the end of the year." (He laughs.) "On December fifth. Do you like this date?"

– "You are sick . . . Do you know Beudet?"[3]

– "The insane asylum?"

– "Yes."

– "Insane. . . . Well, yes, I'm crazy in love."

– "You will never be my husband. Never."

– "And your lover?"

– "Monsieur! How dare you!"

– "Your lover? Hmm . . . Never mind, I don't want to. You will be my wife, for you are young, pretty, and virtuous. You will be clay in my hands. I do not intend to be the 'manager' of a woman who only loves my money, and from whom I expect only pleasure in return. For this purpose, I need a woman with a temper, a diva who measures her love by the number of my dollars. And then one day, she leaves me, or rather I leave her; I always manage to run off first, because I don't like being alone in a bed where we used to be two. And what I hate above all, is to be cheated on.

"Disinterested love is rare, Mlle Laurence, but it may sometimes be found in a marriage where there is fortune or poverty on both sides. There are exceptions, of course. I am rich and want to marry you because you resist me. I shall have the greatest pride in taking you as my wife in spite of you. Don't think I don't love you. No. I've lost sleep ever since I learned that the poor president of our Club had the intention of marrying you. It makes me laugh at times . . .

---

3. The Pont Beudet Asylum in Crois-de-Bouquets, at the time the only psychiatric facility in Haiti.

"Could you forget that Monsieur Vanel's ancestors were the slaves of yours? Would you dare put this beautiful white hand in that of this poorly whitewashed individual, and say to him, kneeling before God's altar: 'I am yours forever'? You won't do that, Mlle Laurence, the colonists would roll over in their graves. Can you forget, or rather ignore, how cruel the rebellious Haitians were to the poor, helpless settlers? Haiti, the ungrateful Haiti, was the first Black territory which encouraged the revolt against and massacre of the whites. Were it not for his temerity, your father would be rich and Guy Vanel, the object of your love, Guy Vanel, who is today a famous lawyer and the president of our Club, would only be a vulgar pickaninny[4] serving a white person . . . you perhaps, who knows?"

– "Enough," said Myrtana suddenly, "our ancestors were not the only enslaved Blacks in the world, but they alone have the glory of having conquered their freedom."

– "Yellow fever was their most powerful ally," said Leabrook.

– "You're lying," continued the Black woman, "the men who made 1804[5] possible, who later helped Bolivar[6] to win his country's independence after he guaranteed to free the slaves of his territory, these men would not need such a poor ally. Yellow fever! Nonsense!"

Turning toward Mlle Desvallons, she said:

– "Laurence, regardless of the grievance I feel talking about the colonists, your ancestors, I must defend the memory of the Black heroes of the Haitian independence."

– "Go on, go on, dear friend . . ."

– "Thanks to the cannons taken from the French, the Blacks drove out of their land the wicked masters who had kept them in the chains

4. Offensive/Racist term used to describe a small black child.
5. Year of Haiti's independence.
6. Simon Bolivar (1783–1830), known as the Liberator of Latin America, received military support from Haiti in his struggle against the Spanish Empire.

of slavery for three long centuries. Many of them were Napoleon's best generals, they had just finished the campaigns in Italy and Egypt and, upon their return to Europe, they were going to cover themselves in glory at Wagram, Austerlitz, Eylau ... [7] It is at the cost of their blood and their sweat that the Blacks can write on the frontispiece of all their important acts, these three words so dear to the Haitian nation and individuals: Liberty, Equality, Fraternity ... [8] It's ..."

She was about to continue when Lucienne cheerfully announced that the tea was ready.

– "I won't be joining you," said the young Haitian; Mom had asked me to go out with her, I apologize."

– "No hard feelings, Miss," Leabrook said, squeezing her hand.

– "Even if I asked you to stay with us a little longer?" added Watson. "Are you upset?"

– "Not at all. A discussion between good people should end in laughter," concluded Mlle Durand.

– "Well! Laugh, Miss, and have tea with us."

– "I am telling you that I am in a hurry ..." She looked at her watch.

– "Good-bye, then. All my regrets."

After Myrtana had gone, Robert Watson took Mlle Desvallons's arm and said:

– "No hard feelings ... But we'll be married before long ..." (He laughs.) "So, what's the point of getting angry with your future fiancé?"

– "Do not insist, Monsieur. Just now you behaved like a scoundrel. You told me things that a French or a Haitian man wouldn't

7. Significant battles of the Napoleonic Wars.
8. The national motto of Haiti (and France).

say to a young girl he respects, but an American speaks bluntly without going in circles. I will never be your wife. I am already engaged to M. Guy Vanel and will marry him within a year."

They walked together, followed by their mutual friend. Soon, they found themselves under the small veranda flowered with pale mauve bougain-villea.[9] The tea table was already set, and M. and Mme Desvallons were waiting for them.

   – "Guy is late," said Laurence suddenly.

   – "Haitians never hurry," commented Watson.

   – "However, this one is always on time ... Look, speaking of the devil ... M. President, do you know that you must pay a fine for making five mouths wait?" said Lucienne.

Vanel apologized:

   – "I beg your pardon, Madame. I blame the endless preparations for the celebration of our Club's anniversary ... I just came back from Jacquemain's[10] and I was hoping to meet Mlle Durand here. I really need her for the program."

   – "She just left," said Laurence.

   – "I shall go to her in a moment, then. I hope you will excuse me if I take my leave immediately after tea."

Laurence protested:

– "You shall not leave without playing Mozart's splendid scherzo for us, a piece you perform with such mastery, as well as the "Papillons Noirs" by Ludovic Lamothe[11] and the latest composition by Justin Elie."[12]

9. A thorny ornamental vine.
10. i.e. the home of Jacquemain, where the celebration is to be held.
11. Ludovic Lamothe (1882–1953) was a Haitian pianist, clarinetist, and composer.
12. Justin Elie (1883–1931) was a Haitian pianist, clarinetist, and composer.

– "If it should please you, Mesdemoiselles . . . but my visit to Mlle Durand is most urgent."

– "Myrtana isn't at home right now," said Mlle Desvallons. "I will call her tonight."

– "Ah! Thank you, Laurence, thank you, how kind you are!"

The young man sat down at the piano immediately after his last sip of tea, and played all the pieces requested.

– "That's not all," said Laurence, charmed. "Play "Babylonienne" and "Prière du soir" by Justin Elie."

– "Yes, of course."

He leaned toward the girl and said softly:

– "And after that, a kiss?"

She smiled, whispering "Yes." During the performance of these musical pieces in which the composers seem to have put the soul of their soul, Guy was sometimes closing his eyes, to catch in thought the pretty pink, blue, mauve butterflies, and the flowers of all shades which seemed to appear from his fingers.

– "What an admirable boy!" M. Desvallons let out tenderly. "I have never met a young man with a more delicate and more generous soul. I like him immensely."

At a time when musical "machines" are replacing pianos in every house, when a pianist seems old-fashioned, a bit crazy, at a time when anyone with a radio has only to turn the button of their "thing" to hear an orchestra, Guy Vanel stares at his keyboard, and asks the instrument the secret of becoming a perfect artist . . .

Moved, Laurence and Lucienne murmured several times: "How beautiful!"

The Americans, to spoil the pleasure of the other listeners, said loud enough for the musician to hear:

– "Playing the piano is not so difficult."

The two women looked at them, surprised.

———

Seven o'clock had rung. Monsieur Vanel had just left his friends when Watson asked Monsieur Desvallons to schedule an appointment with him.

> – "My dear friend, just name the time," concluded Raoul, "you know very well I am free every day after two o'clock in the afternoon, and so are you, aren't you?"
> – "Very well! Tomorrow at five o'clock it is."
> – "All right!"
> – "OK. Goodnight!"

Robert Watson stared defiantly at the girl and left. She smiled, thinking: "Your efforts will be in vain; my father has already promised me to Guy Vanel."

Robert Watson was originally from New York, but he was a cosmopolitan. He wanted to choose the most hospitable country for his homeland, a place where he could get rich quickly. Haiti, perhaps . . .

He was around thirty years old, blond, and of good height. He always had chewing gum at the back of his mouth and a cigar between his lips, which were widowed of any hairs. His pants always arrived a little below the navel and were held up by a thin yellow leather belt. His shirt was of white or beige silk and his jacket of blue flannel. In his pockets, what a load of sweets! Chewing gum, chiclets, and peppermints competed for space.

His fingernails were immaculate, but his teeth testified to endless visits to the dentist . . . Quite far from ugly. He adored sport, only wearing a jacket and shirt when he went out. When it was hot, he often left his house in Turgeau wearing only a shirt and underwear to go take a dip in the sea at Mariani.[13] Isn't he American, after all? Since 1915, to be American in Haiti means to dispossess the peasants by establishing the Latifundia regime.[14] To declare oneself an expert with salaries ranging from four to five hundred dollars a month.[15] To be American is to drive a car fast, to imprison journalists, to get drunk, to kill the most peaceful Haitian, and to call someone an "idiot." It's walking around peacefully with machine guns aimed at poor students on strike. Finally, to be American is to live in abundance, to die of indigestion next to Haitians whose stomachs have shrunk because of deprivation.

Watson and Leabrook were fervent supporters of Prohibition during the day, but at night, they enjoyed strong drinks. Each of them had a cabinet loaded with about fifty bottles of the best Haitian rums. They pronounced the names of Barrau, Villejoint, Alix Roy, Gardère, Barbancourt, Gaetjens, Seneca Pierre, etc. with respect.

They believed the Good Lord had opened Heaven's doors to these producers.

Leabrook was a poet in his spare time. The bluish mountains of Kenscoff, from which rise the pines with their scintillating needles, needles which appeared to touch the sky, the pretty rivers . . . oh! rivers which meander through the fragrant meadows, the abundant foliage which smiles on the sides of the hills, in the valleys, left him indifferent. Only two things interested him in Haiti: drinks and Vaudoo . . .

Huguette Duflos,[16] back from America, replies to friends who ask her which American behaviors struck her the most: "I've never seen so much drinking except in the land of Prohibition . . ."

---

13. A trip of some twenty-one miles, from the Port-au-Prince suburbs to the Haitian seaside.
14. The U.S. occupation government sought to instill a system of plantation agriculture (or latifundia) in Haiti, transferring landownership from the traditional peasant freeholds into the hands of American investors.
15. The equivalent of $11,415.27 in 2023. Average salary in Haiti that same year was $850.
16. Huguette Duflos (1887–1982) was a French actress.

Indeed, the Research Office of the Association Against the Prohibition Amendment had concluded after very thorough investigations: "The illegal traffic of spirits has become one of the largest industries in America. In 1919, it exceeded the $2,793,166,812 generated by the automobile industry . . ."

Leabrook was a poet, and only two things interested him a lot in Haiti. Why would he resist the desire to sing the rum and clairin[17] of this little Black Island? To write a book about it?

One evening, after having successively drunk fourteen shots of Sarthe Gold Seal rum, he felt the imperious need to concretize his love for the Haitian alcohol and wrote:

There are two drinks in Haiti I adore:

One puts me to sleep with sweet dreams

The other fills up my life, brightens and gilds it.

When I don't have them, I feel unhappy.

One is called Rhum and the other, Virgin clairin. For their longevity, I prayed to the Blessed Virgin Mary.

I'm a fervent supporter of the dry diet, but I think it's good to warm your beak from time to time with a few little shots of Haitian alcohol, the best on earth as it tastes heavenly, the evening before going to bed, slowly drink this blessed liquid.

But we must be sure no one is looking, so we can say to the drunk: "Beware, I respect the Volstead Act, I don't "drink," oh! Never! It's water I drink with my meals."

Alcohol from Haiti,

My soul blesses you!

Y LEABROOK

———

The next day, Yen Leabrook promptly shared his verses with his friends. First was Mademoiselle Desvallons, whom he encountered in her parents' courtyard.

17. A distilled alcoholic spirit made from sugarcane produced in Haiti.

– "How hypocritical you are," Laurence laughed, "you always told us that you knew nothing about poetry."

– "What do you think about my poem?" he asked anxiously, eager for praise.

– "It is good. You should read it at our next party . . ."

– "Never . . . many of my friends think that I don't even drink wine . . . and this piece sings of rum and clairin . . ."

– "No one will know it's yours, let's see."

– "I won't read it, that's for sure. I just wanted to have fun . . . Let's talk about something else. Do you know that Robert loves you very much? I told your father about it, I think. . . . No, I'm certain, honestly."

– "My father didn't pay much attention to his request. Did he tell you that himself?"

– "No. I understand him by his silence. He doesn't care."

– "He nevertheless promised Robert . . ."

– "What?"

– "To marry you to him . . ."

Laurence burst out laughing, but she soon after felt a strange premonition, a vague confusion overcoming her; she felt suddenly unhappy, almost hopeless. She passed her hand over her forehead several times, as if to chase away the sad thoughts that were invading her little brain: what if this man wasn't lying!

She thought for a moment, and said softly, as if talking to herself:

– "My father is the most loyal man I know. I'm not afraid of anything, no, nothing . . ."

She had kept her head down, staring at the ground. She abruptly raised it with bravado, with dignity.

– "I'm not for sale, M. Leabrook. My father will not dispose of me like a head of cattle. And if he forgot, I . . ."

An inner revolt not only made her voice tremble but grew louder with each of her sentences.

> – "You know very well that M. Watson does not love me, that he wants to marry me only because I resist him . . . Well, I won't be his wife. Am I not Guy Vanel's fiancée? Who ignores it? You don't ignore it, do you? I must tell you very sincerely that I hesitate to believe my father, my dear and revered father, has given me to M. Robert Watson without consulting me. It's not true."
>
> – "Come on, you're just a child. Why would he consult you?"
>
> – "Yes, I am but a child. But also, a 'thinking reed,'[18] who knows what it wants."

Mlle Durand appeared.

> – "Hello, Laurence, hello M. Yen . . ."
>
> – "You're not angry with me anymore?" said the American, smiling.
>
> – "Oh! Not at all . . . ," replied the newcomer.
>
> – "Thanks."

He took pleasure in teasing her:

> – "Mademoiselle Durand, do you know," he continued, "that I thought some more about your fierce patriotism? Yesterday afternoon, a Haitian man said in front of me that he would be very sorry to see the Americans leave this country . . ."
>
> – "He said what he believes . . . but I . . ."

---

18. Allusion to a passage from Blaise Pascal's *Thoughts*: "347: Man is but a reed, the most feeble thing in nature; but he is a thinking reed. The entire universe need not arm itself to crush him. A vapour, a drop of water suffices to kill him. But, if the universe were to crush him, man would still be more noble than that which killed him, because he knows that he dies and the advantage which the universe has over him; the universe knows nothing of this." (Pascal, Blaise. *Blaise Pascal.* Translated by W. F. Trotter et al., P.F. Collier & Son, 1910, p. 128)

– "Admit that he is right. Haiti was too unstable: a civil war today, another tomorrow . . . oh!"

– "It was your country, Monsieur, which drove us into a civil war. We accepted guns from you without realizing that each gunshot further fed your lust.

"We were only a puppet in the powerful hands of Uncle Sam.[19] At the time, we still lived with the sweet illusion that France, the beautiful France that Haitians have always sung about in all their tunes, would have stood against Yankee imperialism toward us. What a pipe dream! Since none of the goods, or the French lives, or the American lives even, were threatened, France, our legendary protector, gave free rein to her friend Uncle Sam to occupy us militarily in 1915. The League of Nations remained deaf to our demands. The League of Nations! Such irony and hypocrisy! They smother the voices of the weak with a caressing gesture. If they stretch out their hand to poor people, it is to lead them into the greenhouses of imperialism . . . All white nations are imperialists . . ."

She withdrew, as she had just remembered that Laurence was white and that it would be ungraceful to finish her sentence . . .

– "Myrtana," said Laurence, "I want you to finish expressing your thoughts without fear of offending me. Defend your country."

– "Thank you. As I was saying, all the white nations are imperialist. Africa no longer belongs to the Blacks, white people have claimed it, as they once did with the Mantle of Christ. The poor Africans cannot do anything about it. As for us Haitians, we do not intend to remain eternally under America's thumb, one of the greatest injustices we have suffered since the Lüders affair.[20] We will

19. Common personification of the United States' government.
20. After a criminal incident involving Haitian-German citizen Emile Lüders, the German Empire exacted significant reparations, including monetary compensation,

organize a new 1804. When the Americans began invading our territory, we did not owe America a penny."

Leabrook fired back:

– "Why did a horde of savages enter the French embassy in 1915 to drag out the poor president, already defeated, but protected by the tricolor French flag?[21] Surprised by such barbarism, France could not in good conscience protest the occupation of this country where too much blood had already been shed.

"Not only did the Haitians kill their president, but drunk with his blood, they cut off his head in front of the very eyes of those who had promised to protect him. And you wanted the civilized French to go against the order, the honor, and the happiness that we were bringing you? It's insane. It's crazy."

– "France should not have been so surprised, as you say. A century before our skirmish of July 27, didn't the French decapitate Madame de Lamballe?[22] Did they not parade her head on a pike through Paris with the cruel intention of going as far as the Conciergerie,[23] to make Queen Marie Antoinette kiss it? An already poor, defenseless woman who had been kidnapped, whose children had been taken away, and whose husband had been killed?"[24]

---

a formal apology, a reception, a salute to the German flag, and the raising of the white flag of surrender over the Haitian Presidential Palace.

21. Following the execution of 167 political prisoners, on July 27, 1915, President Jean Vilbrun Guillaume Sam (1859–1915) fled to the French embassy but was dragged into the street and killed by a mob.

22. Confidante of Queen Marie Antoinette. Marie Thérèse Louise of Savoy (1749–1792), Princess of Lamballe, was killed in the massacres of September 1792 during the French Revolution.

23. Mistake of the author. At the time of Madame de Lamballe's passing, Marie Antionette was not yet at the Conciergerie, a former courthouse and prison located in Paris, where she will be taken almost a year after the death of her friend on August 2, 1793. During these events, she was at the Temple jail.

24. Mistake of the author. Louis XVI was still alive then. He was decapitated five months later, on January 21, 1793.

– "I am not French, Mlle Durand," Yen said, looking at Laurence.

– "What do you have to answer?" he said to her. "It's your country that's in trouble."

She had promised Myrtana to remain neutral in this discussion.

– "Monsieur Leabrook," continued the Black woman, "if we are to remain friends, it is on condition that we never speak of these things again ... I am sorry to have hurt my friend Laurence's honor ... I know how much she loves her country; how much she always defends it, and you pushed me to say so many things about it, things which hurt her and yet she listened to without anger ..."

The Frenchwoman took her hands:

– "My poor friend, I understand the resentment and the distress of your soul. To see a foreigner treading on the ground of your fathers, to see their flag flying where yours should majestically unfurl, to be unsure that the land where you sleep will always be yours and will keep its name, it must be cruel to a patriot. I understand your revolt and your thoughtfulness. Dear friend, you have all my sympathy."

– "And me? What are you giving me?" said Leabrook, "Mlle Durand insulted my country, I also deserve your sympathy ..."

– "Let's make peace once more," added Myrtana.

– "Alright," said the American, holding out his hand. "No resentment? I do admire you even if I am not in agreement."

All three got up and went back to the living room where Guy was to join them soon.

———

Today is the splendid celebration of the Haiti-France-America Club, right-fully presided over by Guy Vanel for over a year. A burst of flowers.

A select audience. The session opens solemnly with a magnificent speech by M. Raoul Desvallons, honorary president of the club, and M. Jacquemin then read a poem dedicated to Haitian women by M. Lucien Boyer:

Ignorance

We don't tell you that you are pretty,
The poets never sing your charms,
Your pride is dying in melancholy,
You are adorable, we do not tell you.

We don't tell you that you are exquisite,
In all the songs, in all the sonnets,
We always celebrate a pale marquise,[25]
You are arousing, we never talk about it.

We don't tell you that you are superb,
When we wish to exalt your triumphant charms,
We have but one way to praise you,
Oh we marry you, we give you children.

In the tumult of a love without praise,
Wanting to inspire your fatherly husbands,
You try to look like these beautiful pictures
Printed in color by the newspapers of Paris.

And before the makeup, before the powder,
To lighten your complexion, you use in one evening,
More rice than Guerlain,[26] the enchanter, can grind,
And then you pose in front of your mirror:

Am I pretty like this, am I alright, am I beautiful?
Do I look like Venus with this fair complexion?

25. A stone typically included in a wedding ring setting.
26. French perfumer Jacques Edouard Guerlain (1874–1963) sometimes incorporated rice powder in his creations.

You already think you're blonde like Cybele,[27]
But the mirror is silent because it is polite.

We didn't tell you that this parody
Outrage—that's the word—your resplendent body,
And how foolish it is to mimic anemia,
When you have both sun and fire in your blood.

Well! Me, I sang about white women too much,
And, should I pass for your henchman,
I am now going to build you, because I owe you one,
Another statue with the bronze of your skin.

The poem is met with loud applause from the satisfied audience. Then, the president of the Club introduces in a careful manner M. Emile Jérôme, who is to present a rather delicate thesis.

> "In Haiti, does colorism, the discrimination based on skin color, exist among the natives?"

Concerned whispers immediately fill the room. On all sides, the audience wonders, anxious, if the speaker is going to get out of this without being in some big trouble . . . With panting hearts, they watch him walk to the pulpit intended for him:

> "Does colorism exist in Haiti among the natives of the country?
> "No!" he says firmly. "What some might be tempted to identify as colorism in Haiti is not a kind of dissatisfaction with one's own skin color. Black, griffe, sacatra, mulatto,[28] and so forth are all equally unhappy: the first finds himself too dark, the other two

27. Anatolian mother goddess.
28. Racial classifications used in colonial societies of the Americas, among others. Griffe: a person of three-quarters black parentage; sacatra: a person of seven-eighths black parentage; mulatto: a person of one-half black parentage.

not light enough, the last not authentically white . . . This has been going on since the American occupation.

"Many Haitians, knowing the Yankees' hatred of Black people, decided the least dark would receive the most respect from the occupier.

"There is no colorism in Haiti, this word is a stepping stone for the exploiters.

"Mixed and Black Haitians only resort to it if their interests are threatened and they have no other choice; it is like a *viaticum*.[29] The courts of our heads of state, mixed or Black, are comprised of people of all shades, and courtiers take the same bow everywhere, the light-skinned hand shaking the dark-skinned hand.

"Even if a Black man loves his mulatto friend or relative and vice versa, both wish to escape from the path destiny placed them on. So here come the ointments, the cosmetics, the creams, the pastes, and who knows what else? To bleach the skin, light or dark.

"The Black youth of Haiti have become experts in the art of changing race.

"Half-wits with woolly hair went so far as to straighten their hair with a lye solution . . . which permanently damaged their scalp. Annoyed with their complexion, a few Blacks reached out to an adventurer, who presented himself as a Hindu ethnologist, to find out if the African blood had yet to be erased from our veins thanks to the mixing of different races. After a study many people did not understand, M. Lind, the pseudo-Hindu, fled. As a result, candidates for 'bleaching' do not know where they stand . . .

"This folly to do a caesarean[30] to one's scalp so that it gives birth to straight hair, to damage one's skin so that it lightens up, has worsened since the arrival of the Yankees.

29. Latin for "provision for a journey"; the Eucharist as given to a person near or in danger of death.
30. i.e. surgery for hair replacement and treatment.

"Disappointed by their failure, many promise to take their revenge through their offspring. Yes, they will find a wife abroad in order to 'dominate' . . .

"Do not believe, dear audience, that I disapprove of marriages between people of different races. Oh no! Haiti has always known these unions. Before the American Occupation, white foreigners who came to work in this country almost always married Haitian women regardless of their color, and no one found it abnormal that a Haitian man returned from abroad with a white wife. Love is a gypsy's child,[31] one marries the person one loves.

"Instead, I would criticize these 'arranged' unions, these 'businesses,' in which love is absent. They often have as their only goal the 'standardization' of the offspring; the only way to rise toward great ideals, believe some imbeciles. *Voilà.* Nobody can be more philanthropic than us: our foreign friends know it and understand it.

"The word 'black' is the one that most displeases the Black man. Tell a man of the Black race that he is brown, high yellow, light-skinned . . . but never tell him that he is black, or you take the risk of upsetting him. What to make of this?

"How can we forget that we are all Africa's offspring?

"Some Blacks think that to evolve means to become white . . . No, dear friends, it is not your skin you have to change, it is your frame of mind.

"Of course, elegance is something inherent in women. It is essential: straightening, waving, and curling hair should be a matter of beauty and not a *sine qua non*[32] for progress.

---

31. "L'amour est enfant de bohème," lyrics from "Habanera," which is the popular name for "L'amour est un oiseau rebelle" ("Love Is a Rebellious Bird"), an aria from Georges Bizet's 1875 opera *Carmen.*
32. Latin for "an essential condition; a thing that is absolutely necessary"

"Intelligence is not necessarily found under the best hairdos, nor honesty in the best-dressed man.

"Having a beautiful face . . . a radiant complexion has always been a concern of women since the beginning of time. Of a few men too. But at no time did they believe it could make them superior. Never.

"Hairstyles have known many glorious times, all around the globe.

"Who has never heard of the story of the beautiful, powdered heads that Robespierre[33] did not hesitate to lay on the guillotine to make them fall into the bloody and dirty basket of the Terror in the Place de la Révolution?[34]

"Marie-Antoinette and her famous hairdresser Léonard could attest to this.

Emile Jérôme, after taking a sip of water, wiped his face and continued:

"Dear elite, instead of trying again and again to change your race, help your brothers understand their responsibilities toward themselves . . . They are too 'primitive.'

"*Ne quid veri non audeat.* Let him not fail to say anything true. Obviously, one must have a lot of courage, for the man who said this surely had plenty. I am thinking of Pope Leo XIII."[35]

He stands up to conclude:

"Mesdames, Mesdemoiselles, Messieurs,
"Ladies and Gentlemen,

33. Maximilien François Marie Isidore de Robespierre (1758–1794) was a French statesman and the primary architect of the French Revolution's Reign of Terror
34. A period of extreme violence and mass executions during the time of the French Revolution
35. Reigned from 1878 to 1903; known for his design of the Prayer to St. Michael and his socialist teaching within the Catholic church.

"Thank you for giving me your full attention. If I misused it, please have the extreme indulgence to believe that I did so without malice. I am sick of hearing some of my friends repeat insensibly: "We must save the race" and how to do so! By bleaching their face and straightening their frizzy hair! Black Negrophobia!

"They are a small group, of course, those who have this sad mentality and who feel unhappy not to be of the Aryan race. Many of them do not know our history, which is so beautiful! They will tell you with enthusiasm about Charlemagne, Francis I of France, Napoleon,[36] but what about the Ravine-à-Couleuvre,[37] the Butte Charier,[38] Boirond Tonnerre,[39] Capois la Mort,[40] Lamartinière?[41] They don't know about that. They complain about Napoleon sent by England 'to roast' on the burning rock of Sainte-Hélène. They ignore that Toussaint,[42] our dear hero, the son of the sun, died in front of a fireless dungeon in the Jura region of France, frozen by the cold after three days without bread, three long days without anyone opening or visiting his cell . . .

"When children say, while studying Europe's history or geography: 'Our country,' they think about France . . . and certain educators are quite pleased by this.

"I would point out that all these crusades toward whiteness would remain unknown if the concerned parties had the decency

36. French historical leaders.
37. The Battle of Ravine-à-Couleuvres fought on 23 February 1802, was a major battle of the Saint-Domingue expedition during the Haitian Revolution.
38. The Battle of Vertières fought on 18 November 1903 was the last major battle of the Haitian Revolution.
39. Louis Félix Mathurin Boisrond-Tonnerre (1776–1806) was a Haitian writer and historian who fought in the Haitian Revolution.
40. François Capois (1766–1806) was a Haitian officer in the Haitian Revolution.
41. Marie-Jeanne Lamartinière (dates unknown) was a soldier who fought in the Haitian Revolution.
42. François-Dominique Toussaint Louverture (1743–1803) was a prominent Haitian general and "the Father of Haiti."

to keep their inconsiderate remarks for themselves. But no, they confess: Black is not in fashion . . . and tutti-quanti.[43]

"Many would prefer that the books about our origins were palimpsests where they can rewrite history however they choose. They would make subtractions or additions to it.

"We cannot change the past or even less, destroy it. It constitutes the archives of the present and of the future . . .

"Whatever you do, dear 'wannabe-white Black men,' Africa will forever remain the mother of young Haiti, an unfortunate mother but a mother still. 'The greatness of a nation is measured by the strength of its memories.'"

Following a round of applause, the speaker gives way to Monsieur Paul Ronceville, a Frenchman, who began as follows:

"Mesdames, Mesdemoiselles, Messieurs,

"Ladies and Gentlemen,

"Could Haitians have made more progress during the last century, with their freedom and their independence?

"Yes," he said, "I believe they could have.

"Because they pride themselves on being the most civilized Blacks in the world, Haitians have stopped on the path toward civilization, they have lain down on their laurels and declared smugly: 'We made it: Haiti is the Black France.'

"We made it! How ironic! If France declared this during the centuries of Augustus,[44] Pericles,[45] Pope Leo X,[46] King Louis XIV,[47] the

---

43. Italian for "every single one" or "all the rest."
44. Caesar Augustus (63 B.C.–14 A.D.) was the first Roman emperor.
45. Pericles (495–429 B.C.) was a Greek politician and general.
46. Pope Leo X (1475–1521) was the head of the Catholic Church from 1513 to 1521.
47. Louis XIV (1638–1715), also called the Sun King, ruled France for seventy-two years, making him the longest French reigning sovereign.

country would not have had a Pasteur,[48] a Branly,[49] a Curie,[50] a Calmette,[51] a Roux,[52] a Vida. I blame myself for not being able to name all those who, in the past or in the present, honor the good name of France.

"He who wants to become a scholar must be very strict with himself, just as the people who want a strong civilization must never be satisfied with their progress.

"Haiti, which I love very much, can walk, but must walk faster. She must think of those poor children, brought down from the countryside, servant children who do not always receive the mandatory elementary education . . . Poor kids!

"There are too many illiterates in a country that one wants to call Black France; there is too great a distance between the Haitian elite and the masses.

"The candidate for the presidency of Haiti, that is each councilor of state who has a portfolio full of enticing programs, but . . . let him win the price nailed at the top of a greasy pole.[53] Once successful and powerful, all the fine projects he had conceived fly away with the blue smoke of his cigars, the sparkle of his wines, and the aroma of his meats coming from the kitchen of the National Palace. And little by little, this once energetic man becomes a Sybarite.[54]

"Hear me, Haitians. Your country is struggling! Do not be discouraged, which country hasn't?

48. Louis Pasteur (1822–1895) was a famous French chemist and microbiologist.
49. Édouard Eugène Désiré Branly (1844–1940) was a French inventor and physicist.
50. Marie Curie (1867–1934) was a Polish and naturalized-French physicist and chemist. She was the first woman to win a Nobel Prize.
51. Léon Calmette (1863–1933) was a French physician, bacteriologist, and immunologist.
52. Pierre Paul Émile Roux (1853–1933) was a French physician, bacteriologist, and immunologist.
53. A British axiom that represents the hard work someone will have to do to reach a more successful position within their life and dealing with issues that may arise.
54. A person devoted to the pursuit of luxury and indulgence.

"Wasn't the United States, which oppresses you today, under the grip of England until recently (1783)? Didn't we, the French people, see our old Lorraine and our dear Alsace under the German flag for almost fifty years?[55] And didn't we take these territories back gloriously? You don't have to be ashamed of your origins. Slavery goes back to the most ancient times; the Hebrews, the Greeks, the Romans have known the most ferocious oppression.

"Once the master of the world, and today the cradle of Catholicism where God's direct representative, Rome was iniquitous toward its slaves. In no other place was a man so mistreated as in Rome . . .

"The famous poet Horace was the grandson of slaves; Terence had himself been one. Who else should I name to you?

"The world has never lacked slaves. There were some before Jesus Christ, and while he lived among us, and, as I am speaking to you, there are many places in Asia, Africa, etc. where slavery is still in full swing. Brazil does not even have forty years of freedom.

"In short, Black Haitians can boast about being the most daring, the most courageous, but the most advanced? The question must be studied.

"Having conquered their freedom long before other Blacks received theirs, Haitians should be the exemplar of the Black race. The country should have been at the crossroads of civilization, our wayfinder when we wander off . . . But . . .

"Haitians, 'It's better to find out where you're going than to wonder where you're coming from.' Don't go *bac en arrière*— 'bass-ackward,' as your kids say so well. Keep walking on the endless path to Civilization. Aim for order, economy, work. Educate

55. The region of Alsace-Lorraine was annexed by the German Empire after the Franco-Prussian War of 1871 and returned to French control after WWI.

the masses, respect the leader of the Nation, who will in turn respect the Constitution. Love one another, and you will surpass the great difficulties that you have so often encountered in your life as a people.

"You are disgusted by the presence of the Americans in your country. You may be right, but 'pay, they say, and we will go away' . . . Couldn't you sacrifice a few tires? A few gallons of gasoline? A few movie nights, a few lavish dinners at Lucullus, a few splurges . . . well? And launch a large national fundraiser? There are men in the government who get six hundred, eight hundred, more than two thousand dollars in salaries. It's too much when you live in a country where capitalists kill for a few millions . . .

"You would give your all, and before long the 'Constable of Wall Street'[56] would be on his way out.

"But for these efforts, you shouldn't expect gratitude or fond memories (from whom?). No. Devotion never demands anything in return.

"To conclude, let me share a true story which sounds like a fairy tale . . .

"In 1795, a financier located in Boston named James Swan[57] was concerned by the financial situation of the United States, so he privately assumed the entire French debts of the United States: 2,024,900 dollars.

"Shortly after, James Swan was arrested for debt in Paris, and thrown into the Sainte Pélagie Prison, where he spent the last twenty-two years of his life . . . The United States did nothing."

56. Roger L. Farnham (1864–1951) was the vice president of the National City Bank of New York, which bought a controlling interest in the National Bank of Haiti. For many, Farnham served as the face of the Occupation, especially during the early years.
57. James Swan (1754–1830) was a member of the Sons of Liberty and participated in the Boston Tea Party.

The audience shivered; a mute revolt made hearts beat and faces tense. The speaker resumed calmly:

> "Your country may be ungrateful to you, but never be ungrateful
> to your country. Never!"

The talk ends and Monsieur Ronceville is acclaimed.

After two pieces of music brilliantly performed by two young American pianists, Laurence Desvallons delivers an emotional recitation of the poem "L'Abandonée" by Mme Virginie Sampeur.[58]

Then, Mlle Durand reads a detailed report of all the Club's activities during its first year.

Finding herself suddenly indisposed, Mlle Jefferson, who was supposed to close the event by playing a superb piece on the violin with Mme Leabrook as accompanist, begs her brother to present excuses on her behalf to the public.

The young Yankee rises to the podium and says: "Ladies and Gentlemen, my sister is very tired, and she regrets not being able to play the piece as scheduled in the program. She regrets it even more since it deprives the audience of the pleasure of enjoying Mme Leabrook's talent. I would like to replace my sister, being a musician myself, but I only play the phonograph, and I don't see the instrument in the room . . ."

Everyone bursts out laughing.

Confusing their mirth with encouragement, the man continues despite Mlle Jefferson's glare:

"I have wonderful records. It is therefore with the greatest sadness that I leave the stage without giving you the happiness of listening to my collection which is up-to-date . . ."

Then, a choir of young girls sings the American, French, and Haitian national anthems which the audience frantically applauds before leaving.

---

58. Marie Angelique Virginie Sampeur (1839–1919) was a Haitian educator and poet.

CHAPTER III

Laurence had cried all day. All night too. And having suffered so much had left her pale and gaunt the next day, a sad little face where two puffy eyes were trying to repress the tears ready to spurt out.

Delighted by the success of the party, Guy had run to his fiancée to share his happiness with her. He found her in the living room, reading.

– "Laurence," he said warmly, "the fairies have spoiled us. What a great success we have had! My soul, overflowing with pleasure, pushed me toward yours so that we can enjoy this together. *Chérie*,[1] darling, how gorgeous you were yesterday! I even saw tears in your beautiful blue eyes. It moved me. I'd wondered why you had chosen this poem, too sad for you who expect so many pretty things from the future. *Chérie*, tell me you are happy with the success of the party..."

He grew more and more feverish.

– "Do you remember young Jefferson's farce? Your father's speech was amazing. The talks were successful."

1. *Chérie* is French for "dear."

The young girl did not answer. She looked terrified. He took her in his arms, hugged her, and questioned her.

– "Laurence, my Laurence, you look unwell. Maybe the party exhausted you? Please answer."

She tried to lie.

– "Yes . . . I have a bit of a headache."
– "Poor *chérie*, the event was so long your delicate health suffered. Oh! If I could have guessed that you were so overworked, I would have stopped you from reciting poetry. When I thought you were moved, were you actually unwell, my poor friend?"

Mademoiselle Desvallons looked up at him, her eyes so languorous that he deciphered her secret and cried out:

– "You are sad, Laurence. I can feel it. I'm sorry. What is happening? Oh! Entrust me with everything. Everything."
– "Guy, if you knew . . ."
– "Is our happiness threatened? Oh! How terrified I am!"
– "I am very unhappy. Do you know that my parents . . . ?"
– "I'm afraid to hear this . . . don't tell me . . ."
– "My parents want to marry me to . . ."
– "Robert Watson?"
– "You said it."
– "And you refused, I'm sure . . ."
– "Yes. I told them that, despite everything, I will marry you."
– "Laurence, you are more dear and more indispensable every day. I will fight like a savage to keep you. I'll challenge Watson to a duel. I might die, but so what! Me alive, he won't have you . . . I hate him."

He softened.

– "*Chérie*, don't cry anymore. Your eyes are already bruised. Don't you love me today more than yesterday? Won't you, despite everything, be my adored wife? Answer. I want to hear your voice, your pretty voice."

– "Oh! Yes, I promise."

– "But after all," he suddenly yelled, "what do your parents blame me for?"

– "My mother raised the stupid question of . . . races."

– "Ah! Wasn't it she who drew our attention to these words by Felix Viard:

"'Great heroes have no color. The Unknown Soldier, for whom the flame of Remembrance burns under the Arc de Triomphe, on the Place de l'Étoile, is also the Senegalese Tirailleurs[2] of the Champagne region trying to take back the enemy's guns and forgotten flags. It is also the Poilu[3] of Verdun shouting to the invader: 'You shall not pass!' About our love, she had added: 'You do well to love each other, my children, I am for the union of the races.' Ah! If Madame Desvallons isn't the most hypocritical of creatures, she must have very serious reasons for separating us. I'll know them. I must know them, these terrible reasons. However, if major circumstances, independent of your mother or us, force her to separate us, I surrender here and now."

He thought: "What if there was a terrible stain in my family capable of tarnishing the honor of my future in-laws? What if a troubling past was to defile my fiancée because of me? What if I was unworthy of her?"

– "Guy, my father is a compassionate man. Let's go to him and plead our cause. He's just . . . he has always promised to make me happy. Let's go find him. I'll fall at his feet and tell him about my

2. A corps of colonial infantry in the French Army during World War I, recruited from sub-Saharan Africa.
3. Literally "The Hairy Ones," a nickname for French infantry soldiers in WWI.

distress. Yours as well. I will tell him how much we love each other; you will support me. Facing two lovers in tears, his heart will be moved and his sad project—that of marrying me to M. Watson—will fly away and disappear in the air, like a bubble of soap. Let's go right now."

– "No, I can't, Laurence. I can't. I will explain myself to your parents, but not today."

– "I am appalled by your refusal. I really don't understand what caused it."

– "Calm down, my dear friend. The big mango tree over there—near the fence—has a wide crack. I'll put a note in it for you tonight. You will use the same method to respond to me tomorrow."

He grabbed her hands.

– "Good-bye, *chérie*."

– "Guy, please don't leave. Not before we've begged for the mercy of our executioners. We are so unhappy."

He protested:

– "Mercy? Come on. Only the weak, the martyrs, or even the criminals need it. We are strong. Our love will be our aegis. We will overcome all the difficulties, all the oppositions to our wedding. Mercy? No, I don't want it. Good-bye, dear Laurence. See you tomorrow."

– "Guy, I feel like I'll never see you again."

– "Why are you telling me that? Do you no longer trust me? I adore you. Do you doubt it? Look at me."

– "But . . . your refusal to see my father—after I told you such serious things—worries me immensely."

– "My poor friend, don't worry. I will see you tomorrow."

He suddenly broke away from the young lady and left promptly.

– "Guy, Guy!" cried out Laurence desperately, "*Adieu!*"

Turning around, he waved affectionately to her and disappeared down an alley. Once in the street, the sad fiancé hailed a coachman, who drove him to Monsieur Joseph Vanel, on Rue Férou.

– "Uncle," said Guy, throwing himself into the arms of his relative, "tell me about my father. I want to know the life that he lived. How did he die?"

The old man panicked.

– "What's the matter with you, my poor child?"

– "I am unhappy, very unhappy."

– "And my brother's past is responsible for your misfortune? I don't understand. Regardless, I can tell you right now that Henri was the most generous, the most honest man our country has ever had. He loved to study and was selfless. He became a doctor at twenty-five years old. He then married Mlle Eugénie Lenoir, your dear mother—virtue personified. He lived six years of perfect happiness with her. And then, death came. It was a simple yet fulfilled life! A full life! Yes, my brother mostly cared for the destitute and the children. That's why he left to his widow only a famous name and his clients' regrets as a legacy. What more do you want me to tell you, dear child? I have answered your request, I believe? Now, you must explain your troubles to me."

– "You cannot not believe how relieved I am! When I came here, I thought that I was the innocent victim of a dishonorable genealogy. To hear you tell me the contrary gives me the strength to fight my enemies savagely."

– "Explain yourself, Guy! Explain yourself. Your reluctance exasperates me."

– "Well, here it is. M. and Mme Desvallons have decided . . ."

He hesitated, but the old man encouraged him to continue.

– "Come on, come on. I want to know what is bothering you."

– "They've decided," Guy replied, "to marry their daughter to M. Watson, a rich American who associates with them. They wrote me a nasty letter."

– "What does Laurence think about it? There must be the matter of race."

– "Naturally, she refused her parents' decision . . . but paddling against the current is difficult."

– "Your honor commands that you not insist. Crush your heart and renounce this girl! You will certainly suffer, but your attitude will make M. and Mme Desvallons feel that you are responding with contempt to the insult they believe they are inflicting on you."

– "But Laurence . . . Laurence who loves me and whom I adore . . ."

– "You must renounce her to save your honor! Go. In time, you will forget about her."

– "Uncle, dear uncle! How can I forget Laurence?"

– "Your father would have also advised you to break it off. I will think about it some more! But, I must tell you very sincerely that you deserved this useless affront. There are so many educated and honest Haitian women from good families, many of whom deserve to be called your wife. But you needed a white girl."

– "Uncle, I never wondered why I love this young lady. I'll marry her because she's the one I love. That's all. Love knows no prejudice and, as I strongly love, I forget that Laurence and I are not of the same race."

– "Well, you were dreaming. It's a rude awakening to reality. Forget Mlle Desvallons!"

– "Uncle, if you only knew how much we love each other!"

– "Some hesitations are worse than cowardice. Go, think in the darkness of your room, and come back tomorrow to tell me what you have decided."

The old man held out his hand. Guy Vanel took it in haste and brushed his trembling lips on it.

– "Good-bye, Uncle."
– "Good luck, my child. Place your honor above all."
– "It pains me greatly."
– "It will pass."
– "Uncle . . ."
– "Oblivion cures everything."

Guy left abruptly, turning around to hide the tears on his face.

———

Madame Vanel gave a letter to her son, who had just arrived. He was very distraught after he read it, smoking one cigarette after another. And another. Nonstop, like a machine. She regretted not reading the rude note that the postman had given her earlier. The note which now tormented her son.

Guy read it once more. Why reread it when it so clearly makes him suffer?

He got up abruptly from the armchair and sat at his desk. He would answer it, no doubt.

Guy opened his drawer, from which he took a sheet of paper, then laid on blotter paper, and uncapped his inkwell. Each time he withdrew ink, the nib of his dip pen had dried without his writing a single word. The young man soon held his head in both hands.

Madame Vanel sensed that her son was unhappy. She approached timidly, her soul torn.

– "My son, is it this letter?"
– "Mother!" He tried to hide the letter. "Dear mother!"
– "Don't try to hide it. It tortured you enough. I hate it, and I hate the one who sent it to you. I even hate the postman who gave it

to me. Tear it up quickly and come near and cry over my heart. It is big enough to contain all the tears that you have been holding back for so long. Come. Are you crying? Poor *chéri*,[4] tell me your sorrow. I want to hear it."

– "Mother, Mother, it is nothing."

– "Tell me everything. I beg you. Trust me, my little one."

He handed her the letter.

– "Read, Mother, read."

When Madame Vanel finished reading it, she looked at the young man with deep sadness.

– "My son, my child, renounce Laurence forever!"

– "Forever?" He sobbed. "Mother! Mother!"

Collapsing under the weight of his grief, Guy snuggled against his mother's heart, the last refuge of children in distress.

As she was now engaged to M. Robert Watson, Monsieur Vanel would not reply to the insolent letter that Monsieur and Madame Desvallons had sent, asking him to renounce Laurence's hand. He remembered his promise to leave Mlle Desvallons a note in the trunk of the mango tree. Yes, he would write to her. He would ignore the promise that he made to his mother, to his uncle, to himself. Oh, the power of love!

That evening, when the anxious young girl would look for a long, beautiful letter that she had been expecting from the tree, her only confidant, she would only find a short note, a poor note reading:

Laurence,

It is not without tears that I write to you. Why can't I lie to you? No, I would do it poorly. Listen to me. Your parents sent me a letter which created a

4. *Chéri* is the male version of *chérie*.

great rift between our families. *Adieu, chérie, adieu.* How I love you! It is
in the blood of my broken heart that I dip my pen to write this cruel word:
adieu.

Your unfortunate Guy

She replied that she preferred death to a separation:

I never loved anyone but you, my dear Guy. To renounce you is to renounce
love. Why ask for such a sacrifice from a seventeen-year-old heart? Guy,
you make me whole, and I will die without you. Across the chasm of which
you speak, we can build a bridge. Love . . .

Grant me a new promise, since you have forgotten all the ones you
made to me before. They were so beautiful.

Good-bye, my beloved.
Laurence

———

A month had passed. They kept writing sweet, tender, and often desperate letters to each other every day. No one knew about it.

However, one morning, Laurence did not find anything in their little
hiding place. She searched and searched again. The note might have fallen
by mistake. Maybe the wind carried it away? Or it might be lying under a
dead leaf? Ah! The dear messenger.

She looked everywhere with hope and then with suspicion.

She scrutinized every corner of the large courtyard, questioned all the
trees in the orchard, the little birds, the blue sky. Nothing. Desperate, she
fled the garden and went up to her room, where she reread her correspon-
dence and contemplated the picture of her fiancé.

When the young girl refused to have lunch, Raoul and Lucienne, terrified, went to find her. They took her in their arms and inquired about her
health. They told her that she was wrong to favor Guy and to deny Watson. They told her that you can lift the world with money.

Laurence listened to them without flinching, and they spoke further.

    – "You won't have the same opportunity twice my dear child," Lucienne declared. "Your father is getting old. You are . . . we are, you and I, a heavy burden for him. If the Haitians end up managing the School of Damiens themselves, and Raoul cannot be kept there as an expert . . . what would become of us? Misery awaits us, Laurence. It is unreasonable to foolishly let the millions of M. Watson lying at your feet to slip away, and his heart with it."

Desperate, she turned to her husband.

    – "Raoul, help me convince this child. Without this marriage, we are lost."

Once so honest, Monsieur Desvallons, a man of principle from the Rue Servandoni, an honest student of the Boul' Mich, became a sad vulture. At times, he was conscious of his downfall, yet he could not do anything about it. Lucienne wanted him so, and his brain had followed suit, weakened by the serious illness he suffered in France.

Pressured by his wife, tormented by the fear of poverty, Desvallons said without scruple,

    – "Laurence, don't be sentimental. Robert adores you. You must marry him. Forget the little penniless boy who cannot get us out of trouble. Remember that it was Watson and Leabrook who got me into the Central School of Agriculture. Director Freeman doesn't care much for me. If I were to lose the friendship of these two 'friends at court,' I would be out immediately."

The little fiancée did not bat an eye. Her parents demanded an immediate answer which she did not give them. Boiling with rage, her mother grabbed her by the shoulder and browbeated her.

    – "Wicked girl!"

Raoul, whose heart remained good, defended Laurence.

– "Don't hit her, Lucienne. No!"
– "She is too stubborn, too romantic!"
– "Let's leave her room. She needs to think."

He led his wife out of the room, while Laurence prayed for God's help. Her eyes looked to the sky. The maid brought food that no one touched. Her intuition told her that something strange was happening in the house. Earlier, she had dropped the pepper grinder in the dining room. Perhaps her employers had stepped on the pepper. She heard that it could give rise to quarrels in families.

Her heart tormented by superstition, the maid ran to wash the floor, hoping to bring peace at home, but she suddenly remembered that she had not seen Mademoiselle Laurence's young gentleman at the house for over a month. And for over a month, too, she had noticed M. Watson's assiduous visits. Was it a coincidence? One no longer visits. The other visits too often.

The day ended, fraught with mysterious incidents. No one had lunch. Mlle Desvallons locked herself in her room. Raoul and his wife conferred for hours and, very upset, they made several phone calls. Marie-Jeanne was intrigued. She decided to spy on her masters.

———

The day ended. The twilight butterflies were already alight on the flowers in the garden beds, releasing perfumes into the air. The tuberoses and the jasmines, so shy during the day, had opened their corolla wide, their odors gushing out into the dark cloak of night. The garden was now full of shadows. Still believed to be in her room, Laurence had been wandering there for half an hour, without joy but almost without bitterness too. She walked like an automaton. She walked, she walked, and then sat down on a small bench, close to the kitchen. She thought of nothing.

Suddenly an idea started to form in her mind, an idea that agitated her. She pushed it back, but it always came back. She would not listen to it, this idea. No!

She began to walk again. It was no longer an automaton that ran along the avenues of the large garden. It was an unhappy and rebellious fiancée. It was Laurence Desvallons, who no longer feared the fight. She pointed a menacing finger at her parents' house.

– "I'll have my revenge," she said.

Marie-Jeanne, who watched her from the shadows, approached her discreetly.

– "Mlle Laurence!"
– "Why are you watching me?" she said with anger and surprise.
– "Can't I be of any use to you?"
– "No, thank you."
– "Mam'zelle! Missy!"

Laurence came around, and said gently, "Marie-Jeanne, walk with me to the end of the aisle."

They walked together in silence. They were now in the deserted street.

– "Good-bye, Marie-Jeanne," said Mlle Desvallons abruptly. "You didn't see me this evening. Do you understand?"
– "What? I don't understand ... I am too dull."
– "Don't try to understand anything. Simply don't tell anyone that I went out. I demand total secrecy. Do you understand?"
– "No, that's what I don't understand, Mam'zelle ... alone like that ..."
– "That's my business. Good-bye!"
– "Good Lord! What a dirty business!"

Disheveled, distraught, Mlle Desvallons ran to throw herself into the arms of Madame Vanel.

– "Keep me, Madame," cried the young girl. "Be my mother since you are Guy's mother. Marry us. Make us happy."

Mme Vanel sighed, her soul heavy with sadness.

– "My son is gone, my poor Laurence, gone . . ."

– "Guy? Gone? Without me? Oh! It's horrible. He left?"

– "Yesterday. I will join him at the end of December."

– "Well, keep me! You will take me with you."

– "Alas! I cannot. I do not have the right to do so." She thought of the terrible letter. "No, my daughter, I cannot."

– "What can we do, oh Lord?"

– "I'm going to walk you back to your parents. Be brave!"

– "Guy doesn't love me anymore? He left me."

The two women wept for a long time in each other's arms, and then they returned to M. and Mme Desvallons, who were terribly worried.

– "Where were you, Laurence?" they asked.

– "I wanted to ask Madame Vanel to marry me to her son, but . . ."

Guy's mother left, without giving an explanation.

Gone are the fine literary and musical evenings in Madame Desvallons's salons. Gone also, the grandiose meetings of the Haiti-France-America Club, which did not survive the departure of its president.

———

Two years had passed since Watson began tirelessly courting poor Laurence, and what a courtship! The American still hoped to become the young girl's groom while she had convinced herself she would marry Guy Vanel, even though she had not heard from him.

Life was continuing peacefully when one morning, an overexcited Robert Watson visited the Desvallons to tell them that he intended to get married immediately or to leave without delay. Leave! This word threatened Lucienne's cupidity. She asked Robert for three days to settle everything.

But three days later, a general strike began. A strike! A troubling event, a revolt as reckless as it was unexpected, a brutal, savage awakening of the 1804 ancestors' blood, running in the veins of young Black men, misunderstood and mistreated by a white educator.

The strike led by the students of the Central School of Agriculture changed the country and had repercussions all the way up to the White House. It began on October 31, 1929, without any warning signs. Who would ever forget the day that these young people, tired of abuses, abandoned their institution to chant "Freeman Out"?[5]

Freeman was their director, an accomplished Negrophobe, one of the most arrogant Americans employed by the United States in the American administration in Haiti. Freeman might have had some talent, but his arrogance had driven a chasm between his students and himself.

The protests of the strikers were heard in Washington and the special Forbes Haitian Investigating Commission was sent to Haiti. It witnessed a lot of political filth. It is even said that some people had privileged access to the commissioners "to testify." But what they said publicly was different from what they said in private in the antechamber of the Yankee senators.

From that moment on, the strike took on a moral character that served as a springboard for the politicians of Haiti: the "strike" this, the "strike" that . . . everything led to it.

The opponents of M. Borno's[6] government conspired openly on behalf of the strike. Some "pushed" or "broke" the strikers. They were promised the moon when M. Borno left. Later, pressured by the elders, they founded newspapers and poured their frustration into them, against Freeman, against the Occupation, and against the government. Many of them experienced jail and a thousand other troubles. They refused any agreement

5. George F. Freeman (1978–1930) was the American director of Haiti's Agricultural School located in Damiens.
6. Eustache Antoine Francois Joseph Louis Borno (1865–1942) was a Haitian lawyer and politician who served as president from 1922 to 1930.

with the authority, thanks to the promises of a "Monsieur Prud'homme" still developing. It was anarchy at Damiens.

Freeman, now undesirable, was replaced by Colvin,[7] another American. The students at the Central School of Agriculture had created a maddening disorder in the American world, and for the Forbes Commission, a terrible disappointment.

Yen Leabrook and his wife had serious fears, both being "experts" (the first in pest control, the other in culinary arts) who earned together six hundred and fifty dollars a month. They could not tolerate the idea of being thrown out one day. Lucienne's world was turned upside down. Her husband's job was more threatened than ever, so when Watson returned home a few days after the turmoil to query when he was to marry Laurence, she said to him without flinching, "My daughter and you will be officially engaged in a month."

When evening came, she informed the young girl while they were having dinner. Laurence refused again, protested, but Lucienne did not budge. In vain, she begged her mother to change her mind. Enraged, Laurence said, "I emphatically refuse."

One day, Monsieur Desvallons returned from Damiens three hours earlier than usual, so his worried wife inquired about his health, "Are you sick, *chéri*? What's the matter with you, *chéri*?"

– "I submitted my resignation."

Lucienne revolted. Once a darling husband, Raoul was now an abomination. "Your resignation? But that's crazy!"

– "This lifestyle we have may be everything you want, but I can't take it anymore."

– "We're ruined, and if Laurence does not sacrifice herself . . ."

---

7. Carl C. Colvin (1889–1976) was an agriculturalist, educator, and writer who served the U.S. government in developing agriculture education in Haiti.

Desvallons looked at her and cried out in revolt.

– "Leave this poor child alone. We have tormented her enough. Does money lead to happiness?"

– "Ah!" sneered Lucienne. "Are you disillusioned? Well, I am ready to eat all the sick cows except the Haitian ones. I'm leaving you . . . I'm leaving you! I'm going back to Neuilly.[8] Unworthy man! Lazy! Coward! I'm leaving you."

– "Go 'head, go 'head, leave. I'll still have my dignity."

– "Ungrateful man. I wasted my youth raising your child, and you are not even moved to hear that I want to leave. Go ahead, you say? Well, fine, this is the reward for my tireless devotion. If Laurence really was my daughter, if my blood flowed in her veins, she would have thrown herself into my arms. But she is cold, colder than marble. I'm dealing with two ingrates. So be it!"

Madame Desvallons stormed out of the drawing room and locked herself in her bedroom. After she left, Laurence approached Raoul and whispered to him, "Father, I agree to marry M. Watson."

– "What did you say, my child? Would you be capable of a single sacrifice?"

– "Yes, when I attended the boarding school, the Reverend Mother always told me that good people must live on sacrifice and renunciation. I am just following her advice."

– "My child! My child!"

– "I sacrifice myself so that my mother does not leave us. She accuses you of having wasted her youth bringing me up. Well, I sacrifice mine to whatever she desires. Call her back, tell her that I'll marry M. Watson any day she wants."

8. Neuilly-sur-Seine is a commune in the department of Hauts-de-Seine in France.

– "My poor child, I don't want you to. Lucienne wants to leave me because I no longer have the prospect of fortune. Why does it matter? You will stay with me. Oh! Come into my arms."

– "Father, you cannot live without her."

– "You are wrong. Let her go."

– "Alas! Don't be fooled, Father."

– "It would be too painful to know that you are unhappy because of our desires. To live comfortably at the detriment of your happiness."

– "A devoted soul shares the joys of those that she loves as her own. Their pain as well. Father, I wish to forget myself, to concentrate on the gratitude I owe to my mother. My mother just said: 'I'm dealing with two ingrates,' and I hope to disprove her right away . . . Leave it to me, Father."

She left and knocked on Madame Desvallons's door.

– "It's me, Mother, your daughter, Laurence."

– "What do you want from me?" asked Lucienne calmly.

She opened the door. The martyr fell into her arms. "I've come to ask you to go to the Sacred Heart Church to save the date of my wedding with M. Watson."

———

Laurence and M. Robert Watson's wedding took place with a bang one evening in April 1930. All Port-au-Prince was there. After a majestic tour of the city, the guests went to Turgeau,[9] where they were received in the salons of M. and Mme Desvallons.

Fine liqueurs gushed out, while the decorated cakes competed in elegance with the pretty flower baskets scattered everywhere, and whose scent enchanted the guests.

9. An upscale section of Port-au-Prince.

Everything was poetry, flowers, and beauty: not a face without a smile, nor a beautiful body without an admirable ensemble and beautiful jewels, nor a hall without a bouquet of flowers.

Couples twirled around to the captivating music. The brightly lit living rooms took on various shades thanks to the dimming lampshades.

When eleven o'clock rang, everyone was still having fun. Laurence had charmed the guests with her graceful smile, exchanged kind words with everyone, but when a pianist began playing "Babylonienne" and "Prière du Soir" by Justin Elie at the request of two young girls, she lost her composure, and her eyes filled with tears. She tried to use her folding fan to hide her sadness, but Myrtana noticed it and whispered to her, "Be brave."

– "Myrtana . . . I'm hearing Guy playing. It's him in the flesh. If this man knew how much pain that he is causing me, he would close the piano. How I suffer! This music, ah! This music . . ."

– "Encore! Encore!" shouted guests from all sides. "Encore!" Like a sword, this word pierced her heart.

– "Myrtana, is this a test? A punishment?"

– "Let's leave the room, shall we? Let's go up to your bedroom," suggested Mlle Durand.

– "Oh! Yes, yes, take me away. I suffer too much. Take me far, far away. I want to forget who I am, to run away."

Leaning on her friend's shoulder, the young woman went to her little bedroom, a room no longer hers, where her once-beautiful dreams had now vanished. She burst into tears.

A jazz tune brought everyone to the dancefloor. Guests were dancing with such enthusiasm that no one noticed the absence of the bride. Watson, however, worried about it.

– "Where is my wife?" he asked Lucienne.

– "I'm going to look for her. She must be upstairs refreshing her makeup."

A servant reassured Mme Desvallons: "Yes, Mme Watson is in her room."

Laurence walked in with the young Haitian woman.

– "What is it?" Laurence asked, trying to smile.

– "Robert thinks you are tired and wishes to take you home," replied her stepmother. "It's past eleven o'clock."

– "I am ready." She blushed. "Let's go."

The newlyweds got into their shiny, decorated limousine. Several cars followed them.

The American was kind to his wife during the short journey from Turgeau, in Pétion-Ville.[10] The party lasted for another hour. The weather was splendid.

When midnight struck, friends and relatives had just left the bride and groom. They were now alone, standing in front of one another, hesitant.

– "Laurence," finally said M. Watson, "allow me to admire you again. How beautiful you are, dressed in tulle, crowned with orange blossoms!" He stepped forward. "*Chérie*...what's wrong? You're crying? Are you too hot? Do you want me to help you undress? Tell me."

– "No, no, thank you, I can do it alone."

– "Can I not even take off your crown and veil to kiss your beautiful blue eyes?"

– "No, no, Monsieur. Please, leave me alone. I feel sick. The heavy scent of the living room's flowers is nauseating. I'm suffocating."

– "*Chérie*, I will take care of you, my poor darling. Am I not your most devoted protector? Your husband? Laurence, forget everything, I adore you. I am not demanding. A little love will be enough

10. Suburb of Port-au-Prince.

for me. Do you love me a little? Oh! Talk to me. I need a word of forgiveness, what am I saying? Of pity."

She remained silent.

– "Laurence," he continued, "you are going to be the most adored woman. All your most futile desires will be my orders."

She was still silent. Madly in love, he took her hands. She stiffened and glared at him with contempt.

– "Leave me."

Robert had fallen into an armchair, but immediately stood up to face the angry young woman.

– "Please leave, Monsieur," she said.
– "Calm down, Laurence, you know that wanting to make you happy is not the only reason that I married you. I love you. You don't ignore it. What's the point of turning me away like this? I adore you, I idolize you. God gave you a throne, my heart, so be my adored queen. I only demand a word, a smile, a look from you to be happy. Your mother always told me that you have a good heart. I know my tears will move you. Look, they are already falling. Won't their warmth have the power to fight your pity? I suffer so much! Laurence, think of the happiness of an unfortunate man, one who chooses to surrender his power as a master for the docility of a slave. I am your slave. No, less than that . . . your thing. I throw myself at your feet. Dear Laurence!"

Having calmed down, she raised her beautiful eyes to him.

– "My friend, your words really make me shed tears . . ."
– "No, it's not my words that explain them. While everyone was having fun, your eyes were already full of tears at the Town Hall.

Full of them at the church, and even at the reception. My words aren't the cause of your tears."

– "It's true. My pride is wounded, and I am suffering. You know I don't love . . ."

– "Don't finish. Please don't finish. Do you forget that you are forever united to the man that you are brutally pushing out of your bedroom on the wedding night?" His face turned red. "What do you have to say for yourself?"

– "I dare not admit it to myself, but I will never be your wife, except by name."

– "You could have refused to sign the marriage license this afternoon and could have answered 'no' to the priest this evening, when he asked you to swear to be faithful to me until death do us part. It would have been more loyal. What plan did you put together?"

With a look full of contempt, she turned her back on him. He ran toward her.

– "Stay."

With the gesture of a master, of a tyrant, a gesture that tolerated no resistance, which seemed bound to smash everything, he grabbed her, bruised her shoulders, bit her, tore the white veil whose beauty he had just praised, trampled upon her crown, broke the pretty trinkets that adorned the bridal room.

– "You're insane! What you're doing is crazy," cried out the bride.

– "Yes, I'm crazy, you can see that. My violent gestures toward you are only natural. Reason alone would have prescribed others to me."

– "M. Watson, I don't know why I keep believing you will protect me against yourself. I know you are a gentleman. Let me go!"

– "The heart wants what it wants, and I love you."

– "I don't love you. I'm done defending myself. Leave. You are not unaware, Monsieur, that possession without love is a filthy act, a rape, which turns a man into a beast and a woman into a victim. Into two beasts when there is mutual consent. We must think of the little one who may come from it."

She thought about this child as some kind of stranger, an unexpected intruder who would also demand the affection of a woman that he would call mother by convention, and she would be obliged to call him her child. She looked at her bleeding arm.

– "You are a savage. Admit it."
– "When an American cannot enjoy something, he destroys it," he sneered. "You will see . . ."
– "Destroy me? Certainly not."

He drew his revolver and pointed it at the young woman.

– "Monsieur Vanel will not have the pleasure of seeing you alive again."

She glared at him in defiance.

– "Go ahead. Shoot me, beat me. I'm not afraid of you, vile assassin."

He stared at her for a long time, his arm holding the gun still pointed at her, his right index finger on the trigger. A small movement away from shooting her, from turning the white silk wedding dress into a burial shroud. A defenseless woman would collapse under the murderous bullet of her husband, followed by prison, the criminal trial, Assize Court, one more name blacklisted.[11]

---

11. During the American Occupation, Americans were subject to their own tribunals. Hence the penalty for Laurence's murder would not be death or incarceration, but rather Watson's blacklisting and deportation from Haiti.

A murderer! No, the idea disgusts him. Slowly lowering down his gun and no longer angry, he was now crying and begging for mercy.

– "Laurence, I was violent. Forgive me."

– "It's alright. Allow me to be alone so that I may recover from this scene."

– "Good-bye, Madame. I'll give you time to think."

– "*Adieu*, Monsieur."

All night, Laurence heard Robert pacing up and down in the adjacent room. Lying on a divan, she tried to sleep in vain. Hours passed, and morning came. A gold ray entered the room through her white curtains, reflecting on her messy blonde hair. She wore a beautiful pink silk kimono, adorned with flowers, not unlike a mosaic. The sunny gold ray gleams on the fabric, making it even more sumptuous. Oh, the gorgeous pink kimono. How happy Robert would have been to admire the woman wearing it so majestically! She was grateful to the radiant sun, which frolics in the trees, for sending her its golden kiss even in the solitude of her bedroom. But this room, the sad witness to such an unfortunate scene, this room where death had almost touched her, caused her nothing but dread, nothing but disgust. She would like to leave forever and immediately.

Laurence opened her window slightly. Oh! What a torment to see a man pacing in the bushes over there, a man whose ravaged face showed great pain, a man who should be with her at this hour . . . a groom, married yesterday!

To know that he was unhappy disturbed her infinitely. Tears started flowing, thick, burning. A feeling of pity washed over her. But she could not help it.

Alas! Whom to confide in? Who can tell how much she suffers? She looked everywhere, looked for a friend, a confidant, a consoler.

Her gaze fell on a large silver crucifix that M. Watson had hung above the head of her bed. She fell to her knees.

– "God, my God, thy will be done! I'm asking you, like your son once did. if you are willing, please take this cup of suffering away from me."

She felt stronger for having prayed, but she needed to keep herself busy: writing, reading, sewing . . . anything. Idleness weighed on her.

Her husband, who was not Catholic, had nevertheless had the foresight to place on the shelves a rich collection of religious books and virtuous novels. He knew the refined tastes of the young woman.

She picked one up and opened it randomly.

– "Life is hard for many, mediocre for most, but it is happiness and joy for the privileged few who love. But such is the imperfection of human nature that we love by giving ourselves to someone while wishing, expecting, reciprocal feelings. Nothing is rarer than a totally mutual love; the one who loves to the point of devotion, to the point of sacrifice, often encounters nothing but indifference, sometimes ingratitude and betrayal. The feeling that inspires our best hopes might also be (almost always) the source of our worst disappointments and our deepest sorrows."

She stopped for a moment to meditate and repeated these words, like a chorus: "Nothing is rarer than a totally mutual love." Wasn't the author mistaken? Did Guy not love her as much as she loved him? "But his desertion . . . he forsook me." Why did it matter since God allowed it?

Someone knocked on the door. She pretended not to hear. They knocked louder.

Then, she heard a small voice through the lock.

– "It's Chérisna. Yes, Madame . . ."

She let out a "phew" of relief.

– "What do you want?"

– "I bring Madame the breakfast that I just made, yes."

Laurence unlocked her door.

– "Chérisna, thank you, but I'd rather have an orange juice."

– "Oranges are not in season anymore, Madame."

– "Ah! A cup of herbal tea then . . . I feel a little . . . a little unwell."

– "Yes, Madame. Monsieur told me to take good care of you, Madame."

– "Tell me . . . has he had lunch?" It's her duty to know. "Where is he?"

– "He didn't eat anything, no. He's reading the newspapers. He feels a little . . . a little unwell."

– "Very well. You may go now."

She could feel that the servant was aware of the miseries of her home, her hopes nipped in the bud. Queasy, she fell on the sofa and cried uncontrollably.

———

A month had passed since Chérisna had begun knocking daily on Madame Watson's door to bring her errands or to take orders from her. During this lapse of time, Laurence had caught a glimpse of her husband in the garden only eight or ten times. One morning, as she gave way to the maid, Robert burst into her room, dismissed the servant, and closed the door. Their eyes met, like two swords.

Standing, the surprised young woman did not flinch. He moved forward, she moved backward.

– "Do not be afraid, Madame," he said calmly. "I've just come to ask if your grievances against me have not diminished."

– "My grievances? But I don't have any, Monsieur."

– "All right, I've had enough of this strange life. To everyone, you are my companion, the future mother of my children, yet you are a stranger to me, as foreign as the day I was introduced to you. I want to end it."

– "Done. I didn't give you this life. You are aware that a young girl my age gives herself only to the one she loves."

– "Cruel woman! I see that you haven't changed."

– "You married me without my consent, thanks to the authority of my parents and their intrigue. It was very painful for me, but I would have perhaps consoled myself over time if my delicate nature had not been damaged beyond repair. I'll always remember that you swore to make dance for your dollars. I cannot bear this thought. It has been chasing me, obsessing me, for a month now. I can't have an honest desire, a happy memory without it imposing itself, screaming at me that this marriage has tarnished me. What am I saying? Destroyed me. Oh! So let me forget under what circumstances I became Mme Watson. I suffer so much! At least, try to understand me, Monsieur . . ."

– "I'd forgotten all of this. I am asking your forgiveness."

– "Thanks. Even your generosity hurts me. But who knows? Maybe time will . . ."

– "Laurence, I'm very unhappy—believe me—so let's join our two sufferings together and make a small happiness. I cried tears of blood—who would believe it?—but those that I have yet to shed are of fire, they remain within me, burning my soul mercilessly. No one would tolerate the life that I lead. I am deeply in pain."

– "I know. Is it reasonable that we waste two lives which could have, on their own, created an Eden for themselves? Ah! If I get you in trouble, blame my parents and your stubbornness. I've told you this before, Monsieur. You bought me like one buys a trinket. Enjoy your purchase, but don't ask me for anything. A trinket gives nothing back."

– "Ah! Because I do not share the secrets of my life, M. and Mme Desvallons themselves have not guessed the full depth of my torment. I can no longer endure this compromise which forces me keep a smiling face, while a sharp weapon lacerates our hearts. Let's be true to ourselves. I endured this life for a month. That's enough. I have lost hope of even appealing to your pity. M. Guy Vanel will always keep us apart, standing between us. But for as long as I live, you may only be his mistress."

– "Enough, Monsieur, enough."

– "You still love him. And I will never divorce you."

– "You have no right to use this name against me. When you asked me to marry you, I was unofficially engaged to Monsieur Vanel, and you knew that. So, what are you complaining about? I had declined the chance of marrying you because I was against the horrible bargain that was this marriage, but I was sold regardless."

She fell into an armchair and added, "Yes, I am your slave. But I'm begging. I know your generosity. Give me back my freedom."

With these last words, she felt the beginning of a revolt.

– "No. Enslaved people, like any oppressed individual, do not ask for freedom. They take it, even if they shed their blood or die conquering it. I will avenge myself on you and your dollars. I want to be free. I want to escape this golden prison. I want to get my surname back. I want to finally live. Your money is the deepest tomb for me. Haven't you already enriched those who wanted it, to the detriment of my happiness? Don't they plan to return to France to set up a department store with the proceeds of the big check you signed for them? Don't they drive fancy cars? Aren't they finally happy? Well! I don't care about all that, I just want freedom. If you are not a tyrant, you will not oppose the fight which I will undertake to earn it."

– "Laurence, I'd always told you that because of my fortune, I would marry you despite your refusals. I did so without letting you know that behind the dollars of the proud American was hiding the sad soul of a lover. I adored you. I did not know how to let you see that my soul is not shallow and avaricious, but deep and in pain. I was wrong. I release you from all the commitments we solemnly made at the Town Hall, at your church, and before our God, this cruel God you made me worship."

The young woman looked up at her husband with astonishment. Robert suddenly left the room, slamming the door without waiting for an answer.

– "Free!" repeated Laurence. Free with such a small fight! It seemed like a dream to her. Free! This word she had been waiting for, this happy word fell on her heart like a stone. Free? Does it mean getting a divorce? The roses in the window box were wilting. Their petals fell heavily to the ground, weighed down by some invisible weight. Laurence watched them fall with a pull of her heartstrings, wondering why everything she loved was crumbling, sinking in despair. These roses had been given to her the day before by her friend Myrtana. They were so fresh. Oh, cruel disappointment! The poor woman had looked forward to the pleasure of smiling at them during many mornings. But alas, after only two days, those roses were now just a few dead petals on the floor. Dead petals!

She bent down, gathered them up, took a deep breath and whispered,

– "God . . . we 'make' nothing. We can arrange, unite, disunite, count, weigh, measure. But 'make' something? What a word! 'The smallest grass perplexes human intellect.'"[12] She associated this

---

12. "The smallest herb perplexes human intellect. So true is this that the aggregate toil of all men could not create a straw unless the seed be sown in the earth. Let it not be said that the seed must rot in the earth to produce. Such nonsense should not be listened to now." From Voltaire. *The Sage and the Atheist*. Interactive Media, 2016. Voltaire (1694–1778) was a French Enlightenment writer and philosopher.

thought of Voltaire with her inability to make bruised petals turn into very fresh roses, roses that would embellish her lonely room. Someone knocked. It was her maid. Laurence invited her in.

 – "A letter from Monsieur to Madame, yes," said Chérisna.

 – "From M. Watson?"

 – "Yes, Madame, from himself."

 – "Give it to me." She read:

Madame,

An urgent matter forces me to leave immediately. My journey may be long . . .

Robert Watson

Laurence, who should have been swooning with happiness, was terribly distraught.

She ran to the phone, which she waved nervously.

 – "Hello! Hello! Leabrook, M. Watson just left for an unknown destination. I'm worried. Come and reassure me, oh! Quick . . ."

 – "Are you worried?" repeated the Yankee at the other end of the line.

 – "Yes, my friend, very."

 – "Of what?"

 – "Of this departure. Do you know anything about it? Where is M. Watson going?"

 – "I know he's going to . . . well, it's a secret. Listen, he's going to . . ."

 – "Ah, just say it, I am so anxious, where is he going?"

 – "I'm coming to you, Laurence. I have a lot to teach you."

 – "But you must share your information with me right now, can't you see that?

 – "No, I don't see you. I hear you. And the phone, even if it is practical, is not a discreet confidant. I'm coming to you."

In less than fifteen minutes, the American arrived at Laurence's. She ran to meet him as soon as the sound of his car reached her.

– "My friend, my concern is boundless. Did M. Watson give you the reason for his departure? His address?"

Leabrook was American in every sense of the word. He was not moved by Laurence. He sneered. Laughed at her.

– "What are you worried about? I don't understand you. What do you want to know?"

– "What happened to my husband, Yen."

– "And you're asking me?"

– "Yes, you are his confidant, our friend . . ."

– "What are you to him?" He laughed. "Answer me."

– "Leabrook, you are doubling my anxiety. Why?"

– "Because you are a stranger to Robert, despite the name and the fortune he has placed at your feet. I know that."

– "Monsieur, you do not have the right to insert yourself into our intimacy or to blame me."

– "Privacy? Who can you fool? If Robert left, it's because of that. Married to him, you remained the fiancée of the little n——Guy Vanel."

– "Ah! Leabrook! Leabrook! You are a traitor. It was you who made M. Watson leave?"

– "Yes, I advised him to do so, so that remorse gnaws at you, and it's already gnawing."

– "Wretched man! Leave!" She was crying. "I hate you!"

– "See you tomorrow."

He chuckled and left. When she found herself alone, the young woman thought about her situation. Her father and her mother came running after hearing about the event. The first whispered, trying to cheer her up.

– "Laurence, I married you to the most generous, most loyal man there is, I made you a . . ."

– "A martyr," she added, "less than a slave. It's the truth."

– "No, a woman who could have been happy if she didn't cling to unhappy memories. Many times, we've seen people marry even though they did not love each other, and they discovered unsuspected qualities, unexpected delicacies of souls during their life together. Laurence, the law obliges you to follow M. Watson."

– "The law of marriage? But it is barbarism. We can clearly see it was designed by men to terrorize women, to maintain them in a state of eternal childhood. Don't talk to me about it . . . Oh! No."

– "You must be obedient to your husband. Dear little one, think about it . . ."

– "As lawyers, jurists, congresswomen, senators, and ministers, women will soon bury this word in their briefcases. Obedience! Oh! If you could know how much this word hurt me when the mayor pronounced, it . . . It's time for the institution of marriage to no longer turn a free woman into an oppressed one. Thanks to my marriage, I am a slave whom only divorce will set free."

Lucienne, who had remained silent, ventured, "Laurence, you are off topic. We would like to know why your husband decided to leave without giving you an address, not what women are going to do in five or ten years. You've fallen too deep into feminism. What are you going to decide?"

– "I'll stay home."

– "And if the unfortunate man never returns?"

– "That's my problem. With every misfortune, I become more emancipated, Mother."

– "Raoul and I were supposed to leave the country soon, but we shall remain here a little while longer to deal with this."

– "Oh, don't mind me, please leave! I'll handle the situation."

- "Certainly not! Us leaving would look like a desertion."
- "I'm sorry to cause you so much trouble, Mother. Leave."

Moved by these words, Desvallons looked at his child with sadness, despite his apparently austere advice. Laurence saw his grief and suddenly threw herself in his arms out of despair.

- "Father, oh my dear father!"

He caressed her beautiful blonde hair while wiping his tears absentmindedly.

- "Console yourself, dear child."

The scene moved Madame Desvallons, who murmured, "All will be well, Laurence. Raoul will soon learn what happened to M. Watson. Would you like me to send my maid to you? She can sleep here with you until his return."

- "No, Mother. Chérisna is very devoted to me."
- "As you wish. But I shall keep you informed by telephone of the steps that your father will take. Good-bye, my girl. In life, there is no shortage of hardships."
- "Good-bye, Mother. Good-bye, Father."

They left. But as Madame Desvallons stepped into her beautiful blue automobile, a gift from Watson, she felt lightheaded.

- "What's the matter, Lucienne?" asked Raoul, terrified.
- "I feel that this dearly sought-after luxury"—she looked at the car—"is beginning to weigh on me. Laurence's life makes me remorseful."
- "Remorse is a slow but harsh venom. My heart is now full of it," he said.
- "Alas, mine too . . ."

CHAPTER IV

After M. Watson's departure, Laurence sat every day at dusk under the flower-bedecked veranda, which had been decorated so tastefully before her wedding. How many times had she sat there, alone and desperate? Hadn't she shed tears of blood? But how many beautiful memories had she created here as well? Even though the flowerbeds were glowing, no plant without flowers, no bee deprived of honey, she was very sad. The tops of the tall trees in the orchard were spangled with silver, for in the distance the moon had appeared victoriously from behind a large snowflake-shaped cloud, and it now smiled at nature.

The young woman sat in her usual spot.

Out of the blue, and despite her torments, she felt surprisingly relaxed. She could not explain why. A sweet sensation of feeling, a sun of hope was shining in her despondent heart. She became serious, even worried. Was this moment of happiness a trap? Didn't it insult her grief? Her grief! It had become a familiar feeling to her, she almost loved it. She suffered in memory of Guy! Wasn't it a fair compensation for the evil that was torturing him? He who was so generous? Amidst the pink night, she looked to the horizon, eagerly searching for the cause of this happiness. Nature was, it is true, gorgeous, but wasn't it always so in Haiti? Why would it influence her now more than ever? Mystery!

Slowly, Laurence fell asleep. Insects passed through the foliage in little mad rages and walked amid her hair.

She slept . . . She looked like a goddess, her head thrown back, adorned with a bouquet of wild jasmine, her body in a simple pink satin dress with white lace.

Her two blonde braids, like two pale yellow ribbons, casually fell on her bare shoulders. She slept soundly, in an unconsciously lascivious and naturally seductive pose, a smile on her pink lips.

All is silent. It's night, a night full of mystery.

Suddenly, Laurence thought she heard the driveway's gravel being crunched under someone's footsteps. She looked around. Nothing, nobody. A butterfly perhaps, a malevolent insect had undoubtedly brushed past her and awakened her. Oh! The mean one. She was dreaming. But Morpheus[1] returned, and she surrendered to him. Laurence slept. Another small noise. This time she was not mistaken. Someone was walking close by. She got up quickly to run but found a man standing in front of her. He grabbed her and held her close to him and embraced her. Instinctively, she let out a cry of terror, and pulled her scarf over her neck.

– "Laurence, I was told you are unhappy, so I came. Don't be afraid, it's me. How beautiful you are!"

– "Guy? Guy? You scared me! You, here? Am I dreaming?"

– "Yes, I came to take you with me, let's go!"

– "I am not free, my poor friend." (Her honor had spoken.) "I . . ."

Anger filled his loving heart, and he cried out, "Ah, so you care about your torturer? You love him?"

– "Guy, don't be mad, listen to me. M. Watson is hostile toward me . . . however . . ."

---

1. Greek god of sleep and dreams.

– "Laurence, how dare you insult our love by accusing yourself? Would you dare to love the tyrant who sequesters you and abandons you, after having degraded you? I want you to myself, my love. M. Watson does not understand you. No, you don't love him. You are not his wife. Let's go, oh my dear fiancée, let's flee this cursed place."

– "Guy, my poor Guy, but my name is not mine anymore."

– "Forget it, let's go. Come with me, my car is on the other side of the wall, it will carry us away . . . Come . . ."

After hesitating between her duty and her passion, she exclaimed, distraught:

– "Alright, yes! Take me away, I suffer too much in this house where I have neither duty nor right. Let's run away. Let's fly away quickly . . . oh so quickly . . . M. Watson is not my husband . . . I love you, yes, let's go, my beloved."

– "Oh, I knew you would follow me. I knew it. Let's go."

Hand in hand, they left the veranda and ran toward the car which would take them away. Laurence suddenly stopped. Guy questioned her:

– "What's wrong, Laurence? Why this sudden sadness? Those tears? This hesitation?"

– "Alas!" (She sobs.) "What torment! My poor Guy."

– "Do you feel sick? Let's hurry up and leave . . . a few extra steps and we will be in the street . . ." (He worries.) "Why do you hesitate?" (He wants to drag her away, but she stiffens.) "What is it? Are we leaving?"

– "I . . . I can't come with you. No, I can't . . ."

– "Do not be like the *cocottes*,[2] the courtesans who take pleasure in testing passions, who make a thousand promises and then

2. Courtesans.

refute themselves. Laurence, let's make a decision ... time is running out! Shall we leave?"

He stopped talking to give her time to respond, but she remained silent. Vanel, angry, burst into flames. She refused. Then he begged. Still, she refused. Then, he said to her coldly, his mouth tensed:

– "I thought you loved me enough to renounce your transaction with M. Watson. You seemed to have enough repugnance about the stupid deal that is your marriage to run towards the happiness I offer you ... but you remain attached to the memory of a man who no longer wants you. You call yourself a slave to his name, but you are rather the slave of his dollars, admit it. Give me an answer ..."

– "Oh! Guy!"

– "You committed moral and spiritual adultery by marrying this man. Your heart, your thoughts, your soul all belong to me. You swore to love me until death do us part, but you are a cheater, a ... no words can describe how I feel ..."

– "Enough, enough, you insult me unnecessarily ..."

– Unnecessarily? Go on. You've come to prostitute yourself. Oh yes, you can't abandon this luxury I can never give you. I understand you now."

He becomes more and more enraged ... His eyes are those of a tiger, he tears his hair:

– "Perhaps a little monster grows inside you, the fruit of whim and contempt. M. Watson does not love you ... He ..."

– "Guy, protect me ... I suffer so much! In the name of our love."

– "Unfortunate girl, you never loved. Silence ... do not profane the word 'love.'"

– "If only you knew," said Laurence in despair, "if only you knew."

– "I know everything: you were cunning, you were deceiving me when you refused this marriage. Your protests were nothing but a deception. What I know, is that when your mouth protested, your petty, servile soul coveted the Yankee's dollars. If only I knew. I know you sell pleasure. M. Watson has paid you amply for his ephemeral flame, for his golden caprice. It has passed, and he despises you as one despises a whore."

– "Enough, enough! Don't you know that you wound me terribly . . . that I suffer from your attacks. Stop stabbing my heart with such refinement. You don't understand the depth of my feelings, Guy. I suffer too much to add the torments of adultery to my miseries. I do not want to . . ."

– "But you committed it by marrying this man. Didn't you promise me, swear me fidelity?"

– "Yes, your love is all my happiness: it consoled me when the gust of fate swept away my most beautiful dreams. It kept me alive. Loving you in silence was as sweet to me as your words are now cruel to me. Enough. I only ever loved you . . ."

– "Liar, hypocrite! You deceived me."

– "Never doubt my love and my honesty, Guy."

– "Your love? But where would I get enough dollars to buy it? Besides, haven't you already sold it?"

– "Guy! Is this really you, speaking this way? It's horrible! Tell me your heart refutes what your mouth said. How greatly you offend me."

The poor woman uttered these words with the same astonished, sad, despairing tone that Caesar certainly had in his voice when he said *Tu quoque fili mi!* (and you too, my son!) after seeing Brutus among his assassins.

– "Is this really you?" repeated Laurence, panicking. She wanted to flee, to drown to her death. "Guy, leave, leave," she repeated.

Revenge dominated his heart. The lively blood of African savages boiled in his veins: he wanted to be harsh, cruel. To do stupid things. To profane everything he held dear. He went from hating God to joining Satan. To defeat Laurence. To crush her under his feet. To laugh at her complaints, to drown his hatred in her tears:

> – "I want to torture you," he said.
> – "Go ahead. To be tortured by you would be my last happiness."

His desire soured, turned bitter, tenacious, angry. He wanted to turn the body he adored into a pile of crushed, genderless, rotten flesh, so his rival would feel nothing but disgust. He jumped up, grabbed the young woman, shook her with fury. He raised his arm to hit her . . . but, like a flash, he thought: "Don't hit a woman, even with a flower." A voice screamed from the depths of his suddenly appeased conscience: "Coward!"

Distraught, ashamed, he looked around like Cain after his crime.[3] He wanted to run away, but Laurence collapsed at his feet, passed out, dead maybe.

He looked at the immobile body of Madame Watson, and Vanel softened. He hugged her and cried in her hair.

> – "I love you," he murmured, getting lightheaded from the soft fragrance emanating from her body. "Forgive me for my cruel words. I'm jealous. I was mad."

He was afraid as the young woman slowly regained consciousness. Should he call for help? But how to explain his presence at Madame Watson's at such an odd hour?

The day began to dawn. He took out his handkerchief, ran to a small fountain to dampen it, and placed it to Laurence's burning forehead:

> – "Laurence, how do you feel?"

She didn't move. The henhouse's roosters let out their shrill songs, which then flew away in the air, dawn's unmistakable arrival. The nocturnal

---

3. In the Bible, Cain murdered his brother Abel and was exiled from Eden.

birds, singing at the top of their lungs, mad, hastened to regain their shelter . . . The sky gradually turned pink.

Laurence lay there, barely dressed, unconscious, at the mercy of her admirer. Was he going to abuse this defenseless body? No, rape horrified him. He was, however, tormented by this brutal instinct, this barbarous idea which arose in his thoughts. . . . Should he abandon the young woman like a coward? Wait for her to come back to her senses? Alert the servants? What a dreadful dilemma!

He immediately understood the horror of the last option. To stay with her was to tell everyone he was her lover. It was to uselessly feed M. Watson's hatred, because he would think he had been deceived. It was unfair to turn her into an adulteress.

– "I want her to be respected," he suddenly said to himself, "better she is found dead in two or three hours. At least then she would die without a stain, without being accused of impropriety. No matter how small."

He took a few steps before turning back to Mme Watson. He shook her frantically, in desperation.

– "Laurence, Laurence, I would rather look like a coward than compromise you."

He shook her again and again, and . . . oh happiness! He thought he heard her mutter a few words. He whispered:

– "Laurence, dear Laurence. Sorry Laurence, my love."
– "Huh? What is it? Where am I?"

She opened her eyes, tried to collect her scattered thoughts. After remembering, she bid him good-bye as she left. He didn't try to hold her back. He climbed over the wall and returned to his car.

    – "I have insulted the most honest of women," he said to himself. "I renounce to her forever . . . as I could never in my life sustain her gaze."

Mme Watson rushed over to her house and, still in shock, ran to her room where she found her bed just as the maid had left it the day before.

Suddenly the poor woman felt the need to go to bed and warm up. She was coughing. When Chérisna entered to bring her coffee around six o'clock, Laurence was running a high fever.

    – "Give me an infusion of linden," she prayed.[4]

    – "Madame is sick!"

    – "I'm cold. Get me the thermometer . . ."

The small glass stick frightened her; she had a fever of 106°F.

Worried, the maid ran to warn Mme Desvallons, who immediately telephoned Leabrook to ask him to bring Watson's doctor over to see Laurence, who was seriously ill.

After less than fifteen minutes, the poor woman received the most devoted care, from both Dr. Maning and her mother.

Her overall state, however, was increasingly alarming.

    – "I wish to talk to Robert," said the doctor, in English, to Leabrook.

    – "Watson is not here."

    – "It might be necessary for him to come back."

The two men moved away so that Raoul and his wife wouldn't hear their conversation.

    – "Is she in imminent danger?" Leabrook inquired.

    – "Imminent, yes. She asked for a priest. Bring one to her."

---

4. Linden tea has traditionally been used as a homeopathic cough and cold remedy.

– "Ah! And what is she suffering from?"

– "From bronchopneumonia.[5] It's serious, very serious."

– "All right, I will send a telegraph to my friend Watson."

– "Time is of the essence."

– "Is Laurence going to die?"

– "Medicine has many resources, my friend. Who knows."

– "If you save her, Robert will reward you. He is going to inherit millions."

But the preoccupied old doctor had stopped listening to him.

---

5. A respiratory infection that causes fever, cough, shortness of breath, and, in extreme cases, death.

CHAPTER V

Six days after the patient received the viaticum, Laurence was finally out of danger. Each day lasted for what seemed an eternity, but Dr. Maning declared Laurence out of danger after she regained consciousness from her thirteen-hour coma. Among the people gathered at her bedside, she distinguished Robert, his face ravaged, watching her every move. He inquired:

> – "Laurence, are you feeling better?"

It was as if nothing had happened between them.

> – "Oh yes, much better . . . thank you, thank you," she replied.
> – "It's time for your medication; allow me to give it to you."
> – "Yes, yes, my dear, I agree."

He ran out. The nurse came forward and said:

> – "I must take Madame's temperature at this hour."
> – "Let me do it," implored Watson, "would you let me, Laurence?"
> – "Certainly."

Every day after she woke up, he helped the nurse with an incomparable dedication.

It had been eight days since the visits of the old doctor had stopped, but he predicted that a relapse would be extremely dangerous for the patient. A relapse! What effort would Robert not deploy to prevent it! Since

Laurence had coughed a lot the day before, he discreetly went to sit next to her and watched her all night. At dawn, however, he felt a faintness, and fought against it. Surrendering at last, he laid his head on the patient's pillow and fell asleep.

In the morning, the young woman's head brushed against something abnormal. She sat up startled and looked around. She was very confused by the situation. Robert, in her bed! The unfortunate man's head close to hers? Her sudden movement woke him up and he apologized:

> – "I heard you cough relentlessly, my darling, and I came. Here, I put a poultice on you that I forgot to remove. It must have damaged your skin. My poor child! My Laurence!"
>
> – "You did this? I didn't know. How to thank you!"
>
> – "I want you to recover without delay, and I must treat you myself. Maning doesn't come by very often anymore. The nurse and I replaced him . . ."
>
> – "Thanks. I would like to go to the garden for a moment, since it is sunny."
>
> – "Ah! No, I protest! You coughed too much last night."
>
> – "Can I go there in three days?"
>
> – "It would still be too soon. Nevertheless, I will ask Dr. Maning for some advice." He grabbed her hand. "Nothing reckless."
>
> – "Thanks, thanks."
>
> – "Poor dear."

Having reconciled with Laurence since her serious illness, Leabrook had come to announce his imminent departure for the United States when he heard Exantus, Watson's servant boy, telling a friend that he was going to perform a *devoir*, an important duty. His attention was piqued.

Exantus had been preoccupied for some time, so he hadn't made the necessary preparations.

He owned *plates-marrassas*, plates dedicated to the divine Marassa Twins,[1] since his girlfriend gave birth to twins, twins he had the misfortune to not spoil from birth (by giving them healthy green vegetables).

The *loas*, Vodou spirits, had cursed him as he hadn't prepared a *mangé les anges*, a *mangé marassa*, or any other food offerings for the divine spirits of the Marassa Twins in a while.[2]

Exantus, a penniless peasant, already destitute, had struggled to find three hundred gourdes[3] to accomplish a *devoir*. A great duty! And it was barely enough.

The day of his departure to the countryside, Exantus bought all the utensils and ingredients he needed: half a dozen small hollow dishes made of terracotta, filled with clairin, sweets, pistachios, corn, etc. At the pharmacy, he also bought "repelling waters," "expedi," "stay-away," "repugnance" . . . as well as "stay-here" magic powders.[4] The latter was to bring Sor Tiza, his girlfriend, back. She was not very faithful.

Last, but not least, he bought madras handkerchiefs, red scarves, several shades of camisoles, depending on the *loas's* tastes. Over the past year, Sor Tiza had bought several hens and two big goats for this sacred duty.

Leabrook asked Exantus to grant him permission to attend this *candianhoun*, this ceremony, in the company of his chauffeur (who was an Americanized Haitian).

The poor peasant was quite happy to have a white man, a citizen of the great America, and a well-born Black man as his guests.

The American offered to drive Exantus and his precious luggage. What an honor!

---

1. The Marassa Twins, or the Marassa Jumeaux, are divine twins in Vodou. They are the personification of divine power and human impotence. They may also be invoked to guard children.
2. In Haitian Vodou, food offerings such as cake would be required to appease the Marassa Twins.
3. Approximately US$45 in 2023.
4. A variety of Vodou materials.

When Sor Tiza saw her man get out of the automobile, she clapped her hands and called the whole neighborhood so they could witness this great phenomenon: Exantus driven by a white American. Leabrook, who understood Creole very well, said to the woman:

> – *"Moin-minme Vini nan mangé-loi ici."*
> – "Yes, Monsieur, *ça vé di, ouap dòmi tout avec nou . . ."*
> – *"Moin-minme descende, lò ça va fini. "*
> – "Yes, Monsieur. (Then to herself.) *A la nomme gain chance cé Exantis."*[5]

All the half-naked children of the neighborhood came to greet the Yankee and to receive change and sweets. It was funny to see Leabrook and his driver barefoot among the peasants, trying to gain their trust.

Ti Noël, however, was suspicious:

> – *"Messié, moin pas nan calbindage avec blanc . . . pas toléré nomme çaa nan service nou à."*[6]

Angry, Exantus defended "Mouché Libouc," which is how they referred to Monsieur Leabrook:

> – *"Ce Mouché Libouc, zammi moin nan point jou pour li allé."*[7]
> "Mouché Libouc is our friend!"

Since Exantus was the master of ceremony, Brother Ti Noël complied. They brought down the drums from the attics, where they had been hidden because the police did not like to see them, and they liked even less to hear them . . . [8]

---

5. – "I have come to the *loas* offering service."
– "Yes, Monsieur, that must mean you're staying the night with us too."
– "I will return when it's over. "
– "Yes, Monsieur. (Then to herself) That Exantis is one lucky man."
6. Listen! I don't fraternize with white people. Don't welcome him to our service."
7. M. Leabrook is a friend. There's no need for him to leave.
8. During the American Occupation, drums of all kinds were considered contraband, and often seized by the Haitian Gendarmerie.

Small arbors had been built throughout the estate to protect the dancers against the weather.

The ceremony began with the sacrifice of the hens and the goats, followed by their cooking, etc. Soon the *loas*, the Vodou spirits, possessed several people, who opened the dance. Oh! What a rhythm! They danced, drank tafia,[9] sang the *loas* songs, sometimes fast, sometimes slow.

During this time, Leabrook was plying the entire audience with strong whiskey, and during this time he got drunk and mischievous. He photographed the unfortunate participants. Suddenly, he said to Sor Tiza:

> – *"Oy minme fait moin ouè zombi, moin minme ba ou dolà."*
> – *"Ça védi, ou crè nou cé dinmon?"*
> – *"Apa gnou zombi? Li sori Lacayé, hein?"*[10]

He saw a poor sickly woman, eaten away by tuberculosis and lying on a mat.

> – "No," replied Tiza, *"cé pitite Chéristin avec Sor Genette que yo fait mal . . . Yo voyé mò toussé sous li. Si cé pa té papa Guédé et papa Legba qui té moutré nou gnou baingne, li ta mouri déjà."*[11]

Alas! The poor child was to die the next day in the greatest suffering.

> – "So," the American continued, *"nan point zombi ici?"* "There are no zombies around here?"
> – "No, Mouché Libouc," said Sor Tiza, friendly, *"cé mystère nous servi, nous-minme, par permission Grand Maître. Moune qui guin*

---

9. A type of unaged rum made from sugarcane juice.
10. – "You showed me a zombie, so this means I owe you money."
– "So, you think we're demons?"
– "Isn't that a zombie? It came from Lacayé, right?"
11. "No," replied Tiza, "this is the child of Cheristin and sister Genette, who has been cursed . . . They sicced a cough demon on her. Were it not for Papa Guede and Papa Legba who showed us a bath of leaves, she would have already been dead."

Zombi, cé mauve moune qui bésoin yo pou gadé hounfort, ou pou travail nan jadin. Nou pa nan ça, nou-minm . . ."[12]

The American took notes while the naïve Sor Tiza spoke. They were still dancing at three o'clock in the morning when the police arrived, alarmed by the loud noises of the dancers. They were very generous with their baton; police officers do not joke around. Desperate *"sauve-qui-peut"*[13] Screams. Arrests. Many mistreated. Louis-Jean Beaugés.[14] Three wounded: two broken jaws and a broken foot. The food for the *loas* was knocked down and the special plates made for the Marassa Twins ended up broken.

Leabrook, a perfect city rat, and his driver had time to flee, and all the *mama-loas*[15] who could not escape in time were taken to jail. And they got fines!

Exantus swore it would not happen again. Since the *loas* did not protect him even as he served them, he would forsake them. He decided to place himself under the protection of the Christian God, the Lord of all.

Yen Leabrook had the intense desire to write a book for American simpletons, a book that could earn him thousands of dollars in a short time. He swore to write about the zombies of Haiti.

————

Laurence's priest came to see her one morning, after she was well, and he had a long talk with her. As he left, the pious old man gave her a book: *The Valiant Woman.*[16]

12. "No, Mouché Libouc," said Sor Tiza, friendly, "we serve mystery over here, with the Almighty's permission. People who own zombies are bad people who need them to keep watch of the Vodou shrine or to work the fields. We don't do that over here."
13. French for "run for your life."
14. Haitian mythical figure whose name is an expression for "fierce person."
15. Women associated with certain *loas.*
16. *The Valiant Woman: Conferences Addressed to Ladies Living In the World* (published in French in 1862, translated into English in 1886) by Jean-François Anne Landriot. Landriot (1816–1874) was a French archbishop.

As it was sunny, she went to sit in the garden with a little embroi-
dery. But she didn't sew; instead she thought of the priest's advice . . .
M. Watson's devotion moved her greatly. No one could have cared for her
better than him, even though he would probably have been better off if
she had died. Her soul would not have known the torments that tortured
her now. But he'd saved her.

She had as much gratitude for Robert as she had love for the other
one . . . Would she break her heart and renounce Guy, or like a coward
leave the one who consoled her with his kind words when bits of her lungs
seemed to come out of her mouth? Would she abandon him? This man,
who spent nights watching over her, applying poultices to bring her back
to life? Would she say to him, "I don't love you!" with unequaled cruelty,
like she did on the evening of their wedding?

Laurence raised her eyes to the sky, called God, questioned Him:

> – "My Lord, I am but a frail boat, lead me. Where are you lead-
> ing me? . . . I don't want to know, everything you do will be well
> done, give me a viaticum."

She heard M. Watson take the car out of the garage.

> – "Where is he going at lunchtime?" she wondered.

Suddenly, she saw him coming toward her with a sad face. He spoke to
her without looking at her, fearing that his tears would betray his
emotion:

> – "Laurence, I come to say good-bye. Maybe forever . . ."
> – "Where are you going, my friend?"
> – "Since you are cured, I'm leaving . . . but I don't know where
> I'm going . . ."

He held out his hand to her:

> – "Good-bye!"

She pulled the cord of her kimono, embraced his wrist. Surprised, the American looked at her:

    – "What if this small cord made you a prisoner, my prisoner, and that my soul let out this cry of distress: 'Don't abandon me anymore' . . . What would you do?"

    – "Laurence!"

    – "Stay, yes, stay, your devotion has made a place for you in my heart. I am in your debt, a debt of gratitude. Please stay . . ."

    – "Laurence!" He passed his hand over his forehead. "Am I dreaming? No, I can't . . . I'm a gentleman . . ."

    – "Stay, I'm begging you."

    – "Darling, do not feel that, because I took care of you, you have to sacrifice your youth and your love for me. No, be careful. Your delicate soul would suffer too much if I stayed here . . . You told me yourself that possession without love is the sister of bestiality. Darling, you don't love me, and I wish to spare the one I adore the horror of degrading herself. Good-bye!!" (He takes a step forward.) "Farewell!"

    – "Robert!"

He trembled. It was the first time Laurence had used his first name, and with such a delicious accent! Robert!

    – "You're going to make me believe you don't love me enough to forget" . . . she continued, "to forget my mistakes . . ."

    – "Laurence, Laurence, how I love you! Sorry! Let's forget then . . ."

They both cried, one overwhelmed with happiness, the other with resignation.

The young woman said to herself, like a prayer: "Happiness is of the soul and not of the body. Its source is in devotion, not in enjoyment, in

love and not in voluptuousness..." She had sacrificed her love for
security.

––––––

Mme Watson woke up a few months after her and Robert's reconciliation,
feeling a detestable pain. She couldn't get out of bed and thought she had
gastritis. Her stomach was so upset . . . Without telling her, her husband
called Dr. Maning, who came at once:

> – "Feeling sick, little one?" he asked.

The worthy man kindly listened to her, said a few words in Robert's ear,
smiled and left without prescribing anything. Without prescribing anything! It was strange; Laurence felt terrible!

Laurence, worried, asked:

> – "Doctor, you are not prescribing me anything? And you're
> leaving?"

As the old scholar was already in the corridor. He turned around:

> – "Walk along this path five or ten times a day. Enjoy the fresh
> air of your garden and then, when you're not too tired, sew pretty
> little nightgowns . . . Good-bye!"

"What a fool!" thought Laurence. She complained to her husband, who
laughed at her words. Distraught, the young woman stood up and said to
him:

> – "Do you love me so much less today that you make fun of me?
> And because I am sick? You surprise me . . ."
> – "My dear . . . Your illness is the prelude to so much happiness!"
> – "It's true?" she asked, suspecting the truth.
> – "Maning told me we will soon be three."

Robert took her in his arms and laid her down again, as he would have done with a baby:

   – "There. I don't want you to worry, my love. How happy we're going to be, huh? Say, Laurence?"

   – "It's true . . ."

A gleam of resignation mixed with an imprecise happiness passed over the deep, blue eyes of the future mother.

———

April! April! The sun shines in the foliage, and the flowers, wide open, shed their scent in puffs, following the wind.

April! Such sparkles in the golden corn cobs, in the blonde and dark hair, in the hearts! Oh! April in the Antilles! April in Haiti!

April! What banter! So many pranks! So many pleasant surprises! April! Hope for the young, consolation for the old! Dear April, you evoke for people pretty aquariums where cute pink fish dance, eager for space! April, youngest son of Spring, who doesn't love you?

Instead of a beautiful little fish, Laurence gave birth on an April morning to a charming baby who filled the room with her cries.

   – "Oh! How pretty she is," exclaimed the young mother when the nurse handed her the baby after the first bath.

Robert timidly approached the bed:

   – "Thank you, Laurence, thank you for giving me so much happiness. You love me? It's our April Fool's Day. Are you happy?"

   – "Oh, very. I love her. She is worth living for."

He asked the nurse for permission to hold the baby for a moment, to kiss her little feet, her little hands, her nappy:

   – "My daughter! My beloved child! My everything!"

Then, apologizing to his wife:

– "My love, don't be jealous ... Do you still feel tired? You no longer blame her for torturing you?"

– "My God, no, I forgot all my suffering as soon as she cried. I would endure these pains all my life to make her happy."

– "It's true? It's true? How grateful I am!"

– "Thanks, my dear. Thank you!"

– "Listen. If you don't mind, I would like to call her Eveline."

– "Done. I quite like this name."

– "My little one, I'm not imposing it on you, but I would be very happy ... if you have not already settled on another name, of course."

– "No, I promise ... why do you like this name so much?"

– "It's my mother's. I told you once, I think."

– "Really? It's funny, I don't remember that."

– "She will be happy, come on!"

– "I believe you."

– "I bet Myrtana is the baby's godmother ..."

– "And I am sure Yen is the godfather ..."

– "You are correct!"

– "And so are you."

– "Laurence! How happy I am, I want to forget everything that isn't this child and you ... Let's love one another, us three, without sharing."

– "You selfish man, if only your mom could hear you ..."

– "She would forgive me ... Won't we go and see her as soon as Eveline is able to bear the journey? Will you love my mom?"

– "Of course. I want to know her."

– "Dear old mother! She will spoil all three of us!"

– "Oh! Yes, yes, I hope so ..."

– "Let me take Eveline again ..."

- "I beg your pardon, Monsieur," said the nurse, "the child is tired."
- "Alright, alright, I'll leave her, but can I kiss her?"
- "Of course."
- "Oh! If I could make myself very small, I would lie next to her in the crib. (He laughs.)"

———

Leabrook returned from the United States, where he had made a fortune after publishing a book as mendacious as it was daring: *The Zombies of Haiti.*[17] The zombies of Haiti?

Yen walked the Haitian countryside at all hours of the day and night; he never encountered an "evil spirit," he never felt frightened, not even in the midst of the many peasants he so frequently bribed so they would let themselves be photographed as savages, as "zombies," and whatnot. He slept and ate in their huts without worry.

Yen Leabrook knew well that zombies were mythical creatures, given thousands of powers by African superstitions. He knew the worship of Vodou was forbidden in Haiti and that those who transgressed this interdiction were severely punished. But he had to make money, and for that, he had to lie in order to deceive the American simpletons who believed everything, even the worst nonsense:

He saw zombies in Haiti.

The *mange-marrassas*, or ceremonies, that the naïve like Exantus performed were jokes in which the diabolical spirit had no part.

Everywhere, all over the world, when hysterics get drunk, get excited, they misbehave. It is the same with the uneducated country people who still believe in mysteries and who gather to drink, sing, and dance lustfully. Many of these unfortunate people realize their error eventually, and join the Catholic religion, or Protestantism, or Adventism, or Methodism, etc.

17. This invented novel alludes to William Seabrook's *The Magic Island* (1929).

One must go to the countryside of Jacmel, Léogâne, in the confines of Kenscoff,[18] etc., to see the number of believers who dream of having their children take Communion. Supported by the propagation of schooling in the most remote towns, and by the catechization of the masses, Haiti will be successful in sweeping away the remaining superstitions still alive in the countryside.

But then, let's say right away that all countries have their beliefs, their superstitions, their magicians . . . Some have plenty: gangsters, professionals in fraud and kidnappings, like Al Capones, and John Dillingers . . . [19] The belief in the evil eye, the *mal d'ioc* in Creole, is a popular superstition in Italy . . .

As soon as he returned from the States, Yen Leabrook ran to his friends, the Watsons, to tell them about his triumph:

– "My book has been translated into French, Spanish, and German . . . I sent you two copies. Did you receive them?"

– "My friend," said Laurence, "what an imagination you have! What a tissue of lies!"

– "My book invaded, in just a few days, the shelves of all the buildings of New York. And it crossed the ocean with the same rapidity."

– "Lots of dollars?"

– "Fifty thousand net profit . . . in six months."

– "Why do you so hate poor Haiti?"

– "I don't blame the country. On the contrary, I love it."

– "And you wrote all those lies about it?"

– "To make money. I would write about America itself if I could profit from it. Some said, like Vespasian[20] when he deemed it necessary to introduce a urine tax on public toilets, that the money had

18. Haitian communes.
19. American gangsters.
20. Vespasian (9–79 A.D.) was a Roman emperor. He imposed a tax on the distribution of urine collected from public urinals.

no odor. I would add that it should not have any loyalty or fidelity either. It must leave safes or pockets to go to others without regret, and no matter how."

– "I like your sincerity, Yen. You are a good rascal . . . more rascal than your godfather, the Chinese whose name you bear."

He laughed and spoke:

– "It is my opinion, and I don't mind sharing it. But I'm not useless like Joseph Prudhomme.[21] I write books, I earn a living. And then my books are . . ."

– "Lies . . . it's true."

– "My books make money. So?"

– "Here, look at my daughter. Isn't she beautiful?"

– "Very. And rich, huh? Your husband, Robert, will likely inherit millions . . ."

– "Let's not talk about money, you know very well it disgusts me . . ."

– "You are wrong: in life if there is support, it is money. A resistance? Money! A springboard? Money . . ."

Robert, knowing the young woman's sensibility and his own (he had ceased to place dollars above everything, even friendship), exclaimed:

– "Yen, I know you have only one love, that of family, a racial prejudice. I educated my heart at Laurence's school."

– "So, you have stopped being American? I can't imagine a son of the Stars and Stripes without the intense desire to possess millions if he has none, or to earn more by any means if he already has some . . ."

– "Millions don't always lead to happiness, my friend . . ."

---

21. French caricature of the nineteenth century, meant to represent the bourgeoisie.

Robert said suddenly: "Oh, I have some good news!"

– "Come on, come on . . . your reluctance offends me . . ."

– "Do you know you are my kid's godfather?"

– "I assumed so," Yen said. "I will give her a gift."

– "Thrilled?"

– "Of course. We are going to have a lot of fun, eh, my old friend, the day of the baptism!"

– "Ah! Yes. Myrtana, with whom you were supposed to share responsibilities, declined this honor. She is a little unwell . . . Laurence is sorry about it."

– "I'm not sorry. We don't get on well together, Mlle Durand and me."

– "So, Mlle Jefferson will be Eveline's godmother."

– "All right! She is supposed to be quite rich. It will bring happiness to the kid."

– "I would like the baptism to take place on April 15. A beautiful date!"

– "Sure, old friend. I'm at your disposal."

– "A beautiful date, isn't it, Laurence?" continued Robert.

She nodded:

– "Yes, it is."

– "Bye-bye then," Leabrook said, taking his leave.

Back from Cuba, Guy Vanel was quickly carried away by current political events. He hadn't attempted to see Laurence since the terrible scene in her garden. As a fervent supporter of an honest and very sympathetic candidate, he participated in the presidential campaign, his soul overflowing with a fever of excitement. But his political candidate was defeated. A tough test! After love, it was politics that tortured him . . .

He did not retreat or join the opposing party, as certain politicians systematically do as soon as they are no longer part of a government . . . No, starting in 1930, he wholeheartedly wanted to help his candidate seriously prepare for the 1936 campaign: the last step left in Pandora's box of the presidential elections . . .

It was, of course, a little early, but when one has been defeated, one must figure out how many obstacles must be overcome in order to finish ahead, while the winners count their laurels from the top of the ladder. As a result, Guy Vanel founded *La Lutte Sincère*, a local socio-political newspaper denouncing the abuses certain leaders may have committed (and who does not commit any?) and making useful suggestions to them.

Well-educated collaborators ensured the smooth running of the daily publication which, despite its youth, had more than five hundred paying subscribers (among which a hundred never paid) but had three or four thousand readers.

La Lutte Sincère defended the interests of the working class, so despised by the Haitian elite. It demanded that, alongside the canteens that distributed "meat" to poor children, others, many others, should be established to share freely the bread of knowledge.

There were still too many children in the streets during school hours, laboring in the homes of their "masters." Too many ten-year-old children, who will be men soon enough, were condemned to remain ignorant and incapable of self-sufficiency. There are illiterates everywhere, even in France (let us take a moment to say that the completely illiterate European peasant is as backward as ours), but the number of those who have never attended school in Haiti was astronomical.[22]

Guy Vanel loved journalism. He put his whole soul into it, but his newspaper rankled his opponents. They plotted against it. They all thought they recognized themselves between the lines of his belligerent articles. They denounced him to the authorities as a troublemaker. They did so much and so well that, one morning, *La Lutte Sincère* was nothing more than a sad memory . . . "We continue to replace one sadness with another . . ."

---

22. Then, the literacy rate was estimated at 5 percent and school enrollments at 3 percent.

In 1930, three large organizations were founded in Port-au-Prince: Exequi, Deputare, and Gerousia. Vanel became an elected member of the second, but the shared premises brought together the members of these three associations. They discussed major social, economic, and political issues. Having solved these issues, the members organized various literary sessions focused on dramas, comedies, and tragicomedies.

In just a few months, they successively put together *Le Roi s'Amuse* by Victor Hugo, as well as *Le Roi se Promène*, *Les Discours de Duracé*, *Les Millions de ma . . . Pauvre Mère Noire*, *Le Budget des Travaux de Monsieur Toulmonde*, and *Monsieur Joseph Prudhomme*. These plays, all written by Haitian authors except the first, were the most successful. Never had theatrical performances attracted so many people in Haiti. As for the comedy *Monsieur Joseph Prudhomme*, it brought tears of joy to the most hardened. Encouraged by the ever-renewed enthusiasm of the spectators, the actors promised to play it continually until 1936.

They hadn't lied. Not a week passed during which this hilarious play was not being performed at the "Milk-Colored House" Theatre or at the one of the Rue du Chemin Faisant des Corbillards.

One day, a member of Gerousia invited colleagues from the three associations to an unconventional day trip to Mariani.[23] He wrote on each invitation: "We shall not talk about politics."

The day dawned, smiling and promising, so the guests swore to enjoy it to the fullest . . . Oh! To lie down in pajamas on the green and fresh grass, where snakes never nest. To be *oneself*, free from any conventional artifice, and to have the strong conviction to be better today than yesterday! To contemplate the undulating blue sea, on which glide small boats not unlike those paper ships children make, these fragile vessels entrusted to the water of the gutters.

Go to the shore, stick your bare feet in the warm sand, collect pretty pebbles with varied shapes and delicate shades! Let your eyes get lost in

23. A costal town about twenty-five miles outside of Port-Au-Prince.

the infinity of the vast garden, admire the palm trees' stems which majestically rise like the colonnade of a cathedral!

To think of the loved one abandoned for a whole day, with the consoling certainty to find her more lovable, more amorous upon one's return! To forget Haitian politics for a whole day, to believe that this sweet idleness may last forever! What a memorable picnic!

This is what the one-day vacationers had dreamed of. They were delirious.

After their arrival, they kept their word until noon. They joked, recited verses, sang... But as soon as they finished enjoying their Duracé[24] cocktails, they became agitated, excited. Their tongues, too, as one can imagine. They became *duracéennes*.

Lunchtime turned into a fraternal feast, and governmental and political opponents shared sentimental confidences.

Destilus suddenly exclaimed:

> – "Gentlemen, I have been promised a government job, and if the ministry does not give it to me, I am starting a newspaper. I need a Mathie."
>
> – "A Mathie?" asked Charitable.
>
> – "It's the name of the American who issues checks... they are the checks themselves."
>
> – "Oh! It's true. Do you want to become a 'check-servant'"?
>
> – "Be patient, old friend. There are a lot of people to place, and the Minister must," replied Jacquemin, "help first those who helped him during the bad days... out of their own pockets."
>
> – "But I'm starving, can't you see? And I spent all my money 'fixing' the elections. I am going to establish a newspaper, I'm telling you..."

---

24. Duracé was an eccentric who gave do-you-want-some-here-you-go speeches, often on the graves of people he did not know... (Note included the original text.)

– "It's not a bad idea, Destilus. We must help the government in any way we can during its six-year lease of the Republic."[25]

– "Ah! Didn't you guess, Jacquemin, that my daily will be a newspaper in the opposition? I just need to launch it, and I'll be set . . . you'll see."

During this period, an endless number of newspapers and magazines sprung up in Haiti.

– "That might be true. Journalism has become the biggest industry in the country, as well as a serious threat," concluded Jacquemin. "People don't like being . . . *badine min, badinin pa péché.*"[26]

A mean voice rose unexpectedly:

– "A serious threat to whom? I have friends in high places."

It was Chanterelle who had just spoken.

– "So," said Latour, "you support President Sténio Joseph Vincent?[27] You are now a 'Vincentician'"?

– "Thank God, yes! I've always been. Ever since I was in my mother's womb . . ."

Latour protested:

– "That's not true, Chanterelle, you use to be a 'Sannonist'[28] like me. I met you every day at Pauleus."[29]

– "It's true," concurred Charitable.

25. The Haitian presidency was initially fixed at a six-year term.
26. Translated from Haitian Creole: "I'm only kidding, kidding is not a sin."
27. Sténio Joseph Vincent (1874–1959) was the president of Haiti from November 18, 1930, to May 15, 1941.
28. Horace Pauleus Sannon (19870–1938) was a Haitian presidential candidate in 1926 and in 1930.
29. A bar named after Horace Pauleus Sannon (1870–1938), who was a Haitian historian, politician, and diplomat.

– "I also went to Pradel's every evening during the electoral campaign," said Jérôme, "my seat during dinner was next to Chanterelle's who, as a regular, encouraged me to eat well and drink well."

Jégu exclaimed:

– "Chanterelle was a 'Mayardist'[30] just like me, I can assure you."
– "Impossible," said Millebranches, "I saw my friend Chanterelle
carrying Nau's shoes from the basin where he had forgotten them,
to his bedroom."

Price-Mars,[31] very courteously, affirmed:

– "You are wrong, my dear colleagues, this man is my most loyal
friend. Don't misrepresent him like that."
– "I am sorry to correct you, my dear colleague and my friend,
but Chanterelle is like an extension of myself," declared David
Jeannot to Price-Mars.

General Thézan,[32] who had listened in silence, got up abruptly, opened
his eyes, which sometimes were feline-like but also contained so much loyalty, and said, putting his hand on his heart:

– "Here is Chanterelle's man. Me, my friends!"

The guilty party was silent. Hudicourt eyed him up. Loubeau did the
same. Justin Latortue was furious and nervously adjusted his glasses.

– "Defend yourself," commanded Henry. "We will say that you,
you are a 'toutiste,' an 'everythingist'! A man who is all things to all
people . . . and this will make you a bad man, political filth . . ."
– "I have nothing to say," whined the tall man.

---

30. Constantin Mayard (1882–1940) was a journalist, a politician, and a main contributor to *Le Temps*, a daily Haitian newspaper.
31. Jean Price-Mars (1876–1969) was a Haitian physician, teacher, writer, and
statesman.
32. Emmanuel Thézan (dates unknown) was a candidate for the Haitian presidency
in 1930.

- "Defend yourself . . . Are you really a 'toutiste'?"

- "Well, fine, I played you all . . . to have better luck. But then, were the candidates for the presidency loyal to each other? Didn't they attack each other? First with small sticks then with swords? I took everything I could from these naïve men. . . . In politics, you must know how to get money from people's wallets. Yes, I skinned Pradel, but he is tough."

His imposture knew no limits.

- "And I tricked Professor Pradel like the fox tricked the crow;[33] I got plenty of cheddar! Ten dollars today, twenty tomorrow, and add to that nice roasted chicken legs, good wine, fresh green vegetables, nice cigars, and sweets. He didn't seem to mind.

"As for Mayard, I quickly abandoned him the day he was disgraced without pity in the public opinion . . . Could I be more royalist than the king? or rather more 'Mayardist' than Mayard?"

- "You are a wretch!" said Price-Mars and Jeannot together.

Thézan looked at him with a smile worth a gunshot. Paultre, his hand to his chin, stared at him with the commiseration of a pastor. Then, with bloodshot eyes, Chanterelle stood up and said:

- "I was hungry! I haven't worked for the past eight years, sometimes I did odd jobs at the police station . . . but . . . living is a mystery to me. My family is used to going two days without bread. To be a 'toutist' is to be flexible for a living? Well, I was a great gymnast! My wife and daughters tried to do work. Alas! They lost their little savings, and what savings!

"My two sons are in business, but their salaries are wasted in cafés, dance halls, and luxurious Dominican and Haitian brothels. When I saw the candidates throwing away so much money (at least

33. Reference to the fable " The Fox and The Crow" (1668) written by French poet Jean de la Fontaine (1621–1695).

those who had some), I thought it would be only right to enjoy some before it was frittered away in endless extravagant, pantagruelian dinners, in the purchase of quickly withered flowers, and what else?

"I was hungry, and when you suffer, all trades are good. Isn't political wisdom a kind of compromise between opposing opinions? Aren't today's 'Vincentists' yesterday's 'Bornoists,' 'Pradelists,' 'Marsists,' 'Mayardists,' etc.?[34] When you're a beggar, you must make the best of the circumstances. So!"

Furious, Vanel exclaimed:

– "Was Elie Guérin happier than you? Tell me! He knew all the deprivations, all the vexations, however . . ."

– "Oh sure," admitted Chanterelle, "Guérin was a saint, I was not. To stop me from doing *this*, he paid me out of his own pocket, he who had nothing! If he had ten gourdes, he would give me eight, thinking that since he was single, he could endure the lack of comfort, hunger . . . but I have a wife and children. But did his honesty get him? . . . Isn't he dead? Leaving his country under the Yankee boot and the striped flag?"

– "Why didn't you have the strength to die when you should have?" said Vanel sadly. "Some say you denounced your compatriots to the Americans right after they arrived in the country. Some even say that if the Provost Marshal[35] mistreated so many honest people, it is thanks to your denunciations . . . and that you are still to this day colluding with the Yankees . . . Ah! Chanterelle, we can forgive everything but that."

– "It's not true! Oh, oh, oh! Oh! My friends, oh!"

---

34. Followers of various Haitian political figures.
35. The head of military police.

– "Wretched man!" cried out the young Jean Brierre in a sob, while the talented columnist Stéphen Alexis took notes for the newspaper *Le Matin*.[36]

Professor Seymour Pradel arrived in a hurry and said with a rhythmic but playful young voice, a cigar in his mouth:

– "What's up, old friend? What have you become since the famous battle, my dear Chanterelle? Gentlemen, sorry I'm late."

– "I'm in trouble, M. Pradel . . . ," murmured Chanterelle.

– "Ah! Yes, no 'place' for you, huh? Come to my house, there is always room for friends like you."

– "I need . . ."

– "Money," he whispered in his ear. "I know. One more reason to visit me!"

– "I went bust on November 18 . . . you understand . . ."[37]

– "I understand. I understand."

Someone risks:

– "There is the discrete charity fund of the National Lottery."

– "I would rather rely on M. Pradel to find me a place . . . ," concluded Chanterelle.

Accustomed to being duped, the Prince de la Jeunesse, the Prince of Youth, shook the hand extended out to him, squeezed it warmly, did a pirouette, said a kind word to everyone, and ran toward a checkerboard table where a few members were waiting for him.

Henry, the youngest of the picknickers, continued:

– "Is it true you denounced your brothers to the occupier?"

– "On the contrary, my friends," answered Chanterelle, "before the Americans began beating us down, so around . . . well, before they

36. Founded in April 1907 by Clément Magloire, *Le Matin* was a daily newspaper published in Haiti.
37. November 18, 1930, was the end of the Louis Eugene Roy presidency.

took over the legislative chambers, I dedicated myself to helping with the difficulties that arose between Haitians and Yankees. I swear to you. I am the one who told the High Commissioner[38] to invite some more or less important Haitians to the big banquet he gave before leaving . . . I can prove it to you, that's a fact. But our countrymen, haughty and insolent, declined the invitation with unexpected brusqueness and astonishing bluster. It made me angry, that I can say. Jacques Roumain,[39] Antonio Vieux,[40] Max Charlmers, etc., men who ought to have been admitted to such high places, thought they could intimidate the Honorable M. Russell by returning the invitation to him with forceful insults. Such a rare insolence!"

Monsieur Fouchard Martineau, whose intransigence was well known, stood up and said:

– "Gentlemen, I'm disgusted . . . Chanterelle is like an emetic . . ."[41]

Nau, Mars, and Jeannot, indignant, cried out together:

–"Enough! My friend, enough!"

But he continued, God knew why, his mouth seemingly controlled by a machine:

– "Gentlemen, the country is lost. I am one of those who agree with Moton:[42] nothing can be done without the help of the white

38. John H. Russell (1872–1947) was a Major of the U.S. Marine Corps who was appointed American High Commissioner to Haiti with the rank of Ambassador Extraordinary. He served in this position until 1930.
39. Jacques Roumain (1907–1944) was a Haitian author, political activist, and diplomat.
40. Antonio Vieux (1904–1961) was a Haitian lawyer and diplomat.
41. A substance that causes vomiting.
42. Robert Russa Moton (1867–1940) was an African American who served as second principal of the Tuskegee Institute. He was chairman of the U.S. Commission on Education in Haiti, which advocated for close and continued ties between Haiti and the United States.

man. I am against 'Haitianization.' It is the prelude to a civil war ..."

– "Excuse me," said Thézan, "this word is improper, we have never stopped being Haitians. Instead, why not say that you are against the 'de-Americanization' of Haitian public services? Please, go on."

– "Well, either. Americans gave us peace, they gave us ... work. They developed our national industry more than we ever did ..."

– "Work?" asked Jacquemin, astonished, "national industry?"

– "Yes ... now we make wonderful hats. The president wears one of them. We make sisal bags, stoves ... a lot of things."

– "Better left unsaid," added Vanel, "it's true."

Telemachus was silent, but his face showed how sickened he was.

– "My friends," Jérôme said suddenly, "that's how we forget politics today? So much for a pleasant picnic. We did not keep the promise we made to our colleague Jacquemin. You should all get a ticket!"

– "We lied. How do you expect politicians to spend a whole day without talking about politics?" Vanel asked. "Here comes the night," he continued, "we will now leave, but not without thanking our colleague Jacquemin for giving us the opportunity to know Chanterelle's true colors. He is an unworthy man. He did, however, follow the advice of Protagoras,[43] who said somewhere: I would rather show myself as I am than be unmasked ... We must be grateful to him for his frankness. Gentlemen, I will tell you that Chanterelles are not rare in this world, but it is difficult to find in abundance some Jacksons, Jn-Charles Presoirs, Lallemands (nicknamed good-boy), Georges Sylvains, Elie Guétins, Nossirehl Lhérissons, Rosalvo Bobos, Gandhis, Sandinos, Pastor Albert, Raymonds

43. A Greek sophist philosopher (490–420 B.C.E.).

Cabèches, and so and so forth.[44] Dear friends, if I weren't afraid of startling your modesty, I would continue the list."

– "Stop," said Trafalgar, "you might regret it . . . There are so many people who have spent their lives being honest and who, one day, are intoxicated by gold, honors, and what else? They suddenly become more a 'rascal' than the most hardened scoundrels. Plus, a serious man is not always an honest man. Since actions speak louder than words, they are the ones who will glorify us or damage us after our death."

Night came, a pink night, hesitant, frightened, distraught, a night which advanced and stopped, conquered yet triumphant . . . Suddenly, it chased away the persistent twilight which had tried to fight it. The night was beaming.

Pink just a moment ago, and then blue . . . Queen Nature was very capricious; she wanted to adorn herself with all the pretty shades in a single evening. Merry fireflies, in crowds, left their hiding places and mingled the shine of their diamonds with the phosphorescence of the sea and the sparkle of the moon.

– "Oh! How beautiful!" exclaimed Guy Vanel.

– "How beautiful!" repeated everyone at once.

Suddenly, Vanel felt overcome by a deep sadness: he remembered the sweet evenings he had spent in the company of Laurence Desvallons, when she was his adored fiancée. His eyes filled up with tears.

But immediately, a feeling of pride overcame his sadness and he cheerfully suggested:

– "Shall we leave? It's getting dark . . . oh, the beautiful night!"

---

44. Haitian political figures, with the exceptions of Sandino, a Nicaraguan revolutionary who opposed the American occupation of Nicaragua in the early 1930s.

They packed up and checked the engine and the brakes of each car. A purr here, a purr there, the noise of the doors being slammed shut, the horns, big laughs, a few short amusing sentences people found pleasant even though they could hardly hear anything, followed by a lot of dust as the cars left . . .

At the Léogâne gate,[45] Vanel said:

> – "Gentlemen. I raise my drink to the Hotel Majestie. *Adieu!*"

When raising his glass, Titi, one of the thirty-six members of the Deputare Association, said:

> – "Gentlemen, Senators, and Deputies, allow me to leave the hovel that's my language to climb the building of your eloquence and your morality; I want to ask you to defend the policy of the government and to vote on all the contracts presented to you."
>
> – "Rogue!" said M. Hudicourt, adjusting his glasses.
>
> – "I approve!" cried out Chouchou.

Everyone laughed out loud. Suddenly, Jacquemin came up with a riddle:

– "I'll bet you a twenty . . . a hundred . . . that you don't know what they're playing this evening at La Gaîté."[46]

All confessed to ignoring it.

> – "Well," said Jacquemin victoriously, "they play *Le Roi se Promène.*"
>
> – "The king walks, long live the king! Hip, hip, hurrah!" said Titi.

———

The Central School of Agriculture had received a makeover. After compensating all the American "experts," they had been fired from Damiens,

---

45. A coastal commune in Haiti.
46. Haitian theater.

thanks to a compromise between the American and Haitian governments.

Watson, as well as Leabrook and his wife, had been thanked. Once the "de-Americanization" had been accomplished, Haitian directors were hired. But a wind of disintegration blew over the school with such violence that Monsieur Charles Moravia, an outraged high-profile journalist, wrote in *Le Temps*:

"We must close Damiens, this gobbler of millions, this unbridled spendthrift . . ."

The poor establishment was successively directed by M. E. Turnier, aide of S. Nicolas and L. Déjoie, Dr. Pressoir, M. Ganot (temporarily) without success. It never reached the goals for which it was created.

Motivated by the disturbing promises of a few politicians, many strikers got into politics and aspired (despite their youth) to the highest public offices. As leaders of the movement which had changed so many things, they chanted, "The youth make the future!"

Two or three were hired by the government of Mr. Rog, some returned to Damiens, and the rest went adrift, having missed their vocation and being mistreated by unemployment.

The strike of the students of Damiens was perhaps necessary, indispensable, because Freeman had not known how to tell himself (like Nietzsche) that there is a shame in being happy in the presence of so much misery. He displayed his luxury and his finery in front of the suffering children. It was wrong. He treated them haughtily, like pariahs. The students of Damiens never found in the person of their white director the benevolence, the protection, the honest and good leaders use toward their subalterns. Oh! Never.

Let's say it once more: the strike was perhaps indispensable, because it freed Damiens from Freeman, who seemed to have signed a lifetime lease with the Republic. But if the system made some people happy, it was not the young people . . .

What an irony! The eternal affair *bourique travaille, choual galonnin.*[47]
A strike? A beautiful and necessary mess, but . . .

Because they did not return to Damiens, many strikers who should be great agricultural engineers, valuable technicians, were nothing but poor unemployed people without a profession, in search of a public office. Illustrious failures!

It is true that going back to Damiens remained a very delicate problem for a while, given the lack of discipline that reigned there.

Since the strike, an evil genius transformed the Central School of Agriculture into a Gordian knot[48] for the government. They did everything to untie it.

The school changed its name to make people think it had new masters. It was baptized the "National Service of Agricultural Production and Rural Education." Such a big name! But alas!

Last but not least, Belgium gave birth to a son, and Haiti adopted him. He crossed over the Atlantic, and the little black island opened its arms to him:

"Monfils! Monfils, save Damiens!"

Did M. Monfils do a better job than his predecessors? Only government inspectors can answer that. What I do know, is that this Belgian man is one of the tallest men on earth . . . a colossus.

Mme Leabrook, having lost her job, felt desperate, despite the large compensation Haiti had been forced to give her and the other fired white experts and employees, before the end of their . . . lease. She shared her grief with the Watsons, crying.

Robert, suddenly seized with remorse, exclaimed:

– "My friend, let's be honest and admit that our country has been without pity for poor Haiti. Before leaving for the United States, I

47. "The donkey labors, the horse gets the glory."
48. A complex or unsolvable puzzle.

hope to give to all the Haitian charities ... I will at least have the satisfaction of having given something back to this small country: part of the funds America unduly stole from it. Isn't that true, my dear Laurence?"

– "I applaud you for your noble project, my friend," said Mme Watson.

A deep melancholy had crept into the young woman's gaze; it pained her to speak of the misfortunes of Haiti, as these thoughts were associated with those of Guy Vanel.

– "A man ousted and whining is very ridiculous," thought the young man. He'd looked for appeasement in the activities of Gerousia, since he was a member of the organization, and in journalism, the fourth estate ... The fourth power! How ironic in a country under siege.

Guy Vanel was not as unhappy as Laurence had assumed. No. His pride as a Haitian, as an insulted Black man, had prevailed over his love.

After the closure of his newspaper *La Lutte Sincère*, he founded *Le Défenseur*, which lived for a very short time. He then asked for hospitality in the columns of friends and continued to fight. When M. Sténio Vincent put Port-au-Prince under siege, almost all the independent newspapers disappeared, *Le Défenseur* included. Vanel sheathed his pen and left.

(Monsieur Vincent, the current president of the Republic of Haiti, is the honorable citizen who, on February 11, 1930, shouted in an indignant voice at the end of the mass held in Notre-Dame Basilica:

"Long live freedom!" in honor of the victims of the Cayes massacre[49] perpetrated by Yankee troops against a crowd in front of which M. Moravia Morpeau was giving a speech)

49. On December 6, 1929, U.S. Marine battalions in Les Cayes opened fire on 1,500 peaceful protestors.

Many months after the "de-Americanization" of Damiens, nothing had been accomplished.

———

It is the end of 1933. Eveline is now two and a half years old. Her father wants the most beautiful life for her. She already speaks French relatively well; she understands English as well as Creole.

Oh! The little rascal! When Watson anxiously asks her: "Whom do you prefer?" she mischievously replies, "Daddy." She knows this answer always pleases him, without causing grief to her mother, who is not jealous.

She not only confesses that she adores her father, but she also throws herself into his arms, kisses him and kisses him again, snuggles against his heart and stays there, sometimes until she falls asleep. And when she wakes up, she finds herself in the same place.

Robert doesn't trust anyone to take his child out for walks. Oh! It's a pleasure to see a man and child together, walking, stopping, lying on the grass, running after dragonflies, with the same enthusiasm.

Eveline also loves long car trips. Often, M. Watson and she leave in the morning and do not return until the evening, after visiting one or two provinces.

Laurence sometimes protests. She is afraid of so much happiness:

– "Robert, it's wrong to satisfy all the desires of this child, no matter how extravagant they may be," says Laurence.

– "Let me spoil her . . . in case I should be . . . 'absent.' Oh yes, the great absence from which no one can return, and which causes so much pain in the hearts of those who remain. It is so cruel and treacherous. I want Eveline to be the happiest little girl, just as I would like you to be the happiest . . . ," says Robert.

– "I am happy, my dear, I show my happiness badly, but . . ."

– "Laurence, dear Laurence! How to thank you for being the mother of the angel that is Eveline. I love this child more than anything." (He apologizes.) "Don't be angry when I say more than anything in the world. My love is stronger than me."

That day, Watson gathered some friends to celebrate his birthday.

The reception coincided with the news that Utah, after Pennsylvania and Ohio (once terrible adversaries of alcohol), had just voted in favor of a wetter regime . . . This news was an event! The American settlement in Haiti welcomed it like the Messiah.

Yen Leabrook and his wife exulted. Finally! They were going to be able to drink as much as they wanted without hiding . . . And, when they returned to the United States, they would no longer need to use tricks when the demon of intemperance gripped them, to end up drinking some adulterated alcohol, some eau de cologne.

What a delight to be able to bid *"Adieu"* to the Volstead Act![50] There will be fewer cases of drunkenness, poisoning, and smuggling with the new regime in the United States.

The American guests arrived with their hearts full of joy at the Watsons's where, for the first time, the Barbancourt rum cocktails would be served legally.

Yen suggested:

– "Let's see who's going to drink the most tonight . . . Haiti has a new rum, gentlemen, Nazon Rum . . . I promise it doesn't get you drunk . . ."

– "I'm a record breaker," Jimmy said. "But not this one."

– "All records are glorious," opined the young Dick Jefferson. (He became serious.) "If I weren't so young, I would take part in this competition. But surely, my sister is going to stop me, but . . . M. Benjamin De Casseres[51] claims to be the first American who drank alcohol on federal territory, in front of a witness . . . It was reported that he took his first sip at 3:34 P.M. on the day Utah voted

50. The National Prohibition Act.
51. Benjamin De Casseres (1873–1945) was an American journalist and poet.

to end Prohibition, exactly one minute after the vote of the delegates. Are you going to tell me it's not a good record? All the newspapers talked about it. Well, they'll talk about me now."

– "I won't get drunk," continued Jimmy, "because I read that President Roosevelt[52] asked American citizens to use the right to drink alcohol with moderation, due to the thirteen years of withdrawal. He said:

– "'I trust in the good sense of the American people that they will not bring up themselves the curse of excessive use of intoxicating liquors, to the detriment of health, morals, and social integrity.

"'The objective we seek through a national policy is the education of every citizen toward a greater temperance throughout the Nation.'"[53]

Yen said, mockingly:

– "Bravo Jimmy, you are a good and honest citizen. A total, pure American, as we say here. Me, I'm Chinese . . ." He laughed.

They were playing bridge when Watson said to his wife:

– "Laurence, I received a letter for you this morning. I forgot to give it to you. It comes from Martinique . . ."
– "Ah! Thanks." (Turning to the players.) "Do you mind?"

She read it.

– "Robert," she said suddenly, "is it a dream? Someone wrote to tell me he is my late mother's great uncle and that he will bequeath me his fortune since he has no children . . ."

---

52. Franklin Delano Roosevelt (1882–1945) was the thirty-second president of the United States.
53. Extract from the Presidential Proclamation acknowledging the repeal of the Eighteenth Amendment and Prohibition, signed by President Roosevelt on December 5, 1933.

– "Bravo! Bravo! Long live the millions of the old man!" screamed the excited guests. They all wanted to read the letter at the same time. The interested party remained calm. A dark presentiment tormented her . . .

Dick Jefferson, an avid philatelist, picked up the envelope, saying:

– "I want the stamps." (He was surprised,) "Oh! The envelope still contains something . . ."

A photograph fell out . . . Surprise! Shouting!

– "The photo of a n——?" exclaimed Mme Leabrook.
– "Of a n——?" echoed the Americans with repugnance.

All eyes were on Watson, who took the portrait, examined it carefully, and read the dedication Monsieur Luc Pausis had written to his great-niece:

– "In memory of an old uncle who offers you an honestly earned fortune. Luc Pausis."

Laurence, without malice, suddenly said:

– "This must be a mistake. My father never told me that my mother had African blood in her veins."
– "It's still a big blow if that's true, for both you and Robert," Yen agreed. "The Watson family will not accept this union."

The poor husband was silent, harassed by his friends' comments, his heart full of love for his wife and child, his soul tormented by the sad revelation. With his teeth, he tore his handkerchief . . .

– "My friends," Jimmy advised, "let's have mercy on Mme Watson, let's promise to keep this a secret."

Laurence proudly told him:

– "No, Monsieur, keep your pity and your silence. I don't need it. What's the misfortune or shame in having in my veins a few drops of the blood of these men whose genius and courage have surprised the whole world? I'm talking about Toussaint Louverture, Dessalines, Pétion, François Capois, Boisrond Tonnerre,[54] and so many other illustrious Black men. Their story is beautiful, I know it and I love it. I feel in no way diminished to learn that among the noble French blood, which courses within me, there is another just as noble. Keep your pity, Monsieur. I am proud to be the daughter of unhappy Africa. However, I must tell you sincerely that I will only believe in the authenticity of my relationship with the old man when my father confirms the origin of my maternal relatives. I admit I don't know much about it, having been motherless when I was born."

– "M. Pausis's letter is, I believe, quite convincing," affirmed Mme Leabrook, harsh, cruel.

And it was true:

"Around 1892, Monsieur Ménard, a Frenchman, came to Martinique, fell in love with my niece, Annite Pausis, and married her. They had two lovely children: Anna and Paul. But alas! After four years of a happy marriage, my niece went mad. M. Ménard was desperate. He went back to France with his family and tried in vain to cure the disease. Many years later, I learned that Paul had left for Canada, where he made his fortune, and that Anna had married M. Raoul. This was around 1909.

"Since then, I had no further news from France. But, having grown old without children, falling sick and thinking I was dying, I wrote to my little

54. Haitian historical figures.

niece to share my plan of bequeathing my fortune to her. Alas! Silence was
her answer. She had been dead for almost twenty years . . .

"I investigated to find her direct heirs, and I learned that Anna Ménard
only had one daughter: Laurence Desvallons, today Mme Watson, etc."

Mlle Jefferson said:

> – "I would kill myself if I were Laurence: she is therefore a white
> negress. Oh! I regret having baptized Eveline."

Myrtana, for whom the atmosphere had become unbearable, got up
abruptly and left. The other guests immediately followed her example, as
it became obvious the fun was over and had been for an hour. After everyone had gone, Watson approached his wife with condescension, the condescension that penetrates, lacerates the body and the soul with the
sharpness of a red-hot iron, the condescension that outrages and embit-
ters more than an offense, and said to her:

> – "My poor darling, because of this letter and this photo I should
> never have married you, and I should not have fathered Eveline . . .
> Ah! But the damage is already done, I will provide you with the
> means to get out of this dilemma, with the least possible
> bruising . . ."
> – "Explain yourself," said Laurence.
> – "I am leaving for the United States, with no hope of returning.
> When you deem that my stay has been long enough to be a cause for
> divorce, you will send me these documents . . . Do you understand?"
> – "I understand," said Laurence.
> – "What do you think?"
> – "I won't try to hold you back, no, this revelation seems to have
> caused a terrible rift between us, but Eveline, this child of whom you
> are the legitimate father, who adores you and who will suffer so
> much because of your absence, will be. . . . is she not enough to
> keep you? Will you have the courage to abandon her? Answer me!

You have no right to flee like a vile deserter from the home you have created yourself. Remember your happiness the day you heard Eveline's first cries in our bedroom . . . Until death do us part? What about these promises? Were they in vain? Oh! How happy I was, eager for peace, to see you, leaning over the little cradle, contemplating this extension of ourselves! Since then, I have only lived for my family . . . you know that. So, it's stupid of you to want to break a chain that you have firmly welded, for such a banal reason. I say to you, like I did once in the garden: 'Stay.'"

Robert replied:

– "I love you as much as I respect you, dear, because I know the temptation you resisted and the struggle you fought to keep the name I gave you intact, despite yourself. Yes, I know all the steps Guy Vanel took to get you back, I know verbatim the conversation he had with you, over there in the orchard, the evening you fell ill. I know everything."

– "Sad man! What are you saying? You spied on me? The servants in whom I had so much trust were only vulgar spies? Minions at your service? Did you do this? Ah! That's horrible!"

– "What do you want? I was jealous . . . Laurence, forgive me . . . I know you are the most honest woman there is, but fate, by putting this drop of Black blood in our veins, made you for someone else . . .

– "For another?" he said in despair, "For another? . . . Oh! I'm going crazy . . . No, I don't want to, I don't want to . . ."

– "Listen, dear, I can stop being your wife, but Eveline. . . . Eveline, how will she cease to be flesh of your flesh?"

– "Don't you think I didn't ask myself this twenty times since the terrible revelation? Do you believe I do not suffer from it? Unfortunately, I cannot continue living with you, without losing my friends' respect and my parents' affection . . . Only God knows how unhappy I will be after our irrevocable separation. Oh! How I pity you, Laurence, how I pity you!"

She felt the start of a revolt:

– "If there is someone to pity, it is you. Let's break it off here."

She made a movement to leave. He held her back, and said in a sad voice:

– "Laurence, if you wanted . . . We could arrange our life so we would be less unhappy after the divorce. How about this: you could retire to the countryside, or better still, to the provinces with Eveline, and there we could see each other very often, without my being the laughingstock of my compatriots. What do you think?"

The young woman sneered, and answered coldly:

– "Is your racial prejudice nothing but a hideous lie? Snobbery? Hypocrisy? Come on! So, are you lying when you said that the Yankee has a real sexual antipathy for the Black race? You lie, you abandon me. I, your worthy wife, and you ask me to become your mistress in the same breath. Well, no, once the divorce is granted, there will be nothing between you and me, do you hear?"

– "Laurence! You refuse to understand the delicacy of my situation . . . If my parents and friends were unaware of the fact . . . but they know! However, according to your religion, you will still be my wife after the divorce. Are you thinking about that?"[55]

She turned her back to him without saying a word. Passing by the table where stacks of cards were spread out—memories from the bridge—she saw the letter and the old man's photo, grabbed it, and left.

---

55. According to Catholic doctrine, the dissolution of a marriage only impacts its legal status in civil law, and has no impact upon one's status in church law.

Robert, left alone, murmured: "Laurence, as Mlle Jefferson said, is really a white negress. What a tragedy! But how much I love her!"

———

The year 1933 had just ended, and everyone had let out a "Phew!" of relief. It had been so fertile in repugnant and painful whimsical events.

Having received news his mother was seriously ill in Cuba, Guy left abruptly, his heart heavy with grief.

A mischievous thief had released a perverse blow on Port-au-Prince that year. It was strange. Very simple things, in appearance, had taken on extraordinary proportions in 1933. This is how a small twirling piece of wood, going up and down a string, appeared out of the blue: the yo-yo. The yo-yo! Where to find words high enough to describe its power? Our humble pen recuses itself. The yo-yo fascinated young and old, poor and rich, so much so that people did nothing but yo-yoing. Some yo-yos were even made of porcelain, gold, diamond, etc., reflecting the rank of their possessors.

People were yo-yoing all over the world. Emperors, kings, presidents, congressmen, senators, dictators, ministers, etc., signed important acts with one hand and yo-yoed with the other. Listen to this:

One day, a man met a friend who was returning quickly home even though he had just left:

– "Are you sick, old friend?"
– "No, I forgot my yo-yo at home."

The first felt his pocket, panicking, then exclaimed:

– "Thank God! I have mine."
– "Lucky you! I envy you . . ."

Reader, to better tell you about some of the events of the year 1933, we must jump from one topic to another. Please forgive this detour.

Listen. In 1933, we saw a reputedly honest American named David P. Johnson, a U.S. Collector of Customs at Port-au Prince, end up at the National Penitentiary after confessing that he was accepting bribes from the Zrike Brothers, rich Syrian American merchants. American leaders took turns hiding him, even sending him to a hospital under the pretext of an illness, but eventually handed him over to Haitian authorities before facilitating his departure to avoid a trial . . .

The honest M. A., a simple customs inspector in Port-au-Prince, took the fall as a scapegoat. He was arrested and thrown in prison for more than a quarter of a century for Johnson's thefts . . . Rightly indignant, M. A. shed all his tears and died, while his wife herself was in agony the entire time.

We saw Japan flood the market with its cheap goods (which sold for quite a lot of money sometimes) without Haiti, saying: "My friend, what do you buy from me? It should be 50/50."

We saw, during this same fatal year, a grassroots movement revolutionize the Legislative Chambers, pushed for a motion of no confidence against the Ministers, broke them apart, and then beget a revolting reconciliation . . .

We saw Minister Lescot[56] discover several communist plots, attempt to expel many undesirable foreigners, and seize some very dangerous documents to safeguard the State.

We saw Port-au-Prince under siege despite the peace; journalists were arrested and sentenced for violating the press laws; former "frank and loyal cooperators" joined the rank of the nationalists to mistreat their own. This is how the supreme authority arrested M. Joseph Jolibois Fils,[57] took him to a madhouse, brutally closed his printing press, and sealed it thereafter.

The year 1933, I tell you, was amazing.

56. Antoine Louis Léocardie Élie Lescot (1883–1974) was a Haitian statesman. He was the president of Haiti from May 15, 1941, to January 11, 1946.
57. Fils was imprisoned for four years and seven months over the course of seventeen incarcerations during the Occupation.

We saw scenes we will never forget. Who would not remember all their life the amount of dollars the country spent on illustrious outings and returns no less illustrious?

We saw, during this fatal year, a tie merchant (to speak like Monsieur Emile Roumer),[58] a weaver as well, going beyond the distaff to become the most skillful policeman in the world . . . It was he who would later tell the police to shoot drivers whose cars made strange noises. Ah! These political renegades, how excellent they are in courtship and how much they exaggerate the meaning of the words:

to serve!

We saw the priests waging a merciless war on the sleeves of women, and they (the women) responded with bold stubbornness.

Listen. A reputed red nationalist, a talkative orator, was giving a lecture one Sunday morning at X, when a member of Gérousia leaned toward him and whispered:

– "Be careful, old friend, don't attack. You might replace Judge Arty who died in France . . . so watch your mouth." Suddenly, the fellow took off a few passages on his little notes and his talk, which had promised to be a stemwinder (always a crowd pleaser), became a poor crippled thing. This eloquent gesture earned him, not Arty's place, but one of the five most influential seats in the Exequi organization.

Whew! The year 1933 was therefore a tragicomedy whose final act was THE AFFAIR OF THE WHITE NEGRESS.

The most galvanized devotions, the most sacred duties, like the most ardent passions, crumble before American snobbery.

Robert, after oscillating between what-will-people-say and his love for Laurence and Eveline, had chosen separation. A month had already passed since the reception of the dreadful letter. Meanwhile, Robert had tried to

58. Émile Roumer (1903–1988) was a Haitian poet.

be sweet to his wife, but he could only be polite. However, he was less indifferent than he appeared. At night, he devoured his pillow, raging against fate.

Eveline, once his adoration, saw him barely an hour a day. Surprised by this sudden change, unhappy, she demanded an explanation. One morning, she said point-blank:

- "Mom, why doesn't Dad go out with me anymore?"
- "He is tired, very tired . . . sick almost."
- "Yes, but he does not stay in bed. When we are tired, we stay in bed."
- "Listen. Well-behaved children do not ask questions."
- "I miss my dad. I love my dad . . ."

Then Mme Watson took her tenderly in her arms, pressed her to her heart, kissed her until she was out of breath, hiding her tears. Robert had gotten into the habit of spending his days outside and sneaking in at night when everyone was asleep. He demanded of these unusual and prolonged absences the oblivion of his unforgetting family. In vain. His brain, his heart, everything about him longed for her.

The Americans monopolized him, bruised his pride. Some made fun of him, like a clown; others pitied him. Such mocking complaints!

The most jeering nicknamed him the "husband of the white negress" . . . This hell lasted a whole month.

After an anxious wait, Laurence received her father's answer. This was the coup de grace for her husband, there was no longer any doubt. She really was Africa's little girl.

Robert, in despair, read the letter because he had, just yesterday and in spite of himself, nourished the sweet hope that they would end up discovering that Luc Pausis (the Black man) was only the namesake of Anna Ménard's old uncle, Laurence's mother . . .

But unfortunately, no! M. Desvallons cannot be wrong nor lie to his daughter: "Yes, your mother was of African origin," he wrote.

How to reconcile his love with his prejudice? The unfortunate man, oppressed by Yankee norms, approached his wife and grabbed her hands. She stiffened:

– "Let me go."

He dominated her and forced her to listen:

– "I'm going crazy, Laurence. I must leave in two hours."
– "Well?" (She looked at him with pride.) "Leave," she said.
– "If you wanted, I already told you, we could organize our life differently. In everyone's eyes, we would be divorced, but we would remain dear spouses in reality, devoted to each other . . . what do you think? I would buy you a beautiful country house, shaded with flowers, near a river whose crystal-clear waters would often reflect our closely entwined bodies, and while together our eyes would rest on the same pretty little things in the countryside. I can already see us in our little home, shaded by flowers and foliage, intoxicated by the scents of the night. Yes, Laurence, there, alone, hidden, we would laugh at the indiscreet rays of the silvery stars, the nocturnal birds, singing of their happiness, of passersby, of everything . . . And, when the evening is charged with mystery, when in the shadows we hear the heart speaking to the heart, when the hand seeks the hand, when in the end each breath becomes intoxicating, we would wander through the surrounding woods . . . Our muffled, hesitant steps would lead us to unsuspected regions, perhaps to happiness . . . Laurence . . . promise me, otherwise I might kill myself. If you could only know, my darling, how many letters I have received from my parents in the past month, and what letters! Here . . ." (He took a sheaf of papers out of his pocket). "Read, you will forgive me later . . ."
– "No, keep your letters, they cannot interest me. I've let you speak without interrupting you, telling myself to be indulgent

toward madmen, but don't think for a second that I share your opinion. No, I don't accept your deal. It disgusts me. A separation is imminent between us, you are right, because we were not made for each other ... I sacrificed my love, my modesty, my life, for a movement of recognition, I don't regret it ... Destiny is a tough adversary, I gambled my happiness and I lost, well, I'll pay ... Your regrets are fruitless and superfluous, dear, leave ..."

– "But ... We can't part without kissing ... I love you, Laurence, Eveline is my whole life ..."

– "Would you be an emulator of Judas? What reason can you possibly have for playing me like this? Affection?"

– "I love you, Laurence ... I adore you ... you know it."

– "Enough!"

– "I love you!" (He falls at her feet, kisses the bottom of her dress.) "My Laurence!"

With courage, she suppressed her emotion, repressed her tears, embittered her words:

– "Your buffoonery tires me ... an actor could not play this role better ... Leave now."

– "Not without a promise ... not without your ... pardon?"

– "A promise, no! My pardon, yes. *Adieu!*"

– "My dear wife! My dear wife! My beloved Laurence and ..."

Eveline, hearing her father's voice, rushed over:

– "Daddy, I am surprising you today ... Take me with you. You go outside every day ... I want to go for a walk with you ... Where do you eat? Let's go ..."

– "In a moment ... Come, come, *chérie* ...," whispered the Yankee.

– "Listen. Why don't you laugh with me? Please laugh!"

– "My poor child."

– "I'm not poor, look at my beautiful silk dress, my pretty brace-let, my big doll. Look, poor kids don't have toys. Mom always tells me to give some to them. Do you want to?"

Robert throws himself on a couch. She gets on his knees, kisses him and snuggles up, eyes closed, against the paternal heart: "My little daddy, take me with you."

Laurence, revolted, exhales her anger:

– "Let her go, let her go, vile hypocrite . . . Enough! Enough! Don't force me to unmask you . . ."

She wants to spare the child the atrocious reality.

– "Go away, Eveline, your dad is going out, he'll be back in a moment . . ."

– "No," said Robert in despair, "let her stay, let me enjoy this last moment, let me look at her to engrave her beautiful image in my memory, let me get drunk on her little caresses . . . Oh! I almost want to stay with her."

– "Wretched man! Who do you think you are fooling?" (Taking the little girl.) "Come, come into my arms, come, my love. You no longer have a father."

He snatched the girl from her.

– "She's mine! I want her and I adore her . . ."

– "Liar. Give her back to me." (She draws him toward her.) "Give me my child."

– "I don't want to, I don't want to, she's my child . . ."

– "I've had enough of your posturing . . . Leave now."

He presses the kid against his heart bitterly, crushes her with mad kisses: "How I love you!"

– "It's not true!" screams the furious mother.

Robert begs:

- "Laurence, be kind to the end, don't reveal the sad truth to her;
protect her illusions, as you tried so well to do just now. Have pity
on the unfortunate child. Here, Laurence, do you want us to disappear without a trace? We can run away from everything and
everyone . . . we can start a life together hidden from everyone . . .
we can . . ."

They heard the horn of the automobile waiting to take him away . . . He
gets up as if electrocuted. He is about to leave, but Eveline has clung to
him, begs for a caress, calls him sweet names . . . She makes him sit down
again:

- "Liline wants to ride you like a horse (the child took his hat).
There, stay with me . . . (she kisses him). *Chérie*, little daddy, daddy
Roro."

He has freed his neck from the two little but tenacious white arms, but
Eveline grabbed hold of one of his legs by letting go of the hat.

- "Take me with you, I want to go in the car with you . . ."
- "Boohoo! Buaaaa!"
- "And then we'll go to Bolté or Simon Vieux to buy sweets
before the walk." (Turning to Laurence:) "Mom, are you coming
too?" (To the maid:) "Chérisna. Chérisna, come with us . . . we'll all
go . . . Quick, quick . . . We'll leave you behind if you don't hurry."

Another blast came from the car parked outside, then two . . . three
blasts . . .

Feeling his emotions were gaining more and more ground, Watson violently detached himself from the kid, crossed the threshold, and
whispered:

- "*Adieu.*"

He ran away, got into the car, and slammed the door. "Daddy! Daddy! Wait for me!" screamed Eveline painfully. She rushed over and stretched both her arms out to him: "Daddy."

His anguished call was lost in the noise the machine made to leave. She let herself fall, made a racket, fumed, but after a minute, she could only see dust on the gray road to Turgeau.

– "What a coward!" whispered the poor mother. Two tears gently ran down her face and joined those of little Eveline.

If Laurence is crying at this moment, it is not because of pain, of love, of regret, or even because of some hatred. Her soul has calmed down to face her great sorrows. She cries because it's human, because departures leave those who stay behind with a feeling of emptiness, which very often hurts.

When the evening came, the young mother pulled herself together, telling herself she must be strong for Eveline, and choose the shortest route to manage, alone, to bring her up well. She would like to take advice from a loved one, from an experienced relative . . . She would like to have someone who protects her, who is devoted to her.

She looks at the large silver crucifix she had prayed to not long ago, during her first days of anguish, and murmurs:

– "God, protect Eveline. If I am guilty toward Guy, punish only me."

———

Mme Watson receives a cablegram, and since then, she has been wearing a mourning dress. Myrtana, her heart swollen with bitter happiness, came to see her this morning and found her very sad:

– "What's the matter, my poor Laurence? A new grief?"
– "Robert died three days ago."
– "Dead? Is it possible?"
– "He killed himself with a bullet to the heart."
– "The unfortunate man!"

– "Myrtana, it's strange, I thought I could remain indifferent to his corpse . . . but the news of his death saddens me infinitely. Here, I'm crying . . ."

– "Beautiful souls forgive quickly. And then, between Watson and you, my poor friend, there was this living hyphen." (She points to Eveline, who is playing in the distance.) "You are free now," she continued, "your trials are over. You will be able to rebuild your life after an appropriate period of mourning . . . Guy must already know that you are a widow."

Laurence stops her friend.

– "Myrtana, I want to devote myself to Eveline, just to her."

– "Laurence dear, don't give up on Love because it hurt you horribly."

(Doesn't it hurt all women?) "Guy never stopped loving you and you love him . . . You will get married . . ."

– "No, no, it's all over between us . . . over, you know that."

– "But you still love him . . ."

– "No, no . . ."

– "My poor friend! Your doubts in confessing your love are very honest, but do not crush your heart, do not lie to yourself. You still love Guy, don't pretend otherwise . . ."

– "That's not true . . ."

– "After your mourning, Guy and you, poor lovebirds, a fog chased away from the regions of Cythera, will return, together, to enjoy the happiness that awaits you, this fleeting happiness that you had so vainly sought."

– "Happiness! But I found it, Myrtana . . ."

– "Please, Laurence . . ."

– "Happiness? But why would I look for it further than in my child's eyes, in her two little arms around my neck, in that sweet word she repeats through her laughter or her tears: 'mom.' Happiness! It is in me when I think that I must turn a chrysalis into a butterfly, when I think that I am the only pillar, after God, on which Eveline can build a house of dreams until she's self-sufficient, until she can gradually separate her pretty dreams from the great human realities. Happiness! I will find it in the struggle to guarantee my daughter's future."

– "Think about it, Laurence. Love is a fluid that seeps everywhere, that attacks everyone, even the most hardened. Of course, it would be too early to think about it, if Robert hadn't hurt you so much, but . . . you never loved him. Your seat at the banquet of love is waiting for you . . . Prepare your heart again, before swearing you will not remarry . . ."

– "Marriage should not be the only goal, the only ambition of a woman. There are many other goals a woman can aim for which give as much happiness as marriage (when it gives any), dear Myrtana. For example: the nun who leaves her friends, her beliefs, her family, her country, everything she loves to go far away, to teach children or to care for the sick, doesn't she feel happy?

"The nurse who, while some outside are giving balls, organizing sumptuous parties, playing amazing films, voluntarily shuts herself up in a hospital to treat diseases, from the simple cold to the incurable cancer patient, doesn't she feel happy?

"The lawyer who defends the widow, the orphan, who rehabilitates the innocent unjustly condemned, the doctor who saves a child from the claws of death and lays him cured in the arms of his mother, these women, aren't they happy? Did they look for their happiness only in marriage? Myrtana, why don't you admit it . . . I never stopped loving Guy, but I will not marry him. As I told you before, I want to devote myself to Eveline . . ."

– "Love cannot harm maternal love, dearest friend . . ."

– "It's true, but the woman who places her love on the altar of immateriality is almost certain to keep the heart of the one who

loves her longer than any other . . . Idealized, my love can reach a
sky higher than the one we see, this sky is far away, no doubt, but
we get there by renunciation and devotion. It's there that I wish to
unite myself with Guy Vanel . . ."

  – "You are a good woman. Good luck!"
  – "Thank you, my friend, thank you."

They embrace each other effusively and tears stream down their cheeks.
Chérisna discreetly enters the living room:

  – "A letter for Madame, yes."
  – "Give it to me," says Mme Watson. (She opens it.) "Myrtana,
my old uncle is dead, alas! This news saddens me immensely, for I
was hoping to go and pay him the homage of my affectionate gratitude before the end of the month. This letter invites me to present
my papers to inherit the two hundred thousand dollars that the
dear old man bequeathed to me . . ."

She got up. Mlle Durand too. Her voice full of emotion, she said:

  – "Myrtana, I never looked for fortune. God gives it to me, I
accept it, but may Heaven give me with it the strength to fight
against . . . abuses! May I say, 'I am here' every time there are miseries to relieve!"
  – "Oh! May God hear you, dear friend, but never forget the
friendship that binds us."
  – "Dear, dear friend, your friendship? It supported and consoled
me in the days of trial. It's precious to me. I love it. I know its full
depth. Oh worthy daughter of Haiti, be blessed! Dear Myrtana, I
know how much you have suffered from my great sorrows. I know
how many tears you shed because misfortune knocked at my door.
I know everything. How many times have I not seen you, sad
yourself, exhorting me to consolation! Such dedication! I know
everything, my friend. Don't say anything else. Let's be quiet. I love

these sacred silences where the soul speaks to the soul! I know your fears. Do not torment yourself so much: suffering has made me stronger. I don't fear the future, come on.

"The memories of my beautiful childhood attenuate my present misfortunes. Oh! When I close my eyes, I see the dear images of the past: they enchant me. The past! It was not always happy. Alas! No, but my friend, I only want to remember the beautiful, intoxicating things it gave me and which I enjoyed. How good it is to live on memories! I can still see Guy take my hands to recite beautiful verses, I hear the graceful notes he let fall from the keyboard. I kept the trace of his first kiss on my lips. I still remember all the loving words he said to me, all his emotional promises. I can still hear his pretty voice, his nice voice that sings like music . . . Myrtana—Oh incomparable memories!—I hear my child's first cries, I can still see her first smile, I clearly remember the day when, for the first time, she said to me: 'Mommy.'

"Hold on . . . there she is." (She goes to the child, her arms outstretched.) "Come, come my darling, why are you running like this? Come, my treasure, my reason for living, come . . . Let me press you to my heart. How I love you!"

Breathless, Eveline says: "I saw my godfather passing by . . ."

– "Ah! Have you seen Leabrook?"

– "I asked him about my daddy . . ."

– "And what did he tell you? Oh! Speak, speak . . ."

– "He told me like that, that my daddy will be back next week . . . that I'm going to play with him! Is it true that he will come back? He will bring sweets, toys for me? Tell me, Mom?"

– "Yes, my child, but tonight, like yesterday, we will pray . . . for his soul . . ."

– "But why do you cry while praying? Promise me to be less sad . . ."

The two women take the little orphan in their arms and kiss her while she whispers, "God, bless my daddy and make sure he doesn't forget to buy the big doll he promised me, as well as the pink, red, yellow candies, all the candies they sell in the United States . . ."

Suddenly Laurence says:

– "Myrtana, what do I hear? Sounds like an outcry."

– "It's nothing, or rather it's a lot of things: the street is full of young people who rejoice, because they have just been told that soon there will no longer be a Yankee sailor left on the soil of their fathers."

– "Oh! I was not mistaken . . . Looking at you earlier, I saw a flame in your eyes . . ."

– "Yes, I came to tell you the news, but having found you so disturbed, I didn't want to insult your painful emotion . . ."

– "My friend, how happy I am for you, you who are always protesting against the American Occupation!"

Mme Watson takes her friend's hand:

– "Myrtana, the ghosts of your ancestors must shiver with happiness at the news of this second independence . . ."

– "No, on the contrary, they must tremble with shame and horror to hear that their Haiti, once so proud, says thank you to the honorable and generous M. Roosevelt for an independence that they themselves had won with the thunder of grapeshot and cannons, at the cost of their blood and hitherto unsuspected sacrifices . . . Let's not compare 1934 to 1804. They are two historical dates, yes, but so different from each other. 1804: the glorious proclamation of Haiti's independence after continuous struggles by mixed and Black citizens of the small island oppressed by the French! 1934, alas! Freedom . . . the peaceful evacuation of Haiti . . . thanks to the

political intervention of the president of the United States[59] . . . and,
oh irony, a second independence . . ."

    – "I have never doubted your patriotism, dear Myrtana . . ."

Laurence listens and inquires:

    – "What is this song that the young people are singing? Let's
listen."

    – "It's "La Dessalinienne" . . . ,"[60] replies Mlle Durand.

Pretty voices—oh! so many!—enthusiastic, proud, rise to the sky:

For the Country,

For the Ancestors,

Let's march together,

In our ranks, no traitors,

Of the land, let us be sole masters,

Let's march together

For the Country

For the Ancestors.

    – "You're crying?" says Mme Watson suddenly.

    – "Yes, I am thinking about Charlemagne Péralte,[61] Raymond
Cabèche,[62] Pouget,[63] about the little soldier of the Arsenal, about
the victims of the Cayes massacre, and about so many other

---

59. Roosevelt announced the withdrawal of American troops as a result of his new
Good Neighbor policy, which favored multilateral economic cooperation rather than
military intervention to maintain stability in the Western Hemisphere.
60. "La Dessalinienne" is the national anthem of Haiti.
61. Charlemagne Masséna Péralte (1886–1919) was a Haitian nationalist and the
leader of the military group The Cacos. He was killed by American troops on October 31, 1931.
62. Raymond Vilaire Cabèche (dates unknown) was a Haitian congressman. He quit
his post after the adoption of the Haitian-American Convention.
63. Louis-Edouard Pouget (1870–1934) was a Haitian educator, statesman, and
diplomat.

anonymous heroes of the American Occupation, martyred and mowed down."

– "Oh! Unfortunate people!"

– "No, Laurence, let's not pity them; I envy them because they fought well for the Nation, they tried in spite of their weak means to protect it against the white invader; my tears are tears of gratitude and pride."

Acknowledgments

We are most grateful for Dr. Sarah Robbins and Dr. Ben Ireland (both of Texas Christian University), who proved instrumental in connecting us to work together on this project. Appreciation is also due to Lamar University and Hollins University for their academic and financial support over the past few years. At Lamar, many thanks to Kirk Smith, Valerie Key, and the rest of the faculty and staff at the Mary and John Gray Library, whose tireless effort brought many necessary resources to our disposal, and to Adam's students who aided in proofreading, translation, and annotation of *The White Negress*: Jennifer Do, Reilly Smith, Sydney Raughton, Kelsey Provost, and Jasmine De la Rosa-Bonilla. At Hollins, we are thankful for the outstanding work accomplished by Jeanne's students: Arlene L. Ayuk, Madison Brousseau, Hannah E. Chaikin, Julia L. Mouketo, and Vivian D. Urda. They conducted incredible research to set up Cléante D. Valcin's Wikipedia page in French and English, and assisted in the proofreading, translation, and annotation of *Cruel Destiny*. *Mési anpil* to Zeus Sumra and Stanley Dumond for their help translating the sections in Haitian Creole.

We must, of course, offer an abundance of thanks to Rutgers University Press for taking on this project and providing guidance along the way: Kim Guinta, associate press director and editorial director; Carah

Naseem, assistant editor; and Isabel Guzzardo Tamargo, an editorial intern who has a bright future in the business.

We are especially indebted to the generosity of Courtney Abrams for her careful reading of early drafts of these translations. To Haseeb and Penny, *bohot shukria* for their continued encouragements. And to Adam's loving wife, Lauren, who has been very supportive throughout this process.

About the Author

Cléante Desgraves Valcin (January 13, 1891–January 26, 1956) was a Haitian feminist, activist, and writer. Born in Port-au-Prince, Haiti, to Hector Desgraves, a Haitian pharmacist and pianist, and Alice Cunningham, an American citizen, she attended a girls' boarding school directed by the teacher, writer, and poet Virginie Sampeur. Valcin was a teacher until her marriage in 1917 to Virgile Valcin (born 1885) who owned a government-affiliated printing press. A founding member of the Ligue Féminine d'Action Sociale (The Feminine League of Social Action), she is credited with having published the first novel written by a Haitian woman, *Cruelle Destinée*, in 1929. In June 1955, a year before her death, she received the key to the city of San Juan, Puerto Rico, for her work at the 10th General Assembly of Women, during which she led the delegation and acted as a representative for her home country, Haiti.

About the Contributors

Myriam J. A. Chancy is a Guggenheim Fellow and HBA Chair of the Humanities at Scripps College in Claremont, California. She is the author of multiple academic works and novels, including *Framing Silence: Revolutionary Novels by Haitian Women*, *From Sugar to Revolution: Women's Visions from Haiti, Cuba and the Dominican Republic*, and *What Storm, What Thunder*.

Jeanne Jégousso is an assistant professor of French at Hollins University in Roanoke, Virginia. Her areas of specialization include the French-speaking Caribbean and Indian Ocean. She coedited the collected volume *Teaching, Reading, and Theorizing Caribbean Texts* and the special issue *Les Mondes d'Édouard Glissant*. She is the author of several peer-reviewed articles on the work of Édouard Glissant, Alfred Alexandre, and Mauritian comic books, as well as Haitian literary journals and poetry.

Adam Nemmers is an associate professor of English at Lamar University in Beaumont, Texas, whose research focuses on multiethnic American literature. He has recently published on Richard Wright, William Faulkner, Harper Lee, and the Harlem Renaissance. He is the author of *American Modern(ist) Epic*.